The Ransom Drop

Book 1 of The Response Files

Rob Phayre

To Ursie, India, Juliet, and Kira.

Thank you for your love and support.

Rob Phayre
Limited

Forward

I consider myself fortunate to have worked with some of the finest professionals in the world, doing things that make a difference.

From my military service to my years working on the African continent I have seen, and occasionally done, things that as a boy I would have been blown away by if I had only known what the future had in store for me.

The subject of piracy, and the payment of ransom is highly emotive, and contentious. This fictional tale is not meant to glorify and will, I am sure, contribute to the debate.

Do take a moment to share your thoughts at TheRansomDrop.com where there are lots of bonus materials, images and articles.

Prologue
November 3rd, Hobyo, Somalia.

Abdi's face was in the dust, his heart hammering in terror. Every fibre of his scrawny body tried to burrow hard into the ground. Through fearful eyes, wide open in shock, his brain had tried to process so many details that he had glitched-out, frozen, incapable. The automatic gunfire. The harsh crack of fragmentation hitting concrete and rock. The acrid sweet smell of cordite. The occasional wet slap of bullets hitting flesh. The screams of the wounded and the dying.

What the fuck is happening? Am I about to die at the age of 25? Allah be merciful! Please don't let it hurt.

His brain cropped out the excess stimuli, a survival instinct, desperately trying to process. His eyes focussed on a face that was staring at him from only a few meters away. The face was shouting at him, but Abdi's ears weren't working. It took intense effort to reconnect them to his brain and to focus on what was being said.

'Abdi, you are no good there! You are curling up like a baby in the womb. Pick up your weapon and fight!'

Through the fug and noise Abdi understood what Dalmar had shouted even as Dalmar stood up from behind the wall they were hiding behind. Dalmar fired several shots from his AK-47 in the direction of the attackers and then ducked back down laughing maniacally. To Abdi it seemed that the crack and whine of bullets passing over their heads increased momentarily before fading away again.

Amongst the traditional, light Somali build, Dalmar was a brute and in this region, he was feared by many. He was mean and grumpy and had spent much of his youth as a gun for hire. He never went anywhere without his AK-47 and his rotten, gap toothed leer. His pride and joy was his faded green 'webbing', a system of belts and pouches that allowed a fighter to carry magazines, spare ammunition, a first aid kit and a water bottle. In short, all you needed for a brief contact battle. It was rumoured that Dalmar's webbing had been taken from the body of a US Marine killed during a disastrous recovery mission in Mogadishu in 1993.

Dalmar was one of the fighters under the pay of Abdi's father who was the clan chief and ruler of Hobyo. Less than thirty minutes ago one of the fighters had burst into Mohamed's house shouting to the chief that one of the neighbouring warlords was about to raid the camel coral on the Northern boundary of the town. Ten minutes later, after a mad dash across the town in battered old pickup trucks, Abdi found himself with a group of other men hiding behind a wall with a rifle in his hand and beginning to panic.

Abdi was born in Hobyo but hadn't been home for a few years. Until a week or so ago Abdi had been living in London. None of his family has ever gotten a Master's degree, let alone from a prestigious school like the London School of Economics. His certificate was sitting in his bag still back at the house and Abdi was proud of his achievement despite the fact that the piece of paper sometimes felt like an IOU note to his family. They had given up a lot to send him away for his extortionately expensive education. Nothing in that education had prepared him to be where he was right now.

'Abdi, get off your belly and come with me!' Dalmar was crawling past Abdi using the low wall as cover and heading towards an irrigation ditch. The harsh honking of camels had joined the cacophony of noise but somehow Abdi's brain was functioning again. He grasped what Dalmar wanted to do and staying close to the ground crawled after him. His adrenaline levels kept his muscles moving with strength he didn't know he possessed and together he and Dalmar followed the ditch. It flanked wide and to the west of the attackers' positions. After about a hundred meters, Dalmar slowly lifted his head out of the ditch, looked left and right and then ducked back down.

'Ok, there are perhaps six of them, behind the wall of the camel shed. We will go another fifty meters and that will give us the chance to come up to the side of them.'

Trying to control his breathing, 'What would you like me to do?'

Dalmar looked at Abdi and spoke calmly, 'I want you to fight, I want you to kill, I want you to show me you are not just the spoiled precious son of the chief.'

'But I have never done this before.'

'Well, this is where you prove that you are a man or not. This is where you prove that you will one day be fit to lead this clan. Today you can grasp your future by the balls, or you can go back to hiding behind that wall holding your own limp dick.'

Dalmar moved off down the ditch without looking back. Despite his terror Abdi followed him, muttering a prayer to Allah all the way. The crescendo of gunfire had peaked again but there was no tell-tale snap indicating rounds coming in their direction. Dalmar stopped and looked back to see Abdi only a meter or two behind him.

'Good, we will attack now. Is your magazine full?'

'Yes. I haven't fired yet.'

'Were you waiting for a personal invitation? Do you not want to protect your clan?'

With growing defiance, Abdi answered back. 'I will do everything to protect my clan, now let's get this done.'

Dalmar glanced at the rifle in Abdi's hands. 'You will need to take the safety catch off first.'

Abdi glanced down to see that the safety catch was already off. Embarrassed that he had looked and obviously still scared he said. 'Fuck you Dalmar.'

'Let's see boy. I will attack the men behind the wall. Your job is to watch my back. Can you do that?' Without waiting for a reply, Dalmar stood up and started to crouch walk towards the enemy clan fighters. Six of them were lined up behind the white stone camel coral walls firing towards the Hobyo clan less than a hundred meters away to the South. None were looking at Dalmar as he advanced with his weapon ready in his shoulder. Abdi followed, heart thumping, adrenaline pumping, sweat pouring off his face caking the dust above his eyes.

The first men behind the wall didn't know that death was with them until Dalmar opened fire. Thirty rounds from his magazine spat along this side of the wall and back again. The man last in line knew death was coming but only had time to half rotate his weapon before bullets thumped across his chest. Blood and gore spattered the white stone walls and Dalmar kept firing until his magazine was empty. He dropped to one knee and was reaching for another magazine in his webbing when two new men arrived from behind the camel shed. There was a moment. Dalmar saw them coming but was still helplessly fishing. The men saw their dead colleagues, comprehension dawning as they raised their weapons. Abdi screamed to self-motivate and started firing. The first man died immediately, flopping to the ground. The second tried to jump behind the cover of the wall but was caught by a shot to the side of his chest. Abdi ran towards him, firing relentlessly until that man's chest was a mess of splintered bone and blood.

With an empty magazine, Abdi turned to look at Dalmar. All the shooting had stopped now and whoops of victory were coming from the other side of the coral. Dalmar clicked a new magazine into his weapon and stood up. 'Not such a limp dick after all.'

Chapter 1
March 12th, Hobyo, Somalia.

The East coast of Somalia. A desolate place where the Indian Ocean rolls onto a thousand-kilometre-long beach. The parched sand merges into a granular dusty soil that stretches far inland. If it's lucky, it receives 20 centimetres of rain a year, but somehow tufts of rough grasses cling to life. Not a lot else does.

Under the breaking surf, sea life thrives, from shrimps to sharks they have had a brief respite from humanity. A long civil war massively impacted the local fishing industry. That's changing now though, with the foreign industrial fishing ships that have started pillaging their way up and down the coast.

Four months after the camel coral incident, Abdi is sat on a tussock staring out to sea. He's wearing faded pale blue jeans and a light linen shirt that's frayed around the edges. He has high cheekbones and is skinny, though that's more genetics than poverty speaking. Abdi is luckier than most, his father is a warlord. One of the lesser warlords, but still ruler of Hobyo and one day Abdi will inherit the title if the elders agree. Like so many young people, Abdi has a strong desire for more, for better. He wants to make his mark on the world. He wants wealth, security, and power, for his clan, for himself. He wants a reputation; he wants freedom, and he has a plan.

To a Westerner, Hobyo is a nowhere place, three hundred or so houses sprinkled haphazardly around a few dusty tracks that pass for roads that parallel the coast. The houses are made of what looks like a white stone. If you look closer though, it's not stone, it's compacted and fossilized corral, bleached white and left on land during the retreat of the sea a million years ago. It's everywhere and it is cheap. Just kick up a few inches of dusty sand and you have a quarry. The houses are mostly single story with rusting tin roofs that you can quite literally cook off under the blazing heat of the sun. Most of the houses have a compound wall around them, more to keep the goats under control than to prevent crime. The clan structures deal with the latter. Theft is not tolerated in this community. Abdi's father provides brutal and swift justice and blood feuds go on for generations. Of course, pride of place in the centre of the town is the mosque. It has a domed white painted roof, but just the one minaret as that is all the inhabitants could afford to build at the time. That said, the intricate carving on this tall symbol of their faith from which the call to prayer came five times per day was a huge source of pride.

Hobyo sits back about 200 meters from the shoreline. A band of beach lies between the sea and the town. It provides security from a surging tide and it's somewhere for the population to do their daily toilet. Magically, twice a day, nature cleans the beach with the tide and washes away the filth, stench, and the flies.

Around the town, there are no fields growing an abundance of crops. There are not even many trees. Most were cut down years ago for firewood. What Hobyo does have though is priceless to the community. A naturally formed stone breakwater juts out to sea. It sticks out for about 300 meters, and whilst it is broken in places, it provides protection to the fleet of simple fishing boats moored by the beach.

Abdi watched the fishermen at work, mesmerized at how hard it was to make a living from the sea. In the last few years, it had become even harder. Huge factory fishing vessels sailed thousands of kilometres from China and the far east to hoover up every fish in the sea before returning home.

Abdi has come home with a degree and a plan that he has spent months preparing in his mind. He needs the support of his father once more, and his father will need the support of other much more powerful men. Abdi wasn't worried about getting the money to finance his plan. Good ideas always attract investment, and he knows that this is a really good idea, he has done the math.

Chapter 2
March 14th, Hobyo, Somalia.

Abdi's father's short, dark, curly hair was going grey at the age of 45. Mohamed's beard though was stained an unnatural bright orange. He had been treating it with henna since the day he assumed responsibility for the clan and in part it denoted his status as an elder. Mohamed had stained yellow teeth with the two top front ones missing creating a gaping gap. Some of the others were black and rotting, the result of chewing khat for 30 years. Chewing was what Mohamed was doing while he was squatting in the shade in the courtyard of his house when Abdi walked in.

'Father, salaam alaikum,' Abdi greeted his father cautiously, never certain how responsive he would be when chewing the intoxicating leaf.

'Wa alaikum salaam,' his father replied, surprisingly sprightly and in a good mood. 'How was your morning?' he continued.

'To be honest, even after these months I am still getting used to not hearing the London traffic. It is good to hear the sound of the sea again and it is good to be home.' If Abdi was really honest, he missed the bustle of London. He missed the women; he missed the whiskey, but he couldn't say that to his father.

Abdi's father was shrewd though and with his eyes unreadable continued to probe, 'And what do you miss about that part of your life?'

'I miss how busy my life was there. I miss the learning, not just from my academic studies, but studying the infidel. I never got used to how frivolous life was for so many of them. Living from one immediate gratification to the next with no thought of how hard life can be. If we had the tiniest fraction of the wealth that they have in London here in Hobyo, we could make Hobyo a trading city and the pride of Somalia.'

Abdi's voice had become more passionate than he had intended during that short speech, and his father chuckled. As he did so, he tore another bunch of fresh green leaves from his twig of khat folded them up and popped them in his mouth, 'And so my son what would you do? How will you use your learnings to not just be 'busy' but to be productive? What do you need to bring greatness to our city and esteem to our clan?'

'Father, that answer is both simple and difficult. I need several things. I need you to have faith in my abilities. I need you to allow me to walk my path knowing that I seek to bring both wealth and power to our clan in your name. I need you to protect me from those forces near us that may seek to stop me. And finally, father, I need to borrow one hundred thousand United States dollars for a period of one year.'

Abdi's father didn't reply. He hawked a great globule of black phlegmy juice that had slowly been collecting around his tongue and then propelled it, through the gap in his front teeth to a place on the dirt about two meters to his right.

Chapter 3
August 5th, Hobyo, Somalia.

It turned out, getting the money hadn't been that hard. Repaying it would be. In Islamic finance, money had no actual value in its own right, it was just a medium of exchange. No one was allowed to make a profit from lending or borrowing money but there was always a cost.

Six months later Abdi was recalling the conversation he had had with his father in March. Mohamed had told Abdi that he had made an agreement with one of his associates to fund a joint venture under the system of Musharaka. Abdi knew from his studies that this meant that a person had lent the money with a specific agreement on the sharing of any proceeds from the business enterprise. When Abdi heard that the arrangement was for 75% of the entire project earnings he nearly exploded. Of course, his father had calmly told him that to achieve 25% of whatever it was going to be from holding nothing in his hand to start with, was a fair deal. Abdi had taken the money and spent much of it equipping his business. He was still fuming about the rate of 'tax' but wasn't going to let it spoil his day.

Today was the start of it all. Abdi's plans and his dream were coming together. In front of him now, driving down the track towards the beach was a battered old Mercedes truck. Its garish blue paint just about held the rusting box shaped cab together. The tyres were down to the wire and threads and the exhaust was pumping out more black smoke than some of the ancient old boats that plied their trade up and down the coast.

Of course, the truck wasn't the dream. It was the flatbed trailer that it was pulling. On that was a 50-foot shipping container, the contents of which had been put together by his father's associate in Dubai about six weeks ago. The container had been shipped to the port in Mogadishu and had just completed a nearly 900-kilometre drive along the coast. It was only because his father had let it be known that it was his that they hadn't had to pay extensive 'taxes' to let it pass through the territories of the other clans. It was a privilege that the leaders afforded each other most of the time whilst charging a transit tax for everyone else. This faded green metal container held everything that Abdi needed to get his new enterprise up and running.

It was four o'clock in the afternoon and there was the normal slow but efficient bustle of the fishermen who were tending to their nets and boats, preparing for the evening tide to go out and fish. Abdi had already arranged for ten young men to help him as labourers. He needed their help in unloading the container, but he hadn't told them what was in it yet. They would see soon enough.

Despite having just driven such a long way, the Mercedes found the final 200 meters across the sand dunes to the beach to be the hardest work. After much shouting and cajoling the driver finally said the truck had had enough and stopped like a beached whale about 80 meters from the shoreline so it wouldn't get bogged in. The young men crowded around the back waiting with anticipation to unload. Abdi walked up and with a pair of bolt cutters, clipped the seal on the container. With a screech of protesting metal he tried to lift the door lever but it wouldn't open on the first try. Abdi became conscious of all the young men who had grown up on the sea with salt in their veins and strength in their arms. How foolish would he look if he, the academic, couldn't open his dream? He gave a mighty push again, pulling a muscle deep down inside his shoulder blade but thankfully the door opened. Honour restored, he walked in letting his eyes adjust.

With the evening sun shining into the dark space, but with the heat of the day still radiating off the hot metal of the container, Abdi's heart raced. In front of him were 4 brand new boats. They were not the wide, stable, fishing tubs that the men used here for bringing their catch home. They had their purpose, but they were not suitable for his needs. These were 'skiffs.' Sleek boats that were 30 feet long, with pointed noses, slim and fast. The hulls were all a pale grey colour with a black line painted all around the gunwale. Further towards the back of the container Abdi could see the crates containing the engines. Four brand-new 110 horsepower Yamaha fuel injected petrol engines with enough power to propel these skiffs to 25 or 30 knots. Beside them, lashed down were four much smaller 15 horsepower engines. No one wanted to go far out to sea relying on just one engine, no matter how new, how shiny and how powerful. Tucked into a back corner of the container were some heavy-duty waterproof boxes made out of a solid black plastic. Abdi knew what was in those but didn't go to open them just yet. Instead, he stepped back outside to get some cooler air and his sweat started to instantly evaporate, he was approached by Zahi.

Zahi was about 30 years old, one of the more experienced fishermen who had led his own boat since he was 16. As a result, he was powerfully built, sinew and muscles showed in his shoulders and forearms. A deep scar on his left cheek gave him a bit of a lopsided look so he wasn't an attractive man. His father had become too ill to take the family boat out anymore but rather than sell it and lose the one source of family income Zahi had stepped up to lead. His father had needed a lot of money to pay for the medication for his illness and so the priority for maintaining the boat had fallen down the list. Unfortunately, that meant that the boat hadn't had a new engine for many years. It was now so unreliable that Zahi and his crew could never go too far out to sea for fear of not making it back, or worse, suffer the embarrassment of having to be towed back in by one of the other Captains. That had happened last night and so Zahi knew that he wasn't going out tonight. He needed the work to pay for spare parts and so he had approached Abdi.

He called out loudly, 'Abdi, what shiny new toys have you got in there?' the crowd of labourers hushed in anticipation. They respected Zahi and they respected Abdi. Everyone knew that something was happening, but no one knew what yet. The rumour was that Abdi was building his own fleet and the other Captains were not looking forward to the extra competition.

'Zahi, I see you there. I heard you had a rough night; you and your crew are welcome to help.' Abdi didn't need the manpower, but he knew that he could use Zahi to manage the unloading, and that was worth the small extra expense.

'But what are we unloading?'

'Well, if you and your crew want to manage the unloading and get all of it down to the shoreline over there, then you will find out!' Abdi pointed to a spot about 100 meters away. Zahi looked at the spot, then back at the container. This was going to be hard work, but he had nothing better to do this evening.

Having nodded his agreement, Zahi's voice suddenly took on the tone and volume of a ship's Captain projecting across the beach. 'You lot! Stop standing there gawping like you did the first time your saw a woman's tit! You won't get paid until everything that is inside that container is over there! If one of you scum breaks anything, or drops anything, I will personally ask Allah to make your wives infertile!' Pointing to his regular crew he followed up more quietly with 'Tadalesh, Yuusuf, split this sorry bunch of fish food into two groups and let's get this lot unloaded!'

Two hours later just as the sun was setting over the ocean Abdi was unpacking one of the black plastic crates. He had paid off the workers and they were heading back to Hobyo gossiping about what they had seen. Inside one of the crates were items not usually associated with fishing. Satellite phones, small solar panels to charge them, reverse osmosis water filters capable of taking sea water and producing drinking water, kerosene cookers and tarpaulins. In addition, some other items were laid up alongside the skiffs and they had caused the biggest stir. There were four, five-meter ladders fashioned out of iron bar and with a hook mechanism welded to the top. There were some four-pronged grappling hooks, with a thick knotted rope already attached. Finally, there were more empty fuel jerry cans than could possibly be needed for a simple night's fishing.

Zahi stepped up behind Abdi, looking at the contents laid out around them and spoke. 'With all of this you are not going fishing, are you?'

Abdi replied, 'Actually, yes, I am in a way. How would you feel about you and your crew taking one of these skiffs for me and hooking us the biggest fish you have ever seen?'

Abdi and Zahi sat there as it grew darker, deep in conversation, watching lights bobbing up and down on the waves out to sea as the community fishing boats tried to lure squid and other prey to the surface from the depths.

Chapter 4.
August 15th, Hobyo, Somalia.

Abdi's could tell that his father was nervous. They were in the family's battered old white Toyota Landcruiser and Abdi was driving. Pale white dust was flying up behind the 4x4 creating a plume that could be seen for miles. Inside the car, Mohamed kept stroking his beard, stopping only to hawk and spit out of the open window. Abdi himself was unsettled just because his father was nervous and his armpits were damp with sweat. Sure, the humidity and the heat weren't helping, but he wasn't in London anymore and couldn't just turn up the air conditioning.

They were driving to meet his fathers 'Associate', the man who had lent Abdi the money. The Associate had called this morning to say that he was flying to Mogadishu on business but would stop at the small airstrip in Hobyo on the way. He wanted to meet Abdi for the first time and talk.

Hobyo airport was only a kilometre or so away from the town but in that short journey Mohamed had wound himself up so much that he was a wreck. Abdi tried to calm him down.

'Father I am sure it will be OK. He is just coming to check on his investment.'

'Son, I have only met this man once before. He is immensely powerful, extraordinarily rich. I don't understand why he is spending valuable time coming to look at what you are doing. It doesn't make sense.'

'But he has invested his money with us. If I had invested money, I would want to meet the person who I had invested in. Its OK, I will speak to him, answer his questions, make sure he is happy, and then he can get back on his little plane and leave us to make him richer.'

The car pulled up as it approached the airport. A simple chain was raised across the road and a dishevelled looking guard was sitting in the shade of a tin hut on the left-hand side. The guard had seen the car approaching and even though there were no flights scheduled for today, and this was probably the one interesting highlight of his day, he was obviously disinterested and lethargic in his movements.

Mohamed, normally a patient man, let the stress get to him and snapped out of the window, 'Move! Or I will feed your balls to my goats!'

The guard stared, spat, and walked in an insolent way just short of total disobedience to the chain where he unhooked it, letting it fall to the ground. Abdi drove forward about another 100 meters and parked on the side of the cleared aircraft apron. There was no one else around and they sat in the car waiting.

The Hobyo airstrip was simple. The bush had been flattened and cleared for just over 2 kilometres and about halfway along its length, an apron for the aircraft to load and unload passengers and cargo had also been cleared. On the southern side, nearest the city, were two buildings made from rusting corrugated iron sheet. A couple of roof panels had come loose from the incessant coastal wind and were flapping noisily.

As they sat and waited Mohamed continued to fidget. The wind was blowing strongly from the south, causing dust devils to rise and track across the terrain. Old plastic bags caught in the bushes flapped angrily as they slowly tore themselves to shreds.

The wait wasn't long, and just before mid-day Abdi saw the aircraft approach from the North. It touched down lightly on the strip and taxied towards the apron. Abdi didn't know his aircraft, but he did see that this wasn't a little run about. The aircraft fuselage sat on top of a low wing base. Pale cream in colour there was a flamboyant red sash painted along its length that ended in a swirl on the tail. The twin jet engines were aft of the wings and set high on the tail. It was a clever design that allowed the aircraft to land on rougher strips and not swallow all the dust that the wheels kicked up, preserving engine life.

The aircraft pulled up on the apron and shut down. The door opened in two parts like a clamshell, smoothly lowering the internal staircase as well. A petite oriental woman immaculately uniformed and with long black hair coiled smoothly on top of her head, stood at the top of the ladder and beckoned Abdi and Mohamed to come.

Leaving their car, they walked to the aircraft and up the stairs. As they entered the lady asked for their cell phones, which once handed over were locked in a cabinet. Abdi led the way into the cabin trying really hard to conceal his surprise at the opulence he saw as he did so. The lady pushed a button and the aircraft doors closed behind them with soft thump. The interior was brightly lit. Anything that wasn't white suede or leather was gold. At the far end at a table sat a short, thin, bald man wearing a navy-blue pin stripe suit and an emerald, green tie. The man was on the phone speaking in a language they didn't recognise and indicated for Abdi and Mohamed to sit. Abdi felt a ridiculous urge to brush the dust off his clothes before he sat down on the pristine white leather executive chair. That of course would have pushed the dust onto the floor which as he looked down, he noticed had a white carpet about three inches thick. His grubby, hairy toes, sticking out of his walking sandals looked ridiculous sinking into the floor.

When he looked back up The Associate had finished his call and was studying him. In an accent that he couldn't quite place, somewhere between Japan and Nigeria he said. 'So, you are Abdi. Have you spent my money well?'

Abdi, a little shocked at the lack of an introduction or even common courtesy greetings quickly recovered and said, 'Yes, everything has arrived as planned, would you like me to brief you on what I plan to do?'

'No. I know that you intend to send the vessels out at the end of this month when the monsoon weather has cleared. Have you found reliable crews?'

Abdi was even more unnerved that this man should have taken the time and effort to find out the detail of what he intended. 'Yes. I have some good Captains and have allowed them to pick their teams. I felt that they should be both familiar and comfortable with each other as they will have a difficult job to do.'

The Associate nodded his agreement and said, 'If they are successful in their expedition, how long do you think it will take to get a return on the investment and how much are you modelling?'

Abdi's confidence was growing, financial returns and business plans were his strength and he had spent many months refining this one. 'The return depends greatly on the size of the prize captured. If it's a Chinese factory fishing ship, then we should negotiate for about one million dollars. If it's a container vessel, then depending on the cargo we should be asking for about three million. Having studied the insurance market and the ransom returns in the Asian market I would expect negotiations to take anything between 2 and 6 months. I think therefore, that even though we may lose some crews to the sea, we should be able to repeat the project several times over, replacing skiffs and crews where needed. I will make sure that successful crews are well paid, and in line with our customs I will make some compensation payments to the families of those who die.'

His turn to be surprised, The Associate looked at Abdi while he considered all this information. 'Very well, you may use the funds for one year. You may manage them as you see fit. I will expect a strong financial return after each successful project, and I expect at least three successful projects in the year.'

Abdi nodded as The Associate continued, 'If you do well, then I will look after you. If you don't, then...' The Associate gave a little shrug, but there was no amusement in his eyes which stared coldly. 'One final thing before you go. Don't underestimate the ability of the international intelligence community. They can monitor most electronic communications. I won't speak to you for a while. If you prove yourself to me then we will work out a way to communicate more regularly. Go, with the grace of your god.'

Abdi and Mohamed, who hadn't said a word, stood up and walked back down the plane as the oriental woman gave them back their phones. She pressed a button and the doors opened again letting light, heat, and some of the incessant dust back into the plane.

Abdi walked down the steps shielding his eyes against the bright sun. He shivered slightly, despite the heat and he realised that it was not because of the cold airconditioned environment he had just left.

Chapter 5.
August 30th, Ras Laffan Oil Terminal, Qatar.

The Hibernia III was a VLCC. A Very Large Crude Carrier. As far as 'Very Large' goes, compared to the modern vessels she was actually quite a small one. Built in the 1990's her hull was 300 meters long, painted a deep red below the water line and a simple matt black colour above. The superstructure was all the way aft and was painted cream. The Hibernia III was well maintained. She was well loved by the 24 crew members who cared for and operated her, and she was well loved by the owner. She was his first mistress and his most expensive mistress too. Since buying her second hand 15 years ago, Mr Papadopoulos the Greek shipping magnate and owner of The Aphrodite Freight and Shipping Company (AFSC) limited, had come to realise that the 105 million USD that he had borrowed from the bank to finance her, was well worth it. In all that time of ownership she had managed a faultless charter uptime rate. Considering she cost about 100,000 US dollars a day to run and finance this was just as well. Mr Papadopoulos had built his shipping company from her hard work, and he was proud of her.

The Hibernia III could carry just over 2 million barrels of refined oil products in her holds. Give or take, at today's market rate that was 120 million US dollars' worth of petroleum. Today she was loading for a regular run, from Ras Laffan oil terminal, on the very tip of the Qatar peninsula in the Persian Gulf. Her route would take her across the Indian Ocean, to Mombasa in Kenya where she would unload half of her cargo. Then she would carry the rest down to Dar es Salaam in Tanzania.

Watching the loading procedure from the bridge wing on the port side of the ship, Captain Oleksiy was growing impatient. It wasn't his crew who were causing the delay, it was the vessel that had loaded before them. The harbour master had complained about paperwork and in his belligerence had refused to take a bribe. Oleksiy hated jumped up officials who didn't know their place and who wouldn't look the other way for a fist full of bank notes. Of course, back home in Ukraine he would have solved the problem in good time, but here in the Middle East it didn't work that way anymore. The Captain reflected that not much of the world worked 'that way' anymore. It used to be that you could always trust a corrupt official. Well, you could of course, if you also showed them that you knew which bar they liked to drink in at night, and casually mentioned that you always carried a knife.

Captain Oleksiy was stocky, with short cropped greying hair and tattoos up his arms collected from ports that he had long forgotten. He was still standing there fuming when the bridge wing phone rang. He picked it up and answered with a curt 'Yes?'

On the other end of the line was the chief engineer Marko. 'Captain, looking at the loading volumes we are nearly at the contracted rate. Ambient air temperature is +40 degrees centigrade and the average fuel temperature through the inlet valve is +30 degrees centigrade. We need to load for a little longer to make sure we are within tolerances. I have spoken to the Deck Officer and the head office and confirmed my calculations.'

The Captain paused for a moment before replying. He and Marko had worked together in a former life in the Ukrainian Navy. He trusted him and his mathematical ability though Marko was getting old now and soon he would retire. Oleksiy thought he probably had a few more years left in him though and whilst his body was getting arthritic, and his liver was getting pickled, his brain was still as sharp as a tack. The funny thing about loading bulk fuel was that it expanded or contracted depending on its temperature. An 8 degree increase in temperature of the fuel resulted in a 1% expansion in volume. When loading two million barrels that meant that for this load, he needed to collect an extra 20,000 barrels, or 1.2Million USD worth of fuel. If he didn't, and he turned up in Mombasa with the fuel having cooled down and shrunk as a result then his career was over.

He spoke down the phone. 'Understood Marko, I will tell the Steward to make sure the crew get fed before we slip our mooring. Have you loaded all the other stores we ordered?'

'Most of it Captain.' Marko always called Oleksiy 'Captain' when they were embarked. They would get absolutely wasted together onshore, get tattoos together and were the best of friends, naturally on first name terms, but as soon as they were aboard, they addressed each other formally. Marko continued. 'There were a couple of items the useless supply company couldn't get here in time, some new water filters, a replacement pump for the toilet system, but nothing that we can't make work for the short trip to Mombasa. They have promised me that they will be waiting for us when we get there.'

Captain Oleksiy acknowledged and hung up the phone. Then, he picked it up again and called the Steward. 'Andres its me.'

Andres, down in the Galley stuck a finger in his ear to block out the noise the Chef was making. It wasn't his cooking; it was his singing. He wondered for the thousandth time why the hell the Ukrainians loved Elvis so much. 'Yes Captain, what do you need?'

'Andres please tell Chef that we will be loading for about another hour and then we will depart. Can he get dinner for the crew sorted before then?'

'One moment Captain' Andres replied as he turned to the Chef.

'Chef! The Captain needs dinner on the table in half an hour. Can you do it?'

The Chef without breaking a note replied, 'Uh huh huh!' and started pulling plates of pre-prepared sandwiches out of the fridges.

'Captain, that's a yes from Chef. On the table shortly.'

'Good, make sure he doesn't trip over his blue suede shoes.' The Captain hung up the phone. Andres was a Filipino. Small, thin, dark haired, incessantly polite, but outstanding when it came to enduring any form of hardship. Sometimes the Captain thought he should mentor Andres to stand up for himself a little more. Not always say 'yes', express his opinion more. Oleksiy reflected on the number of vessels he had worked where the Filipino crew were in the service jobs on board. No doubt, saving money to send home, enduring hardship, and not letting the menial jobs get them down. Always so polite and so bloody happy! He smiled to himself. It was probably just as well that Andres was here. He balanced out the Alpha-male element of much of his Ukrainian crew!

With one final professional eye cast over the vast bulk of his ship he stepped back into the bridge and walked down to the Galley to get something to eat.

Chapter 6.
August 30th, Hobyo, Somalia.

At the Southern end of Hobyo, Zahi's house nestled in amongst a number of other small houses made from a combination of coral, sticks and corrugated iron sheet. His house had one room and he shared it with his parents, his brother, and his sister. His mother and 19-year-old sister did everything to run the household, cooking, cleaning, and collecting drinking water and firewood where they could find it. His sister should have married by now, but she was very plain to look at having a face heavily scarred by a measles breakout when she was young. Zahi's family name was not a good one.

Zahi's younger brother made a small living selling telephone airtime vouchers in the market. He was one of those people who was naturally cheerful and always had a smile. He never let the fact that he had lost his leg to a landmine when he was seven get him down. The explosion had damaged his right arm too, but the doctors had managed to save it. He walked with two crutches crudely made from wood and padded under the arms using rubber strips torn from old tyre inner tubes. If the family's small earnings were not all being used to pay for their fathers' medications, then they might save for a simple prosthetic leg. The harsh reality of remote parts of Somalia was that it was a tough place to be sick or disabled.

Zahi had discussed the opportunity that Abdi had offered him with his family. His mother and father were concerned for Zahi's safety naturally. What if Zahi wasn't successful and so didn't earn anything, or worse, didn't come back, who would provide for the family then? The family would have to sell the fishing boat which would provide them some money for a short time, but then they would really be in trouble.

Zahi's brother on the other hand was obviously cross that Zahi wouldn't let him go with him. He had hobbled off in a huff when Zahi had asked him how on earth he was going to climb a rope or a ladder with only one leg and a bad arm.

Zahi was now sitting outside the door to the hut mulling things over. Tomorrow he and his crew would depart on their voyage and he was restless and a little uncertain about the decision he had made. A couple of his neighbours' chickens were scratching around in the street, pecking at nothing, trying to fill their stomachs. Zahi couldn't help but draw a parallel. Sometimes he felt like that. What was the point? Where was the opportunity? How could he, a simple fisherman, with a broken engine, not only fill his families' bellies but pull them up out of this never-ending poverty? That's why he had jumped at Abdi's offer. They had discussed the risks and Abdi had said that if Zahi and his skiff crew didn't come back then he would pay their families compensation. They hadn't agreed an amount and Abdi wouldn't be drawn on what it would be, but Zahi did take some comfort from that. Zahi was inspired though by the possible opportunity and his dreams of success. Abdi had told him that if he was the first person on board a vessel, brought it back to Hobyo and they were able to collect a ransom for it, then he would make him a rich man. Again, they hadn't spoken about numbers, but Zahis' dreams included a house with at least 4 rooms, medicine for his father, a new leg for his brother and happiness for his sister. For him? With wealth? Well, he would be able to afford a new engine for his boat and the dowry for a pretty young wife, though not necessarily in that order.

Chapter 7.
September 1st, The Indian Ocean

The Hibernia III weighing in at about 400,000 tons was making easy going. The monsoon seas that lasted from June to August had cleared up and now there was just the gentle but steady swell. The Greek head office had sent through the detailed weather forecast and there were no major issues. Captain Oleksiy was looking at a weather map with the track from the AIS marked clearly on it. The Automatic Identification System was an automated tracking system that all large vessels installed and subscribed to. Working through a VHF radio frequency it showed the vessels' location, speed, and course direction on the global map database. The shipping office could add data like the name of the ship, the flag state, where the ship was sailing from and where it was destined for. It could even include approximately what date and time it would get there and what the draft of the vessel was. All this data would help the customs clearance agents or anyone with an interest and an internet connection, plan their workload given the tens of thousands of ships constantly moving around the world.

Currently, the Hibernia III was about 200 kilometres East of Socotra Island, a large nature reserve which guarded the entrance to the Gulf of Aden, about 400 kilometres from the tip of Puntland. She had escaped the busy shipping lanes passing East West heading to the Red Sea and the Suez Canal. Now the Hibernia III was heading 230 Degrees South West at about 15 knots on a beeline towards Mombasa. The weather looked really calm and there were only a few major vessels with a transponder in the immediate area. Not one to be complacent, Captain Oleksiy surveyed the bridge instruments whilst he sipped his coffee.

Chapter 8.
September 1st, Hobyo, Somalia.

Dawn. The waves were rolling onto the shore in a kaleidoscope of brilliant blues. Where they broke, a pinkish white foam raced up the sand towards the bows of four brand-new heavily laden skiffs. Their bows, facing the sea, were dug deep into the sand. They flirted unmoving with the water as the waves lost energy around them. Gathered around the skiffs was a bubbling crowd. Most had just returned weary, from a hard night's fishing. Some were the crews that were about risk their lives on this adventure, and the rest were families and friends come to say farewell.

Abdi was there, talking to the four chosen Captains. They had spent days preparing, planning, testing but finally there was nothing further to do except to head out to sea.

All the Captains had been given a zone at sea to try to maximise the chances of coming across a suitable ship. Zahi and his crews' job was to push as far out to the East as he could and see if he could find a Chinese factory fishing vessel. The other Captains were spread, with two heading due North toward the busy shipping lanes up towards the Red Sea and the last vessel due South to try to intercept any vessels heading into Mogadishu.

Abdi was a little skittish, making an attempt of leadership, repeating details that had been gone over countless times already. 'Remember, don't risk the skiff unnecessarily, make sure you call in using the satellite phone each morning and each evening. Send me your location using the inbuilt GPS on the phone so that I can see where you are. You have enough supplies to stay out for about two weeks and the long-range weather forecast is good. Any questions?'

None of the Captains had anything left to say.

'Ok, it's time to go.' And with that the four Captains walked towards their skiffs.

Zahi, had made peace internally and was now impatient to get on with it. He had stayed out for two nights once before, but never for this long. The sea, from which so much was given could also demand the final price, and often without warning. Zahi had his fancy new satellite phone, and Abdi had told him he would make sure he shared the weather forecasts. But, to put so much trust in another man didn't suit Zahi all that well. Still, he walked towards his crew now with an expression of determination. His crew depended on him for their lives, and he on them.

Standing near the bow was Tadalesh, just turned 19, still very boyish in looks and trying hard to grow his beard. His Manchester United T-shirt faded from the sun and about three sizes too big for his frame was his pride and joy. Tadalesh meaning 'Lucky' in the western tongue had only been working with Zahi on his family boat for about a year, but Zahi was confident that this fearless youth was just right for this voyage.

Yuusuf on the other hand was an old salt. Nearing 60 with a face hammered from working all those years under a harsh sun he was a quiet, solid, and dependable man. In his youth, when Mogadishu had been the tourism capital of East Africa, tourists had flocked from Europe to the extravagant hotels and beautiful white beaches. Yuusuf had worked in a hotel. He had picked up some Italian and some English and earned a good living for a young man. The rise of Barre Adid in the 70's had destroyed the tourism industry and forced Yuusuf back to his hometown of Hobyo where he went back to the sea. Having worked for Zahi for many years, he was a great impromptu mechanic and had fixed engines whilst at sea in terrible storms doubtlessly saving the lives of all onboard. He had looked suspiciously at the brand-new Yamaha engine fixed to the back of this skiff and had grimaced when he took the cowling off to see something so shiny and new and covered in grease. Being a grandfather, he was the old man of the skiff. It was his responsibility to pilot it and make sure that he gave the crew a solid platform from which to board anything that they came across.

The final crew member was Dalmar. Dalmar wasn't a fisherman, he was a fighter and he was Abdi's contribution to the crew.

Zahi hadn't wanted an unknown element in his crew but had been clearly told by Abdi that Dalmar had done well in the battle of the camel coral last year and it was a requirement, so Zahi had done his best to make it work. About a week previously Dalmar had taken the team for a walk down the beach and they had spent a day doing weapons training. By the end of it Zahi had learned a couple of things. Firstly, Dalmar really was a fighter and he should never come across him on the opposite side of any battle. The second, surprisingly, was that Tadalesh who had never fired an AK-47 before, was a really good shot at close range. Finally, they had all learned that throwing a grappling hook any distance was really difficult. If you failed in the throw, wasting time pulling it back in from the water, put you at a disadvantage as well as making it heavier for the next throw. Zahi had tasked both Dalmar and Tadalesh to practise and practise with the grappling hook and the ladder whilst he and Yuusuf prepared the skiff and supplies.

With the surf gentling around him, Zahi gave his family one last embrace and reassuring comment before he instructed his crew to take their positions. The skiffs loaded as they were would never move under just their own efforts and Abdi called out to the fishermen and families standing around to come and help them launch. It prompted much laughter when even with more men and women helping to push, the skiff still wouldn't move. Comments such as 'Are you sure she won't sink?', and 'You will never get any speed up!' whilst meant to be amusing were uncomfortably close to the bone. Eventually the young children that were 'helping' but which were preventing a stronger man from pushing were shushed out of the way and inch by inch the skiff was pushed into the swell.

There was a great cheer as she floated and then a moment of wet and dangerous pandemonium in the breaking waves whilst Yuusuf got the engine started. There were a couple of experienced men holding the stern to make sure the bow kept pointing out to sea and making sure the skiff didn't go broadside on. They avoided the danger of the propeller and the moment passed as Yuusuf nudged the skiff well beyond the turbulent surf.

With Yuusuf at the stern and steering using the engine, Tadalesh was in the bow sitting on the ladder which protruded forward a little. Zahi and Dalmar sat amid ships in amongst the vast quantity of fuel jerry cans, food and drinking water bottles. Carefully secured were three AK-47s in a waterproof bag to protect them against salt water and rust. The ammunition was in a box, also waterproofed and lashed down. As Yuusuf gunned the engine a little, they all looked to shore and gave a brief wave to their friends and family on the beach. Then, each determined for their own reasons, they headed out to sea.

Chapter 9.
September 3rd, Indian Ocean.

The sun was scorching, the wind non-existent, and the sea was flat. So flat that it was a lake with small, sparkling ripples on the surface and only the slightest trace of a swell. Dalmar was lying on the bottom of the skiff groaning. For the 20th time in as many hours he was wondering why he had volunteered for this job. Dalmar liked land, good solid sand under his feet with dust and mud between his toes. This 'living thing' called a skiff, that moved in a completely different direction to what his eyes and brain were telling him was just awful. How could he fight anyone feeling like this? He was certain that despite the retching there was nothing left in his stomach to bring up and he just felt so weak.

Zahi was watching him with a slight smile on his face. He and the other men had taken the piss initially, of course. They recalled the image of Dalmar lying draped headfirst over the side of the skiff this morning violently heaving and retching whilst Tadalesh gutted the fish he had just caught. Zahi had nearly pissed himself with laughter when Tadalesh threw the fish guts into the water just upstream so that they floated past Dalmar's nose inches from the water. Dalmar's whimpered reaction seeing what he thought were some of his own insides floating past was priceless.

Of course, the crew hadn't been completely merciless. Now that they were in the area where they thought they might have success; they were just floating and conserving fuel. They had rigged up an awning using some long wooden poles and were enjoying the shade.

Tadalesh was in the bow on lookout duty, Yuusuf was still sitting at the stern next to the outboard engine. His original suspicion of something so new had been completely overturned. His arthritic shoulders liked the simple ability to use a push start button, and his senses liked the complete lack of fumes and the way the engine just purred quietly when idling. His curiosity getting the better of him, he asked the question that was on his mind. 'So where did Abdi get the money to buy four brand new skiffs, with such good engines?'

Zahi wasn't completely sure, and Abdi hadn't told him, but being the leader, it was fair to express his opinion first. 'I am not certain, but it might have come from Nairobi. There are so many brokers there. My old neighbours brother managed to enter Kenya last year and now he works there importing and exporting.'

Tadalesh piped up 'Really! Now that is lucky. Wish I could live in Nairobi. What does he trade in?'

Zahi said, 'My neighbour says that our Somali smuggling routes are particularly good for getting tax free goods into Kenya. He buys them from the Middle East, lands them in one of the Somali ports and then just drives them across the border paying a few bribes. He has taken electronics, pharmaceuticals, cigarettes, all sorts of things. But being a good businessman, when the trucks come back, he brings goods that are made in Kenya like plastic bowls, coffee, maize meal, whatever he thinks he can trade!'

Yuusuf cut back in, 'But that sounds like he has a lot of money. I know your neighbour. He wasn't rich!'

'That is exactly it.' said Zahi, 'The broker in Nairobi went to many Somali brethren and they invested a small amount of money each with him.' The broker made his agreement and set the terms of the business partnership and my neighbours' brother got his funds. Now that there are so many wealthy Somali's in Kenya it's easy to raise money if you have a good idea.' Yuusuf nodded and Zahi continued, 'but this is the really clever bit. With Somali brokers all around the world now, they can move money from one country to the other, never having to actually send the real money by a bank, or even by cash! They send it from one broker to another just on a promise and with a mark in their ledger. On a different agreement, the other broker might 'send' money back to the first broker, who lends his original money back to someone else. It's become so big that if you need the funds, and are willing to make the agreement, you can get the money in any country in the world. The western banks with their stupid money laundering laws and rules can't touch it. The infidel American government can't trace it and can't do anything about it either.'

Tadalesh spoke up again, 'So is that how Abdi paid for this skiff? What happens if this idea is not successful? What happens if Abdi loses all the money?'

Zahi replied a little grimly, 'Well, firstly if that happens then I suspect Abdi will not be long for this earth. Secondly, if that has happened, we will have died trying to make his idea work, and we will be in paradise surrounded by beautiful virgins!'

Dalmar looked up about to say something but then thought better of it. He burped a noxious bubble of bile, groaned, and just lay back down in the shade.

Chapter 10.
September 5th, Indian Ocean.

Night-time on the Indian Ocean. A complete lack of light pollution meant the stars were brilliant against a blue-black sky. The moon was near full and its brilliant white light flooded down. The skiff kept no running lights and continued to bob on a calm sea. The men had taken turns to complete their prayers, with Yuusuf maintaining the prow of the skiff to the East. Dalmar was feeling better, much better, so much so that his natural scowl and grumpiness had come back. It was his shift on lookout duty and he sat in the bow moving his head constantly. The men had eaten using their simple fuel stove to cook. It was fixed carefully to the hull in a specially built frame. A smaller meal of rice and fish stew was allowing them to push their rations further so that already they were thinking they might be able to stay a few more days at sea. Their water purifier was doing its job and the solar panel kept the satellite phone charged. Zahi had spoken to Abdi as promised twice each day. So far none of the other skiffs had seen anything but Abdi said he wasn't worried. The weather forecast was excellent for the next week and he was sure something would come up.

The problem for Zahi and his crew was it was just boring. Floating, watching, catching the odd fish, cooking, watching, and then more floating.

There had been a lot of talk of course. Lots of discussion of who should do what when they actually found a ship. None of them had ever done this before and the main thing they were worried about was that if they could find a ship, how would they actually get on board? Could they actually sneak up on it before anyone even noticed? How high were the sides of the ship? Was their ladder long enough? Could they throw the grappling hook that high? Would their small skiff sink whilst approaching the larger ship just because of the wake created by the more powerful engines? These were all unknowns. They had agreed that once on board, with weapons, they would have the advantage, but there were other uncomfortable questions too. If someone fell into the water whilst trying to board, would they all stop the attack, or would they throw that man one of the empty fuel jerry cans, keep going and then come back?

There had been much debate but eventually they came to an agreement on who was going to do what. Now all they needed was a target.

Chapter 11.
September 6th, Hobyo, Somalia.

Abdi was getting worried. This morning he had spoken to all four Captains and still there was not a single sighting worth getting excited about. He was agitated and he had spoken cross words with his father this morning who had simply asked how it was going. His father had barked back at him and put him in his place, reminding Abdi that it was his connections that had gathered the money and so his reputation on the line. Deep down Abdi had known he was right, but that didn't stop him from leaving the house in a huff. He had gone for a walk to try to settle down a bit and think.

The ocean was a huge place, but it seemed in Abdi's mind that those big Chinese factory fighting ships had a permanent presence just offshore Hobyo, so how come there hadn't been one for nearly a week now? Where were those huge cargo ships carrying containers? Where were the bulk grain carriers? He just didn't understand it and he was getting increasingly stressed.

He pulled out his phone and, in his petulance and frustration Googled 'Where are all the ships?' He started to scroll through a number of articles, skipping most of them but then something caught his eye. He went to a website called vesselfinder.com. As soon the page came up his heart started racing. In his hands he had a live global map showing every single major ship in the world. Where it was, what type of cargo it was carrying, which port it was heading too, and its exact current course direction and speed!

For 60 US dollars a year he could subscribe and see almost real time data based on the ships Automatic Identification System or AIS. As he learned more, he saw it was just like a transponder on an airplane, but for surface ships instead!

Even with the free version in his hand he could click on a ship in the Indian Ocean, see where it had been, where it was heading, and what date it was expecting to get there. Given the site also published the ships current speed it was amazingly simple math to see roughly where it was now.

He rushed back to his house to pull out his laptop rather than work on his small phone screen. Opening it, he pulled up Google Earth and entered the last coordinates that Zahi had sent him from his satellite phones GPS. Then he started searching for vessels due to leave the Middle East with a destination of either Mombasa or Mogadishu. He found twenty or so that were either in transit or due to leave shortly. With a beating heart he quickly started planning. Now this was phishing!

Chapter 12.
September 6th, Indian Ocean.

Another long day had passed with nothing seen. Night had come again and Zahi's crew had settled into the routine. The sky wasn't as clear tonight and there was a thin veil of cloud which obscured the brightness of the moon, taking some of the sparkle off the gentle swell. There were no running lights on Zahi's skiff. They had agreed that whilst a lantern was good for fishing, it destroyed night vision on these darker nights. As the crew had enough fish for tomorrow, they had agreed to sit there in the dark of the evening looking for the lights of a passing ship. For a few hours they chatted, but no one had any news.

Later, Tadalesh was in the bow on lookout duty whilst Dalmar and Zahi were sleeping. Yuusuf was dozing, leaning over his engine with a blanket over his knees. Tadalesh was busy thinking, as young men do, of all the things that might happen if they were lucky to find a ship. Various heroic actions came to his mind that would bring the praise of Zahi and perhaps even Dalmar. Conscious that he was daydreaming he focussed his attention again and took a long slow look around. He missed it on the first sweep, perhaps because of the slightest dip in a long slow swell, but as his eyes passed to port on the second sweep there was an unmistakable sight in the far distance of the lights of a ship. Brighter and yellower than the stars behind them, he couldn't tell how fast the ship was travelling but it was definitely a ship. Pointing at it he shouted 'Wake up! Wake up! It's a Ship! Yes! It's a ship!'

Zahi came out from under his blanket, mind fugged from a deep sleep, not quite understanding at first. Dalmar was up a little quicker, but the winner was Yuusuf who had now spotted the ship, switched on the engine, and was already gunning towards it on an intercept course.

The sudden increase of speed didn't help the men to balance as they tried to clear the decks. The discipline they had had for the first few days of always tidying things away had faded over time and blankets, food plates, and water bottles were strewn everywhere. Whilst Yuusuf drove the skiff, the other men frantically tried to keep their balance as they packed things away. With lots of excited chatter they finally got everything stowed and the last thing they did was unpack the weapons and fix magazines.

'Yuusuf slow us down a little!' called Zahi over the engine noise. 'I don't want them to hear us until the last moment.'

Yuusuf throttled back a touch. It was obvious that they would be able to catch up with this ship at its current speed. After a couple more minutes what looked to have been one bright light on the water split in to three separate lights. As they closed on the target further it looked like a bow light and two bright sodium floodlights. One light over the stern and one over the starboard side. Excitedly Dalmar said 'I think it's a fishing ship!' and Tadalesh with his younger eyes agreed.

Zahi thought for a moment, 'OK, if it's a fishing ship it might be trawling and have large nets out the stern. We should approach it from the side. Yuusuf, do you think you can bring us alongside so that we can try and get the ladder up?'

Yuusuf spoke over the quieter engine noise, 'Yes, but we will have to be careful as we go over the bow wave. We need to be sitting low in the skiff as we go over the bump so that we don't capsize. We must stay there right until we are alongside. I don't know how she will handle when we are alongside a larger ship and moving at speed, but I agree that that is the best plan.'

'Ok,' said Zahi. 'Just like we practiced. When we get alongside, Dalmar, you hook the ladder over the gunwale, Tadalesh you hold the base of the ladder steady whilst Yuusuf keeps us alongside. Then Dalmar, you head up first while I cover you with my weapon and when you are up I will follow. Once we are both up, we will hold the top of the ladder in position whilst Tadalesh climbs up and then Yuusuf can steer the skiff clear. After that Dalmar and I will run like crazy for the bridge. If anyone tries to fight, just shoot them. Tadalesh, you stay on the main deck and make sure there are no surprises. Is that clear?'

Dalmar, Tadalesh and Yuusuf all acknowledged with an excited but nervous 'Yes!' and now came the worst part. They were still about a kilometre away slowly coming to bear and so far, the fishing vessel didn't appear to have seen them. The moments stretched. That initial boost of adrenaline had worn off slightly and a little bit of fear was feeding into Zahi's mind. He had to work hard to keep himself calm, acknowledging internally that this was what courage felt like. It was ok to be afraid he thought, but it's how you dealt with that fear that determined if you were brave. Looking at Tadalesh who looked like he was about to throw up he realised that the others were probably afraid too. 'We are ok my friends, Allah is with us, be strong.'

Dalmar piped up, looking the calmest of the lot and grinning for probably the first time ever. 'It's going to be Ok. They are not even shooting at us yet!'

Tadalesh held down a retch, Yuusuf clenched his teeth with a determined look on his face and steered the skiff closer.

With about one hundred meters to go now, the fishing vessel looked huge. A clunking great rusty green ship with a black funnel spewing out dirty, oily smoke. Above the engine noise of their own skiff, the noises coming from the ship were a blend of rumbling engines and clanking equipment. There were indeed thick hawsers trailing taut from the stern of the fishing ship. She was trawling something and if they got caught up in that then their journey in this world would be over. The deck was fully lit and the Zahi felt his fear spike as they closed on the ship with the skiff lit up, naked. They could see a couple of Chinese men working on nets or ropes or something. There was something else that they could sense now over the noise and the bright lights. It was the smell. The smell of a thousand years of fish innards cloying the air. Nothing sweet about it. Just rotting scales, intestines, and fish shit.

With the vast envelope of yellow light around the vessel, Zahi's crew felt as though there was a huge spotlight tracking them as they approached, but there was still no sign that they had been seen.

Yuusuf could see the bow wave approaching on their port side and spoke quietly. 'Stay low, hold on!' With a deft flick of his arm, he angled the bow of the skiff to the best angle of attack to pass over the bow wave of the fishing ship. Given how calm the sea had been for the past few days, this wave felt huge. The skiff pitched and rolled as it went over and the ladder sitting propped up against a fuel jerry can shifted and landed on Dalmar's ankle. He swore loudly and winced, closing his eyes. Within moments Yuusuf had the skiff up against the hull of the fishing vessel and was holding it there. Crazy flows of water made it difficult to stay steady but already Tadalesh, Zahi and Dalmar were balancing trying to lift the ladder. It was heavy and the three of them bunched together in the narrow skiff, muscles straining. The hooked end waved up into the air as Dalmar tried to lift it over the gunwale towering about 4 meters above them. The skiff lurched and Tadalesh lost his balance, falling on his arse back into the skiff. Zahi and Dalmar had to take the strain with the ladder waving precariously. Zahi shouted 'Yuusuf for the love of your mother hold her steady, Tadalesh get up and help you son of a whore!'

With a huge grunt of effort Dalmar lifted the ladder again and hooked it over the gunwale just as Tadalesh got back to hold the base steady. Zahi raised his AK-47 and aimed high above his head, almost pointing at the stars whilst trying to keep his balance and looking for trouble.

Dalmar, weapon on a sling over his shoulder, leapt onto the ladder and started to climb. It wasn't easy, the ladder shifted and moved, and he had to be careful not to trap his fingers as it slammed back into the ship's hull. He could only just get purchase with his toes on the ladder's rungs for the same reason. As he approached the top, he took a deep breath and prepared himself, muttering a short prayer to Allah. His hands reached the top and went over the gunwale and then his head popped up and into the brilliant flood light.

In a fraction of a second, Dalmar saw a lit deck, fishing tackle everywhere. There were two Chinese fishermen almost opposite staring at the ladder and at him. He looked to the right as he kept climbing but never saw the evil hook of the fishing gaff as it swung through the air, hooked through his left temple and deep into his skull.

Below on the skiff, Zahi hadn't seen what had happened. All he saw was Dalmar's body stiffen at the top of the ladder and start twitching. A moment or so later Dalmar started to lean slowly back, falling. Sensing something was wrong Zahi screamed 'look out!'.

Dalmar was dead in an instant. His body fell the four meters onto the skiff below. His head with the gaff hook still wedged firmly in it struck the gunwale on the starboard side. As his body flipped over the side, the skiff teetered precariously drawing in some water. Zahi avoided being crushed but lost his balance and landed on his arse inside the boat. The shock of the fall caused him to press his finger onto the trigger of his AK-47 and a stream of bullets snaked up the side of the fishing ship in a roar of noise and plinking metal. Yuusuf, trying desperately to stop the skiff from sinking steered away from the side of the ship. He was deeply conscious of the great cables hanging out above their heads dragging the trawling nets. He gunned the engine forcing the skiff out and over the fishing ships bow wave as he moved at speed to get clear. Tadalesh, in shock, was shouting 'Dalmar! Where is Dalmar?'

Finally, the skiff was clear and Yuusuf cut the engine. They looked back and saw the bright lights of the fishing ship as it ploughed on through the seas as though nothing had happened. They saw one of the Chinese men come up to the side where the ladder was still hooked on, lift it up and drop it into the water with a casual disdain.

It was quiet again now. The skiff floating calmly while hearts were hammering. Zahi looked at the spot where Dalmar's head had crunched onto the gunwale. The gunwale had a slight crack in it and the only proof that Dalmar had ever existed was a splash of blood and a lump of grey gloop with some matted hair in it sliding down the inside. Without even thinking what he was doing Zahi picked up a bailing bucket and started to sluice water over the spot. Where the mess was inside the boat, he used his hand to pick up the matter and flick it over the side. When the skiff was clean, he washed his shaking hands and sat down on a bench athwart ships. Remembering his duty as a Muslim and as the ship's Captain he intoned 'Verily we belong to Allah, and truly to Him shall we return.'

Internally he swore.

Chapter 13.
September 7th, Hobyo, Somalia.

Abdi had been to dawn prayers, naturally, and was now striding through the city towards the beach with his satellite phone in one hand and a piece of paper in the other. On it he had written the latitude and longitude that he wanted each of his skiffs to go towards to try and improve their chances of finding a target. He had worked through much of the night using the internet and Google Earth to come up with a plan. By his calculations, his skiffs only had three or four more days at sea before they would have to return home to refuel. He desperately needed someone to be successful.

As he extended the antenna on his phone, he pulled up Zahi's number and pressed the green dial button. It was picked up almost immediately.

'Dalmar's dead.'

'What!'

'I said Dalmar's dead.'

Abdi paused and then replied 'How? What happened?'

Zahi proceeded to tell Abdi a brief version of the story, conscious that this call was being billed at about 15 dollars a minute, more that he normally earned in a day.

After a couple of questions Abdi said, 'Well you had better come home.'

'No. We are not coming home until we succeed!' Zahi had discussed it with his crew, and they fully agreed, what was the point of going back with their tails between their legs? They had so nearly succeeded and were determined to try again.

'Zahi, you are the Captain of my skiff, so I hear you. Now though you must listen to me. I won't tell you how I know but I believe you have a ship coming your way in about a days' time. I will send you a location through the satellite phone as a text message. Use the phones GPS to take you there and wait for a maximum of two days. I do not know if you will be able to take the ship that is coming, but if Allah wills it then you will bring a great prize back to Hobyo and huge honour for your family.'

'Ok, but one more thing. Don't tell anyone about Dalmar yet. I want to tell his family myself.'

'As you wish.' And then Abdi hung up. He had always known that there was the chance that some of the skiffs might not come back, but he hadn't considered an individual dying in such a brutal way during an attack. He thought that they must have been so close to success. To add insult, it was one of those cursed Chinese fishing ships too.

He studied his piece of paper and carefully typed in the latitude and longitude into a text message. He rechecked it and then addressed it to Zahi. He closed his eyes briefly, said a short prayer and pressed send.

Chapter 14.
September 8th, The Indian Ocean

The Hibernia III was fully settled into her sailing routine and was cruising at just over 15 knots, her most economic speed. It was early evening and there were still four days to go until she would arrive offshore Mombasa. Marko the Chief Engineer was on the bridge using the satellite phone. He was having a language problem with the ship's supplier in Mombasa. His thick Ukrainian accent and short temper was hitting up against a very casual Swahili voice at the other end.

'No! I was told you would have the replacement pump for the ships toilet water system when we arrived, what do you mean you haven't been told!' He listened to the other end and then repeated slowly 'Replacement pump! Ships toilet water system!' he listened again. 'Not shit toilet water! Ships toilet water, ship with a P!' He exploded down the phone, swearing in Ukrainian. 'Listen, at this rate my crew won't be able to take a shit or have pee! The pump is breaking as we speak! My assistant is up to his elbows in it and I was promised that you would have a replacement pump by the time we got to Mombasa.' He paused calming a little as he listened, 'Ok check your paperwork and see where the cockup is, I will call you back in the morning and you had better have good news for me.' Fuming he left, leaving the First Officer on the bridge. The First Officer would have smiled except for the fact that his own cabin was beginning to stink of poo.

Szymon, the First Officer, was 28 years old, highly competent and had served at sea since he was 18. He was working towards his Captains exams and he never went anywhere without one of his coursework books. Szymon was tall and thin with short cut, dark brown hair. He was wearing a crisp white shirt, black trousers, and smartly polished shoes. He had just come on duty and received his handover for this shift. Szymon took pride in his work. Here he was, the First Officer on a 100-million-dollar boat, with a 100-million-dollar cargo. One day he would be Captain!

He spent much of the rest of the evening and into the early morning commanding the ship whilst the Captain rested. Professionally he monitored the bridge crew, always with one eye on his own set of instruments, one ear listening to their communications, an ear listening to the sound of the ship and one eye reading for his Captains exams.

It had been an uneventful night but at about 3 AM the radar operator piped up. 'Sir, contact bearing 020, range 15 miles, it doesn't have a transponder and it's intermittent.'

Szymon stood up from the Captains' console and walked towards the radar. Its green screen was dimmed slightly for night-time running. The never-ending sweep of a pale green line forever rotated clockwise around the screen leaving a faint shadow trail as it passed.

'There it is again sir, it's small and not moving very fast.'

Szymon wasn't worried at the moment. This was the only thing of note in the area and whilst it was almost directly ahead, if it was showing on the radar screen at this distance, they could keep an eye on it. He replied, 'Ok, well done, keep watching it and keep me informed.' Then he went back to his books.

Over the course of the next hour the small white blip that was the radar contact slowly moved from a heading of 020 around to the starboard and a heading of 090. The contact was now at a range of about three miles out into the dark night. Just to be sure, Szymon picked up his binoculars, a prized set of Nikon Ocean Pro's that he had indulged in when he had received his appointment as First Officer. He stepped out onto the Bridge Wing on the starboard side and tried to find the object that was getting his radar all worked up. It was darker tonight than it had been for a while and he decided after about ten minutes of careful looking that whatever it was, wasn't carrying any lights. This far out from the shore it couldn't be a fishing boat. Not a chance.

Chapter 15.
September 8th, The Indian Ocean

For Zahi, Yuusuf and Tadalesh the day had been miserable. They had moved at best speed to the location that Abdi had sent through the text message on the satellite phone, but the freedom to travel fast for the past twelve hours had numbed their bodies, to match their souls. Dalmar hadn't been a likable person, but they had come together as a crew over the short week or so that they had been at sea. His grumpy demeanour had been part of the trip and they missed it now. There was an obvious void in the boat where he had sat. The team had been relying on his courage and skill to help them succeed and they felt highly vulnerable now seeing how easily he had been killed. It was even more depressing because they had come so close to actually succeeding in what they had set out to do. That fishing ship had seemed the perfect target. How the hell had that Chinese crew seen them coming? Not only that but how had they set up such an effective trap? So effective that it had defeated heavily armed attackers!

Now that the evening had stretched into the long night and the skiff had settled in the target area, Zahi was feeling sorry for himself. He kept replaying what he had seen of the incident. He never saw the Chinaman before the spiked gaff had killed Dalmar. He had only briefly seen the man's head peep over the rail of the ship high above them before Dalmar fell and Zahi had fallen backwards off balance and shooting. Zahi was trying to think how they would do it again if they could. What would they do differently if they came across another ship now? Approaching from the side worked! You missed the great mass of bubbling, oily water that rumbled behind in the wake stirred up by the propellers. At the bow, the bow wave was tight up against the vessel and really unstable. About two thirds to the rear there had just been a stable spot on this particular ship and there was no way you could get aboard if the skiff was rolling around everywhere.

Of course, they didn't have a ladder now either and that was a problem. Dalmar had been the strongest man and had been most effective at getting a grappling iron to fly high enough to have a chance of clearing the side rail and snagging. The others hadn't practiced with it as much as they could have. Overall, they were in a shit situation.

Having spent a few hours holding a self-pity party, Zahi finally came out of his morose frame of mind and spoke up. 'Losing Dalmar is tough. He was a good man, but for now we have to get on with our jobs and work out a plan. We only have enough fuel to last for a few days here so we need to talk about what we will do differently next time.'

Tadalesh spoke up expressing his fear. 'But what if we do get onto a ship? Now it's only two of us who can get on board. How do we take a whole ship's crew with only two of us?'

Zahi a little impatiently replied. 'What happened last night was just bad luck. Maybe Dalmar had used all his luck up. We have to succeed. We have to make this work. Have you forgotten why we are doing this? A little hard work now can set us up for all our lives! Don't forget, we have the guns they won't!'

Tadalesh went silent and Yuusuf spoke up, the older voice of reason. 'Well I think we can still do it. If we come across another boat, we all go up the grappling hook line. We don't need to keep this skiff. It's a nice boat but its value is nothing compared to what we can get if we can catch a big ship and sail it home.'

Tadalesh looked over incredulous.' But you are nearly 60! How are you going to climb a rope and up onto a ship?'

Yuusuf grinned, 'You look after yourself young man and get that rope hooked up. I will worry about me!'

Zahi looked at the old man, frail and going grey, wondering if he really could get up the rope. 'Tadalesh, Yuusuf is right. Worst case it's just you and me who can get up the rope but if he can make it, we don't need this skiff. We have to commit to taking the prize. You were the next best at throwing the hook so it should be your job. I suggest we accept that as the plan and now that it's late we get some sleep. I will take the first watch and will text Abdi our position to tell him we are ready.'

Tadalesh and Yuusuf made ready to sleep whilst Zahi pulled out the sat phone and in the green glow of the screen navigated to the 'send location' command. Having pushed the button, it was only a few minutes later that he received a reply from Abdi.

'You are in the best place. Large ship coming your way. Probably in a couple of hours. Stay alert and good hunting.' Zahi read the message to the crew. They were excited and keen, but he still told them to sleep while they could.

Two hours passed and Zahi was yawning. He hadn't seen anything at all during his hitch but had noticed some darker clouds come rolling in from the East. It wasn't windy but without the moon to see by a black sky met the black sea somewhere at the horizon. He woke Tadalesh, made sure he was wide awake before getting under the same blanket that Tadalesh had been using. It was warm and dry under there and within minutes he was fast asleep.

Tadalesh took some water from a bottle and rinsed his mouth out, gargling noisily before spitting most of it over the side. He stretched and started his visual scan. It was only about thirty minutes later that he saw a light on the horizon. Knowing that Zahi had only just gone to sleep he gave him another half an hour before he woke him up.

'Zahi, wake up.' No response. A little louder, and with a nudge of his shoulder to go with it. 'Zahi wake up! We have a ship.'

Zahi roused himself and looked. 'Where?'

'It's over there. I have been watching it for a while. I think it's coming straight towards us.'

Whilst Yuusuf also stirred, Zahi studied the approaching ship for about five minutes and agreed. 'Yuusuf, take us out about three miles to its starboard side and then we will sit and wait for it to pass. We do the same thing, approach from the rear quarter and see if we can get a closer look.'

Yuusuf started the engine and moved them at a reasonable pace out of the direct approach. As they moved to a side position, what had seemed to be one bright light transformed into a string of flood lights along what was obviously a huge hull. There wasn't quite enough light to make out what type of vessel she was, but she was long, imposingly long.'

'Allah be praised. Would you look at that. Tadalesh, you are living up to the meaning of your name. Each time you are on watch you are 'Lucky!''

The huge ship kept ploughing through the gentle swell and as it came at right angles to them, at a distance of only a couple of miles, they saw the bridge wing door open and a figure walk out. Perhaps just for a cigarette.

Zahi, trying to contain his excitement instructed Yuusuf, 'Ok, let's move in closer, try to stay out of the light, and use just enough engine to keep us up with her. I don't want them to hear us coming, but I do want to see where we should try to board her.'

Slowly, over the next thirty minutes or so, Yuusuf steered the skiff with extreme caution into a position at about 5 O'clock of the giant ship at a range of about one mile. Gently he started to move them in closer. The gigantic vessel was now directly to the front and Abdi could see the bright orange emergency lifeboats in their housings, hanging at their crazy downward pointing angles at the back of the superstructure.

Another half an hour and Yuusuf was playing a clever game of cat and mouse. There seemed to be a spot just aft of the vessel where the floodlights didn't overlap at range, and where the ships wake was just off to the port side. He kept moving the skiff forward into that black wedge-like shadow, avoiding the wake, and avoiding as much of the light as possible. There was no more chatter on the skiff, just features set in quiet determination.

By now the skiff was only a few hundred meters astern. Dawn was coming and the sky was lightening up behind them. Zahi could clearly see the words Hibernia III stencilled in huge white letters in front of them. The ship towered above, and the sea was churning behind her, a pale phosphorescence disturbed by her huge propellers. The noise was deafening, and now Zahi realised that he didn't need to have been so cautious about the skiff's engine noises. It was also obvious this close that the Hibernia III was very full. She was low in the water for a ship of her class, but the rail above them must still have been almost ten meters up.

Zahi processed what he could see. He had to shout above the noise. 'The good news is that there is a good strong rail up there that we can try to hook. But we can't try here, that wake will sink us if we do. Yuusuf, take us up the Starboard side for a closer look!'

Yuusuf did so. They crept along the length of the vessel, passing under the bridge wing, and moving forward. Again, there seemed to be a calm space about three quarters of the way down the ship where the wake was manageable. The skiff was so close to the massive super tanker that Tadalesh could almost touch the rough painted side.

'This is what we are going to do. Yuusuf take us out by a meter or two from the hull. Tadalesh, you need to muster all of your strength and throw that grappling hook over the rail. Can you do it?'

Tadalesh replied with a very uncertain 'I think so.' He was standing in the bow of the skiff, legs far apart for balance. He had the grappling iron in his right hand and tied to the metal three-pronged hook he had a long coil of knotted rope which he held in his left hand. The loops of the rope were freely coiled at his feet. As he had practiced, he made sure his feet were clear of the rope on the floor and started to warm up his arm. He muttered a short prayer to himself and with Yuusuf and Zahi willing him on he threw the hook with a huge grunt of effort.

The hook sailed into the air, far higher than the height of the rail, but it flew straight up. He almost lost it in the dawn light above him but at the last moment he saw the glint of steel as the hook came straight back down towards the boat. Zahi swore, Yuusuf hadn't seen it and the almost kilo of metal came down and landed within about a meter of him striking the hull of the skiff with a huge crack. The hook didn't penetrate the hull cleanly, but it did cause a large crack to form and water started to flood in.

Zahi screamed, 'Not good enough! Do it again! For Dalmar's sake, show him that you are strong! Show him you can throw!' Tadalesh quickly coiled the rope again in his left hand whilst Yuusuf steered the skiff, already water was gathering at his toes.

Tadalesh prepared himself again whirling the iron, compensating this time for the angle. With a mighty scream, he threw the grapple again and as it soared into the air it sailed over the rail above them trailing the rope behind it.

For a moment no one moved, they couldn't believe it had gone over. Cautiously Tadalesh pulled on the rope, willing for one of the three prongs to catch. He pulled smoothly and for a moment he thought he had failed but then he felt solid resistance against his pull. 'Yes! Yuusuf bring us up against the hull, I will keep pressure on the rope!'

Zahi was already moving, he had his weapon slung over one shoulder and a small bag with his sat phone slung over the other. He crouched carefully moving up the skiff trying not to lose his balance and thinking how stupid it would be to fall out now, to drown in failure. He reached the rope, nodded a well done to Tadalesh gripped the highest knot that he could and started to climb.

As he stepped out of the skiff, there was an awkward swing against the hull. He banged his elbow and his weapon crashed with a metallic clang that would have brought Dalmar back from the dead. He held tight for a moment and then started climbing. Once he got into the rhythm, he just had to pull his own weight and the knotted rope helped. He would pull with his hands and then bending his knees wrap his ankles together trapping a knot. Then he pushed up with his legs, lifted his hands and repeated the motion. The rope though was thin, and his hands quickly began to tire. He looked up and saw he was about halfway there, then he looked down, and wished he hadn't. Pure determination kept him going and with hands screaming in pain, he reached a wire and stanchion side rail that allowed him to grip a horizontal strand for his final meter of climb. He dragged himself over, collapsing in his exhaustion and not giving a shit if there was anyone else on deck or if he had been seen.

Next came Tadalesh, working hard, again his weapon over his shoulder and an expression of pure commitment on his face. He had a moment of a wobble when his ankles nearly slipped over a knot, but recovered well, reaching the top and falling in a heap beside Zahi.

Yuusuf, down below didn't have a weapon to carry, but he had to manoeuvre the skiff forward a little so that he could try to grab the rope. The skiff had filled with a lot more water now and was getting heavier to handle. He gunned the engine surging the small craft forward and scraping against the hull of the super tanker as he did so. With his right hand on the tiller and engine throttle he reached out with his left hand. In one movement he committed everything to the rope. As he let go of the tiller, the skiff yawed off to the right and into the darkness leaving him dangling only inches above the waves.

Yuusuf had a light spindly body, with sinew and muscle and extraordinarily little fat. He was a spry old man and found the climb up the rope relatively simple. After only a few moments he appeared at the top and he stepped over the rail grinning. They had made it.

As they recovered from their exertion, the men took a moment to look around. Now that they were on the main deck their view changed considerably. They knew already that the Hibernia III was long, but now they could really see how wide she was. She was an obese ship, fat, wide, low in the water. In the yellow light of the ships floodlights they could see that the whole deck was painted a dark green. The top deck was fairly clear of obstructions except for a long low cluster of pipes that stretched from bow to stern in parallel lines. Amid ships there was a low crane, painted white and folded down into a stowed position. At the tip of the bow, far ahead, was a slightly taller white mast on which several flood lights were mounted. About 100 meters behind them, at the stern, was the white multistorey superstructure of the accommodation. With the long bridge wings sticking out prominently, the structure looked like some kind of precariously perched sea gull with its wings sticking out. Instead of eyes, the bridge, at the very top of the structure had a row of ten large square windows.

Because of the flood lights mounted above those windows, Zahi couldn't see into the bridge, but he did feel very exposed. Pulling his AK-47 off his shoulder he shouted 'Tadalesh, Yuusuf, let's go! – we need to get up there to the bridge and quickly!'

The men ran down the length of the tanker but even with the adrenaline coursing through them it was hard going. Tadalesh being younger got to the superstructure first and found a door. It looked closed but he turned the handle and the door opened easily. The three men piled in. They were now in the accommodation area. White painted walls with framed photos of various ships, bright blue nylon carpets and an odd smell of last night's supper mixed with sweat and engine oil. In front of them was a staircase, with some kind of cream plastic floor tile, one flight heading up, one down. Zahi led now with his weapon raised. He was followed by Yuusuf and they climbed the stairs cautiously. Behind came Tadalesh covering the rear, walking backwards where he could and trying not to trip over. They went up four flights of stairs in total, with each floor marked clearly by a large number painted on the stairwell. On each deck, a large emergency sign showed the layout of the ship and the way to the exits. They saw no one else on the way up the stairs until they reached the very top landing. There was only a small space at the top, and nowhere to go but forward through the door marked 'Bridge'. Just as they were approaching, the door opened and out came a man wearing black trousers and a white shirt marked with the name Hibernia III in blue writing on the front left breast. The man stopped, his eyes wide, mouth opening and his brain unable to process the barrel of a gun that was pointing at his face. Nor did he process the malevolent eyes behind it.

Zahi was almost as surprised when the door opened but quickly recovered. He pushed the butt of his weapon forward and with both arms extended forced the weapon horizontally into the man's nose and mouth as he was about to shout a warning. The man's nose flattened and then exploded in blood, his cry of alarm changed to a shout of pain and he fell back through the door into the bridge room where he tumbled on to the floor.

Zahi stepped in and fired three shots at one of the windows. The noise, deafening in the confined space of the room did exactly what he wanted creating shock and awe. There were another three men sitting at consoles when he entered and they flinched hugely, jumping at the noise. After a moment of shock, they raised their hands. Shouting loudly in Somali and gesturing with his weapon Zahi pointed to a corner of the room near one of the bridge wing doors where he wanted the four prisoners to go.

Yuusuf stepped into the room next and in his broken English, learned so many years ago in an international hotel in Mogadishu he shouted 'All, go there!' The three men who had been seated stood up slowly and moved to the corner. Pure instinct had made them raise their hands. The man who had fallen to the ground crawled from where he was to the same corner and then sat down with his hand over his nose trying to stop the blood flow which dripped onto the floor. His pristine white shirt now looked like a disaster area, stained with bright red blood spots and a clear smear mark where the man had wiped a blood covered hand. Tadalesh had been next into the room. He had a brief check, to get his bearings, and then he stayed at the door, looking out back down the main stairwell.

Yuusuf told the other three men to sit on the floor and then asked. 'Who Captain?' A young man raised his hand.

Trying to make his voice sound strong and in his Ukrainian accent, 'My name is Szymon, I am the First Officer of this ship. The Captain is asleep down below.'

Zahi spoke to Yuusuf and asked what had been said. Yuusuf translated as best he could and then Zahi asked him some questions.

Yuusuf spoke again but this time to Szymon. 'How many men on ship?'

Szymon replied '24,' but seeing confusion on Yuusuf's face he held up ten fingers twice followed by four more.

Yuusuf understood and then said 'Get all men here now. All men!' this last sentence shouted to make sure that Szymon understood they were not messing around.

Szymon slowly stood up and walked to the bridge telephone. He looked nervously at Zahi who was pointing his weapon directly at him but when he got the nod of approval, he flicked a switch for the ship-wide intercom. He pressed a blue button beside the phone and a short, loud, two tone siren filled the ship before he spoke into the mouthpiece. 'This is not a drill. All ship's crew are to muster immediately on the Bridge.' He repeated the siren and the sentence five times to make sure that any sleeping crew would have heard it and then placed the receiver back in its cradle.

Tadalesh spoke up from besides the door. 'I hear people coming!' he stepped back into the room and took a place out of sight from the stairs and just to the side of the door. He was in the best place to make sure that people would enter but couldn't leave.

The first man through the door was Captain Oleksiy who was shouting before he even reached the top of the stairs. 'Szymon, what the hell kind of order is that? Half the crew is asleep, you have the engineers down below and...' He stopped as he entered the room, saw blood on the floor and then saw the armed men. Zahi, with a flick of his rifle barrel as a gesture, indicated where he wanted the Captain to go. Oleksiy moved to the same place where the rest of his crew were. Eyes watching carefully and trying to work out what was happening. Over the next five minutes the whole of the rest of the crew arrived and soon the corner of the bridge where they were all forced to sit was crammed with men, wide eyed and watching.

Finally, Zahi felt in control. He tried not to show his excitement at what they had achieved. He spoke to Tadalesh and Yuusuf in Somali. 'Allah be praised, we have done it! Now you two, guard these men whilst I go and tell Abdi.'

Zahi stepped out through a door on the bridge wing opposite from where the crew were detained. It was breezy out here, the vast bulk of the ship below and in front of him. To the rear, the sun was just rising above the sea, a gorgeous orange and yellow dawn reflecting off the remaining cloud. He wasn't looking at the view though as he pulled the satellite phone out of his pouch and dialled Abdi's number.

Chapter 16.
September 9th, Hobyo, Somalia

Abdi had been to morning prayers where he had fervently and devoutly done his duty. He had picked up some breakfast consisting of a chapati and some stewed beans from a street vendor on his way home where he had collected his satellite phone for the morning check-ins with the skiff Captains. He was walking down to the beach to do his morning shit when his satellite phone chirruped in his hand. He looked at the screen and his heart squeezed out an extra beat. 'Zahi, how did it go? Did you see the ship?'

Zahi exploded down the phone, 'Yes! Yes! And we took her! We have her Abdi! We have her and she is huge! Her name is Hibernia III, and she is full of oil!'

'Allah be praised, Allah is great! That is good news, that is the best news! Well done! Was it difficult? How did you do it?'

Over the next five minutes Zahi gave Abdi a brief version of the story ending with the comment that there were lots of things to be learned and that when he got back, they must talk more about the tactics of how to capture a ship.

Abdi agreed and then asked, 'So how long will it take to bring the ship to Hobyo?'

'I don't know yet, I thought you would want the good news first. We shall turn her around and then get the navigator to do the math. I will text you when I know the answer. Tell me, how have the other Captains done?'

Abdi lost some of his cheer. 'Well, two of them have already started to come back to Hobyo, with no luck. I haven't heard from Captain Mahmoud for nearly two days' and I am worried about him. Still don't worry about the others for now, this is important. You must ask the Captain to remove the transponder from the ship. It's a box that allows the owner to track where it is. When you have done that, bring back your beautiful prize and we shall talk!'

Zahi acknowledged and Abdi hung up the phone to make his next call. He started with trying to ring the missing skiff, but the only answer was an automated robotic female voice. 'The subscriber cannot be reached.'

Chapter 17.
September 9th, The Indian Ocean

Zahi, came back onto the bridge from the bridge wing. As he closed the door behind him and turned around, Yuusuf gave him an update. 'From what I understand she is carrying petrol, not oil, to Mombasa. It's a mostly Ukrainian crew, that man there is the Captain, and that man is the chief engineer.'

Zahi walked up to the Captain and stared him in the eye. Captain Oleksiy, whether because of his cultural belief that men should be confident, loud, and forceful, or because of some miscalculation started speaking loudly, puffing his chest out. 'What are you doing on my ship! What do you want!'

Zahi was having none of it but he didn't get excited. He could see that Captain Oleksiy was upset and posturing. This was something that the skiff Captains had spoken about on the beach during one of their planning meetings. They had discussed all the options. If a hostage became noisy or belligerent, should they just shoot them early on and set an example to the rest of the crew? A bullet for their AK-47 only cost one US dollar in the Bakara market in Mogadishu. It was an easy way to subdue a whole crew, but Abdi had cautioned against it. He had said that the whole purpose of the project was to make money. The fewer people they could hand over for a ransom, the less money they would make. The Captains had agreed instead that whilst they wouldn't rule out killing anyone, they would leave that as a last resort. First up, they had to show who was in charge, and the way to do that was not to get into a shouting match. The skiff Captains were aware that any ransom situation could take months to solve and Zahi was aware that he had to maintain control of this crew for the next 24 hours or so whilst he got the vessel back to Hobyo. Once home, a large number of guards would swarm the ship outnumbering the hostages and bring stability. He had to make them fear him, he had to force them to his will. Without saying a word, he pointed to Captain Oleksiy and then pointed to the Bridge wing door clearly indicating that he wanted to speak outside. Captain Oleksiy went first, opened the door, and then stepped out. Zahi followed him but as he reached the door, he stopped, he raised his rifle aimed and fired one round about a meter to Captain Oleksiy's left.

Again, the noise was brutal and sharp. The crew left inside couldn't see if the Captain had been shot and a cry of fear went up. Captain Oleksiy who hadn't been expecting it jumped out of his skin and turned around sharply, his eyes wide. Yuusuf, who had followed Zahi and who knew exactly what was coming because they had discussed such a situation beforehand spoke calmly. 'You are not the Captain now. You are a hostage. You do what we say. Say yes or no.'

Captain Oleksiy still recovering from the shock nodded and in a hoarse whisper said, 'I will say yes if you do not hurt my crew.'

Yuusuf translated for Zahi and then said. 'You tell crew, if they do what told, then we not hurt them.'

Oleksiy nodded, 'OK.'

'Good, this what you do. First, you tell crew be good. Next you stop the ships transponder, engineer to bring it to me here. Next, all crew will stay on Bridge from now on, sleep here, eat here, shit here. No one goes alone into ship, must go with one of us. Next when transponder off, change course to heading 330, speed fifteen knots.'

To this last instruction Oleksiy was confused. 'What? Why? Where are we going?'

Yuusuf couldn't help but grin his reply. 'That is easy. We go home.'

For the next two hours, 23 members of the crew were sitting on the floor, some in their night clothes, some in their working dress. They were not allowed to talk. Zahi and Yuusuf stayed on the Bridge with everyone except for the Chief Engineer Marko.

Accompanied by Tadalesh, Marko went down below to get some tools. They came back up and after isolating the power on the circuit board, Marko removed the panel from the back of one of the consoles on the Bridge. Once the cover was removed, it was easy to identify which of the small black electronic boxes was the AIS transponder as it was clearly marked. After a few turns of a screwdriver and the release of a couple of cables he had the box unplugged. Tadalesh took it out onto the bridge wing and walked about 30 meters to the far end. Looking out over the side of the ship he dropped the box into the sea. It fell forty meters or so into the blue green swell with an insignificant splash.

With the transponder disconnected, no-one could remotely get data from the ship anymore, its heading, speed, location etc were no longer being transmitted to the satellite above them. Oleksiy told his First Officer to set a new course and to increase speed to 15 knots.

With agreement from Zahi, the first officer and the helm were allowed to resume their seats at their consoles. Oleksiy spoke to Yuusuf, 'I want to get food and water for my crew. How do we do that?'

Yuusuf thought for a moment before replying. 'Who is cook and who is waiter?' When the Captain pointed to the large chef and to Andres the chief steward Yuusuf said. 'Just the thin one, the waiter. He can get water and food.'

Andres had been doing well so far, he had accepted that this was an act of piracy. It happened a lot in his home shipping lanes in the Philippines and Indonesia. He had heard lots of stories, but he had never heard of pirates operating near Somalia before. It was a complete surprise. If these pirates were like the ones at home, then they were just after money. He wasn't a wealthy man, and he wasn't in charge of the ship. If he could keep his head down, then he would be ok. Being singled out to do a job made him very anxious. As he stood up and blood rushed back to his legs, he reflected that on the bright side he might get to move around a bit, stretch his legs, and help his crew at the same time. Accepting his role quite passively, he nodded and went to get some water bottles from the fridge in the Galley.

Back on the Bridge, a ringing sound came over the Bridge speakers, a phone was trilling next to the Captain's chair. Zahi and Yuusuf looked at each other. They hadn't thought about this but with a nod from Zahi, Yuusuf walked over to the phone and picked it up.

'Hi, Hibernia III, its John at the operations centre for The Aphrodite Freight and Shipping Company, how are you today?'

'Good,' Yuusuf's simple and muffled reply.

'We are getting an error message from your AIS transponder could you please reset it?'

'OK.' and with that Yuusuf promptly hung up.

He explained the conversation to Zahi who smiled and said 'Excellent. Now let's get this thing home and let Abdi do his work.'

The Hibernia III finished a long slow turn before settling on her new course. With a couple of key presses by the helmsman on a computer, her speed increased to 15 knots. As Zahi watched he thought that at this rate, in less than a day, they would be 'home'.

Chapter 18.
September 10th, The Indian Ocean

Abdi had been working hard. With the name of the ship and the power of the internet, he now knew a lot about what was heading towards Hobyo. It was loaded with about two million barrels of petroleum; the ship was bought originally for about 100 million US dollars and it was owned and operated by The Aphrodite Freight and Shipping Company (AFSC) limited who were based in Greece. Abdi had been to their website and had the telephone number for their 24-hour Operations centre. He was pleased to see that they were a big enough company to need such a thing.

Abdi had more immediate problems though and he wasn't ready to speak to the shipping company yet. The first thing he needed to do was to organise the guards for the ship that was going to arrive tomorrow morning by the look of it.

By his calculations, he needed thirty men, all with weapons. They would all live on the ship permanently until, if Allah willed it, they would receive a payment from the ship's owners.

Abdi was worried. He didn't have a lot of money left. He had spent most of what he had borrowed buying the four skiffs and their equipment. He laughed inwardly thinking about what he had learned in his business degree. Like all small businesses he was having a major cashflow problem. Abdi however felt that he was on top of it. He had a plan. He was going to offer a lump sum payment to the men who would guard the ship, with a simple structure. He was going to pay them 30 dollars a day or 900 dollars a month. He was also going to pay for all their food, and he would give them a khat allowance each day. Most of the men he intended to employ would jump at that chance. Even regular meals, and khat alone would probably do it. Many of these men probably earned less than 2 dollars a day but he would make it clear that their risk was that they might not get paid at all, if his plan didn't work. He was going to be completely transparent with them, but he was confident that he could persuade enough of the unemployed young men to do the job. It would be their problem to get hold of an AK-47. By paying them so much, he was also buying their loyalty.

His next problem was feeding them and getting enough khat. He had met with one of the largest merchants in town and struck a deal. The merchant would provide rice, fish, beans and would provide charcoal to cook it. He wanted to charge an exorbitant 50% premium for the whole cost but was willing to provide the goods on credit for three months for the 30 or so guards and 24 crew that Abdi was talking about. Abdi's sister and his mother, with a couple of their friends would do all the cooking. He would pay them the same rate that he was paying the guards. If he ever got the money of course.

Khat wasn't so easy. It was expensive and it was all flown in from Kenya or Ethiopia. For khat to be at its best, it was picked that morning, driven to a local airport, where planes, owned especially for the purpose, would fly it to all the regional airports on a daily basis. Two-day old khat was almost useless as a stimulant, the leaves dried quickly in the heat. Khat leaves picked off the bush that morning got a premium because of its increased narcotic effect. Once the daily delivery plane arrived at Hobyo it was loaded on to pickup trucks that would drive out into the regional towns. By lunchtime it was available in the local markets. Much of the trade locally was done by small traders and none of them could afford to subsidise the khat habit of 30 or more men for three months. He eventually struck a deal, on credit with three different traders. Each would provide one month's supply, flown in daily. Abdi winced when he heard the price.

After all that, Abdi reflected that if he never got paid, his life would be worthless. He would owe nearly 400,000 dollars that he didn't have. If he didn't get paid, he would have to worry about the armed guards, the food merchant, the khat suppliers, Zahi and his team, the blood money for the lost crew members, The Associate who had provided the capital for the skiffs and worst of all, his mother.

Chapter 19.
September 11th, The Indian Ocean

The sun was rising on the starboard side as The Hibernia III approached Hobyo. Captain Oleksiy had agreed with Zahi that mooring such a large vessel offshore would be a difficult operation and that he should manage the manoeuvre. Whilst Zahi had watched closely, Oleksiy had brought the ships speed right down to only a few knots for the final part of the approach. At five kilometres out from the shore, Captain Oleksiys' hope died as he saw the town of Hobyo and the pale desolate coastline that stretched in all directions.

Going so slowly, the final kilometre or so took time. But the bulk of the vessel, its length, the lack of tugboats to give her a nudge if needed in these unknown waters, meant huge caution was needed. It hadn't helped that a gaggle of small fishing boats, not yet returned home after a night of fishing were swarming around the super tanker. Some came far too close, but out on the port bridge wing, Yuusuf waved merrily to friends as they shouted greetings and congratulations.

Having accounted for the wind direction and the current as best he could Oleksiy settled the vessel about 2 kilometres offshore. He instructed the helmsman to stop all engines with the ship heading into wind. Once completely stationary, he then entered a couple of commands into his computer which dropped the anchors. Far ahead at the prow of the ship two vast anchors were released slowly on chains thicker than a man. The vessel was allowed to drift, and the anchor chains continued to spool out long after the anchor heads had embedded in the sand and rock about fifty meters below. The weight of the extra chain would help keep the vessel in position.

Doing a double check for sea room, the Captain was satisfied that when the wind shifted, even with the three-hundred-meter vessel, and with the long length of chain, there was sufficient space for the ship to swing on her mooring and not risk grounding. That said, not knowing the mooring location he felt incredibly uncomfortable. One large rock lurking beneath the swell and a strong wind would cause a disaster.

The Captain had agreed with Yuusuf that the Hibernia III needed to keep one of her turbines running constantly, even in low power. Firstly, to provide electrical power to the ship and secondly to be able to drive the ship away promptly in the event of a mooring problem.

With the tense manoeuvre completed Oleksiy turned to Zahi. Knowing he couldn't speak English but using sign language Oleksiy indicated by waving his hands outwards, palms to the deck that he was finished. Zahi cold eyes, nodded and indicated for him and the rest of the crew sitting at consoles to return to the small section of the bridge that had become a kind of nest of blankets where the men had slept overnight.

Leaving Tadalesh to guard the crew, Zahi stepped outside to speak with Yuusuf. He took a moment to gaze in wonder at the thirty or so small fishing vessels that were floating just below them. His senses gorged on the yammer of voices, the multiple colours, the smell of fish, the sparkle of the ocean and the frisson of success on this fine morning. The fishing Captains were shouting a mixture of questions and humorous abuse up at Yuusuf who was replying as quickly as he could. Zahi waved and called greetings to the men below. The fishermen cheered him, making jokes about how the engine probably didn't work on this ship either, or how he was trying to move up in the world. In a moment of pleased recognition, Zahi waived his AK-47 above his head eliciting another cheer from the crowd.

Zahi looked to shore and could now see 5 fishing boats together coming towards him. They were about a kilometre away and filled with men. He spoke to Yuusuf whilst handing him his weapon. 'Look, here comes Abdi and the ship guards! Take the engineer down to the deck and lower the boarding stairs on the port side.'

Leaving Zahi on the bridge wing looking down to chat with his fellow fishing Captains Yuusuf nodded and went to fetch Marko. Marko led Yuusuf down the internal stairwell and out through the door that they had come through two nights before. They walked forward about 50 meters on the port side and there was a set of metal stairs painted white. They were fixed at one end to the deck level and lowered to sea level using a mechanical winch at the other. They were currently raised parallel with the deck. Normally they were lowered only to pick up a port pilot or for the crew change to a tender vessel. Now however with Marko working the stair winch controls, the lower end was slowly dropped down to the water line.

Staying up on deck and keeping a close eye on Marko, Yuusuf waited. He could see Abdi clearly now standing at the front of one of the approaching fishing boats. A big grin on his face as he came under the lee of The Hibernia III and gazed open mouthed at her sheer scale. Abdi's' boat came up alongside the bottom of the gantry stairs with a slight bump. After a brief wobble, but keeping his balance, Abdi stepped across onto the lowest step.

He climbed the stairs shakily, holding a rail in one hand. He couldn't tell if that was excitement or because he was not used to life at sea. Behind him came 6 of his newly recruited guards, with the other four boats behind bringing the rest. When he got to the top of the ladder, he embraced Yuusuf warmly. 'Well done my friend, what a magnificent fish you have brought home!'

'Thank you, it was a difficult fish to catch. We were sorry to see the one that got away, and what they did to Dalmar.'

Abdi was solemn in his reply 'Yes, who would have thought such a thing could happen. It is good that you have been successful though. Now we can pay our proper respects to Dalmar's family. Now lead the way, show me this prize of yours!'

Yuusuf made Marko who had been almost forgotten lead the way and he walked beside Abdi chatting amiably with the six new guards. All were armed with either an AK-47 or an old British Lee Enfield bolt action rifle, left over from the second world war. They wore a range of clothing, some were dressed in a western style, dirty faded jeans and faded coloured T-shirts. Some wore more traditional macawis, patterned sheets of coloured fabric, similar to a sarong and tied around the waist like a skirt. The balance of the material was then thrown over the shoulder as a shawl. A couple of them also wore a koofiyad, an embroidered cap perched on the top of their head. Those that were not wearing sandals were barefoot. As an unkempt, untrained troop they climbed the stairs behind Abdi and Yuusuf following as they entered the bridge.

As they entered a collective groan came from the crew who were sitting, confined to one corner. Somehow, seeing a large group of armed Somalis enter and stare at them was all that was needed to extinguish any last hopes that this ordeal would be over quickly.

Zahi standing by the Captain's chair now and hearing that exhalation, turned as Abdi walked in and gave him a grin. They embraced, with Abdi saying, 'You look tired my friend, but what an achievement!'

Zahi reflected in his reply, 'Yes, we haven't had much sleep for the past couple of days, but we have been successful.'

Abdi grinned back, 'Yes, very. Did you know that the 'famous Captain Zahi' is now a living legend in Hobyo!'

Zahi, always humble, smiled, 'Allah has been kind to us. It's through his will that we have been able to achieve this. He is great.'

'Yes, Allah is great, but you were the instrument of his greatness this time. You too deserve praise!'

'Thank you, I see you have been busy whilst we have been gone. You have found enough men to guard the ship?'

'Yes, we have thirty men who will manage the ship and their crew. They will guard it day and night. I assume you will want to stay on board and manage this until completion?'

Zahi hadn't really considered this at all. None of them had really considered the next steps, but he quickly made up his mind. 'Yes, I want to protect my investment. But I don't want to manage a guard force. I will stay on board, but I will also speak to my brother Hassan, I know he is disabled, but I think he will manage the details of the guards, and he will enjoy the responsibility. I will then stay onboard and manage the crew and the ship.'

Not completely happy but understanding the need to protect his own share and needing someone who would manage the Somali guards, Abdi agreed. 'OK, send a message for someone to go and get him. I want to speak to the Captain of this ship. Which one is he?'

Captain Oleksiy who had observed this discussion, but not understanding Somali stood up when he saw Zahi pointing at him. He was surprised when Abdi started speaking to him in perfect English, with a hint of a London accent. After a brief and overly courteous introduction Abdi continued, 'Captain you have a problem. I and my friends have stolen your ship and all your cargo. For now, we own you as well.' The Captain narrowed his eyes as Abdi continued. 'However, there is as you say, honour amongst thieves. My aim is simple. I want to sell your ship, your cargo and you back to your owner, and I want to be paid an exceptionally large amount of money. I will say this. You and your crew are going to shall we say, be my guests, for several months I expect. I and my men will treat you fairly if you and your men promise to behave. We will feed you; we will not beat you unnecessarily, but have no doubt, we will kill any man who tries to attack one of us. Now, you were in command of this ship, but not any longer. I will allow you to remain in command of your men, and you may speak on behalf of them. Is all of that clear?'

Oleksiy, who had spent the last 24 hours trying to think of a way out of this but finding none was of mixed feelings. Part of him knew that the shipping company didn't want to lose a couple of hundred million dollars of ship and cargo. Part of him knew that piracy, and let's be blunt, that's what this was, was a dangerous game. If he didn't act carefully, some of his crew could die. If he got it right, then everyone might get home one day. 'I understand what you are saying. I will speak to my crew, but there are some things that we will need to do if we are going to live on this ship together for a long time.'

Abdi, relieved that his message had got through, and that there might be a clear path to negotiate replied. 'OK, I want you to think about what is needed, sleeping mats, food, and things and then we will talk again this afternoon. I will stay on this ship for a couple of days while we settle things so we will have a chance to speak later. For now, point me in the direction of your ships satellite phone.' Oleksiy pointed to the Captain's chair and Abdi walked towards it, sat down in it and looked forward out of the bridge windows over the vast bulk of the ship in front of him. He spoke a command in both English and Somali to be quiet, and the chatter stopped. The guards and all the rest of the crew were all outside his peripheral vision and for just a moment he felt alone on the bridge. He paused a moment to gather his thoughts before he lifted the telephone handset and began to dial a number that he had taken from the internet the day before.

Chapter 20.
September 11th, Athens, Greece.

John was sitting in the large open office that was the operations centre for The Aphrodite Freight and Shipping Company or AFSC as it was known by. The centre occupied most of the second floor of a small multi story building that also housed several of the other major Greek shipping company offices in Athens.

The office was located near to the main port in Pireas in a prestigious building that looked East towards a private marina and West towards the main industrial port. The employees joked that Mr Mateo Papadopoulos, the owner of the company, had an office that looked East, towards his awfully expensive superyacht. That left the staff to look West and to the working ships. It was a little unfair, Mr Papadopoulos had built AFSC up from almost the ground, inheriting a small company from his father, but turning it into the large multinational shipping and freight company that it was today. He had shared his success with his staff and was a fair man. If he wanted an office that looked out over his toys, then that was ok with John.

Johns' office didn't have a window. The operations room had a large number of digital screens though, and the reflections would have been irritating. John, an English merchant navy veteran of 20 years had semi-retired to Greece when an old friend had recommended him to AFSC as exactly the right person to run a large shipping fleet. He had let his physique go a little; well, who wouldn't with the diet down there, and his thinning black hair indicated that he should have been brave a few years ago and gone bald. Appearance aside, John was employed to manage Mr Papadopoulos's fleet of ships. Whilst it fluctuated a little, the company owned nearly 70 ships now ranging from cargo ships to Very Large Crude Carriers. From this room, and with his operations staff, John knew what they were all doing and where they were in the world every minute of the day. Every single one of them was displayed now on the screens in front of him. Actually, that wasn't true, one of them wasn't anymore, and that was bugging him. Yesterday, he had spoken to the ship and asked them to reset the transponder, but it hadn't worked. He made a note to speak to the Captain this morning as he looked at his daily tasking sheets. He parked that one for now and prepared for his morning Ops meeting.

Shortly after ten o'clock John had just been to the office canteen and had used the bean to cup machine to make himself a double shot of espresso. He took the small paper cup back to his desk and as he sat down his internal phone rang. 'John, it's the ops desk, I think you need to take this call. It's the Hibernia III calling in and something is very wrong. The guy on the other end says he has taken control of her. It's not Captain Oleksiy, but the accent is educated English.'

'Ok, thanks Ops, put it through.' There was the slightest of clicks and then the crystal-clear comms of a high-quality digital satellite call. 'Hello, good morning, you are speaking to the duty operations manager at AFSC, how can I help you?'

There was a fraction of a delay as the landline signal went up into space and then came back down to the vessel some 8000 Kilometres away. 'This is the man who has taken control of the Hibernia III, I want to talk to the man in charge.'

John, frantically searching his hard drive file directory for his vessel hijacking response sheet replied. 'Hello sir, today I am the duty manager so I think you are speaking to the right person, could we start by sharing our names? My name is John.'

Abdi at the other end thought for a moment, he didn't want the other man to know his name just yet, so he replied with. 'John, my name is not important. What I am about to tell you is important. You can just call me Hibernia, after your ship.'

'OK Mr Hibernia, what would you like to tell me?' John had found his response crib sheet by now and was trying desperately to read it whilst focusing on what the man was saying.

'Well John. This is the situation. I and a large number of my friends have taken your ship, and right now it is parked somewhere in the Indian Ocean. I have all of your crew and they are alive for now. If you want your ship back, your cargo and your crew alive, then I want 100 million United States dollars and I want it by the end of this week.'

John was frantically typing into his response card but was trying not to be focused only on the paperwork, whilst trying to think about the problem. He knew that response tactic 101 was to repeat back what had been said. 'Mr Hibernia, I believe I have heard what you are saying, but I want to double check with you. You say that you want 100 million US dollars by the end of this week in return for the release of the Hibernia III, her cargo, and her crew. Is that correct?' After an affirmative from the man known as 'Hibernia' John continued. 'Mr Hibernia, I understand what you have said. I have to tell you that I will immediately speak to my superior but please understand that such sums are beyond my ability to agree. Please can you tell me how I should contact you, and I will call you back later today.'

Abdi kept his voice calm and said 'I am on your ship; you can call the phone number that is on the Bridge. If I do not hear from you, I will be extremely disappointed and will have to take some other.... action.' Abdi thought the pause for dramatic effect was a good, and it left him the ability to get angry later if he needed to.

John came back on, having read the bold type at the bottom of the response form. 'Mr Hibernia, I would like to speak to a member of the crew, or the Captain please. You understand I need to verify the situation?'

Abdi paused, and put his hand over the microphone on the phone. 'Oleksiy, you can say one sentence down the phone to this Mr John. Tell him the ship is captured, the crew are well and immediately pay the money. Anything else and I will be angry.'

Oleksiy stepped up to the phone. Abdi handed it over and stared coldly into Oleksiy's eyes. 'John, its Captain Oleksiy. I have been told to say that the ship is captured, the crew are well and please pay the money immediately.'

'OK, Captain, can you tell me where you are?'

But Abdi had already taken the phone back and replied sharply. 'That wasn't reasonable. The price has just gone up. I want 110 Million dollars now. Don't Fuck with me again!' and then he hung up. Abdi thought the call had gone well considering. Allah be merciful, what a crazy amount of money! He was sweating profusely despite the air conditioning on the bridge.

In the offices of AFCS John was breathing heavily trying to calm down. What the hell was he meant to do now? Like all ex-mariners, he knew there were procedures to help people in difficult situations. The first thing he did was collect his thoughts and fill in the form. Who the hell wrote these things anyway? Did the voice sound anxious at the other end? Not really. Educated? Yes. Background noises? Now that he thought about it, he thought it didn't sound as though the ship was underway. The man definitely spoke good English, and it appeared that Captain Oleksiy was alive. 110 Million dollars by the end of the week. Seriously? How the hell was that going to happen? Having filled in the details he went further down the form, which told him to open a response plan called AFCS Emergency Response Plan – Hijack at Sea.

With a click of his mouse the word document opened and the third page after the front page and the document control page was a flow chart. It told him exactly what he had to do. Firstly, call the boss. The boss should then form the incident management team. Secondly, if the hijack was confirmed, he should call the response company. Ok, well he could do that, but he was going to check with Mr Papadopoulos first.

He picked up his phone again. 'Mr Papadopoulos its John in the operations centre.'

'Hi John, tell me how our empire is this fine morning?'

'Umm, well sir I have to report an incident to you. It seems that The Hibernia III has been hijacked somewhere in the Indian Ocean. She is fully loaded with a cargo of petroleum products and was on her way to Mombasa. I have just received a ransom demand by a phone call. The hijacker wants 110 million US dollars by the end of the week.' John had blurted this out, feeling a little out of his depth and the enormity of the situation.

'Oh dear.' He paused and then said 'John, tell me is the crew ok?'

Wow! John wasn't expecting that, but he reflected later that that was why the man had built a successful company with employees that loved working for him. 'Sir, I spoke to the Captain briefly. He told me the crew were ok. I have checked the Hijack response plan and it tells me that you need to authorise me to assemble the incident management team and that I should call a global phone number for a response consultant next. Is that OK?'

'Yes, yes, certainly. We must work out how to solve this little problem. It looks like our day has just changed for the worse. Form the Incident Management Team for mid-day and I will be in then.'

'Yes sir.' At which point they both hung up. John breathed for a moment, then picked up the receiver and called the number which was in big bold letters in his response plan. It rang just twice before being picked up by a very calm and cool female voice at the other end.

'Good Morning, this is the hotline for The Global Response Company Limited, how may I direct your call?'

'Hello good morning, I am the duty manager at AFCS, I need to report a vessel highjack.'

'Very good sir, I will put you through to our duty response manager.' John was put on hold for a about a minute, during which he was subjected to listening to an instrumental music track, that if he had to bet on it was based on music written by Enya.

A gravelly male voice came on the phone. Definitely one that still smoked 20 cigarettes a day and definitely a voice that had grown up having gone to an English public school. 'Hello good morning, my name is Finlay. I am the duty crisis response manager for TGRC. To whom am I speaking to please?'

Feeling that he was finally talking to someone in the right space, John introduced himself and briefed Finlay about the problem that had just landed in his lap.

When John had finished, Finlay asked a couple of follow up questions. 'Tell me, what was your gut feeling about this when you received the call? Did you think it was legitimate, serious?' There was no doubt in Johns' mind, and he said so.

Finlay continued 'Ok, so the bad news is obviously that we have a situation that we have to deal with fairly sharply. The good news is that now you have informed us, we will support you all the way. Your company is fully insured with us, and it is our job now to help you manage this from a negotiation perspective and to work with your vessel insurance company. I assume you have formed your own incident management team or IMT? Yes? Good. I will join you via the phone for those meetings so that I can advise your leadership team. As soon as I can, I shall join you physically in Athens, I suspect I can get there by tomorrow morning. In the meantime, I will need you please to share with me the response form that you have filled in. From now on a couple of ground rules. No matter the reason for the hijackers calling, we will need to set up a way that they will always be transferred to the same person as yet to be identified in your organisation. For now, that should continue to be you. No one else must speak to the ship at all unless you and I have agreed it in advance. I will prepare a short note so that you can call them back and that we fulfil your agreement of someone coming back to them today. When we meet tomorrow, we will need to develop a negotiation strategy. Are you happy with all that?'

'Yes, certainly.' John had been scribbling notes furiously and was actually incredibly happy with that. From feeling distinctly out of control, especially given all the information he had just received, he now felt that there was someone on his side, who not only knew what to do, but who had obviously done it many times before.

'Excellent, I will text you my email address now and if you send a copy of your notes in the response form, I will send you a broad overview of next steps.'

'Yes, no problem.'

'Perfect, well let's chat later today John once I have had a chance to review. Chin up old chap, we shall work this problem together.' And with that Finlay hung up.

John reflected for a moment not really processing what had happened in the whirlwind of the past 20 minutes of his life. He didn't give himself too long. He now needed to mobilise all the members of the incident management team for a meeting that was going to start in just over two hours' time.

He pulled up todays' duty manager sheets and started with the first name on the list before picking up the phone and dialling again. 'Hey Martha, it's John. We have a problem.'

Chapter 21.
September 11th, Hobyo, Somalia

Later that afternoon, after Abdi had a call back from John, he was sitting on a sofa in Captain Oleksiy's stateroom. It was on the floor just below the bridge and had three oval windows which looked forward over the deck. There was a TV with a DVD player on a low piece of furniture in front of the sofa, and on the other side of the room, a small wooden dining table that would sit up to 6 people. Through a door on the right was the Captains bedroom with an en-suite bathroom. It wasn't too bad Abdi thought, but he also reflected that if you were going to spend half of your life at sea, you needed the creature comforts. He thought that this room would suit him very well when he was on board. As he was sitting there, the door opened and to his surprise his father walked in.

'Abdi, this is amazing! Who would have thought it!'

'Father, it's great to see you here, but I wasn't expecting you... Why have you come?'

'I had to see the success of my son's little project, I haven't set foot in a fishing boat for years, but it was worth coming out here to see this ship. Its gigantic! It's all we can see from Hobyo. You should hear what the elders were saying this morning. We talked of nothing else!'

'Well thank you father I am delighted that you are happy, but we still have a long way to go. So far, we have a ship, and we have a crew, but we haven't even started to work out how we are going to turn that into real hard cash. It's going to take many months yet.'

'Abdi my son, you have made me proud, and I know you will work this through. So, tell me, what do you think you will get the owners of this pretty vessel to pay for all your hard work?'

'Father, come and have a seat and let me tell you. Would you like anything to drink? The Captain has his own fridge which is filled with sodas and drinking water.'

Abdi's father sat at the other end of the sofa whilst Abdi took a can of Coke from the fridge, opening it for the old man before handing it over. 'Father, unbelievably, this ship is worth 100 million US dollars, and that is just the ship! With the fuel that is on board, add another 100 million dollars. Then we have 24 crew members, let's say half a million per person. Call it a round 210 million dollars in value. Then we have the greatest thing of all. Every day this ship is not working, it costs the owner 100,000 US dollars in lost chartering fees. That means, every day that the ship is under our control, it costs them even more money and that will be extremely helpful to apply pressure when it comes to negotiating. I made my first phone call to the owners this morning and I demanded 110 Million dollars for them to get their ship and crew back!'

Abdi's father sucked his teeth noisily, extremely impressed. As a sum of money, you could probably buy every property in Hobyo and the surrounding towns, every fishing boat on the beach for 20 kilometres in every direction and the airfield as well. 'Do you really think they will pay such a sum?'

'No father, this is just like going to the market. The stall selling you beans is going to ask for three or four times their worth to start with. We are going to haggle, and we will be talking large numbers. They will come back with an incredibly low number and we will go back and forth. The best thing is that we have the advantage. If we go quiet for a couple of days to apply pressure to them, its costs them hundreds of thousands, just for us not answering the phone!'

'It sounds like you have everything planned out. So how long do you think this will take?'

'The simple answer father is that I do not know. I have planned for a couple of months, but I really do not know. At the moment we have the benefit of surprise and things are in our favour. I would like to complete for a high price, and quickly, but I just don't know.'

Abdi's father turned serious for a moment. 'You know I have been told by some of the elders that this is a criminal act and that you could bring unwanted Federal attention to our city.'

'Yes, I have thought of that. The crime was committed in international waters, the ship is now in Somali waters, but with all the political infighting in Mogadishu and the complete lack of government up here I think we will be ok.'

'But son, I am the responsible man for government up here!'

'Yes father, and that means that you are best placed to deal with any interest that might come from the central government, or anyone else for that matter. We will have sufficient money to be able to grease our way out of any problems I am sure.'

'If you get paid!'

'Yes father. If we get paid.'

'You know son, I was thinking that the mosque needed to be redecorated.'

'Father, if we get paid, I will take care of that, and much more. We need to make sure that if we are going to make a business of this, that we have all the community on side. I believe we can make this work, but for now I need your support with the elders. Can you give me that?'

'Of course my boy! Now I am sure you have things you need to do. I am going to take a look around and then I will head back to shore.'

'Good and thank you.' Abdi gave his frail father a hug and then helped him out into the corridor before heading up to the bridge again. When he got there, he found Hassan talking with his brother Zahi. 'Hassan, has Zahi told you what he needs you to do?'

Hassan, leaning up against the Captains' console and with a crutch under one arm nodded and replied, 'Yes Abdi, he has told me that I am responsible for managing the guards. He has told me that I must make sure they don't beat the crew unnecessarily or kill them. He has also told me that I should take instructions only from him or from you.'

Abdi stared at this young man, a little uncertain if he really wanted to hand over some of the responsibility of this critical phase to him. On the flip side, he certainly didn't want to be on this ship all the time himself, so he decided he would brief all of the guards together that Hassan was working directly for him and that if there were any issues then they would be thrown off the ship without pay. 'Very well, but I want to be in close communication with you and Zahi each day, if there are any problems you let me know immediately.'

Abdi spent the rest of the day walking around the ship, his ship. He walked into various rooms and bedrooms and saw decadent wealth all over the place. Mobile phones, TVs, laptops, wallets, all sorts of things. He made a mental note to make sure to tell the guards not to steal everything but wasn't sure how successful that would be. He strongly suspected that before the night was out, there would be a lot of 'new' TVs in houses in Hobyo.

Chapter 22.
September 12th, Athens, Greece.

Finlay had had an early start. He had flown from Heathrow to Athens, landing at 08.45 local time. His new client, AFSC, had sent a car to pick him up and he had just been whisked to the offices near the port. He had been given a seat in a medium sized meeting room on the second floor just off the operations centre and had been told to make himself at home whilst he waited for today's incident management team meeting.

Finlay had waited a while but then managed to sneak out to the smoking area where he inhaled a cigarette in almost one drag. That and his fourth cup of coffee for the day, along with a dodgy pastry of some kind served on the airplane had been breakfast. He had picked up all three habits during his service with the metropolitan police which he had left about six years previously. He had led the kidnap response unit in the specialist organised crime command. He had been successful and aside from his pension had left with an MBE for his hard work too. Whilst he smoked, he mused to himself; it was about time he should give up that filthy habit. Those pastries just were not good for his waistline. He was just reviewing his slide deck for his presentation as the clock in the room showed 11.20 and in filed Chloe, an old friend.

Chloe was a lawyer and she worked for Stratton Parker Insurance, SPI, the global insurance behemoth that was one of the leading agencies providing maritime all risks insurance. There were not many that specialised in piracy related risks, but it was a demonstration of Mr Papadopoulos's care for people that AFSC paid the extra premiums. It didn't hurt his business that he had made the right decision from a financial perspective either.

Chloe had short dark red hair worn in a bob which suited her pretty oval face well. It gave exactly the right no nonsense, intelligent look that she was after. The fact that she dressed immaculately in a black business jacket, knee length skirt and a cream blouse reinforced the effect. Chloe and Finlay had worked together on numerous occasions and they worked well as a team. Chloe worked for SPI and SPI paid for Finlay's services as a response consultant. The fact that Chloe's company was on the hook for potentially a large sum in this situation meant that the personal attention of her legal expertise and

Finlay's negotiation expertise were going to be crucial to get the best outcome.

In a voice far brighter and more cheerful than it deserved to be after her early start she piped 'Hi Finlay, how was your flight?'

'Chloe! My dear lady, it was awful as always, but those stresses have faded away now that you have waltzed into my morning.'

With a smile that she genuinely meant she replied, 'Always the charmer Finlay.' Finlay was twice her age and was always bordering on a little flirtatious, but never anything inappropriate. She continued. 'So, tell me, have you initiated contact? What did our opponent sound like?'

Finlay was about to reply when the door opened again and in trooped about 10 people, all of whom said good morning, or shook hands with both Finlay and Chloe to the point where names became a blur. The one name that stuck was Mateo Papadopoulos. Finlay went straight up to him and after saying good morning he leaned in and quietly asked if he could very kindly have a quick word outside the room. Mr Papadopoulos agreed, and they ducked back out of the room for a moment.

'Mr Papadopoulos, I appreciate that we have literally only just met, but I would like please to ask for a simple ground rule before our first meeting.' Mr Papadopoulos raised an eyebrow and Finlay continued. 'Sir, in my experience, the most effective team to resolve a problem of this nature is a small, very discrete team. You need to have a few highly trusted managers with certain skill sets in the room, and they will need to do a lot of the legwork themselves on this one in order to keep confidentiality at the highest level. Once the key strategy decisions are made, if we must, then we can open it up, but I would suggest you don't want the parameters of any negotiation to be widely shared or leaked. It would jeopardise not only your company reputation but also the managers that make the decisions. Worst case, the opposition could get wind of things through a media article and suddenly increase their demands, because they may hear you might have agreed more generous terms.'

Mr Papadopoulos looked at Finlay with his round friendly face and in his heavy Greek accented English, 'That is why you are here Finlay, so that you can advise us on how we should deal with this awful situation. Which roles would you suggest we have in the room?'

Delighted that he wasn't going to have to push his experience aggressively as a persuasive tactic Finlay rattled off the key roles.

'Well, I would suggest you want your legal counsel, media relations, your HR director your operations manager and a highly trusted person who will log all events and decisions. Along with you as the crisis manager I would say that that's it. If I may, we might also want to get a video conferencing screen into the room, some whiteboards mounted on the walls, a couple of telephone lines, flip charts and stationery.'

'Ok, anything else?'

'Yes, one more and it's one of the most important.'

Mr Papadopoulos raised an eyebrow. Finlay continued, 'You need one of your team to take the primary role as the communicator with the hostage takers.'

'But isn't that your job?'

Finlay smiled. It was a common misconception that the 'response consultant' did the negotiating with the opposition. Not only was that not true but it was a dangerous line of thinking. 'No. My job is to advise you as the Board and to help you liaise with the insurers. I will coach the person that you nominate as the communicator, so that they have help all the way, but there is a long list of reasons why it should be someone close to your company and to the team on the highjacked vessel and not me as the response consultant.'

'Ok, tell me more.'

'Well, you need to nominate someone of sufficiently high decision-making capability, but not the final decision maker. They should be familiar with the ship and crew and the way the company operates. They should have good communication skills and the right level of gravitas so that the opposition believe that the negotiation is happening in good faith. They must not be part of this crisis management team, and the information we give them must not put them in a place where they are compromised. They will need to work privately, away from internal staff for the duration to help maintain confidentiality. Somebody else will need to cover their day job.'

'OK, that's a long list and I will think about who in the team has the necessary skill set. Let's discuss that later today.'

They both stepped back into the crisis management room with Mr Papadopoulos starting immediately. 'Right, let's begin' He gave a strong hint as to how he had grown such a great shipping empire as he reeled of Finlay's instructions absolutely verbatim, adding his own reasoning for keeping the team small, and without causing offence to all of those other senior managers who had come into the room with him and who now had to leave.

A few moments of disappointed shuffling of chairs as some people left, and those who had been asked to remain were now seated around the board room table. Mr Papadopoulos opened the meeting with some suitable senior management type remarks on how serious the situation was. He stated that his main priority was to save the lives of those seamen who had been taken hostage, and his secondary priorities were to manage the reputation of the company for the long term and to recover the assets if possible. He then handed over to Finlay who had agreed to give a broad overview of how this type of problem usually got resolved.

Over the next hour Finlay gave an induction into the hostage resolution business. Having established that none of them had ever dealt with a ship hijack before, he explained what each of the persons around the table's roles would be with Mr Papadopoulos nodding his assent or querying if something needed clarification. Finlay issued crib sheets to each person with some reminders of what they might need to focus on, giving reassurance to those who were looking wide eyed and uncertain.

Over the course of the rest of the day and after a break for a working lunch, Finlay and Chloe detailed what the next few months might look like to the leadership team at AFSC. As expected, there were a lot of questions, but by the end of it the team were feeling a lot happier about how to manage the problem and what might come up as a result of it. They all realised that the work was only just starting though.

At 19.30 that night Chloe and Finlay who were both staying at the Marriot Hotel in Athens were sitting in the bar and having a drink before supper. They were discussing their client and Finlay commented, 'You know, it never ceases to amaze me how many organisations don't take time out to practice responding to incidents, even when they are clearly at risk of having them. If AFSC had trained their staff properly and run a desktop exercise or two, then we wouldn't have to spend the whole of today giving quite so much instruction and we might have got on with resolving some of the issues.'

For Chloe, this was just as familiar a problem and she nodded her agreement. 'Well at least this team are listening, and at least they have the right insurances. What was the name of that company last year who lost a vessel to pirates in the far East and then went bankrupt?'

Finlay thought for a moment, 'I can't remember....'

'Exactly! That's my point! At least AFSC will bounce back from this one provided we do our jobs. Now, I am hungry, let's go and get something to eat.'

Chapter 23.
September 13th, Athens, Greece

It was 07.30 and Finlay was in a small office on the 4th floor of the AFSC office building. An incredibly nervous looking John, the Operations manager was sitting with him. The room was quite large, had a large bay window looking out to the West and the port. There were a couple of white boards on the walls but perhaps most importantly the internal wall to the rest of the office was solid so no one walking past could see into the room. There was a standard office desk, with a single landline phone, but no computer or monitor. There was no other digital or electronic equipment in the room other than a specialist tape recorder that was attached to the phone. In front of the whiteboard was another plain white rectangular table and three chairs. Finlay and John had met briefly yesterday but Finlay had started again with some simple introductions and his background.

'So that's enough about my experience. I know Mr Papadopoulos gave you a call last night, but did he fill you in much about what he wants you to do?'

John took a sip of his coffee and replied with his best merchant mariner attitude. 'Well apparently he wants me to negotiate with the bastards that took our ship.'

Finlay laughed. 'Well yes and no. We would like you to be the face of the negotiation to the hostage takers. We want you to create the relationship with the opposition negotiator so that we can get to a reasonable outcome for everyone.'

John, taking the cue, 'But you don't want me to call him a bastard again?'

Finlay smiled, 'It would be immensely helpful if you didn't, especially to his face. We need you to create a positive working relationship with the hostage taker, and as you coincidentally were one of the first people to talk to him that's a positive.'

John still nervous replied, 'Ok, but I have never done anything like this before. How does it work?'

'Well, we are going to try to gain trust with the hostage taker. That may sound odd, that we want him to trust us, but we ultimately want to negotiate to a successful conclusion. We have to think of it as a business discussion. He will have demands and so will we. We need to get to a solution saves lives and gets the company assets back. The best solution for them is most likely to get a large sum of money as quickly as possible, without any military intervention.'

'Ok, so why don't we just say we will give them a lot of money tomorrow and get this over with?'

'Well, think of it like this. If you go into a car dealer to buy a car, and the sales rep offers you loads of things for free that you hadn't even thought of, within the first five minutes what would you do?'

John thought and then replied, 'I would ask for more. If they are that desperate to sell, I could get a better deal.'

'Exactly! If we offer too much to begin with, they will ask for more money and it takes longer. The other outcome, if we pay too much, is that they will target us in the future, or other vessels and so the whole industry gets stuck paying more and more money.'

'Ok, I suppose that's logical, but it's looking a long way into the future.

'Again, yes and no. If we offer too much too early, they might change direction. It's not like any normal transaction. We don't just go gently towards each other and meet in the middle. External factors will happen. They might get nervous about being able to hold the vessel safely, a crew member might get sick, the military might arrive. And in the same way, we might get an unhelpful family member saying publicly that the company has hundreds of millions of dollars and should pay up. If you were on the other side, you would immediately raise your demand wouldn't you.'

'Yes. I suppose so, but how is this going to work? Procedurally I mean.'

'Well, the crisis management team are going to develop a strategy. You won't be party to that whole strategy. It's important that you are insulated from it and don't know the full agreement, or any target settlement figures. You will need to do your best to create a relationship with the hostage taker away from the bigger picture. In the strategy, you will be able to agree certain small things within parameters and based on your own judgement, to keep the negotiation going. But you won't be able to approve or agree some big-ticket items. Over time, the crisis team will approve slightly higher numbers in terms of the ransom or other concessions, and it will be your job to insulate the final decision makers from the emotional impacts of dealing with the hostage taker.'

John asked, 'Is that going to be difficult? The emotional part?'

'I won't lie to you. It will. But your ultimate goal now is to save as many lives as possible, ideally all of them. Mr Papadopoulos has probably already told you that your deputy will take over your normal day to day operations manager role, whilst you focus solely on this. You are going to need to take time out to get your headspace right and to think meticulously about every phone call you are going to make. What I can tell you is that getting this right is hugely rewarding from a job satisfaction perspective.'

'And getting it wrong?'

'Well, in so many ways it's already gone terribly wrong. We are in a recovery and response process now and so any improvement from the current situation is a big win. The good news is that you and I will work closely together. You should never have to make a call on your own unless they call at two AM when you are at home. Once we are into a rhythm though we will always plan the timing of the call and get the oppositions' agreement. That's all part of the trust thing. Before each call we will come up with a tactical call sheet. In the early days we will do some role play and before long you will find that you are much more comfortable with the process.'

John was still a little uncertain, 'OK....'

'So, to help during live conversations to start with, and for any critical calls in the future, we are going to put some key lines for you to use on these white boards. You can hang whole parts of the conversation off some of these lines. On the other board, over here, we are going to put some key emotive words. As I can listen in to the calls as they happen, I will point to some of the words to help guide you.'

'What do you mean?'

Finlay stepped over the white board nearest the window and started writing a number of emotions by name. 'Ok, so, if the conversation turns aggressive or angry – you might start to rise to it, and I will recommend that you change the tone of your conversation I will point here to the word 'soothing'. You can actively change track, stroke the guy's feathers, get him to calm down a bit. But, if I think that you can take control and make one of our demands, then I will point here to the word 'demand' and then you can make one of our demands. This way, it's all silent between you and I, and I can help shape the conversation if needed because I can stay emotionally detached.'

'So how often do I have to speak to the hostage taker?'

'To start with we want to set up a call every day, ideally at the same time. As I say, we want to build trust and a relationship, but we also want to exert some subtle control influence. We want to manage the call scheduling if possible. It's a powerful subconscious control that an inexperienced hostage taker won't realise puts them in a subservient position. We will also insist that we only ever speak to the hostage taker on the bridge phone. That way we know at least where he is, and if we need to get a proof of life from a crew member, they should be on hand. It's a subtle way of getting them to keep the crew on the ship, rather than onshore where we lose them.'

Johns' eyes were wide as he was seeing an uncomfortable part of a subversive underworld that he had never even considered before.

Finlay continued. 'There are a couple of other negotiation techniques that we shall use as the situation progresses, things like using delays to apply pressure, passing key demands from them upwards for decisions etc. Of course, we have to be aware that the other side will likely use some of these tricks too, but that's ok. I have been around the block a few times and again will help you. What I would like to do next though is to hear you have a short introductory call with the hostage taker this morning, just to touch base.'

'Wow, that quickly!'

'Yes, it's OK. It will be a relatively short call, and I have already drafted the strategy. If its ok by you, shall we go through it and practise?'

Feeling a little more confident, but not much, John nodded his head. 'Sure, let's do it.'

Chapter 24.
September 13th, Hobyo, Somalia

Abdi had slept in the Captain's cabin overnight but hadn't slept well. The noise and the vibration of the ship, the slightest movement on the water and the endless questions running through his mind. Two of the other skiff crews had come back having not been successful, but the third hadn't been heard from for about a week now. With the loss of Zahi's skiff, which he knew had been for legitimate reasons, but which still hurt, he was down to only two skiffs. He wouldn't be able to buy any more until he had received payment for the Hibernia III. He wondered if The Associate knew yet that he had a fish on the line, but that it wasn't landed yet? He also wondered if The Associate would get pissed off that 50% of the assets bought with his money had most probably ended up in the bottom of the sea on their first expedition. Abdi knew that there were risks, but the losses wouldn't stop him from sending the remaining skiffs out again as soon as he could refuel them.

Abdi had eaten some breakfast, tea and chapati and was now on the Bridge sitting in the Captain's chair when unexpectedly and interrupting his musings the satellite phone rang.

'Good morning my name is John, I am a manager at the company that is responsible for the crew on board the Hibernia III. Who am I speaking to please?'

'John, we spoke on the phone yesterday. My name as I said then is Mr Hibernia.'

'Mr Hibernia, it is good to speak to you again. Though I would like to request that we get going on the right foot. Please will you tell me your real name.' Finlay nodded to John approvingly in the background.

Abdi considered it for a moment and decided. 'Fine, you can call me Abdi.'

'Thank you, Abdi. Next, I would like to make sure that we are able to communicate well. Are you able to understand my English clearly?

'Yes, I have spent time in London and can understand you very well.'

Finlay raised an eyebrow whilst John continued. 'Great, and how are the crew?'

'Your crew is fine. I am looking over this huge ship and wondering when you are going to deliver the 110 million US dollars that I asked for?'

'Well Abdi, as I suggested yesterday, this has obviously caught the company by surprise, and I can tell you that yesterday we were in meetings to discuss exactly this subject.'

'OK, so what did you discuss?'

As per his brief, John read from a sentence that was on the white board in front of him. 'Abdi, we are obviously deeply concerned about this situation. We are concerned about the safety of everyone onboard including you and your team. Ships carrying hydrocarbons are extremely dangerous places and I think it's particularly important to emphasise that to you.'

Abdi retorted quite quickly, 'So pay me the money that I demand, and your crew and your ship will be fine!'

'Abdi, Abdi, I am sure you mean what you say, and I appreciate your saying that the crew will be fine. I will speak to my superiors and pass that message on to them. What I wanted to do today was just to make sure that our communications work, that you know how to get hold of me, and I you.'

'Yes, yes, you can call me, I can call you. Now tell me about my money!'

'Abdi, I am working on that for you, in fact after this call I have another meeting with the shipping company, and I will pass on your message. This is an area of great importance to me, and I will call you back at this same time tomorrow on the bridge phone.'

Feeling that he wasn't getting quite what he wanted from this conversation Abdi said 'Fine, call me tomorrow!' and then he hung up.

Back in the office in Athens John let out a huge sigh of relief. 'Wow, that was intense!'

Finlay leaned across the desk and pressed stop on the tape recorder. 'I thought you did really well there, you led the conversation, you set a couple of parameters. You got his name, or at least a more realistic name in the first call. Sometimes that takes days! Most importantly though, he agreed to speak tomorrow from the bridge, that was a real win. Well done!'

'Thanks, is every call going to be like that?'

Finlay grinned. 'It will get easier for most of them, but it will take a while. The good news is that we now have 24 hours to prepare for the next one!'

John tried to muster some enthusiasm. 'Oh good.'

Chapter 25.
September 13th, Athens, Greece

Finlay walked downstairs to the main boardroom at the AFSC offices after Johns' conversation with Abdi and as he entered, he looked at Chloe, the only person in the room. She didn't say a word but raised a questioning eyebrow. Finlay replied to her with a 'Oh that was fine, he is a little tense, but otherwise fine.'

Chloe brushed a strand of her red hair behind her ear as she asked. 'And what's the hostage taker like?'

'No complaints. Relatively easily manipulated on that first call, we now have a name for him, Abdi. My gut feel from those few moments is that he is an amateur, punching above his weight. Definitely educated, spent some time in the UK. Probably comes from a wealthy Somali family and must have some real backing from someone to be able to take a ship like that.'

Chloe paused, 'Interesting, we can use some of that. Shall we get back to planning the negotiation in detail?'

'Sure, have your company come back to you with the target settlement figure?'

Chloe who had a yellow legal pad on the table in front of her replied, 'No not yet, this TSF is a complicated one and the finance team are getting into the numbers. I know off the top of my head that the total asset value including vessel and cargo for which we are liable in the event of total loss is 226 Million US Dollars, but it's complicated by the potential environmental impact in the event that the ship is lost or damaged.'

'Yes of course, if they dump two million barrels of petroleum into the Indian Ocean that would be about 8 times more volume than the Exxon Valdez disaster in 1989. How much did that cost their insurer to clean up?'

'It was around 8 billion dollars, not including the fines.'

'Wow! I bet that is really messing with your numbers. Part of you wants to settle quickly, which of course goes in the pirate's favour, but your shareholders do not want to spend a 110 Million dollars doing so.'

'Yes, but there are a couple of other factors we need to consider as well. There is no previous history of other ransom payments made for vessels of that scale held in Somali national waters. A couple of fishing vessels were held and released in the 90's and I do know that onshore a number of NGO's have paid ransoms for staff who have been kidnapped. There was one from a Kenya based NGO who had their staff taken hostage, and that was settled quite quickly. Given that Somalia is a failed state, there don't appear to be any legal issues on the payment of ransom there, but one of my legal colleagues is just checking.'

Finlay nodded whilst Chloe continued. 'Staying with legal issues, the vessel is registered in Greece, the crew are from Ukraine and the Philippines. Whilst we might have to think about where we source the funds from, I am comfortable that there is no issue with the payment of ransom in international waters for humanitarian purposes and to save life.'

Finlay took a sip of his coffee, resisted the urge for a cigarette before replying, 'Yes, and stating the obvious for the record, I think that this is a credible threat. There is no messing about here by the pirates and given the complete inability for the Somalia state security services to do anything about this, I don't think we can rely on any state intervention to solve this one for us. I would even go as far as to say that we should actively avoid that.'

As Chloe wrote a note on her legal pad she nodded and said, 'Yes, I agree.'

'With regards to the safety of the hostages, I am concerned that there is direct threat to life. Firstly, their negotiator made a physical threat on his initial call, but I am just as concerned with the fact that the value on human life is so low in that part of the world. We will need to make sure that we negotiate carefully, so that we focus on saving life, without letting them know that it is our primary concern. I am worried that they might do something vicious just to apply pressure.'

Chloe wrote another note on the legal pad, 'Agreed.'

'OK, so when we have the Target Settlement Figure, we can set the 'Initial Offer'. Ideally, I can make that to their negotiator tomorrow during our call. I think we should set something that is enough to make sure that no harm is going to come immediately to any hostages, but it also needs to be low enough to bring down their lofty expectations. Let's aim for a figure of around a third of the TSF whatever that ends up being.'

Again, Chloe wrote in her immaculate cursive script on the yellow legal pad. 'Agreed, I am quite sure I will get a number signed off by the end of the day. We can have a quick catch up later this evening to confirm.'

'Excellent, I am going to spend the day working with the AFSC team and I will also draft the negotiating plan which we can also discuss this evening. Now, unless there is anything else, I am going to find somewhere I can smoke.'

Chloe looked at her old friend, knowing that any comment about his health would just bounce off him. She smiled, a little sadly around the eyes and said, 'See you later.'

Chapter 26.
September 14th, Athens, Greece

Finlay hadn't slept very much last night, there was a time constraint and some anxiety. He was surprisingly good at managing his stress levels whenever he was negotiating and had learned over time, that excess stress wasn't an effective driver to good decision making. Sure, a little stress was great for motivation and efficient work, but he never enjoyed presenting an Initial Offer to a hostage taker. It was the absolute test of his skill at preparation that he got it right most of the time. Too low and the hostage taker would get really pissed off and could turn dangerous. Too high, and there was a strong risk of the hostage taker making new demands thinking that there was an unlimited pot of money at the other end. He had tossed and turned in his bed for a while before he finally got to sleep.

The numbers from Chloe's' team hadn't come in until 22.00 last night and so they had worked till just past midnight finalising the negotiating strategy and checking the initial offer, which they both had to sign off on. Finlay had spoken to Mr Papadopoulos early this morning, told him what they were recommending, and he had agreed immediately. Ultimately, Finlay felt comfortable with where the numbers had fallen, but how professional was the negotiator at the other end? Would Abdi see that this was a negotiation, or did he think his demand would be met with no resistance at all?

It was about three hours until the next scheduled call and then, Finlay mused, he would find out. He was meeting John in the designated call room in the office in an hour and a half. It was a good setup, and he was glad there wouldn't be any distractions. He had his notes prepared on his laptop and he locked it away into the hotel safe, whilst he went up to the club lounge to get breakfast. A full English he thought, screw the cholesterol, and a barrel full of coffee.

After breakfast, and a quick cigarette, Finlay went back up to his room and hung the do not disturb sign on his door handle. He walked over to the windows and opened the curtains fully, looking out at the view of the park and cultural centre just over the main road. He took a couple of deep breaths focussing into the moment, double checked that his reserve project phone had enough battery and mustered his thoughts whilst admiring the view. After about fifteen minutes, feeling much better and in the zone, it was time to go. He collected his laptop from the safe, went down to the intricately marbled lobby to see that the company driver was already outside with the car in the pickup area. A short drive later in frantic traffic and Finlay arrived at the AFSC offices.

John was already there when Finlay walked in, 'Good morning John. How did you sleep?'

John with big bags under his eyes and a cup of coffee in his hand was surprisingly sprightly. 'I didn't sleep very well, but I processed a lot of information last night. I think this is going to be really interesting. Stressful? Yes, but really really interesting.'

'Great, the stress will be a constant, but you should find that you will get back into a sleep pattern soon enough. Of course, if you don't, then antacids will help in the short term.'

'Oh good.' John sighed.

Finlay continued. 'So, we have a call to do in about an hour and I thought we would go through the preparation for that first. Then after the call, we can take a break. Later this morning, I have some training materials that I want to take you through. Things to do, things to avoid saying, negotiation tactics, manipulation techniques, things like that.'

'Ok, sounds fine. Let's get started.'

The time zone in Athens was the same as in Somalia and so it made Finlay's job a little easier. He hated projects where the time zone was so out of whack from where he was based that he ended up working all hours.

On the dot at 09.00 Finlay pressed record on the tape recorder and John dialled the ships satellite phone. He listened to the ring tone for a couple of rings and then the phone connected. 'Abdi, good morning its John, how are you this morning?'

Abdi, had also been up for a couple of hours, stressing about a meeting he was going to have later that day with the families of the dead skiff crew. 'I am fine, but I have been waiting for your news.'

'Well thank you for being there to take this call. I do appreciate it. As I had said yesterday, I had meetings with the shipping company all day and we are trying to work out a plan.' Abdi only grunted an acknowledgement and so John continued. 'There are a couple of things that I need to check with you. I am told that a couple of the crew are on various medications which if they run out of them could be profoundly serious to their long-term health. I would like to request that you ask them if they have enough of their drugs, and if they don't, then as an act of good faith would you be able to procure more of those drugs at all locally?'

Abdi was a little put off by John making a request of him before John had answered anything on the financial demand, however he could see the reason for the request. 'I will ask Captain Oleksiy to check.'

'That's really great Abdi, I appreciate it.' Then trying to personalise the hostages a little and make them seem more human, rather than a commodity he added, 'And I know their families will too.'

Abdi saw through the ruse though, 'John, what concerns me is that you sound like you will not be getting me my money by the end of the week as I required.'

Finlay had briefed John on this and so he had been expecting this from his call plan. It allowed him to get to the meat of what he needed to say. 'Abdi, I have been told that I can make you an offer and I have tried really hard to find some middle ground here. The company is simply not able to find the sum of money that you are looking for.'

'Well, they are going to have to try harder. I have their ship; I have their cargo and I have their crew.' Abdi was getting a bit more heated now, all the pressure of the past six months coming to bear.

Finlay pointed to the emotion grid on the white board and to the word 'soothing'. John nodded and tried his most soothing tone, 'Abdi, Abdi, I do understand your frustration, but this is what I am authorised to offer. I am able to agree to 2 Million US Dollars in return for your releasing the entire crew completely unharmed, the ship and the full cargo.'

Abdi wasn't happy. 'What! You think I will give you everything that you want for that tiny amount of money! You are out of your fucking mind! I think you are underestimating who holds all the cards here!'

Finlay, expecting some push back was happy to listen to Abdi continue to vent and he held up a hand to John not to interrupt. 'I have your ship! I have your crew! And I have 100 million dollars of your petrol. You go back to the company and tell them I demand more, much more!'

Abdi appeared to have finished and so John spoke in his most reconciliatory voice 'Abdi, I hear that you are disappointed, and I will of course pass that back up to the owners. In the meantime, if we can get to a point where we agree, have you given any consideration as to how we can get the money to you?'

'Yes, you will bring the money in cash, in 20-dollar bills to Mogadishu, to an address that I will give you. When you hand over the money then I will release the ship and her crew.'

Finlay knew immediately that that was not going to work and pointed to the phrase 'do not commit'. John, conscious that he didn't want to cause a second explosion from Abdi's end answered silkily, 'That's an interesting idea Abdi, I will certainly look into that. Now it's going to take a couple of days for me to speak to the shipping company on your request for a little bit more money, but I will check in with you tomorrow morning and see if that's ok?'

Abdi's voice started cold but ramped up over his short speech to full vented fury. 'Mr John, I didn't ask for a little bit more money, I asked for all of the money! All of the Money! In Cash! In Mogadishu, In one week!'

And with that he hung up.

Finlay reflected for a moment, whilst he wrote his post-call notes. 'Well, that could have gone better.'

John a little stunned looked at him and spoke. 'What happened?'

Finlay replied with a quick, 'Just a minute.' Whilst he kept writing. He knew it was really important to keep as clear a log as possible of the calls made. Not just the words of course, but the emotion, the inflection, the words, or phrases that caused the most angst. He had always used a series of coloured pens to annotate in his own code important sections. He underlined in a red pen 'Cash – Mogadishu Delivery'.

Then with a wry smile, he pulled out his calculator, A million dollars of 20-dollar bills weighed about 50 kilograms, so he did the math and started chuckling.

John, not getting the joke asked 'What?'

Finlay replied with mirth in his eyes. 'Ha! Our friend Abdi has just asked for five and a half tons of 20-dollar bills in cash delivered to some back street in Mogadishu.'

'Wow! How do we do that?'

'Well, that's just it. We don't, and the muppet doesn't even realise what he has asked for. We, my friend, are dealing with an amateur!'

Chapter 27.
September 15th, Masai Mara, Kenya

If you wanted an image imprinted forever in your mind, this was it, thought Max. Here in the Masai Mara, the giddy concoction of wild animals, intense bird life, air that had that unique 'Africa' smell to it after the rain, and a sunset that turned the entire sky marmalade orange.

Max was standing with his head and shoulders sticking out of the top of his specially customised land cruiser. It was parked on top of a small hillock and he had his binoculars in one hand and a Bombay Sapphire and tonic, with ice and a cucumber slice of course, in the other.

To his front, in fact all around him, was the gentle hubbub of the plain. Animals were getting more active in the cooler part of the day, heading for water, a little twitchy and looking for predators. A pair of giraffes were grazing on an acacia tree about 50 meters to his right, and in the water hole a pair of wrinkly old grey elephants were taking a long cool drink.

The sun was sinking rapidly over towards the West, setting behind the distant detritus of a thunderstorm that had at one point threatened their safari, but in the end hadn't come close.

Max and his wife were camping if it could be called that. They had booked one of the private camp sites, which in reality was just a patch of grass, beside the Mara river. There were no guards, no fences, no running water. Just their tent, pitched in the centre of the patch of crudely cut grass, pure heaven. Of course, the noisy troop of baboons that seemed to live in the trees near the site had tried over the past two days to raid their stores, but Max was a seasoned camper and had brought his catapult. It was a pain in the arse having to pack the tent up each day, but if they didn't it would get trashed, or shat on or both.

The ice tinkled in his glass as his wife popped up beside him, gave him a refill and balanced a large bowl of salty crisps on the roof sill beside them. Camping this way was a luxury. Proper camp beds, safari chairs, a portable BBQ, cold drinks throughout. It took about as much planning as a military campaign but was much more pleasurable.

Max who was slim, and just over six feet tall, had thick wiry blond hair and trimmed pork chop sideburns all of which was just turning grey now that he was approaching 60. He still had strength in his upper body, his arms, and shoulders still good but his formerly muscled chest was fading a bit and his legs, which had always been a bit thin, were looking old and freckled as he stood there in his safari shorts. In his younger days Max had served briefly in the Parachute Regiment, a short 5 years' service finishing as a Captain and commanding a platoon in Iraq in Operation Desert Storm. His 'war' had been exciting, but on reflection afterwards not as fulfilling as he had hoped. Once he had got back to England, he had had this feeling that he could do better, be something more. So, he had resigned. His Commanding Officer was sad to see him go and through the old boy's network got him an interview for the Foreign Office. He sailed through the interview process and having had certain key skill sets identified was swiftly passed on to the Special Intelligence Service or MI6 as it is better known. This was much more Max's style. Interesting, enjoyably subtle, meaningful, much more intelligence cloak than parachute dagger.

To Max's good fortune he spent much of the next 20 years of his professional life working and living in the Middle East and then Africa working out of a High Commission here, an Embassy there. Totally contradicting his original military roots, he became a commercial specialist. Pushing her Majesty's Government aims with the weapons of commerce instead. It wasn't glamorous, but the ability to influence through nefarious means if needed, a multibillion-pound arms contract away from an Eastern state and towards a British contractor instead meant jobs and technology growth at home.

The fact that it reduced cash inflows to opposing forces was a double win. Of course, every now and then a much more interesting project came up that suited his old skill set more but eventually he just left that sort of thing behind. Max had spent the last three years of his government service, his sunshine tour, based in Nairobi and had then retired there. He used some of his termination grant to establish his own company leveraging off his past endeavours and contacts. To be honest, that was when the really fun stuff had started. He had quickly become 'known' as the UK's man at arm's length in Africa, who could resolve problems to which Her Majesty's government was perhaps wary of getting too close.

He enjoyed this lifestyle. Fun projects, his own hand-picked team, some money to boot. The problem was that even on holiday he would get interrupted.

His phone rang, causing the nearest giraffe to stare at him belligerently whilst still slowly chewing. It was an unknown number from a country code he didn't immediately recognise. 'Hello?'

'Max, its Finlay, are you in the UK at the moment?'

'No.'

'Ah, I um, I wonder if you can get to Athens tomorrow?'

'Tomorrow night, probably. Anything you can tell me on this means?'

'Not really no, a sticky situation that I think you are ideally placed to resolve.'

'Sounds great, I will see what I can do. Can you let me know which hotel you are staying in? The Marriot? Fine. I will confirm tomorrow morning what time I can get there.'

The sun was just going down over the horizon and Max's wife, Arianna, looked at him, her beautiful Italian eyes and long brown hair lit up by the stunning glow. Having been married for so many years she could tell by Max's voice that the faintest, most imperceptible tinge of excitement had just entered his mind. Max hung up and said simply. 'Off to Greece tomorrow, probably only for a day or so.'

'How wonderful for you dear.'

Noting the obvious sarcasm Max looked his wife in the eye. Her face was sparkling, and he considered for the millionth time how lucky he was to be married to her. 'Now all we need to make this a perfect day is to see a cheetah hunt!'

Chapter 28.
September 16th, Hobyo, Somalia

Zahi was pissed off. He didn't like living on this ship, and he had been on it for less than a week. He and Hassan had eventually worked out a plan for managing the crew. It had been hard to do given that only Yuusuf could translate how it was going to work to Captain Oleksiy. It was easier now that he had all of his guards though.

There were, Zahi had discovered, a number of things that had to be constantly worked, monitored, or maintained on board this ship. He had wanted to keep all the crew in the same place to make guarding them easier but that just wasn't happening. The chef and the chief steward had to clean clothes and make food. The Bridge crew were active making sure the vessel was safe and prepared to pull away if anything happened to the mooring. The Chief engineer and his crew really did have to be in the engine room apparently for much of the time that an engine was running. Captain Oleksiy went nuts each time he saw someone lighting a cigarette. It took a while to get the guards to understand and eventually an agreement had been made. All cigarettes and lighters had been taken and held on the bridge, it had caused a lot of angry conversations, but ultimately, everyone agreed that there was no point getting paid a ransom if they had all been blown sky high before it was delivered.

Now, the Bridge was always under guard, making sure that only Abdi used the satellite phone so that was relatively easy. The kitchen had a couple of guards too and the engineering compartment had a guard, but more guards were needed there because the engineers had to work the ship, manage the repairs, and do whatever else was apparently needed. Those crew not working were kept in a corner of the bridge. With his contingent of guards, broken into ten men on each of three shifts that didn't leave a lot of slack.

Right now, there was a bigger problem. The ship stank of shit. In this heat, it really did. A miasma of poo permeated every room and corridor. The Chief Engineer Marko had reported yesterday that some pump or other had finally broken and now the toilets were not able to flush. Of course, that was only discovered after people had taken a dump in a number of them, leaving pleasant presents that the vacuum system was no longer able to remove. The Somali guards hadn't understood how it all worked anyway and were not using the toilets, they were shitting over the side, or as Zahi had discovered after a complaint from the Captain, a couple of them had decided to take a dump in some of the crew cabins, spreading their turds out using the curtains or bedding in some kind of symbolic 'up yours' to the West.

Zahi and Yuusuf had gone with the Captain to take a look and had seen the state of one of the rooms. Part of Zahi had been disgusted with the smell and the state of the room, and part of him had been impressed with how they had managed to smear it all over the ceiling. Knowing that this wasn't sustainable, he had come up with a plan with the Chief Engineer for another option. They had used a blow torch to cut a hole in the floor of the bridge wings at the far end on both sides. The deal was that they would open the toilet only on the downwind side. It was an odd thing to take a dump and then look down to see the mess falling into the sea below. Of course, sometimes, with an errant gust of wind the turd would be blown back onto the deck below instead. Because the Somalis culturally didn't use toilet paper, the Chief had rigged up a water hose, with a shower head on it so that the user could wash their ring piece and hose down the bridge wing deck. Given there were now sixty or so people on board the one working toilet was almost constantly in use. Still, it was a solution that looked like it would work in the longer term.

The next problem Zahi had to deal with was khat. Every day as promised, Abdi's contractor delivered a boat full of fresh khat to the vessel as partial payment for the crew. The green leaves that you chewed into a paste and then held between your teeth and your gums, or as some people preferred, under their tongues, was a stimulant, similar to chewing tobacco, though much more powerful. When actually benefiting from chewing you were more alert. After the effects wore off, similar to a hangover you had to come back down, and then you could be drowsy and sleepy. Neither being hyper alert and stimulated, or drowsy and sleepy were good traits for guards with guns.

The habit in Somalia was to chew khat socially. Men who could afford it would sit on their haunches in a common space, chatting, and chewing. The thing was, it was bad for you to swallow the spit which formed in your mouth when you were chewing. So, you spat. Not only that but you spat anywhere and everywhere. The plants sap turned brown, so you spat great big balls of brown mucky phlegm. On board, after a few days of the guards spitting everywhere indoors, Zahi had designated an area forward on the deck outside for those off duty to go and chew, chat and spit. This of course had turned in to another mess and a different kind of problem. All night and all day the area was packed with guards, some of whom should be sleeping, but who were stimulated like a cup of coffee on steroids, and some who should be guarding, who were snoozing like a sleepy thing. Zahi's brother Hassan had tried his best, but it eventually took Zahi, with his new celebrity status threatening to take the khat ration away before there was some semblance of order.

Zahi didn't know the history of the old sailing fleets, where in the old days a rum ration was issued, and the occasional Pirate Captain made the mistake of withdrawing it. The last thing Zahi needed was a mutiny.

Chapter 29.
September 16th, Athens, Greece

Max walked into the lobby of the Marriot hotel in Athens and queued up at the reception counter to check in. The white marbled floor, brown walls and bright chandelier lights looked like the lobby of many other hotels that Max had stayed in. However, it was a cool and pleasant environment after his 7-hour flight from Nairobi. As he waited, someone brought a tray with small glasses of juice and a pile of ice-cold white towels to wipe his hands.

Having checked in seamlessly he took the lift up to the second floor and went into his room where he dropped his small overnight bag on the floor. He quickly found the remote control to stop the wall mounted TV that had somehow sensed him coming in. It was blaring away with some hotel advert or other. Why did they do that? He wondered, a little irritated. He pulled out his phone and messaged Finlay. 'Just checked in. See you in the business lounge at 20.00?' He took off his navy-blue double-breasted blazer and draped it over the double bed. His shoes were next to go and then he padded over to the window. The room was pretty standard, a decent sized bed, a long wooden counter that doubled as a desk, a small sofa under the window and a free-standing lamp. As Max looked out into the evening light, he saw he was opposite some kind of conference centre, obviously an expo of some kind was happening as there were a lot of banners, lights, and advertising. He looked at his curtains briefly, relieved to see that they were full blackout curtains and that he wouldn't get bothered by any of the lights. Max used to be able to sleep almost anywhere, but now he enjoyed his creature comforts. His phone pinged with a message in reply. 'Sure, see you then.' Max looked at his watch and worked out there was just enough time to take a shower.

At 20.00 on the dot, dressed in pale cream chino trousers and a pink pastel checked shirt with the collar open Max walked into the business lounge. There were only a couple of business people in there and he didn't see Finlay immediately so walked to the fridge and grabbed himself a beer from the complimentary bar. He browsed the grey marbled food counter and took a small side plate adding a couple of snacks for good measure. The sushi selection looked particularly good, so he picked up some pickled ginger, wasabi, and a couple of chopsticks too. He found a table in the corner of the room with a sofa on one side and one of those curved hard backed chairs that look fashionable but are not all that comfortable to sit on. Max took the sofa.

A few moments later Finlay walked in, fresh from the AFSC office and still in his lightweight, hot weather, single breasted blue suit. It had obviously been tailored once but that was a few years ago now. Max observed that Finlay had probably spent too much time travelling, staying in hotels, and eating tasty food. Max grinned as he stood up and shook Finlay warmly by the hand, it had been a couple of years since they had last seen each other. Max and Finlay had once both successfully worked the problem of a particularly sensitive kidnap of a British Ambassador in the Middle East, and both had come to appreciate each other's skill sets.

Finlay spoke in his sometimes loud but gravelly voice. 'Max, how are you? And how is Arianna?'

'All well thank you. She sends you love.'

'Very kind, very kind. You know I do appreciate your dropping everything and getting here so quickly. Was it much trouble? Were you busy?'

'Well, exceedingly early this morning I was in the Masai Mara. We managed to break camp quickly though, connect almost directly with the flight and here I am.' They made chit chat for a short while, occasionally nipping to the bar for another drink and filling up on finger food. There was a moment when they had to dash to stop the waiter from tidying everything away as it was getting late, but suitably quenched in food and ale they then got down to business.

Finlay started. 'We have a really interesting problem in your neck of the woods that we haven't seen before. Before we talk about it though I need you to sign this non-disclosure agreement.' Finlay rustled out of his inside jacket pocket a one-page NDA. Max read it and fishing around for a pen looked up to see Finlay brandishing a metallic blue Montblanc fountain pen. After he had signed, Finlay continued. 'About a week ago, one of my clients had one of their super tankers hijacked off the coast of Somalia.'

Max, over his many years of sensitive discussions had become a master in absorbing information and getting people to fill the voids that he intentionally created in conversation. He had learned that a simple nod of the head, or an 'uh hum?' was enough to keep people talking. People usually liked to talk, especially if it was a subject that interested themselves. Once people were talking, they could go on for hours and hours, stepping over the boundaries of whether or not they should be talking. Now in this case it didn't matter too much. Finlay needed Max's help and so was going to tell him anyway, but there were countless people who didn't want to share information with Max or shouldn't, who ended up going home that night with the thought that they had told him too much and regretted it.

Over the next twenty minutes or so, Finlay filled Max in on all the details and then came to the reason why he had called Max to Athens. 'Right then my friend, in a month or so's time we will have concluded the negotiations, come to an agreement with the hostage takers and we are going to need you and your team's skills to do a couple of things. Firstly, I suspect we are going to have to deliver a ransom. A large one, in cash, to somewhere in Somalia. Secondly, we are going to need to secure the Hibernia III as soon as we have paid the ransom, making sure that the pirates have all left her, and that no one gets the opportunity to pick her off again. It's possible that the Hibernia III won't be able to move under her own steam, so we need to factor that in as well. The question is, is this something that you can do for us?'

Max's mind was firing in overdrive. 'Finlay what a fascinating problem. Its complex, there is large risk to life, there is a huge capital sum involved and the reputation of a multinational shipping company too. My immediate thought is yes, of course. My other thought is who on earth would you have gone to if I wasn't around? There are not many operators on the African continent with the resources that I have!'

'Max, I completely agree. There are a couple of people who say they can, but I don't believe there is anyone else actually who can in your neck of the woods, and especially in Somalia. Now to be clear. This doesn't mean you can write your own cheque on this one! You need to let me have a detailed plan and together we will present this to the shipping company and the insurers here in Athens in two days' time. If we think it's reasonable then it's probably a go.'

Pretending to be hurt, but with a sparkle in his eye Max came back, 'Finlay, me? Write my own cheque? Heaven forbids. Now, how large did you say your target settlement figure was?'

Chapter 30.
September 18th, Athens, Greece

Max had spent the past 36 hours doing what he enjoyed most. A client had come to him with a problem and now he had to present a solution, estimate how long it would take to implement and then cost the whole project.

This problem was a little more complicated than most and was innovative for East Africa. Max started with some research. Using a number of online resources, he looked at piracy issues globally seeing that much of it was occurring in Asian waters. He looked at the geography of Somalia and the distances involved to get there which made it logistically challenging. He contemplated the ransom payment. Any operator can physically pay a ransom, but which ones did it within the complex boundaries of law, with the minimum of risk either to the hostages, the hostage taker, or the consultants that would physically carry it. The final piece of the puzzle was the collection of the vessel once released. That would need some clever planning too. Sailing another ship into harm's way would require some very specialized maritime security skills let alone the risk of cross decking the rescue team, whilst at sea, onto a ship that may or may not have been evacuated by the pirates.

Having come up with a wide range of potential courses of action, Max refined each phase down to the ones that he thought were the best. Without doubt the ransom payment method was most challenging, he came up with three different solutions that could work, but which would need a lot more thought process before he could settle on the right one. That meant that his costing scenarios varied widely. He knew that clients liked to be given an accurate costing scenario before agreeing to use Max's services, but for now he couldn't give a detailed figure. He also knew that clients needed a confident individual to tell them the credible solution before even talking about numbers. He wasn't certain that he had all the solutions ironed out there either, but he certainly had some plausible options. He decided not to produce any slides for this pitch. He would take the conversation where it needed to go and use his skills to adjust, as necessary.

At 15.30 that afternoon Max walked into the lobby of the AFSC offices and waited whilst Finlay came down to collect him. They went up to the small boardroom and Max was introduced to an attractive red head called Chloe who told him she was the legal advisor for the insurance company. They made pleasant chit chat until 16.00 when a number of people walked into the room including the owner, Mr Papadopoulos. After a series of introductions Mr Papadopoulos gave the meeting over to Finlay.

'Good afternoon everyone, the agenda for today is twofold. Firstly, I will give you an update on my most recent call with the hostage takers and then I will hand over to Max who has some solutions that we should discuss.' After seeing some nods of assent around the table Finlay continued. 'This morning we had a further conversation with Abdi, the pirate leader. According to him the crew are all well. There are some mechanical issues with the Hibernia III, but nothing major. I have briefed your ops team separately on those. Abdi is a quite frustrated that the offer value is lower than he wants, but that is perfectly normal. As per our strategy, remember we need to make sure we are not seen to be willing to pay immediately, or the hostage takers can up their demands. On my next call I will be offering a small increase and again we let him consider the final implications of that. Next up, we still don't know the exact location of the ship at this point. I haven't pushed to ask this yet, and won't until we get near to the target settlement figure. Whilst we would like to know, it's not the nearest crocodile to the boat at the moment in terms of its importance. With regards to payment, so far Abdi is determined to be paid in cash face to face in Mogadishu, but I believe that that will simply be impracticable. There are also issues in making payments and securing release simultaneously which are important and which we will need to plan for. The less time delay between the two the better and the less potential for any funny business.'

Mr Papadopoulos interjected in his heavy Greek accent, 'Is that a real risk, could we pay the ransom and then they still don't release the vessel?'

Finlay replied. 'To be honest with you yes, a number of things could happen with these hostage takers. They are not professionals at this, and my gut feeling tells me this is their first gig. It's possible that they will renege on the deal, even after receiving payment. It's possible that they could steal some or all of the cargo, and finally it's possible that they could hold on to some or all of the crew even after we pay the ransom. They are all risks that we will need to manage, and that leads me nicely into Max's part of the presentation. Unless we have any other questions at this stage?'

Mr Papadopoulos wasn't looking particularly happy. He hadn't really considered that this could go on longer than the ransom payment being made, or that these crooks were really, well, crooks! Still, he recognised his naivety and waved a hand for the meeting to go on.

Max stood up from the table, not for gravitas, or because he needed a white board but because he knew his mind worked better when he was on his feet, when he was moving. Giving a pitch to a client gave him a natural buzz and he loved it. 'As Finlay says, the art of solving a problem, to get the resolution that is needed, comes from exceptional planning, immaculate execution and extensive experience. I am not going to stand here and give you a sales pitch. What I am going to do is give you a number of potential options for resolving this problem. That said though, I am not going to tell you which one is the best solution at this point in time, because it's counter intuitive. The situation is fluid, but by the time Finlay negotiates a settlement we will have identified and tested the best course of action.'

Over the next half an hour Max broke the resolution methodology into different phases. With very few speaking notes he outlined the pros and cons of his different solutions. He took questions on the fly, answering reasonably and only very occasionally did he need to make a note to come back with a follow up. At the end of his impressive slot, one of the other team members around the table, the finance manager if Max remembered correctly asked; 'So these solutions you suggest look both complicated and expensive. Are you able to give us a ballpark figure for your fees for your services?'

Max gave his most charming smile. 'Yes, there is risk for us in offering our services to you, especially as things are evolving. We are going to have to guarantee a solution that works and yet we don't yet know definitively what that solution is. I do however guarantee that we can resolve this for you. Our standard terms are 7.5% of the Final Settlement Figure with 50% of the Target Settlement Figure on signature of contract as a guide, 25% on mobilisation of resources and the balance of 25% on proof, provided by us that the ransom is in the hands of the pirates.'

The finance manager queried, 'Why at that point and not when the vessel and crew are safe?'

'Well, the simple fact is that we can't guarantee what a 3rd party criminal organisation is going to do. Our task as far as the delivery goes will be complete once the quantum, that's the money, is in the hands of the hostage takers. If you wish, we can separate out the vessel recovery service from the main project, but I will need more time to develop the detailed plan and proposal.'

Mr Papadopoulos came in. 'Max, thank you for coming all this way at short notice. I think your presentation was impressive, but we need now to speak internally so I am going to ask you to leave.'

Max, a little surprised, but not outwardly phased by this abrupt end to the meeting said, 'Of course. Thanks very much for listening and do please get in touch if you have any other questions.' He then proceeded to go around and shake hands with all of the attendees before making his way back down to reception where they kindly organised a taxi to take him back to the hotel.

About fifteen minutes later the cab arrived and just as he entered the lobby his phone rang. 'Max, its Finlay, good presentation. It looks like it's a go for you and your team, but Mr Papadopoulos would like a little more detail on the ransom drop methodology before signing. Could you please work something up over the next week and get a detailed proposal to us?'

Max smiled, 'Yes of course. Please tell him I appreciate the trust he is putting in me and we will work something up in detail. I should just have time to get back to Nairobi tonight and we will start mapping it out tomorrow.'

'Great, have a safe flight and chat soon old chap.'

Chapter 31.
September 19th, Hobyo, Somalia

Abdi was feeling the pressure. He had expected the owners of the vessel to move faster than this, to offer a better opening bid, to be keen to do a deal. He couldn't work out what he was missing. How could they have only offered 2 million dollars so far! He had been speaking every morning to John, and he was getting used to the rhythm of the calls, but he always felt that he was conceding something and not getting much in return. This morning Abdi had decided he was going to be more forceful, was going to demand an increase in the offer. He was just waiting for the phone to ring so that he could get his point across.

At 09.00 when the phone did ring, Abdi snatched it up.

'Abdi, good morning it's John, how are you this morning?'

Abdi took his opportunity, the one he had been stewing on all night. 'John, it doesn't matter how I am, but if you really want to know, I am upset. For a week now you haven't given me anything more than your first offer. So, this morning I am going to be truly clear.' Abdi slowed right down and pronounced each word very clearly, 'I, want, more, money!'

'Abdi, I understand, and as it happens, I have some better news for you this morning. The owners have worked out that they can sell their other ship and are able to give a slight increase in what we can offer you. But I was wondering if we could chat first about the logistics of paying you. I know you said you wanted 20-dollar bills, but I have checked with the banks here is Europe and they say that getting such a large number of them is going to be exceedingly difficult. It's also going to be extremely heavy not to say bulky. It would be great if you took my word for it, but if you want to do some online research you will see that a million dollars' worth of 20-dollar bills is very heavy.'

'Ok, so what about diamonds?'

John was flummoxed for a moment, 'Um, what?' Finlay frantically shook his head no and started writing rapidly on the board.

'Diamonds, you can pay in diamonds, they are not traceable.'

John, talking slowly and stalling for time recovered, filling in the gaps between Finlay's words on the board. 'Abdi, do you really want to be paid in diamonds? There are lots of problems with that. Assuming that we can actually get hold of that many, then it comes down to trust. We can measure, we can weigh, we can have experts who can value each individual stone, but if that's what we deliver, do you have experts at your end that can value them for you in a reasonable amount of time so that you are confident that we have fulfilled our end of any agreement? Also, how are you going to spend them? If you flood your market with that number of stones. Then the resale value of any one stone will plummet through the floor and you won't get back in cash what you are expecting.'

'Hmm Ok, that's a fair point.'

'So, I was thinking, what would you prefer instead? A bank transfer, or 100-dollar bills?' Finlay had briefed John to use a simple ruse that often worked on stubborn toddlers. Offer them a false choice, so that they feel they have some control, but manipulate the choices, so that both of them are acceptable outcomes from your perspective.

Abdi didn't quite spot it for what it was. All he knew was that there was no way he was going to take a bank transfer for this, and the idea of a large volume of 20 dollars bills being heavy wasn't something that he had considered. 'Fine, 100-dollar bills delivered to an address in Mogadishu. Now what is this increase you are talking about?'

Finlay was delighted to have potentially removed what might have been a real logistical headache and gave John the thumbs up to proceed. John continued but was careful in his tone now. 'Abdi, so the owners considered what you have been telling me, and I have really tried to push your case for you. They have agreed to increase the payment to 3 million dollars.'

Abdi wasn't happy. 'What! That isn't an increase! That's an insult! You spend a whole week and when you do come back to me you hardly move an inch. This isn't a negotiation this is a robbery!'

'But Abdi, I am doing my best here. The owners are deeply concerned and want to try to solve this in a way that is good for both sides. Can you let me know if you are able to move at all at your end? Then I can go back to them and show them that you are trying to be flexible?'

'Fine, I want 90 million dollars, in hundred-dollar bills and I am going to give you one more week.' With that Abdi hung up again.

John was rapidly learning and knew now not to speak to Finlay until he had finished his notes. Finlay switched off the tape recorder and then sat down and completed his log. He paused for a moment thinking. He doodled a diamond in a green pen whilst he considered that overall, that was a good call. Finally, Abdi had started to climb down from his initial demand. That was an important phase, he mused, perhaps this one wouldn't last too long after all.

Chapter 32.
September 19th, Nairobi, Kenya

About 40 Kilometres South of Nairobi, and near a small rural village called Oloolitikosh was the small very private airfield called Orly. Carved out of the bush originally by some sports aviation enthusiasts who had bought 230 acres of land for the purpose, it was the perfect place for Max and his team to run a discrete office and keep some of their more sensitive kit and equipment. Along the southern boundary a small river ran nearly dry in the summer but flowed freely and noisily during the rainy season. The air park, as it was known, was home to roughly 40 light fixed wing aircraft owned by private flying enthusiasts wanting to be away from the hustle and bustle of Wilson Airport in Nairobi. There were also a couple of rotary aircraft with some highly specialised stabilised video kit that supported everything from wildlife documentary filming to particularly sensitive contracts for organisations that could find a purpose for them across East Africa.

The whole plot at Orly was fenced and there were two runways. One was a grass strip and one made from 'cabro' or grey concrete bricks, laid finely, similar to some carparks in Europe. There was technically no night flight capability because there were no runway lights or approach lights. However, there were a number of ex-military pilots who had once flown extensively on Night Vision Goggles during their time in service. On exceedingly rare occasions, where human life was at risk, there might be a need for them to ply their old trade as part of a medivac from a remote location. Usually, a tourist had been trampled by an animal, or a there had been a particularly nasty road traffic accident.

Internal to the perimeter wire there was a long line of trees and scrub on the southern side of the airfield and interspersed amongst them were some residential houses built by the original founders. One of these had been bought by Max and converted into his very discrete operations centre. The facility had a combination of storage sheds, offices, a common room allocated as a dormitory, a kitchen and a veranda that overlooked one of the runways. The veranda was a great spot for post-project BBQs.

Max had arrived back at Jomo Kenyatta international airport in Nairobi and had come straight to the office using one of the company cars. He had had enough sleep on the Kenya Airways overnight flight but still needed another coffee. The car deposited him outside the house and Max used the biometric hand scanner beside the door. It opened automatically with an audible clunk and a pneumatic hiss. The whole house on the outside looked to be made of wood. To look at it, it wouldn't have been out of place in some Alpine valley. It was pretty to look at, but Max had added some special upgrades internally. Firstly, physical security. The access doors and windows had all been upgraded with bullet resistant glass. The doors and windowsills reinforced. The walls rebuilt with an internal layer on the ground floor of steel and concrete. Max had gone the extra mile and added a faraday cage around the Ops room, which occupied most of the ground floor, as well as an additional reinforced door. Air conditioning systems had been added, and the IT server which was housed in another reinforced enclosure in one corner of the Ops room was thus at the centre of the 'onion.'

The Ops room was always a bustle of professional activity. On one wall was a digital tasks board. All the projects that were currently underway were on there and the board included key details like the project name, project dates, current status update and the name of the lead consultant who was managing it.

A lot of thought had gone into designing the room. Three rows of desks were prominent. The front row were the duty operations officers. There were currently two on duty and they wore headsets which were plugged into their IT systems. They managed the numerous tasks which were ongoing, 24/7. Safety tracking of an Antarctic expedition? No problem. A team supporting the safety of a politician who always walked a fine line in a former Russian state? Yes. Managing the security envelope of a particular rock star whilst on a world tour? Ok. Emergency evacuation of 30 or so staff and families from a Coup D'état? Absolutely. The types of tasks Max's company did were always legitimate, always sensitive, and quite often fascinating. The Ops Officers were all Kenyan, highly educated, impeccably trained and very capable.

The next line of desks behind the ops officers, looking at the large LED TV screens on the walls, and using their own IT systems for research were the analysts; two Kenyan women, ex-intelligence service followed by short commercial careers. Their job was both threat assessment, and research. If a client wanted to know what the threats were to their safety when visiting Mogadishu, then this team researched it. They used a mixture of the companies retained network of information gatherers, media reporting, statistical analysis, and published security think tank data. In the event of an incident, they communicated with their human assets, and pored over social media to identify what was going on using live reporting where needed. Their job was to condense vast amounts of information to a useable format and then share it with the consultants who were in the field or the clients directly.

The final desk, in the back row of the room and with oversight over the whole lot was the Duty Operations Manager desk. By day, or during the completion phase of particularly sensitive projects, this desk was always manned. Only a couple of Max's core team filled this role. The ability to respond in the event of a drama took training, experience, and a calm mindset. If there was a problem this was where it was solved. It didn't matter if one project needed an expensive solution if something went wrong, the client's safety was first, and the company's reputation was second. In those exceedingly rare instances, a projects' bottom line didn't matter.

Off the Ops room on the right was the main briefing room. There was seating for an audience of ten in cinema style tiered seating, though it rarely housed that many. The presentation wall at the front was multi-screen and seamlessly interfaced. It allowed either one large picture, or multiple break outs to be shown. Dolby surround sound and about 90 thousand dollars' worth of IT systems which managed the presentation suite and also allowed encrypted video conferencing made this room better equipped than the presentation room of the Kenyan Intelligence Service in Karen on the Western side of Nairobi.

When Max walked into the main briefing room that morning a debrief was just wrapping up. Stood at the front of the room was Tom. Tom was a thin, wiry character with black short cropped hair, a broken nose and dark stubble that grew whilst you were looking at it. He had a Desperate Dan jawline and he rarely smiled, at least with his mouth. Those who knew him could tell when he found something amusing just by the slightest wrinkling of his eyes. Tom was an ex British Royal Marine officer who had been an instructor at the arctic warfare school in Norway. He had completed a couple of operational tours in former Balkan states and in Iraq and that's where he had first met Max. Listening to Tom and sitting in the front row, were two of the permanent team and one of the consultant pilots.

Mike could have been a model but instead he had joined the US Navy Seals. He had specialised in all things airborne. You wanted to jump out of a plane at flight level nosebleed opening a parachute just before the rest of you turned bloody, then he was the instructor who made sure you were safe. You needed an aircraft which could push the envelope to the limits and a pilot crazy enough to do it, then he was your man. Mike had that deeply masculine look that wouldn't have been out of place on a Gillette advert and he also knew it. He really fancied himself and he spent more time in the gym than most body builders. He focussed on his upper body and looking good in T-shirts that were obviously one size too small. Mike was also black. Really black with a deep voiced southern drawl that some English women found extremely attractive. He was uber calm, never panicked under pressure and was a stabilising influence on any team. Despite all that, and a military career where banter and piss-taking were commonplace his weakness was if anyone wound him up about his appearance or his love life.

Raj was also sitting in the front row and was Mike's best mate and gym buddy. He knew how to press all of the right buttons to wind Mike up. If Mike had a slight gym fetish then Raj was one of those guys who took it to the next level. He seemed to exist on protein shakes, protein bars, chicken fillets, a cocktail of pills in the morning and that was about it. Show him a potato chip and he would look at you in disgust, probably walking away to go and do another hundred reps in case he had been contaminated. Raj was huge up top with that narrow waist that led down through tight glutes to massive legs. He was Sikh and an interesting character that through a murky and suspicious past, which he never talked about, had learnt the arts of explosives and weaponry. If you needed anything from a small hole to a large crater, he could work out the how and using what delivery system. He was in his early 40's, intensely intelligent with an encyclopaedic knowledge. While some men kept copies of Playboy under the bed, Raj kept copies of Jane's Defence Weekly. When it came to work, Raj and Mike always worked together and were inseparable. When it came to play, Raj was a good wingman for Mike when he was out womanising, rarely needing to pull himself, but always willing to take the piss and keep Mike's ego in check.

The final team member in the room was Charly. Charly was a consultant pilot and was probably one of the best in the world. She had started flying legally when she was 16 but was already a talent. Her dad had flown for the Red Arrows and she had it in her blood. By her mid-twenties she was flying one of the Red-Bull stunt aircraft in flying displays all over the world. Highly capable at low level didn't even begin to describe her talents. Long blonde hair, nearly always in a ponytail, she had a pretty face with bright green eyes. Mike found her infuriating. He had pursued her from the first day he had met her about 18 months ago and he had had no luck whatsoever. Sure, they kept it completely professional at work, but she was an enigma to him. In his mind, he was absolutely right for her. How could she not fall for him?

Tom was obviously wrapping up the brief when Max walked in, so Max took a seat on the front row and waited for him to finish. When Tom had done so Max stood up and addressed the team. 'Well done on Project Chimera, I have just come off the phone with a delighted client and that was an excellent job. The directors and I have decided to double your bonuses for the active project phase, and you should all have a little bit of time off.'

The team looked around at each other with a smile, rare praise from the boss was always welcome. Max took a deep breath and with a twinkle in his eye spoke again.

'Right, how was your break? Feeling rested?' Max spoke over the groans from the team. 'Great! We have a new task starting and I want everyone back in here after lunch for a planning session!'

Chapter 33.
September 19th, Nairobi, Kenya

Max and the team had moved from the main briefing room into one of the planning rooms. It was set up differently and was a creative workspace with white painted walls, soundproofing and pine veneer wooden floor tiles. One side faced the airstrip and half of the room was set up for planning. There was a map chest with maps of most African countries in varying scales. There was a digital white board on one wall which could be used to sketch ideas and diagrams especially as overlays for photographs and digital maps. End products could be captured by the attached computer and uploaded to the company secure file sharing site for circulating with field consultants, or clients. There was a full stationary cabinet in one corner and there was a light table and navigation instruments for good old manual flight planning. The other half of the room was taken up by an oval table which could seat 6 and Tom, Mike, Raj and Charly were all seated there now. Max was standing by the digital whiteboard with a pen in his hand.

'Ok, so this is one of the more fun projects that we have had for a while but at this stage there is no signed contract. We need to provide a demonstration of concept within the next week to show that we know how to solve the client's problem and that's what I want you all to work on.'

Over the next twenty minutes Max briefed the team on what he knew so far writing key notes on the board behind him. When he finished, he asked 'Any questions?'

Tom spoke first, 'Do we know where exactly the Hibernia III is held?'

'No. All we know was she was taken about 100KM off the Somali coast. I strongly suspect she is anchored somewhere off the coast rather than floating free in the Indian Ocean, but that's not a given.'

Tom, as commercially minded as ever offered. 'Ok, how about we use Charly's skills and see if we can do a run up the coast at low level. It might be a value add to find it for them and demonstrate capability?'

'Great idea, Charly could you work out the flight time and costing to do that? I am happy to take that as a business development cost for this one seeing as we got a free introduction.'

Charly said, 'Sure, sounds fun, I will have that for you this evening.' I would imagine it'll be less than 10,000 dollars if we use a Citation Jet and refuel at Mogadishu International.'

'Great, any other questions?'

Raj went next with his distinct Indian accent. 'So how are we going to deliver the ransom?'

Max smiled, 'Well that's what I want you all to work on for the next couple of days. Give me options, do some research, cost the methods, work out the risk assessment of the different solutions you come up with. I think we have a pretty free run here to resolve the problem and if we can come up with an option that is better than face to face delivery in Bakaara market then we should be on to a winner.'

Raj continued, obviously having had a bit of experience around ransom delivery during his slightly murkier past. 'What sum are we talking about?'

'It could be anything between 5 and 10 million dollars according to the response consultant. Worst case if you do the maths in 100-dollar bills is about 140 Kilograms. Plan on a maximum of 7 samsonite suitcases to move it around.'

Raj grinned whilst he quipped, 'Hey Mike, that's about the weight of that mama you pulled last weekend!'

Mike not rising to the bait replied, 'Yadda yadda.'

Max let the laughter die down and seeing there were no more questions said, 'OK all, have a look at initial ideas this afternoon and let's have a final chat before we knock off for a beer tonight.'

Chapter 34.
September 19th, Nairobi, Kenya

It had been a long day for Max, and he was feeling a little fatigued. It was just past 17.00 and the team had just reassembled in the planning room.

Max asked for updates and Charly started the meeting. 'I have looked at the numbers for trying to locate the Hibernia III. From here, to the Somali border and then flying all along the coastline to the tip of Puntland its about 1800 nautical miles each way. If we take a Citation jet, then we can cruise at high level to Mogadishu and refuel. We can then drop down to 2000 feet, taking a speed penalty but we will have the legs to search the northern coastline. Given the Hibernia III is a super tanker we will easily pick her up if she is at anchorage near shore. We can drop down lower if we want, take some closer images and then return.'

Tom commented. 'I like the idea of covering the northern coastline first, that's nearer to the hijack location and Somalia is more lawless the further North you go. I don't think we should make it obvious if we spot her though. Keep flying at 2000 feet, don't make any turns etc, not give it away that we are looking for her. If you have someone with you with a really good digital camera then that should be sufficient to give proof to the owners that we know where she is.'

Mike spoke 'Yes I agree. Charly, I will come with you and do the spotting for you.'

Charly grinned. 'OK, sounds like a plan. Max if you are happy, we can file this flight plan first thing and have the results by tomorrow night?'

'Excellent, go for it.' Max paused.' Right, what are the initial thoughts on ransom delivery?'

Tom had been working on that with Mike and Raj and he walked up to the digital white board where there were a couple of headings. 'So, we are concerned about doing the mechanics of proof of life for all the crew and then delivering the quantum to a different location to the vessel. We think we should try to work out how to get it directly to the vessel location. Then we exchange the money for the vessel almost simultaneously.'

Max asked, 'OK, How?'

'There are a couple of options and I will take you through all of them. We could in theory, put a team on the ground with a discrete vehicle and drive it there. We discounted that immediately as too high risk. We could use the resupply vessel, which will tow her if she can't make her own steam and we could hand over the money face to face from that. It has possibilities but we need some more thought on how we physically get the money to the ship in a clean timeframe, given that the resupply ship is probably going to need five days or so to sail up there from Mombasa. I don't know what the response consultant will say about that. They may want to execute the delivery as soon as practicable after an agreement is made. The final option is we throw it out the back of a Hercules and on to the Hibernia III' deck.' Tom said this last bit deadpan.

Charly was grinning as she hadn't heard that option before. Max raised an eyebrow. 'Mike, can we get a Hercules?'

'Of course, but they are slow, and we will have to fly it in from the Middle East or Europe.'

Max continued, 'And we can package the money in such a way that we can drop it directly on the ship?'

Mike being the expert replied. 'I think so. I have never done it with cash before, but we should be able to do it. We want to go and run some tests this week. See if we can get the drop precise enough and see if we can package it so that we don't end up with millions of bits of awfully expensive paper floating in the sea.'

'Ok, let's try it. Charly and Mike do the Hibernia III search tomorrow, Tom you and Raj work up the maritime plan and speak to our marine partners to try and cost a maritime rescue mission. Then the day after you can all work on packaging different loads and then we can stress test them. I suppose we had better order a couple of hundred kilos of printer paper and make some dummy money!'

Chapter 35.
September 21st, Nairobi, Kenya

Yesterday had been a good day. Charly and Mike had discovered the location of the Hibernia III flying over her very discreetly. Mike had captured an excellent couple of photos of the vessel, and then the shape of Hobyo town in the background. A quick Google Maps search with the satellite view turned on had been good enough for a comparison and Max had drafted an email to Finlay with the images attached.

'Dear Finlay, found something that you are missing. We have worked up a solution or two that we are going to test, and I will come back to you by the end of the week with the details. Give my regards to the team in Athens. Max.'

Meanwhile out in the back garden of the house the team was rigging a couple of dummy loads using printer paper that had been laboriously cut roughly into the shape of hundred-dollar bills. This 'cash' had then been packaged into 'bricks' of one hundred thousand dollars. Mike was in his element; he had taken a couple of parachutes from the company store but was tutting that they weren't what he would choose for this task. He had carefully repacked them using the manufacturer's data sheets. They had been in the stores for a while and were nearly date-life'd, but a visual inspection of the lines and the canopy proved them good enough for a test. Considering that wet money was useless money he had come up with a basic plan to try to protect it and had gathered together some other items from the company stores as well.

The first test load was a Pelicase, a great piece of kit made from injection moulded plastics and advertised as crushproof and waterproof. Mike and Raj had taken the equivalent of two million dollars and had packaged it inside a heavy-duty dry bag. These bags were bright orange and consisted of a heavily rubberised fabric with a special closing mechanism at the top. You folded this over a couple of times and then clipped the twisted material together with the kind of clip you find on a rucksack. Well trained soldiers usually used them to line their rucksacks, to keep their sleeping bags dry. If you did it properly, the contents of the bag stayed completely dry, in heavy rain, or if immersed in water. If you didn't, you usually got a wet night's sleep.

Mike and Raj had squeezed as much air out as possible when they sealed it and then locked it up inside the Pelicase with a little bit of foam padding to stop the bag moving around. They had then put an external strop around the case and tied it off with cable ties. Mike secured a small static line parachute, via carabiners, to the conveniently integrated loops on the outside of the case and using a light para-cord secured the parachute to the Pelicase. Job done on the first prototype.

The next one, with another two million dollars of dummy money was a slight variation on the theme. This time, Mike and Raj double bagged the cash using the heavy-duty dry bags and then wrapped a small cargo net around the package. It didn't look great, more like some kind of mutant butterfly chrysalis, but Mike wanted to test the solid case concept against something with a bit more freedom of movement. Again, using a small static line parachute and carabiners he secured the load ready for a drop.

With the first two prototypes completed they went back into the Ops room and told Charly they were ready. She had already filed a flight plan for a local recreational flight, for just before lunch, using a Beechcraft King Air. Commonly used for sports parachuting, it was a great aircraft and easy to remove the rear door before flight. They talked through the flight plan and the profile that Mike wanted for the drop. Five hundred feet, 120 knots. The landing zone was a friendly farm owner 20 KM south of the airfield. After a quick comms check on the handheld VHF radios, Tom and Raj hopped into Toms green Toyota Landcruiser and headed off to be the ground party. Mike grabbed a trolly from the stores and loaded the two packages on to it, before wheeling them over to the dispersal. Charly went ahead to complete her aircraft safety checks.

Half an hour later they were airborne. Mike was in the back and had a jumpmaster's safety harness on. A waist strap with integral leg straps and then a long lead which ended in a sturdy clip, which he had attached to one of the aircrafts integral cargo security points on the floor. To complete his ensemble, he had some knee protectors, padded on the inside and solid plastic on the outside. Similar to the type of thing that skateboarders wear, but military spec of course. He had on a set of headphones, with a long lead and male jack, which he had plugged into the female socket near the door at the back of the cabin. The headphones were noise cancelling, but they didn't do much to alleviate the roaring noise of the wind coming in through the rear door space. The door had been removed first thing that morning in preparation for the tests.

Charly, the completely professional aircraft commander, came over the intercom, 'Mike, we are five minutes out. As discussed, we will make a safety pass over the landing site first. Speed 120 knots.'

'Roger that.' Mike made a double check to ensure that the loads were secure, far away from the door space and that there were no loose items, including himself. He then got down on his knees and holding the open-door frame leaned out into the buffeting wind. He looked forward, trying to identify the drop zone.

Over their headsets came Tom's voice on the VHF. 'Five Yankee Lima Lima Zulu, this is ground party, we have you visual.'

Charly's voice: 'Ground Party this is Five Yankee Lima Lima Zulu, conducting our recce pass.'

'Roger that, wind speed is approximately 20 knots direction 080. We have a bright orange drop zone panel on the ground.'

'Lima Lima Zulu, copy that wind speed and visual with the panel.' Charly continued on the internal intercom. 'Mike, with that wind speed, when we drop, I will fly directly into wind, I suggest you count to ten, after overflight of the landing site, to account for drift.'

'Sounds good to me Charly, I figured eleven seconds at 500 feet.'

With a laugh to her voice Charly replied, 'Well babe, I didn't know if you could count that high with your shoes on!'

Mike laughed and looking down he could see Tom and Raj looking up at them. He scanned the immediate area of the drop zone and then a wider arc and then wider again before calling back. 'Drop zone looks clear, recommend we do the first run.'

'OK, hold on, banking right now.' Knowing that Mike was hanging out of the port side of the aircraft, Charly had purposely turned in the direction that, if there was any kind of drama, Mike would fall into the aircraft rather than out. A point that Mike inwardly appreciated.

Having tear-dropped the aircraft around and giving plenty of room for the setup Charly came up again on the VHF. 'Ground Party this is Lima Lima Zulu, starting the first drop run.'

'Roger that standing by and clear at our end.' Tom and Raj were looking up into a brilliant blue sky and could clearly see the white King Air flying towards them. As the aircraft came over the top, they could see Mike in the doorway holding the Pelicase load.

Inside the aircraft Mike had double checked again that the static line was clipped onto another anchor point on the floor of the aircraft. He could see the drop zone pass underneath and started mentally counting. When he got to nine, he leaned a little bit further out, felt the wind suddenly buffet him much more and gently released the load. It dropped like a stone well clear of the aircraft's tail plane, the static line lengthened and went taut dragging the bright orange parachute out of the bag and then snapping, leaving the static line dangling below the aircraft. Mike ignored it for now and watched the canopy deploy. It opened cleanly and started to drift. This time, having agreed with Charly in the brief in advance Mike said, 'Chute deployed, bank left please.'

Charly put the aircraft into a steep turn to the left keeping the plane at 500 feet but allowing Mike to watch the canopy drift all the way to the ground.

Tom and Raj saw the deployment and could see the load descending. A few moments later it hit the dusty savannah with a light bump about a hundred meters beyond the marker panel. As they approached, the parachute was being blown by the wind and was still partially inflated, but the load was secure on the ground. They secured the canopy and the Pelicase and carried them both back to the Land Cruiser. Meanwhile above them Charly was setting up for the second run.

45 minutes later with the second run complete they were all a back in the garden of the house at Orly.

Tom and Raj had unloaded the two dropped packages from their vehicle, having removed the parachutes back at the drop site. Mike and Charly walked in and together they inspected the packages. The Pelicase had done well as expected, and the load that used just dry bags and cargo nets had also done ok. Mike spoke first. 'So, either of these would work. We can pack them into two million-dollar bundles. I would like to get some different parachutes though, rated for lower weight loads.'

Tom replied, 'Fine, so we have a method. What do we think about trying to land these parachutes on the deck of a ship? Can we manage the drift in a sea breeze to an almost certain probability?'

'I don't think so,' said Raj. 'I think it just adds complexity to the drop and there is too much that can go wrong. Why don't we start with the intent of dropping them into the water near the ship? We can tell the pirates to be in the water in one of their boats to collect them.'

'That's a good idea, removes some of the risks, but perhaps creates others.' said Tom. 'What are the weaknesses there guys?'

Mike said, 'I like it actually. We just won't have reliable ground level windspeed and direction, which could throw off our aim. We can make sure the packages are waterproof and have floatation aids in them. It's a better idea than aiming for the ship and missing. It means that we remove the risk of canopy's getting snagged in cranes or other obstacles. It also means less time in the area, as we can drop more than one load per run.'

Charly spoke next. 'That sounds good to me. I have also been thinking about the delivery aircraft. We can't take a King Air all the way to Greece to collect the money and then all the way back again with a door off. That would take days and I would like to suggest a different piece of equipment.'

'What did you have in mind?' asked Tom.

Charly looked a little sheepish. 'Well, I might happen to know of a modified Cessna Citation X corporate jet.'

Mike managed to not roll his eyes as he asked, 'What kind of modifications?'

'Well, it has a smugglers hole at the rear of the aircraft. We can remove an internal panel in the floor during flight, then a further panel which would otherwise keep the aircraft pressurised. It has a small hidden door on the external skin of the plane that we can open in flight, as it's on a mechanised system. Finally, it's got a very discrete externally mounted pan tilt and zoom camera with a really good zoom on it.'

Mike asked, 'How big is the overall hole when it's all opened up?'

'I would have to check but I think it's a circle that's 24 inches in diameter.'

Mike thought for a moment. 'Well, that's a big enough hole to use. It won't take the square Pelicases though. Can the Citation get slow and low enough for us to hit the parachute drop parameters?'

'Yes. She can come down to a couple of hundred feet and right down to a hundred knots if you need it. She will drink fuel at that speed and height though, so we don't want to loiter too much. The benefit is, that for the long runs to Europe from here, she can cruise in the flight corridors at Mach 0.7, more than double the King Air speed. One word of caution, it's a commercially operated aircraft that is mostly used by some agency friends of mine, so I need to check if we can use it.'

Tom chimed in. 'OK, I like the concept. Mike, I know you like the solid case framing for each load. Can we do it with anything else? How about a piece of nylon drainpipe? We could cut it to length, seal up one end permanently and then work out what proportion of floatation aid we need to the relevant dry bags with cash weight.'

'Yes, that would work, we could get some industrial 30-centimetre pipe, cut it into perhaps one and a half meter lengths. We just need to work out how to seal the open end and how to rig the parachutes to it in a way that is fool proof.'

Tom spoke again. 'Right, so that sounds like a workable plan. I would like to test it again before the end of this week. Raj, can you work with Mike and build three prototypes. We will fly them again as a final check, and then I want you to wet test them as well. Charly can you speak to your 'friends' and see if we can use the Citation for the test drops and the project itself, also get some commercial rates for us?' Charly nodded and Tom continued. 'Great work everyone. Let's get the tests done this week and, in the meantime, I will go and talk to Max and tell him that there is a workable solution.'

Chapter 36.
September 21st, Nairobi, Ken

Max was sitting in his office on the second floor o
at Orly airfield reviewing the company accounts for the
Overall, not too bad he mused. That last project in the Central Africa
Republic had gone way over budget but it was a really good new
country entry task. They had not only now identified a good quality
local operator or two, but it had also been a great demonstration of
capability, for one of the big mining companies, which so far had only
given them a few small jobs. If their client won the mining licenses
that they were prospecting for, then that contract could turn into a
really good long-term revenue stream. The Central African Republic
as a country scored poorly, on just about every international metric
there was and trying to do business there was just plain old difficult. It
was just the right sort of environment where risk, managed properly,
equalled reward.

A short knock on the door and Tom walked in. He sat on one of
the comfortable sofas in the corner of the office and waited for Max to
finish what he was doing. It was early evening and his jaw line, which
he had shaved that morning, was already darkening up. Max closed the
screen on his laptop and moved over to a more comfortable chair
opposite the sofa. As he sat down Tom started: 'I thought you would
want to know about the preparation for the Hibernia III project.'

'Great, go ahead.'

'Well, it looks like we have a delivery method. Charly has
potentially pulled a specially modified Citation jet out of her bag of
tricks and Mike thinks he has a solution for the drop. They are going to
do a final test run later this week. We don't think we should try to drop
the packages directly on to the deck. Too much risk there. Instead, we
want to deliver the packages directly into the water, and then let the
pirates collect them.'

'Ok, for the test, will that be over ground or over water?'

'We were going to drop them down at the test site again, but
now you say that I see where you're coming from. Do you want us to
do the practice drops into the water?'

'Yes, let's find somewhere relatively quiet, where we can get
that done and really test the integrity of the loads.'

Tom thought for a moment. 'I know, let's take the aircraft down [...]fi Creek. It's on the coast about 20 minutes flight north of [...]mbasa. The creek is long and wide and there are very few houses [...]at overlook it at the far end. I know the chap who owns the boat yard there. He's a good bloke and will be able to lend us a couple of speed boats, so that we can pick the packages up when they land. It's all very discrete and the team will like it too. They can have lunch there afterwards. They serve one of the best prawn curries on the whole of the coast.'

'Ok, let's make that happen.'

Chapter 37.
September 21st, Nairobi, Kenya

As Tom left the office, Max stood up and went to the window that overlooked the airstrip. It was a quiet day, brilliant blue sky and hardly any wind. The acacia trees on the far side of the runway with their yellow bark and vibrant green, needle like leaves, were as listless as the bright orange windsock that colour clashed behind them.

Max thought for a moment and then turned around to his desk. He looked at his Apple watch which had just reminded him with a faint buzz that it was time to stand, and he pushed the 'up' button on his electrical stand-up desk. With a soft whir the desk rose to a predetermined height lifting the entire surface with the keyboard, mouse, and twin monitors. With that done he picked up a notepad and pen and jotted down a few thoughts whilst he stood there. He was about to pick up his mobile to make a call when he paused for thought. He looked back at his notes, changed his mind, and then reached into a desk drawer to pick up a cheap burner phone that had never been used.

Whilst the burner powered up, he pulled Finlay's number up off his iPhone. Max entered it into the burner and pressed dial.

When Finlay answered it was with a slightly quizzical, 'Good evening, who am I speaking to please?'

'Finlay, its Max, I hope it's not too late in the day for you?'

'Not at all, I just didn't recognise the number. Burner?'

'Yes, don't save it. I wanted to give you a call after that email I sent you.'

Finlay laughed. 'Yes, don't worry, we got that. You always were really good at business development. The owner loses their boat for a week, then totally unsolicited and outside of contract this now legendary consultancy company finds it, before the host government military does and just sends a nonchalant email!'

Max replied with a grin in his tone. 'Yes well, we do try.'

'Mr Papadopoulos was ecstatic. You should have heard him singing your praises. Anyway, needless to say the company is pleased and Chloe said to say thank you on behalf of the insurers too.'

'Excellent, my pleasure. I actually wanted to let you know that we think we have a solution for the release too. Can I tell you about it verbally before I send you a proposal?'

'Absolutely my good man! Let me just stub out this fag and grab a pen.'

Over the next 15 minutes Max outlined the broad plan to Finlay who asked several questions for clarification. Max finished off with, 'Of course if this is what is finally agreed we need to make sure that the 'need to know' on this is held tightly. Ideally, I don't want the client's incident management team to know anything about the methodology until the day of the project. Do you think we can do that?'

Finlay considered his reply. 'Well, we obviously need to tell Chloe, because the insurers need to approve the delivery method, and I assume you will want to take out high-risk insurance for the quantum whilst it's in your team's hands as well. We will also need to tell Mr Papadopoulos, but we may get away with only telling him for his approval. He is the kind of man that would agree to that.'

'Ok. Do you think Chloe will insure us for carrying that kind of cash halfway across the world and then throwing it out of the airplane?

'Ha, I have no idea, but it's their risk ultimately isn't it, if they agree to your plan!'

'Yes, I suppose so. Do you want to discuss it verbally with them tomorrow and I will put it into the proposal?'

'Yes of course. If you send it to me using our encryption keys, I will share it with the client and the insurers. I will come back to you in a couple of days with what they say. Out of interest, what are you going to charge?'

'I think we will ask for the 7.5% of the final ransom as discussed when I met the team in Greece. However, it's a little tricky to say at the moment, but by close of play tomorrow we will know the costs of the logistics. All of those assets on the move for that amount of time isn't going to be cheap I am afraid. I will try to keep to that 7.5% but may have to put a lower boundary on it.'

'That will probably be ok, as long as you also put an upper cap on it too.'

'Let me take a look at the numbers when we have them. There are so many variables that it's not easy I'm afraid.'

'It never is old boy, it never is.'

Max said goodbye and then hung up the phone. Absently, repeating a process he had done hundreds of times before, he pulled the back off it, pulled out the battery and the sim card. He dropped the sim card into the crosscut shredder right next to his desk and dropped the phone in the incineration bin.

Chapter 38.
September 23rd, Kilifi, Kenya

On the northern side of Kilifi creek, opening out onto the blue Indian ocean was the market town of Kilifi. It was a typical hectic African mix of brick and concrete three-story buildings with a large number of tin roofed houses spread haphazardly in-between. Many of the concrete buildings were covered floor to roof with bright paint jobs advertising everything from Coca-Cola to washing machine powder. The town itself was throbbing with the local markets open and trade brisk.

Motorbikes swerved in and out between the minibuses, which themselves mounted the pavements honking their horns to move irate pedestrians aside. Between the Northern side and the Southern side of the creek was the Kilifi bridge; a huge structure that towered over the creek, it was so tall that sailing ships could pass easily underneath. The pilings that supported the bridge were a popular place for the local children to climb on, to jump into the cool ocean below. The Southern side of the creek was a different world from the bustling town on the north, large pastel-coloured mansions on cliff tops with swimming pools that overlooked the ocean. There was a vastly different pace to life on the large multi-acre plots with coconut trees swaying in the wind beside the pools and where cocktails were served under the cool shade of the verandas.

It was over the Kilifi bridge that Tom and Raj were now being driven by a lunatic taxi driver. Tom thought that the car was probably possessed. He was certain that the driver was. But somehow car and driver spoke to each other on a daemonic plane, overtaking, undertaking, driving on whichever side of the road worked at that moment. Occasionally the driver even used the brakes, though given the high-pitched squeal that happened, when he did so, Tom was beginning to wish he wouldn't.

Tom and Raj had just flown in from Nairobi to Malindi on a commercial flight. The taxi driver had driven them the hour from Malindi to Kilifi, and now as they crossed the bridge, they looked inland along the creek, stretching nearly five kilometres away from them. The immediate foreground was occupied by about 60 or so small boats, all at their moorings in front of the popular boat yard.

Sailing boats, deep sea fishing boats, speed boats. All the playthings of those wealthy enough to afford such toys. As Raj looked, he saw a speed boat doing a power turn pulling a large three-seater 'doughnut' with some kids on. Lots of fun being had by all he thought. The car crossed the bridge and then turned right onto a road that may once have been tarmac, but which was now mostly just interconnected potholes. Following it for about ten minutes the car descended on a narrow track down to the creek level. As they drove out of the light forest, they came through a 100-meter stretch of mangroves, where angry brown land-crabs with huge red claws scuttled off the road, back down into their muddy holes.

The taxi pulled up in the boat yard car park and whilst Tom paid the driver, politely refusing the need for a return journey, Raj got out and stretched his legs. Having not been here before he looked around. In front of him going down a concrete slip way was the creek. Over the top of the moored boats, he could see the far side and the clutter of the town of Kilifi. As he looked further inland up the creek, the town gave way to hills covered in trees with larger houses interspersed. To his left was a fully functional boat yard. Boats of all sizes and types were on their trailers out of the water having work done on them by a team of engineers. The sound of grinders and the smell of resin and fibreglass mixed with the salty seaweed smell of the sea. To the right was one of the social highlights of the town for the expats and wealthy residents. The bar and restaurant comprised a lofty wooden structure almost completely open on three sides and with a thick thatched roof. In front of the bar, palm and coconut trees sprouted through the deep sand covered floor of the dining area. Plastic tables and chairs with parasols branded by Tusker, the local beer brand, were raised to keep the clientele cool.

Standing proud of the restaurant area, which was elevated from the sea, was a long, concrete jetty that reached out into the creek. Raj swung up his waterproof day bag and slung it over his shoulder as he walked out onto the jetty. He admired the teeming sea life that darted this way and that as he walked its length. Once at the end, he looked up into the blue sky, rummaged in his bag for a baseball cap and slathered some sun cream over all his exposed skin. Raj thought to himself that there was no way he was going to burn today. Cream applied, he looked over at Tom who was now having a conversation with an expatriate man wearing chino type shorts and a cream linen shirt.

After ten minutes Tom joined him on the jetty. 'Great, so the owner says the boats are ready. He has a couple of good helmsmen who will take us up the creek and he says they'll keep their mouths closed for a small tip.'

Raj looked at his watch. 'Good, Charly and Mike are due overhead in about two hours. I will speak to them and say we are good to go.'

'Excellent, then I suggest we order an early lunch and admire the view.'

With that they both walked back up the jetty took a seat at a table in the shade right up against the tides edge. The waiter came over and smiled.

Tom had been waiting for this moment all morning. 'Jambo my friend. Two prawn curries, extra chillies please and a couple of big bottles of ice-cold water.'

Chapter 39.
September 23rd, Kilifi, Kenya

Charly was back in her 'office' with her long blonde hair tied back in a ponytail. She was wearing a headset, aviator sunglasses, a white shirt with short sleeves and shoulder tabs with her gold and black striped aircraft Captain's epaulets. She spoke through the intercom. 'Five minutes out Mike.'

Mike wearing faded blue jeans and tight white T shirt replied with 'Roger that,' before switching channel and calling on VHF. 'Sea party this is foxtrot yankee zulu over.'

Raj's voice came back a little faint, but readable. 'Foxtrot yankee zulu, this is sea party strength four over.'

'Roger that you are strength three to me but workable. We are five minutes out.'

'Roger, we are about 500 meters West of the location we discussed. There were a lot of mangroves that we didn't pick up from the overhead photos so we have moved slightly. Roger so far?'

'Roger so far.'

'We are in two cream-coloured boats and there are no other boats within visual range. However, please take a look on your recce. There are a lot of sports watercraft and it would be a little embarrassing to drop onto a water-skier.'

Mike confirmed his reply and then spoke to Charly on the internal comm. 'Did you get that Charly? We need to line up slightly to the West of our original approach plan.'

'No problem. I can see the creek clearly now. Slowing right down to 100 knots and opening the external hatch door. We are at five hundred feet.'

About ten minutes ago once they were at low level, Mike had removed the Citations internal floor panel and the concealed removable panel that kept the cabin pressure correct when at high altitude. As he watched, the thin external skin door opened, and he could see straight down to the pristine mangrove and light forest vegetation passing below. Mike switched his attention to the small console on his right where a high-definition monitor sat, with a controller joystick. He slaved the discrete pan, tilt, zoom, stabilised camera that sat in a small transparent dome under the aircraft all the way forward. As he zoomed in, he could see the two speed boats in the water about a mile ahead. 'Awesome bit of kit this camera.'

Charly replied. 'Yes. Believe it or not its military spec.'

'Oh, I believe it. Scanning around the creek I can't see any other water traffic. We have Tom in one boat with a local helmsman near the shoreline and Raj in another about 1 kilometre ahead.'

'Seen, setting up for the recce run.'

Mike mused. An hour's flight from Nairobi to Kilifi was suddenly turning into the high pressure five minutes of the actual task. It was always that way. Lots of boredom followed by the need to switch on, perform to your peak and then switch off again.

Mike looked back down through the drop hole and briefly saw Tom and his boat flash past five hundred feet below. A moment later Raj passed by in a sparkle of blue water.

'Banking left.' Charly spoke just before she pulled hard left on the yoke banking the Citation into a steep turn.

Tom came up on the VHF. 'Wow you guys are noisy. Let's get the drops done and then move you on before the customs team come down the creek start enquiring what's happening. By the way, wind speed negligible.'

Charly replied. 'Roger that, setting up for the drop.'

Mike adjusted his position, kneeling now on the floor in front of the drop hole. He had two loads prepared in the aircraft with one on either side of him. He double checked that the static lines were secured and then as the aircraft ceased its turns and Charly said, 'Thirty Seconds,' he lifted one of the pieces of nylon drainpipe and placed it between his open knees. It didn't look pretty, but it should do the job he thought. His overly large biceps bulged slightly as he held it in position waiting for Charly's drop command. The package weighed about thirty-five kilos with the fake cash, the waterproof bags, the polystyrene floatation aid material, and the parachute. He placed one end of the tube directly over the drop hole now and then held his position waiting.

'Mike, you can drop in five, four, three two, one. Drop Drop Drop!'

Mike released the first package. It fell cleanly through the hole leaving the static line hanging free below but blowing in the slipstream. Quick as he could, he grabbed the second package, lined it up with the drop hole and released that one too. 'Both packages away.'

Tom's voice. 'Package one clean deployment, Oh! Shit! Package two is a malfunction!'

About five seconds later Raj's voice called. 'We are all clear! We are all clear! It's fallen straight into the water. I will collect that one if I can. Boat 2 are you happy collecting the first?'

Charly called on the intercom. 'Mike, banking left!'

Mike held on as Charly pulled the aircraft around again. He tried to get the PTZ camera to follow the first canopy down but wasn't yet good enough on the controls to move it slickly whilst the aircraft was in a tight turn.

Tom's voice came over the VHF. 'Ok, it looks like the first package is down safely in a clear area on the water. I will collect that one. Foxtrot yankee zulu, suggest you return to base and we will get these packages bagged up and couriered overnight to the office. Then we can meet tomorrow morning for a debrief.'

Charly replied with 'Roger that,' before switching back to the intercom. 'Mike, you happy to seal up those hatches? I am closing the external door now.'

'Sure Charly. Doing that now.' As he screwed the panels back in place, he was mulling the task over. He very rarely had a bad drop. He was trying to think of all the things that might have gone wrong, and he knew that it would give him a restless night. He was certain it wasn't the packing of the canopy. He hadn't been able to see if the load had left the aircraft cleanly and so had fouled the canopy at the moment that the static line had pulled it out of the deployment bag. The only thing he could think of was that the parachute had been on the shelf for too long. But he had inspected it yesterday. Hmm. He was pissed off and fumed all the way home.

Chapter 40.
September 24th, Nairobi, Kenya

At 08.30 the following morning, in the garden of the office back at Orly airport, the team were sitting at a picnic table each with a mug of coffee in their hands. One of the Kenyan members of the Ops team was unpacking a freight crate that had just been dropped off in the car park by the overnight courier.

As the two pieces of pipe were placed on the grass, there were surprisingly few problems visible as the team moved closer to take a look.

Raj, who of course wasn't drinking a coffee, but was drinking his morning protein shake out of a sippy cup started off. 'I saw the package that malfunctioned deploy cleanly from the aircraft. It came straight down and wasn't tumbling. The static line deployed the canopy and so my first thought, that Mike had done a shit job releasing the load from the aircraft, was unfounded.'

Mike glanced at Raj but said nothing and so Raj continued, purposely not looking at him. 'I saw the package hit the sea quite cleanly, but at high speed it hit almost perfectly end on. The canopy had deployed but it was a streamer, it just didn't look like it inflated. So, then I was thinking that Mike had done a shit job packing the chute.'

Mike growled in his deep low voice. 'Fuck off.' Whilst Raj continued.

'However, once I got hold of it, I could see that a number of the lines had snapped, all on the same side. So instead of a canopy packing error, I thought that Mike had done a shit job checking the lines before he packed the chute!'

Mike growled again a little louder this time. 'I said Fuck Off!'

Tom and Charly were giggling now whilst Raj was still deadpan.

Raj pulled the still sodden mass of the canopy out of the plastic box it had been transported in and laid it out on the grass. 'Anyway. I looked at the lines and simply put they look to be in good condition but,' and with that, he pulled sharply on what had looked to be a decent line and it sheared in his hand. 'So, looking at this we can see that it probably wasn't a checking error, but we do now know never to let

Mike put parachutes into storage again!' Raj couldn't help himself and he started giggling as well.

Mike puffed up his chest put on his most serious face for a moment, and then also cracked a grin before saying slightly more humorously. 'Raj, you are such a dick.'

Tom brought a little order to proceedings. 'Ok, so we knew it was a risk with those old chutes. We used them beyond their shelf life. The big question in my mind was actually, what if this happens for real. What did the Nylon tubes look like with that kind of impact?'

Raj continued. 'Well, the good news is that the money didn't get wet. The tube fractured of course. And it was a bitch to find it in the water just because I couldn't see it. If the parachuted hadn't been orange, then it would have been even harder. Anyway, the dry bags kept their integrity. But I would suggest that when we do this for real, we do a couple of things differently.'

'Go on?' said Tom.

'Well, firstly we put some floatation aids into the dry bags as well. Just enough polystyrene to make them buoyant in their own individual right. Just in case we get a casing split again. They should still be able to take one million dollars each of hundred-dollar bills. Next, we make sure we use luminous orange or yellow bags not black ones. It makes them easier to see in the water just in case the casing does split.' The team was nodding so he continued. 'Next we paint the tubes with some kind of bright paint. Again, it makes it easier to see them in the water. And finally, we go and buy some new parachutes, with the right ratings so that we don't have another malfunction.'

Tom nodded before saying. 'Ok, that's all logical. Package one as you can see worked perfectly. She only hit the water at about 5 meters per second, smack within limits. The casing wasn't even scratched, and the bags kept their integrity inside. It was a good idea to add the flotation aids inside the tubes, but I agree with Raj on painting them with hi-vis paint. Charly, Mike, what did we learn in the aircraft?'

Charly went first. 'From my perspective, it's a good piece of equipment to do this from. It worked well. Fast at high altitude, reasonable at low level and technically nothing wrong with the drop at all. Mike?'

'From my side, it was really busy at the back end for the drop. I think we need an extra operator in the rear of the aircraft just to manage the video camera. It's a great piece of kit and assuming we want to record the delivery then it needs its own body to manage it.'

Charly commented. 'You men, no multi-tasking skills at all these days.'

'Thanks, gorgeous.'

Charly continued demurely: 'Just saying. I am surprised you can't play with a little joystick whilst sticking something in a hole at the same time.'

Mike was like a bunny in the headlights, his jaw opened as he considered his reply, then closed again as he thought better of it and then continued. 'So, um, as I was saying. Another operator in the back for the camera and perhaps even another to line up the loads, so that the person releasing them through the drop hole can do it smoothly.'

Tom replied, 'OK, that's logical too. It looks like this ransom will be a large one anyway and so the team that does the collection is probably going to be at least three people.' Tom paused. 'So, in summary, we are happy with the drop method. Happy with the tubing. We need some bright coloured paint. We need more people in the aircraft, and we need some new parachutes so that Mike doesn't fuck it up again?'

Raj blurted out with laughter, Charly raised an eyebrow and smirked at Mike, whilst he choked on the last of his coffee.

Chapter 41.
October 10th, Hobyo, Somalia

The town elders were all sitting or squatting in the courtyard of Abdi's father's house chewing khat when Abdi arrived home that evening. He had spent the past week onboard the Hibernia III continuing his daily negotiation calls with John. It hadn't gone well. This morning he had really gotten angry at the lack of progress towards what he felt was a reasonable ransom figure. He just couldn't work out, given the huge value of the assets that he had grabbed, why the shipping company wasn't offering a lot more money. When it came to the people, they just didn't seem to give a damn. So much for western respect for human life. Yesterday the conversation had ended with Abdi threatening to hurt one of the crew if the offer wasn't increased. This morning however, instead of the revised offer that he was expecting, John hadn't even called at nine o'clock. Abdi had sat in the Captain's chair waiting and waiting, for more than an hour, before he tried to call the shipping company. It was then that he realised that something had been done to the ship's satellite phone. It could only call one number now, and that number was off the hook or engaged. Abdi had gotten even crosser, shouted at a couple of the guards for no good reason and then stewed in the Captain's cabin all afternoon before deciding to leave the ship for a couple of days and go ashore.

As he walked into the courtyard, instead of the warm welcome he was expecting, there was a bit more of a hushed tone. He even suspected the odd angry glance from some of the old men. His father Mohamed, who had been holding court, paused, and stood up to embrace his son. 'Abdi, welcome. Just the person we wanted to speak to.'

Abdi went onto immediate alert, a conversation with his father was one thing, but 'we', being the town elders wanting to speak to him was something else. 'Yes father. What's on your mind?'

'Come and sit my son. Some of the elders here are worried.'

As Abdi sat, he tried to exude a confidence that he didn't feel while Mohamed continued. 'We are worried about this project of yours. Yesterday I received a call from the Minister of Interior himself. I tried to cover for you but simply put he isn't happy that he wasn't consulted.'

Abdi interjected. 'Father he has no power here! He is nothing but a puppet of a useless government that can't even keep Mogadishu secure. Why are you listening to him?'

His father continued. 'It's not just him Abdi. As you know, he represents The President. But even much closer to home, the traders and merchants who are providing you all of your supplies came to see me yesterday. They are worried that you might never get paid, or that you might not get enough money to pay them.'

'Father that's rubbish. I have an agreement with all of them. They are charging me exorbitant prices for their goods in return for the credit they are giving me. They will get paid when I get paid!'

'And when will that be Abdi?'

'In the next few weeks, I am sure.' One of the old men chose that opportunity to hawk his throat and spat a huge globule of black phlegm and khat juice into the copper pot at his feet. It was a not-so-subtle insult that indicated that he didn't believe what Abdi was saying. Abdi turned and glared at him.

Mohammed continued smoothly before it could escalate. 'Abdi, you said you would get your money within a week. Do you see the problem? We are now a month into this. We have a huge ship moored off our coast sticking out like the erection on a camel and lots of people are worried that we are going to get screwed.'

'So, let them worry father!' then pointedly looking at the man who had spat, 'They are just jealous that they didn't think of this first. They are jealous that they are not the ones who will earn millions of dollars for taking a risk!'

Mohammed asked his follow up, 'So where are you with the ransom negotiation, my son?'

Abdi, regretting his outburst suddenly became more cautious. 'It takes time father. I have made my demands and they have started to meet me in the middle.'

'In the middle? But that's good Abdi, so they are offering what thirty, forty million?'

'No father.'

'Well how much?'

Trying to look defiant Abdi said, 'They have offered me five million dollars.'

Mohammed paused, looking around the courtyard. There was more balance now. Some of the men were actually looking impressed, there wasn't so much obvious dissent. 'Ok, and are you disappointed with that?'

'Yes! I am! That ship alone is worth a hundred! Its cargo is worth a hundred more. There are 23 foreigners onboard and I should be able to get a couple of million just for them!'

'But Abdi. I think you are going to have to compromise. Think about it. Six months ago, this was just an idea. Now you have proven it. I think, no, we think, you should come to an agreement and soon.'

'But why father?'

'Because too many people are watching. As the elders we can support you and protect you for some time, but soon there will be too much interest. Better to make a deal, better to complete it honourably. Better to send your skiff Captains out again, and again, and again.'

'Yes Father, I will see what I can do.'

'Excellent!' Then, addressing the assembled men. 'My respected friends, I think that concludes today's business. Do please allow me to speak to my son alone now.'

The elders stood up and gave their respects to Mohamed before they left. Once they had gone Mohamed addressed his son again as they walked into the dark cool of the house. 'Come Abdi, let's go and have some dinner. I couldn't tell you with the others here, but I have spoken to The Associate. He says he is pleased. He says that you should complete this project and soon. I am glad that you listened to me outside.'

Abdi looked at his father, recognising that it was actually The Associate who had been pulling the strings here and not the elders.

Mohamed continued smoothly. 'Oh yes, and The Associate has agreed that I should manage any wider expectations from other power houses and to complete some projects that show the town the benefit of your work. So, to help me do that, you will pay me ten percent of the final value of whatever you receive.'

Abdi stopped in his tracks. He closed his eyes and kept his mouth shut, fuming as his father continued to walk down the corridor. This week wasn't getting any better at all.

Chapter 42.
October 12th, Nairobi Kenya.

Max, standing at his desk, had a burner pressed up against his ear. 'Finlay, good afternoon it's Max. You wanted me to call you?'

Finlay's gravelly voice on the other end replied 'Max! Yes, thanks for coming back to me so quickly. It's good news my end.'

'Excellent, I like good news. What sort?'

'Well, subject to contract, blah blah blah, it seems Mr Papadopoulos likes your proposal, and he has told me he is going to accept it. He has asked me to tell you that his contracts and procurement team will be getting in touch with you today.'

'Good! Thank you. I am delighted and I shall wait to hear from them. In the meantime, how is the negotiation going?'

'Quite well actually, the communicator that Mr Papadopoulos has given us is really quite talented. He is managing the nuances really well and the negotiator on the other end is falling for all the usual tricks which is helping us keep the numbers down. We are at the 'I am going to chop someone's fingers off stage.'

'Ha, so naturally you will stop speaking to them for a bit?'

'Quite right, usual policy. If they threaten violence ignore them for a bit.'

'Good, so you are keeping them thinking that you don't value the crew or the assets so that their expectations are lowered. How long before you think you will get to an agreement?'

Finlay paused. 'If I was a betting man, I would say about another 6 weeks. Does that give your team enough time to prepare?'

Max reflected briefly. 'Yes, if we can get the contract signed this week, and the signature payment received then we can start to contract the aircraft, and the shipping.'

'Ah yes. You know I think that was the thing that really swung it for Mr Papadopoulos. I know that the drop itself is quite sexy but offering the solution to escort the ship out of harm's way as well really was the complete package.'

'Yes, it's going to need some meticulous planning, but I think we can manage that.'

'Well Max, if anyone in that part of the world can, then it's your team. Anyway, just wanted to let you know. Let's chat in a week's time and I should be able to give you an indication of the size of quantum that you should be planning for.'

'Good, I think that and an indication of which bank we will be collecting it from would be helpful at this stage.'

'Ok, I'll let you know. Bye for now.'

Max closed down the phone and pulled out the sim card. Again, that was shredded whilst the unit went into the bin. Switching to his desk phone he asked his PA to call Tom into his office. About ten minutes later Tom walked in. 'What's up Max?'

'I think it's about time we gave our little pirate problem a code name.'

'Excellent! We are going ahead with it! What are you thinking?'

'Project Calico.' Max replied. Tom looked at him not quite getting it. Max continued. 'Calico Jack was the name of one of the most famous pirates of all time.'

'Wasn't he caught by the British Navy and hanged?'

'Exactly!'

Chapter 43.
October 30th, Hobyo, Somalia

Two weeks later, Captain Oleksiy was on the bridge with Abdi and Zahi. Over the past few weeks there had been a couple of changes on guarding the crew. Less effort was required in terms of guarding and most of the crew now spent the majority of their days and nights living in the room that was the combined canteen and recreational room, next to the Galley. Zahi had worked out that it was much easier guarding the crew when they were occupied and so they spent most of their days in front of the satellite television.

There was another reason for the move of the crew too. After one of Abdi's noisier phone calls on the bridge with John, Abdi had gotten so pissed off that he had gone and kicked the shit out of one of the crew members who was lying asleep on the floor. It was Symon, the first officer who had received the brutal beating. As far as Zahi was concerned that wasn't on. He didn't care about the crew, but he did care about what they were worth in hard currency. Szymon had had a couple of ribs broken and was still in pain even now. Abdi had had to bring the doctor from Hobyo out to treat him, but some kind of infection had set in and now the man was lying down constantly in pain on one of the sofas in the recreation room. After that incident Zahi had persuaded Abdi that they would move the hostages away from the bridge so that they couldn't hear the phone calls. It was irritating at first to have to bring the men up to use the toilet on the bridge wing, but they had worked out a way of doing that as well in the end.

The problem for Zahi now was that some of the guards were simply crap at being guards. Too many times he had walked in to see the guards cheering along with the hostages just because Manchester City had put one past some club or other. Or there was the time that he had found out that one of the hostages had bribed one of the guards to bring some chewing gum and sweets aboard. To Zahi, it was all becoming just too familiar. Last night though was the most dangerous. He had walked in at about two in the morning to find most of the hostages awake watching some filthy western movie, and three guards all asleep in the corner of the room, their weapons lying beside them.

Zahi was still cross about that and was going to have a word with Abdi. He reflected that it seemed that Abdi had been avoiding him for the last couple of days. Had he done something wrong? Certainly, no longer was Zahi allowed to listen in to the negotiation calls that Abdi was having with John. This afternoon, Captain Oleksiy had specifically asked Zahi if he could have a conversation with him and Abdi. He had some important information apparently.

Abdi was sitting in the Captain's chair, brooding and looking out the front windows when Zahi brought Captain Oleksiy in. Captain Oleksiy was looking a bit worse for wear. He was still keeping his personal standards where he could in terms of shaving and hygiene. But his uniforms were only cleaned once per week now and if the whole ship hadn't been the same, he would have noticed his own stink.

Abdi asked him. 'You wanted to see me?'

Captain Oleksiy's replied in his Ukrainian accent. 'My Chief Engineer tells me that we have a problem coming and that I should tell you about it.'

Tired from the stress Abdi replied, 'What is it now?'

'Simply put, we are running out of fuel.'

'What! How is that possible?'

'Well, we have been running this ship for six weeks now. We have about 4 weeks' worth of fuel left at the rate that we are consuming it.'

Abdi retorted. 'But that is ridiculous. This ship is carrying a hundred million dollars' worth of fuel. How can you be running out?'

'Unfortunately, the fuel in the cargo holds is petrol. The ship's engines run on marine diesel. The two fuels aren't compatible.'

'So why is this my problem?'

'Well, if we run out of fuel, assuming you are able to receive the ransom that you are after, then we won't have enough fuel to sail away from here.'

Abdi paused to think. While he did so Captain Oleksiy became concerned. The Captain knew he was completely bullshitting Abdi. He had seen him become increasingly stressed over the past month and had even heard Abdi's side of a couple of the conversations with the negotiators. The Captain knew for a fact that he had so much fuel on board that he could run this ship for another 3 months at least, but he felt that applying more pressure to Abdi might speed up their release, or at least make the guy crack faster.

Abdi spoke again. 'So, what happens if you switch off the engines?'

'Well, we lose all electrical power. The air conditioning below, the lights, the power to that satellite phone. It all goes.'

'So just switch it off for half the time and then on again when I need it.'

'But that won't work Abdi, the engines are not designed for that. It takes about a day of engineering time to shut them down, and the same again to start them up.' The Captain was really bullshitting now, but he was relying on a complete lack of large vessel knowledge on Abdi's part.

Zahi could see Abdi was getting increasingly agitated. In Somali he asked Abdi what the problem was. Abdi filled him in, and they spoke for a moment about what to do. Zahi didn't know about large vessels either and whilst he was suspicious, he couldn't work out why Captain Oleksiy would lie. Abdi on the other hand was feeling the pressure. Firstly, John was being a bastard and wasn't offering enough money. Then the Associate had told his father that he wanted a speedy end, and now the Captain was telling him that they were running out of fuel. He swore inwardly before saying, 'Captain, I will think about the problem and I will speak to you tomorrow.'

Captain Oleksiy replied, 'Thank you, before I go back downstairs, I will just use the toilet please.'

Abdi gave a flick of his hand to acknowledge and the Captain went out the bridge wing door leaving just Abdi and Zahi on the bridge.

Zahi took his moment. 'Abdi, I want to talk to you about the guards.'

Abdi trying not to show his exasperation replied, 'What now?'

'Well, I am worried that they are becoming too familiar with the hostages. I think if this goes on too much longer, we will have a mutiny.'

'Really? 30 armed guards and 23 unarmed crew members and you worry that we will have a mutiny?'

'Yes. Last night, all three guards who should have been on duty watching the crew were asleep. They had their weapons with them at their sides and were completely out of it. By luck I checked on them, after midnight and found them asleep. But just think. If the crew had been alert, they could have taken those guns and we would have had a real problem!'

Abdi was tired, and he replied. 'OK, so what do you want to do. You are in charge of the ship.'

'I think we should remove the khat that the guards get.'

'What! That really would cause a mutiny!'

'The drug knocks them out. They are all chatting on the deck during the day, and then sleeping all night. They aren't used to it and their brains are fried!'

'We can't do that. We gave them an agreement that said we would include it.'

'Ok, so we offer them something different. We see if some of them want to have their daily pay increased by the equivalent cost of the khat. Some of them might go for that.'

Abdi quite liked that idea. It would reduce the pressure from the khat merchants and no one on board knew that he was paying fifty percent above market rate for the privilege of credit. 'OK, try that, see if it works for you. You can also sack some of them if you need to. I would imagine that you will only need to do that to a couple of them for the rest to get in line.'

'I will try that, but I have to ask, because originally this was only going to last for a week or so. It's now six weeks. Where are we with the negotiation?'

Abdi looked at Zahi and, deciding that Zahi was important to the success of this, he told him where he was in dealing with John. Once he had filled him in, he finished off with, 'So we are at just over six and a half million dollars, but the last couple of increases have been peanuts. Yesterday's increase was only 74 thousand dollars. It's ridiculous.'

Zahi reflected for a moment and then replied. 'Abdi think for a moment. Before this all started, what would you have done to get such a price? When we were thinking about little fishing boats, we might have gotten a few hundred thousand. This price will make you, and me of course, rich men.'

'So, you think I should take it?'

'I think you shouldn't worry about one hundred and ten million anymore. I am sure that your daily costs are high for all these guards and all your supplies of food and khat. I think you should worry about your bills. But on top of all that, I think you should worry about some foreign military coming to rescue their crew.'

Chapter 44.

November 8th, Athens, Greece

Finlay and John were discussing this morning's call strategy with Finlay continuing the coaching of what he thought was one of his brightest students. John had managed to settle into a rhythm of sorts. The bags under his eyes told of the sleepless nights, but that said he seemed increasingly comfortable actually having the conversations with 'the baddie' as Finlay kept calling him.

John had decided a while ago that to do this job, if it had been one of his family, children, or his wife who was being held, would have been the worst form of torture. Finlay had told him that sometimes that happened, though usually a preference would be for an uncle or close friend to do it. Finlay had also said that most cases, involving the kidnap of individuals, were resolved within about a week.

John was finding, that oddly, when you had 24 hours to plan each call, each step, it became easier. The other thing, John thought, was how odd it was for there to be such experience to draw on, so many processes or strategies that were tried and tested. As he had now discovered, there was a vast industry that existed to resolve cases of kidnapping and many of those highly paid skills were now being applied here, with this piracy problem.

As he now knew, it all started with the insurer or under-writer, and by that it really did all end up back at 'the' insurer, Lloyds of London. Of course, there were lots of brokers, some of them quite large, but ultimately there was a place in an office block in London where this was all meticulously planned and controlled. The insurers ran the game, and the game was to manage the risk and make money while doing so. The insurers set the price and ultimately sanctioned the target settlement figures that would become the ransom. The insurers paid for the consultants to respond and guide the negotiation, but actually they were also involved much earlier in the process. They had worked out a long time ago that, funded by a proportion of the premiums that were paid, there was a need to train the people sent to dangerous areas. A need to train the security managers whose responsibility it was to look after them. A need to help the companies write the plans and practice the responses. The more premiums they took, and the fewer incidents they had to pay out for, the more money they made. It was all quite logical when you thought about it.

Finlay had told John quite early on that there was one more trick up the insurer's sleeve. If a person had 'kidnap for ransom' insurance, that covered the actual ransom payment, it was never the insurer that paid it directly. They had discovered that the best way to keep ransom payments low was to insist that the company, or the family of the victim had to pay the ransom out of their own funds first. Then the insurer would repay them after the fact. This meant that the communicator and the response consultant really did have to keep the numbers down and it kept it realistic.

Finlay interrupted John's thoughts with a cough that turned chesty. After a moment or two of catching his breath he said, 'Sorry, I really should give up those fags. Definitely not good for me.'

John poured him a glass of water from the jug on the table in front of them and Finlay gasped his thanks. 'Right, where were we? Oh yes. Today. The main objective is signalling. By signalling we need to make it really clear that we are converging on the final amount that we are going to offer. Over the last couple of weeks Abdi should have started to get that idea, but we need to be clear today that we have nothing substantial left to offer. We haven't given him an increase for a week, and so he will be feeling the pressure. What I want to do now is demonstrate to him that the increments he gets from now on are hopefully less than his costs. So, let's get right down and offer him a final ten thousand. Tell him the boss has sold his car and that's it. If we are lucky, he will do the maths and realise he is spending more than that running his project over the past week and he is now making a loss each day. If that doesn't persuade him, then we will have to try something else, but experience tells me that we're on the right track here. If we get to that point and he agrees then we will close the call at that point. Tell him we will have to check with the owner that he still has the money available and that tomorrow, or the day after, we will call him back with how we think we can get it to him. Naturally, we will leave him for a few days longer than that just to sweat him out. That gives us a few days to plan the next call. Happy with that?'

'Sounds good.'

'Excellent. How about you grab another cup of coffee and settle your mind, while I put the key points up on the board?'

'That sounds good too.' And with that John stood up and went down the corridor to the coffee machine. His mind was working through the phrases he would use, some of the replies he might need. He reflected on some of the stock replies that Finlay had taught him to use if things didn't go to plan. He was so pre-occupied that he didn't notice the machine had already produced his latte and a polite cough behind him brought him back to the present. 'Umm sorry.' He said to the young intern waiting behind him. He took his coffee and walked back down the corridor to what he now termed, in his own mind at least, the Negotiating Room.

There were two clocks on the office wall now and as nine o'clock in the morning Mogadishu time came up, Finlay pressed record on the device next to the phone while John picked it up and pressed speed dial 1. After a brief period of rings Abdi came up on the other end of the phone. 'Abdi, good morning, it's John, how are you?'

Abdi wasn't feeling all that good this morning because the stress was really getting to him. There were just too many problems on his mind. Guards, supplies, council elders, Zahi, the accusing looks of those who had lost family in the first couple of skiffs lost at sea. He drew on his absolute last reserves as he bluffed his way. 'I am fine John, what news have you got for me?'

'Well, the owner told me that there is nothing left to offer. He just doesn't have any more money. I said to him that I didn't think you would find that acceptable.'

'You are right about that.'

'Anyway, he said as a gesture of final goodwill he would sell his car, he could get some small amount of cash for it, but that's really it, Abdi, there is nothing left.'

'So how much?'

John delivered the line in a flat monotone, trying to sound as though he had really done his best but that he was also disappointed. 'He can add another ten thousand dollars.' He paused. The wait grew longer. There was no reaction from Abdi at all. Nearly a minute passed before John followed up with 'Abdi, are you there?'

'Yes John, I am here.' Abdi sounded very tired.

John, increasingly confident, pressed him. 'Just to be clear Abdi, I think I can persuade the owner to pay you a total of six million, five hundred and thirty-four thousand US dollars, in return for your releasing the whole crew unharmed, the ship and its entire cargo.'

Again, a pause from Abdi, but then sounding defeated he said, 'OK. When can you send the money?'

Inside John was stunned, he didn't know how to react. His mouth dropped open, and it was him that paused this time. He looked up to see Finlay pointing at the line that had already been written up on the board. As he came back to his senses, 'Um, Abdi, I understand that we have an agreement, and I will go and speak to the owner. I will give you a call back in two days time, when we have worked out how we can deliver the money to you, so that we can go over the details. Is that OK?'

'Yes John. Call me when you have the plan.' Abdi hung up the phone and sat there in the Captain's chair disappointed, feeling a failure, not actually realising that he had probably won.

John at the other end of the line hung up the phone, whilst Finlay stopped the tape recorder. He looked at John and in his gravelly voice said, 'Well, that went quite well I thought.'

John looked back at him and not for the first time said, 'Christ, and you do this for a living!'

Chapter 45.
November 10th, Athens, Greece

It was 07.30 and Mr Papadopoulos was in his office on the third floor. Not for him, the vast expanse of a penthouse view at the very top of the building. He had a sumptuous office, good furnishings, all the trappings. On the walls hung well-lit oil paintings of some of the vessels that had meant the most to him whilst he had grown his maritime empire, but he didn't believe in ridiculous excess. His overweight frame, perhaps his largest excess, was sitting in his executive chair behind his teak desk. The teak was antique and had come from an old far east tea clipper. Whilst it had once been weathered and salty, it had been crafted by an expert cabinet maker into a creative masterpiece. His old-fashioned post masters desk lamp was on one side and his laptop on the other. Over on one wall away from the windows was a large television screen which was currently showing a golf tournament somewhere in the United States.

There was a knock on the door and Finlay walked in with Chloe led by Mr Papadopoulos's PA. Finlay had put a jacket on today, one of those blue linen ones that looked rumpled the moment you put it on. Chloe, her dark red hair in a bob and some simple pearl earrings was much more smartly dressed in one of her lawyer power-suits.

'Come in! Come in! Finlay, Chloe welcome. Do you want some coffee?' When they both nodded yes, the PA closed the door behind them to order it from the catering staff. 'So, you have good news for me?'

As pre-arranged with Chloe prior to the meeting Finlay went first. 'Well yes, we do believe that we have had a breakthrough, but I want to caution that we must not get too optimistic about this, until the whole thing is put to bed.'

'Yes, yes, I understand.'

'And we must keep this incredibly quiet. If this news gets out to the families at this stage, we can lose control of the narrative. Some of them might go to the media and the baddies might realise that they can try to leverage more money. Then we would be back to square one.'

Feeling a little bit as though his balloon had been deflated Mr Papadopoulos replied with, 'Yes, I can see how that would be a problem. But it is still good news yes?'

'Yes, it is. We have agreed a total sum of six and a half million dollars plus change. But perhaps I hand over to Chloe now.'

Chloe paused as the PA came back in with the coffee but after he had left, she was brisk and to business. It's actually below our target settlement figure which is good. It makes it easier to get the final approval from the underwriter. My boss at Stratton Parker Insurance has already given me a verbal approval to proceed and we will provide that to you in writing by the close of play today. We will need you to sign and return a copy of that document showing your agreement to the terms.'

'Excellent. No problem.'

'I must remind you that it is now your responsibility to organise for the cash funds and that you need to provide certain legal documentation that hands over responsibility of those funds to your contracted security consultancy that will complete the delivery.'

'Yes, I understand, is there a preference do you think for where the funds are collected?'

'That will be up to you and your bank manager. I would suggest that you choose a European country as that will help with the cash export declarations. I would also suggest that you inform the bank soon, as not many of them have that much cash immediately available for collection over the counter.' The last was said with a little twinkle in her eye, a rare chink in her armour.

'OK, and this documentation that is needed, who can help me on that?'

Chloe continued. 'I am happy to do that as part of the service. I am also happy to be present at the time of the collection of the funds, to ensure that we get the right signatures and declarations from the security consultancy. I would suggest that you have one of your finance representatives there as well.'

'Excellent, thank you, yes we will do that. Do you need anything else?'

Chloe shook her head and so Finlay chimed in again. 'So, one of the things that needs to happen next, after your signature of Chloe's letter, is the final approval for the security consultants to mobilise. They will need to get all of the logistics in place and be prepared to collect the funds in just under a week's time. They need to mobilise their shipping assets almost immediately. Please confirm that you approve that I can mobilise them?'

'Yes, I approve. I will get my team to send Max a written approval today.'

Thank you but on that, just a reminder then Sir, as you inform these other people. We really need the fewest people possible to know that this is now in play. If everything goes well it will take about a week from now to get this finished off.'

'Yes, yes, I understand. It's good advice.'

After saying goodbye, Chloe and Finlay walked out of the office. Chloe asked. 'What did you think of that?'

Finlay considered before replying, 'Well to be honest, it was great that he accepted all our advice. I can't put my finger on it though, but I am worried about this one.'

Chapter 46.
November 11th, Athens, Greece

Finlay walked into the negotiating room. He had stopped off for a fag on the way and so walked in reeking of stale cigarette smoke. He was carrying an A4 sized manila envelope and John was already there sitting at a desk.

'Hi Finlay, how did the conversation with Mr Papadopoulos go? - Did he approve?'

'Morning John, yes, we are good to go, no issues. Are you happy with the notes that we went through yesterday? It can be a bit of a tricky conversation to get through this one.'

'Yes, I think so.'

'Good, explaining how the delivery is going to happen can sometimes be difficult. Especially as this one is quite unconventional, though Abdi's English is really quite good, fortunately. Let's write some of the key points up on the board and then we can go through it.' Looking at the table by the wall he added 'Ah, good, we got the fax machine installed then.'

'Yes, the tech did it yesterday. I have put the fax number for the ship on the piece of paper beside it.'

Finlay walked over to it, glanced at the number, lifted the handset to check there was a dial tone and then replaced the receiver. He walked back to John's desk and pulled some documents out of his manila envelope. 'Here we go. This is the final draft of the process that we need to talk Abdi through, and here is the diagram.'

The documents weren't new to John, they had discussed them extensively yesterday and re-drafted them twice. One was a written explanation of how the drop would go, and one was a picture, showing how it would happen. Finlay had kept the physical copies in his possession overnight. He wouldn't have been the first response advisor to have lost vital documents just before a drop.

They spent the next twenty minutes writing key phrases on the whiteboard and then took a quick break. As 09.00 Mogadishu time came up on the clock, as always, Finlay pressed record and John pressed speed dial 1.

The phone rang several times before Abdi picked up. Sounding relieved he said, 'Hi John, good morning.'

'Good morning Abdi, how are you?'

'Well, I was expecting your call yesterday. What happened?'

'Oh, were you? Sorry about that, we had some final detailed planning to do. Hobyo is a long way from most places Abdi.'

Abdi was a little shocked but tried not to show it. 'Um, yes, it is. I hadn't told you where the ship is. How did you know?'

Finlay nodded at John, this was a good pressure card to play and John evaded directly answering the question by saying 'Abdi, we have known where you are for a long time now.' He stopped to let that sink in.

Abdi filled the gap. 'OK, and do you have a plan on how to get my money delivered to me? I won't put any of my men at risk, so if I don't agree the deal is off.'

'I understand Abdi. In a moment I am going to send you a written instruction using the fax machine on the bridge. It's important that we don't have any misunderstandings during the next week. Remember, your aim is to receive the money, and that will be in return for the ship, the cargo and the unharmed crew.'

In a non-committal tone Abdi replied, 'So tell me your plan.'

Over the next twenty minutes John described what he wanted to happen. Finlay and he had very carefully prepared the script, and the written instruction that would be faxed to Abdi. Whilst John was talking, Finlay pressed send on the fax which described the process for the delivery and the release of the ship in detail. The diagram was sent too, trying to put key parts of the plan into pictures rather than words.

There were only a few questions throughout by Abdi, but he asked one important one at the very end. 'What happens if my money sinks to the bottom of the ocean?'

'That's a fair question Abdi.' replied John. 'We have thought about that in detail and I know that the person who is going to deliver the money to you has thought long and hard about it too. They have tested and tested to make sure that this will work, but it does need your team to do their bit too.'

Abdi, not quite ready to give in yet said, 'And what if I demand delivery face to face on land in Hobyo?'

'Abdi, that's a no deal. We looked at flying into the airport there and hand delivering the cash, but that would be too risky for both sides. What if someone else decided that they wanted to steal it from you, what if the government impounded the plane and arrested the crew? We feel that this way you can control the maritime environment. You use your town's fishing fleet to secure the area and keep any, shall we say, criminals away, whilst you receive the money and confirm it all. Then you release our ship immediately.'

'Ok, I will think about this overnight and then we speak tomorrow.'

'Abdi, before you go, we have one further thing that we require.'

'What now?'

'Well, tomorrow, when we confirm everything. I must speak to each of the crew members to confirm that they are all alive.'

'What! You don't trust me?'

John quickly replied. 'Abdi, we have been speaking for weeks now. I do trust you, but my boss told me I have to make sure that everyone is alive before I am allowed to proceed. Can you help me out there?'

'Fine, what do we need to do?'

John told him and Abdi agreed. It wasn't too difficult by the sound of it and Abdi felt that with each day passing, he was getting closer and closer to his money.

Chapter 47.
November 11th, Hobyo, Somalia

Zahi and Abdi had taken a walk to the extreme bow of The Hibernia III. They had discovered that it was one of the best places to be able to have a conversation without any risk of being overheard. Zahi had his AK 47 on a sling over his shoulder and was leaning up against the gunwale which felt hot to the touch. He was looking down at the waves lapping against the hull, thinking it would be good to go swimming. The sea was fairly calm and whilst he couldn't quite see the sandy bottom, he could see fish a long way down through the sparkling clear blue water. Abdi, wearing light three quarter length trousers, sandals and an old, stained light blue T-shirt was next to him. Instead of staring down, he was looking at the shoreline about 2 kilometres away.

Zahi had requested they go up to the bow as he had something to discuss and to get off his chest again. 'Abdi, I am getting bored. I was never meant to spend so much time cooped up on a ship like this. I like the sea, I like being a fishing boat Captain, I like the freedom that comes with that.'

Abdi looked at him. 'You like the freedom of being poor?'

'Well with Allah's help I won't be poor for much longer, but yes I like the freedom.'

'I understand. This project has been going on for a long time, but we are getting near the end.'

Zahi looked across, this was news. 'Seriously? Are we near the end?'

'Yes, but you must keep this secret. In about a week's time, we are going to have millions of dollars delivered to us, right here!'

Zahi, got excited. 'But that is brilliant news! How?'

'Zahi, my friend, I can't tell you yet, but you will know before anyone else, I can promise you that.'

Disappointed and perhaps with a slightly disbelieving tone Zahi countered with, 'But really? We are close now?'

'Yes, but we have an issue that I do want to discuss with you.'

Zahi had noticed that Abdi had turned serious. 'OK, what is it?'

Abdi replied simply, 'The owners know where we are.'

'What! But how?'

'That I do not know, but on the call this morning they told me that they knew where we are.'

'They are bluffing!'

'No, they said Hobyo. First, they told me how they would deliver the money and then there was this sort of threat that they knew where we are.'

Zahi asked, 'Do you think they have told the U.S. navy? The government in Mogadishu?'

'I don't think so. I think if they were looking at a military action, then they wouldn't have told us what they knew. Any intervention would come as a complete surprise.'

Zahi continued staring down at the fish below him as he reflected on that before replying, 'Well perhaps. It's almost a threat isn't it. You agree an amount, and it's followed up with 'we know where you are,' almost to reinforce that this is the last deal or offer they will make. It's meant to apply pressure, get us worried, get us thinking.'

Abdi looked across at Zahi, thinking his ally very astute. 'Perhaps my friend. What it does do is make me cautious and I am worried. We need to make sure that the guards are alert especially the ones on watch outside.'

'Ok, I will see to that. We also need to make sure that no one knows what day the ransom will arrive. How about I confiscate all the mobile phones that the guards have on board? Then they can't communicate with anyone. Perhaps a large ransom like this might be too tempting for some of the other Somali clans as well and they might try to come for it.'

'That's a good idea, lets collect them all in 5 days' time, and make sure the guards are alert and we keep the crew under control. On that subject, tomorrow morning, we need to provide proof of life to the negotiators. They want to know that all the crew are safe and well.'

Zahi looked worried all of a sudden. 'Abdi, there might be a problem there. The first officer, Szymon, that you beat and kicked in the chest. He still hasn't recovered. He has some kind of infection I think, in amongst those broken ribs.'

'Can we move him up to the bridge just to make a phone call?'

'Yes, but he is still in a lot of pain. I think we may need to get the doctor back on board.'

'Ok, do that today so that when they ask this man tomorrow, he can say that we are at least treating him.'

'Fine, and I will work out a plan on how to get each of those men up one by one for the phone call. I have got one other important question though. If the owner is delivering the ransom to us here, are we actually going to release the ship and crew when they do so?'

Abdi had spent quite some time thinking about this one. 'Zahi, I see a future where we have huge opportunity to make money in the long term, not just off one ship. Can you imagine what we could do if we re-invest this money into funding lots more Captains like you, capturing lots more vessels, perhaps even two or three a month.' Zahi raised his eyebrows and he looked at Abdi as he continued. 'If we are going to make a business of this, we need to behave like businesspeople. If we make a deal, then we need to stick to the deal. Then we build up trust.'

'What trust between thieves? Will that even work?'

'Yes, I think so. At the moment we are an unknown entity to the ship companies. But if they see that we release the crews and the ships after they have paid, then we might get to a point where this becomes a regular transaction. We can make a lot of money.'

'But the higher the profile, and the more regular these transactions become the more interest there will be in trying to take the business away from us. Government will pay attention; other clans will want their part of the action.'

'I agree, but if we are making several million dollars a month, we can afford to buy good weapons. We can afford to pay for many men, we can have one of the largest militias in the country and all loyal to my father and our clan. No one would dare to attack us then. If there is anyone that we have to pay, to stay off our backs, then that is possible too.'

'I didn't realise that you had such intentions.'

'I didn't either when we started out and it's only really become apparent to me over the past month or so. My question to you Zahi, is do you want to help me manage and grow this? You have the reputation; you have the respect of the other Captains. I won't be able to manage all of this, if it is going to grow the way I intend. I will need a key lieutenant.'

'Can I have some time to think about it?'

'Of course, you can have until the ransom is paid on this vessel. Then we will need to decide on the future. In the meantime, I need you to protect this investment.'

They lapsed back into silence, staring at the sea, staring at the land, fantasising about the possibilities, and worrying about what could go wrong.

Chapter 48.
November 12th, Hobyo, Somalia

On the bridge of the Hibernia III Abdi was alone and feeling quite calm for once. He was sitting in the Captain's chair, which he reflected he was actually quite beginning to like. In it, with the view of the vast tonnage of the super tanker hull before him, he felt powerful and in charge of his destiny.

Abdi picked up the phone when it rang and after the usual greeting with John they got down to business. John asked, 'Abdi do you have any questions about yesterday's call?'

'The first thing I want to know is what day will you be delivering?'

'Ok, that's a good question. There are a lot of complicated things that need to happen now to get everything in place. But we believe that we can deliver on the morning of the 19th. Will that work for you?'

'Yes.'

'Good, I think it's a good idea that we both agree to make sure we have a phone call every morning between now and then without fail. Do you agree?'

'Yes.'

'Perfect, what other questions do you have?'

Abdi tried to put a bit of steel into his voice with this one. 'I need two cash counters to come with the money.'

John, confused couldn't stop himself from asking, 'Sorry what?'

Abdi asked again. 'I need two automatic cash counters so that I can count the money when it arrives.'

'Um, hang on a second please Abdi.' Abdi could hear John talking to someone in the background briefly before he came back onto the phone.

'Abdi, I am sorry, but I don't think I can manage that. We are going to throw these loads out of the back of a plane and into the sea. When the loads land they will land hard. We know that the cash will be alright, but I can't guarantee that sensitive electrical goods will survive the landing. I can't see how I can solve that one I am afraid. Are you able to get some locally?'

Abdi was a bit irritated that he couldn't get a final demand in but recognised the logic of what he was being told. 'Ok, never mind.' Then after a pause, 'I don't have any more questions. I agree with the method that you have described. But I warn you. If it doesn't work, then we go back to my idea of delivery in Mogadishu, and it will be for twice as much.'

'Let's see how this goes shall we. We are extremely confident that we can deliver as we have discussed, and we need you to hold your side of the agreement and release the crew, cargo, and vessel once you have confirmed the count of the money. Can you do that Abdi?'

'I have told you already. Yes!'

'Great, shall we start with the proof of life demonstration?'

'Give me a minute to get the first member of the crew up here, but first my rules. You may not tell them that we have an agreement. They do not know yet. You may ask them questions about themselves only, and I will be listening in. If you ask or say anything else, then I will disconnect the call. Do you understand?'

John replied. 'Yes Abdi, that's clear.'

Abdi put down the receiver for the phone and went to the Bridge door. He opened it to find Zahi outside with Captain Oleksiy. The Captain was looking much thinner and paler than he had done two months ago, when Abdi had first met him. A poor diet, lack of sleep and stress did that to a man. That said, he still kept his chin up and his pride intact. Abdi indicated the phone and they both walked over to it. Abdi put it on speaker phone and said 'John, I have your Captain here. You may speak to him.'

'Thanks Abdi. Captain Oleksiy, It's John. How are you feeling?'

Captain Oleksiy's eyes lit up a little at the familiar voice of his operations manager back in Athens. 'John! I am ok. It is difficult for us though, you understand?'

'Captain, I do. I am certain that things have been awfully hard for you. All I am allowed to say is that we are making progress and you must bear with me for a little longer. Can you do that please?'

'John, I don't know for how much longer we can do that. The crew are tired, they are broken. Some of them are not well.'

With concern in his voice John asked, 'Captain, who isn't well? What happened?'

Abdi cut in quickly. 'John, that's not our agreement. You will speak to all the crew members today to confirm they are alive. You will not ask any other questions!'

John tried to recover his posture, 'OK Abdi, I understand. Captain, I believe I recognise your voice, but I need to ask you to tell me something that only you and your wife would know. Can you do that for me?'

The Captain paused before saying. 'Yes, the first time I kissed her was at a Christmas party in Odessa.'

John paused as he considered the humanity of it before replying. 'Thank you, Captain. We are doing our best to get you reunited with her again soon. Please keep the crew calm for a while longer and I hope to speak to you again soon.' Then addressing Abdi again. 'Abdi, I can speak to the next person now.'

For the next forty minutes or so John spoke to every crew member on the ship one by one until finally he came to the First Officer, Szymon. As Szymon was carried on to the bridge, Abdi spoke up.

'John, the First Officer is the last man to check. Before you speak to him, I will tell you that he is not well.'

'Why isn't he well Abdi?'

Evasively Abdi answered. 'He has a chest infection.'

'What kind of infection?'

'He has broken ribs that are not mending well. I have had a doctor visit him and he is on some painkillers and some antibiotics.'

'Abid, I am concerned on two issues here. Firstly, broken ribs sounds like you are mistreating the crew, and secondly you haven't told me this before.'

Abdi got heated. 'I don't have to tell you anything. It was your fault that this man got hurt. You should have listened to me more carefully when we were negotiating.'

John, who had received a prod from Finlay backed down a little. 'I hear what you say Abdi, I would like to speak to Szymon now.'

Abdi, indicated to Szymon who approached the phone, and leaned against the chair trying to still the pain in his lungs from the breathlessness that was a result of his climb up the stairs. Szymon had spoken to John a couple of times earlier in the year and thought he recognised his voice. 'Mr. John, its Szymon.'

'Hi Szymon, tell me how bad your injuries are.'

'Well to be honest I could do with a better doctor, but yesterday they allowed a local one to see me and strapped me up. I also now have some pain killers and antibiotics.'

'Well, I am sorry you got hurt Szymon. I hope you understand but I need to ask you a question so that I know it really is you. I spoke to your mother recently; she sends her love by the way. What was the name of your primary school?'

'Thank you, tell her I love her too. It was school number 7 in Chornomorsk.'

'Thank you Szymon. Look after yourself and hopefully we will speak soon. Abdi I would like to have one more word with you before we complete today.'

Szymon was escorted out of the room as Abdi settled himself back into the Captain's chair. 'Ok, what?'

'Abdi, I will make sure to check all the information I have been given here and will speak to you tomorrow morning. Before I go though, remember our agreement. You are remarkably close to getting your cash. My objective is the return of the ship, cargo, and crew unharmed. You understand me?'

Abdi, unfazed, simply replied: 'Goodbye John, until tomorrow.' And then he hung up.

Chapter 49.
November 12th, Athens, Greece

Finlay and Chloe were sitting in the incident management room of the AFSC offices in Athens. Finlay had already told Chloe that the proof of life call had been interesting, but positive, in that he could say with reasonable evidence that all of the hostages were still alive, if not all well.

Chloe asked, 'And how did John feel about that call?'

'Pretty much the same as everyone does. It's an emotional phone call to make, especially for someone who knows many of the victims. They are very real to him and he's seen their names on ship manifests regularly. I told him to take the rest of the day out of the office and to go and do something to clear his mind. I also said he should think about getting some therapy. Talk through some of the emotional side and all that.'

'And what did he say to that?'

'I think he had the same approach that most men do when confronted with the need to look after their emotional health. Denial, and evasion. Most men are still in the ice age when it comes to understanding mental health. Still, I have planted the seed in his mind, and I will continue to recommend it to him. I will also speak to Mr Papadopoulos about it so that he is aware of the need. John doesn't have to live with potential nightmares for the rest of his life, just because of his job.'

Chloe, perhaps more than many, knew the risks here for John, having seen so many communicators in her time. With luck this task would go the right way in the end and John wouldn't have to live with any perceived guilt from any negative outcomes. They would cross that bridge if it ever came up. Chloe asked, 'So we have POL, we have a final agreement, and we have a target delivery date. It looks like we are still on track to complete on the 19th?'

'Yes, I am just going to give Max a call and let him know. His is now the most complex part of the operation. We have a call scheduled in about five minutes and I should pull up the number that he sent me for his burner phone.' Finlay opened up his encrypted laptop and looked through his emails. He found Max's number and digit by digit entered it into his mobile.

Chloe, watching him do it said, 'Max is very cautious with his communications isn't he?'

Finlay snorted, 'Yes it's the 'Service' background in him. If anyone is going to know how capable governments are at intercepting digital mobile phone conversations, then I suppose it's him. I asked him about it once over a beer and he looked at me in a pitying way, as though I was clueless! Eventually I got out of him that the Chinese supported Kenya in developing their entire internet and telecoms infrastructure. Not the basic commercial towers and stuff, but the fact that every signal in and out of Kenya goes through a magical box of tricks, which the Kenyan intelligence service have access to. Oh yes, and there is a big fat pipe that sends a copy of everything back to Beijing too.'

'Really?'

'Well, I was sceptical too, at first, but he is adamant. Every time we have a conversation that might be a little sensitive, he uses a one-off pre-paid burner phone! He only powers it up when he needs to make or receive a call, and then immediately he destroys the sim card and dumps the phone in the bin.'

'Wow, that's an expensive way to make a phone call.'

'I suppose he thinks that a 30-dollar burner and a 10-dollar sim card, all bought for cash naturally...'

'Of course.'

'....is a reasonable cost to pay for leaving no digital footprint. Given how many projects he runs for Her Majesties government I wouldn't be surprised if he had bought shares in the phone manufacturer!'

Chloe smiled as she reflected on this slightly weird conversation as Finlay looked at his watch again. 'On that subject, let's give him a call, shall we?'

Finlay pressed dial on his personal phone and after only a couple of rings Max picked it up. 'Hello, my friend, what can I do for you on this fine day?'

'Well, I wanted to let you know that we have an agreement with the counter-party and that we have set a delivery date of the 19th. Does that work for you?'

There was a brief pause at the other end as Max did some maths. 'Yes, I think we can make that work. So that I can plan, on a scale of one to twenty where did the team end up?'

Finlay paused a moment as he tried to work out what was being asked, and then he replied, 'About six and a half.'

'Oh well done, I am impressed! When you speak to our mutual friend next tell him to expect 4 packages in total when we see him.'

'Will do. I just wanted to let you know as soon as possible so that you can get those first logistical pieces moving. I will drop you a secure email with some of the details later today. Have you received formal written approval?'

'Yes, we got that overnight. All good to go our side.'

'Marvellous, I will give you a three-day warning for the next phase so that the final bits and pieces get moving.'

'Sounds good, lets chat again then.'

Finlay hung up the phone and looked across at Chloe. 'Oh, I do sometimes hate dealing with ex-spooks, understanding the subtle nuances and meanings. But do you know what? Given that that was probably a cheap and crappy phone, and the guy is more than 5000 kilometres away, that was a pretty clear call.'

Chloe playing dead-pan: 'Well, you know, the Chinese intelligence service just wanted to make sure they had a clear recording. Now that they have your phone number and voiceprint too, I think you should stamp on your iPhone just to be safe.'

'Christ Chloe! That's not actually very funny!'

Chapter 50.

November 12th, Mombasa, Kenya

The Sea Dragon was a 20-year-old offshore tugboat. Marine environments were not kind to work horses like that and her original paintwork had been scraped, battered, and patched up so many times that rust stains splattered her what could have once been a blue hull and white superstructure.

To look at, you would say the designer got the balance wrong. All crew accommodation, the bridge, and the smokestacks; that seemed to smoke more than stack, were all weighted so far forward you would think that she would tip forward over her nose. Of course, the long, low, flat working deck at the rear was designed for work. There was a six-foot-high steel wall around most of the rear deck, but she was open at the stern towards the sea to allow her huge tow cables to move freely as needed. In her past glory days, before she had been despatched to Mombasa, she had worked tirelessly in the North Sea. Her job there had been helping to reposition vast oil rigs, fresh out of the building yards to the places where they would anchor for their working lives. She was no stranger to rough seas then, or risky work, but the project she was being prepared for now was a different kind of risk altogether.

At the moment she was birthed beside a thick concrete jetty in Kilindini port, Mombasa. On one side was the large Coca-Cola bottling factory and on the other, the wide expanse of water that was the mouth of a wide, deep lagoon.

Chris was standing on the top deck of the Sea Dragon. He was wearing beige cargo shorts and a matching beige short sleeved cotton polo shirt with no logo. His shirt was darkened by sweat dripping down the centre of his back and his pits were dank and stained. Mombasa's humidity did that to you personally too.

Chris was a British ex-naval officer, top of his class at Dartmouth, just got his Captains ticket but had then shagged one of his junior officers on a tour of duty. He was told to leave under threat of being dishonourably discharged. He had kept his commercial Captain's ticket though and joined a small shipping company for a while before he got bored of that and started freelancing. He was tall, with blond short curly hair and a mousy brown trimmed beard. He had spent the past five years job hopping, disappointed that he never got to command an aircraft carrier and he was just pissed off with the establishment. As he stood on the top deck, he looked out over the carnage of the sea traffic in the port. Ragged vessels, no one obeying the maritime rules, rubbish, oil pollution and every now and then a waft of raw sewage attacked his nostrils.

He was the maritime team leader for Project Calico. Far too overqualified for this one, but happy to take the income to help pay for the new conservatory his wife wanted back in Plymouth. He and his team had flown down yesterday and spent the day today stowing kit and checking the weapons.

The weapons, despite a widely held and common disbelief of mercenary contractors, were completely legitimate. You could get into all sorts of problems carrying dodgy weapons into a country's territory illegally and he didn't intend to spend any time in a sweaty prison in Mombasa, that was for sure. Of course, he had thought, if you knew where to go in pretty much any port you could acquire a weapon, for a few hundred USD. Then you would drop it overboard at the end of the task. Max and his teams thought people who operated that way were just unprofessional wankers.

The Sea Dragon's Captain, Jammo was also an ex-military officer. A Kenyan, he was now in his late 50's. He had dark sun damaged skin that had spent too much time outside near the equator, and short black, now turning grey, curly hair. In his youth he had been a young Lieutenant for the Kenyan Navy but had become disillusioned very quickly with the lack of serviceable ships and little actual sea time. He had left the service and worked his way diligently up the ladder in KMS, the Kenya Maritime and Shipping company which owned the Sea Dragon. For several years now he had been working as a Tug Captain, pulling huge barges up the coast from Mombasa to Mogadishu. Most of the time he was carrying World Food Program grain aid to Somalia and he had a lot of experience of the coastline.

He had also applied for and been granted a private firearms license which allowed him to own and carry personal firearms in Kenya. He was a firm believer in the right to protect himself when at sea and he had a beautiful pair of L1A1 self-loading rifles. For this trip he had also applied for and received a temporary permit to take two AK47s and he had borrowed them from a colleague, who had transferred them to his license. Of course, 'borrowed' in return for an exorbitant day rate, which was the norm.

The Sea Dragon was on charter to Max's team for the next two weeks and Captain Jammo's well-disciplined and diligent crew had done all the hard work in terms of stores, bunker fuel, water, and all that. Chris' job was to direct the vessel safely up the coast, rendezvous with the Hibernia III at a location north of Mogadishu, put an armed team on board it, which he would lead personally and then escort it back down to Mombasa. Chris was going back up to Nairobi tomorrow for the final briefing with the other team leaders. It sounded simple enough. He just hoped that the pirates did the honourable thing and fucked off when they got their money. That would make this job so much easier.

Chapter 51.
November 13th, Nairobi, Kenya

It was 09.00 and the Calico project briefing was about to start in the main briefing room. The room lighting was slightly dimmed, and the cinema style chairs were mostly filled. Present were Tom, Mike, Raj, Charly, JP, and Chris who had just come up from Mombasa.

JP was Charly's co-pilot for this project. He was an ex-Tornado fighter pilot who despite his talent had only joined the military for a bit of fun. His mother was an heiress to a vast multi-national drinks business. He had her looks and he certainly didn't need the flying income. JP loved his flying though and had qualified on a large number of airframes including the Citation model X, an aircraft that the family happened to have at home as well. He was very well spoken and was mostly self-deprecating, he could let you know that he came from a 'good' family in both subtle and not so subtle ways, depending on whether or not he liked you. One of his favourite ice breaking lines when introduced, was to say, 'Hi, my name is Jonathan, but only my mother and the Prime Minister call me that, so please call me JP.'

Charly had introduced JP to Max, because given the total flight time on this project she wanted an extra set of hands in the cockpit. Max didn't like using untested consultants, especially on complex projects like this, so he had used some of his old contacts to do some discrete vetting. He was pleased to learn that JP was an experienced pilot and, in passing, really was as well connected as he claimed. He had been at university with The Prime Minister and was a regular guest at Chequers.

There was a bit of chatter in the room as people introduced themselves. Chris had worked with Tom before but hadn't met any of the others. There was a cool, calm, anticipation in the air that was palpable. No testosterone, just professional operators there to get briefed on the details of a plan.

Max was standing behind a small podium in front of the tiered cinema seating and behind him some of the big wall mounted screens were powered up. One had the power point presentation on it, with the heading slide saying 'Project Calico'. Another screen had a Google Earth map fully zoomed out, so you could see Europe and Africa on one page. There was the smallest of red tags on the map offshore Somalia showing the location of the Hibernia III. The vast expanse of land visible on the screen had the country names in white writing. From south to north were the labels, Somalia, Ethiopia, Sudan, Egypt, Greece. A final screen was rotating through images of the Hibernia III. Stock photos from the shipping company website, and then the photos that Charly and Mike had taken when they had discovered her location.

Max, ready and keen to start on time, cleared his throat and started talking as the room went quiet. 'Good morning everyone and welcome to the briefing for Project Calico.' There were some murmurs in reply, 'Morning' and 'Morning Max.'

He started with a round of introductions, making sure that everyone knew who was who. Once that was completed, he continued. 'So, we all come from different backgrounds as we can see. The format for this briefing takes some of the headers from military orders, but as you know we all left the services a long time ago. Think of this as more of a formal briefing. I am happy to take questions as we go if anything is unclear. OK? Right, then the first slide. The mission is the collection and delivery of a ransom, for humanitarian purposes, in order to release and secure the vessel, cargo and crew of the Hibernia III.' Max repeated that statement before moving onto his next slide.

'We have split you up into two groups. An air team, and a maritime team. Let's start with the air team. Tom is the team leader. Mike is the air drop specialist, Raj will manage project security, Charly is the aircraft Captain and JP is her co-pilot. The mission is broken into a number of phases and you have several key tasks. The overall concept of operations for the air team is this. I want you to travel to Athens and meet with the client's representatives at the bank to sign for guardianship of the quantum. Next, organise its safe transfer to the aircraft and depart Athens. Then whilst in flight to the project area, prepare the quantum in to four packages for the drop. Prior to doing the drop you will conduct a detailed proof of life check using the onboard camera system of the aircraft. You will confirm that you have POL with the vessel owner and with his final approval you will release the packages. You will need to conduct two passes at least, depending on wind conditions. Mission success for you is photographic proof of the four ransom packages being loaded onto the deck of the Hibernia III. Once you have that you can return to Nairobi. Everyone happy with that broad outline?'

The team was and Max continued. 'The maritime team will be led by Chris using the charter vessel Sea Dragon and its crew. Chris' team is aware of the broad task and he will brief them in detail tomorrow after departure. Chris will be supported by Miguel, who some of you know, as well as Bob and Omondi.'

Mike chipped in. 'Oh, is Omondi back from Puntland then?'

Max continued 'Yes. His project helping to coach the Puntland coastguard is having a funding hitch, so he is available for a little bit. I thought we would use his talents.'

Mike addressed Chris. 'You have a good man there. He is one of the most professional Kenyan operators I know. A good hand.'

Chris nodded his appreciation, making a mental note and Max continued. 'The maritime team's concept is this. You will depart Mombasa tomorrow and pre-position to a location approximately 50 kilometres East of the Hibernia III and over the radar horizon. You will loiter there until drop day, at which point you will proceed to within visual range of the vessel, but no closer than 5 kilometres. We need to give the pirates the sea room to collect their ransoms. Once you see that the pirates have vacated the vessel, which might take a few hours, you will immediately board her with your armed team and secure her. You will have to play that timing by ear, but once the drop is complete, I have no issue with you closing to 2 kilometres so that you can better judge visually when the pirates have left. Chris, Miguel, and Bob will cross deck onto the Hibernia III. Once secured, you will then cross load some fuel and supplies from the Sea Dragon and stay on her all the way back to Kenyan waters. Omondi will stay on The Sea Dragon which will escort you home. Chris and his team will then cross deck back onto the Sea Dragon prior to arrival back in Mombasa. Project success for you is the safe recovery of The Hibernia III back to Mombasa. Any questions so far?'

JP asked, 'What happens if the Hibernia III can't get underway on her own? Is the Sea Dragon powerful enough to tow her?'

'Good question. Yes, is the answer, but it will be really slow. We have a secondary vessel on standby that can head up and join the towing effort if needed.'

Raj spoke next. 'Has all this been communicated to the pirates?'

Max replied, 'Yes. We have shared the plan with the communicator, and we have sent diagrams and notes on how it will all work. The testing that you did down in Kilifi was instrumental in that. Their negotiator is called Abdi, and he speaks exceptionally good English. We don't think there will be any communication issues there. That said, we need to be cautious. Anything else at this point? No? The

Hibernia III is a Very Large Crude Carrier, she was hijacked on the 8th of September with 24 crew on board. She is carrying just over 100 million dollars' worth of petroleum products.'

There were a couple of low whistles and murmurs at that as Max changed slides and showed one with a zoomed in image of Hobyo. 'She is being held here and as far as we know, the crew are still all on board. The shipping company negotiator has made it clear that the crew are all to be on board for the next proof of life check, that I will come on to in a moment. We know virtually nothing about the baddies here. Only a name, Abdi, and that he sounds young and speaks with a slightly cockney London British accent. The overhead photos that you can see here showed a large number of armed pirates on board the Hibernia III and we don't know if this will be a satisfactory business transaction at this stage. So, maintain healthy levels of suspicion and caution. A ransom payment has been agreed, to be delivered on the morning of the 19th. The exact quantum is six and a half million and thirty four thousand US dollars in hundred-dollar bills.' Max paused for a moment as he changed slides again. 'The weather is looking good for the next 7 days in the drop location, and the sea state is low, so there shouldn't be any issues with cross decking. However, in Europe there is a large low-pressure system which is bringing snow and sleet. It's likely to hit Greece at some point and there is a low risk that it could happen whilst you are there. Nothing we can do about that for now and we will continue to monitor the situation. On the moon state, it's a waning moon and is only 5 days from a new moon. It will be nice and dark at night at sea for the period of the drop, and the period of recovery of the Hibernia III. Ok, before we go onto phases, any questions?'

Tom asked, 'Max, if the meteorological situation in Europe is iffy, can we collect the quantum from anywhere else?'

'It's a good question, and I have asked.' replied Max. 'I am told that it's too difficult to change locations now, given the specific quantity of cash required. Legal say that we definitely want to collect it from within the European Union.'

'Why is that?' asked JP.

'Well, by doing it in the EU, we fill in the right legal paperwork to export the cash. We will do that with the support of the shipping company lawyer, and we are then legally protected. No chance of being charged with money laundering etc.'

'Thanks.' replied JP who was on a rapid learning curve.

Max continued as he changed slides again. 'Phases and timings. As mentioned, Sea Dragon departs tomorrow morning, the 14th. The air team will depart on the 16th, collect the funds on the 17th and complete the legal processes. Then on the 18th the air team manoeuvres to the air staging area in Djibouti and refuels. That's the same day that the Sea Dragon should arrive at its staging area 50KM from the Hibernia III. There is then a slight pause for approximately 8 hours, which gives us a little slip time then to conduct the delivery on the morning of 19th. After the drop, the pirates will count the money, we've no idea how long that will take, and depart. The Sea Dragon comes alongside for a ship-to-ship transfer of the armed team and cross decking some supplies. Then, Sea Dragon escorts Hibernia III back to Kenyan waters. At that point, our role is over, and we will be clear. She will then come under the shipping company's supervision, and they will conduct family meetings, media briefs etc. Right, Tom over to you I think.'

Tom stood up from the front line of seating and proceeded to hand a printout to each person. 'Needless to say, this is a confidential piece of paper. It's got every single timing, date, and movement for the whole project, so we don't want to lose control of this. My preference is that we don't take it from this room. We should use it now to discuss the details, and then we can shred them. I will share it digitally with you all using our encrypted email.'

The team spent the next thirty minutes or so going through the absolute details of timings, distances, how they would do the collection from the bank, and how the final proof of life process would work. Then they covered the administrative details like the communications plan, what accommodation had been booked and who was providing transport to get them to and from the airports or the port. When they had finished, Max took over the briefing again and summarised the core parts of the plan. He reminded them that he would be based with the client, in the client's office in Athens, in case there were any issues. With no more questions, the team meeting broke up.

As per the normal tradition, Tom, the team leader told everyone to get a coffee and then meet outside in 20 minutes at the picnic table for an informal chat.

A short while later, hot beverage, or protein shake in hand, the team were sitting outside in the sunshine under a clear pale blue sky. The briefing had been comprehensive and there were no residual questions, so the session turned more informal. It only needed one person to ask, and in this case, it was Raj, 'So are we doing the usual?'

JP didn't know what that was and so asked, 'The usual?'

Reeling him in Raj told him. 'Ah yes, ladies and gentlemen we have a virgin amongst us today.'

JP spluttered into his English breakfast tea. 'What, no I am not!'

'Yes, my friend, its nothing to be ashamed of, but as this is your first project, I don't care if you are an Adonis between the sheets, but to us, you are a virgin!'

Charly rolled her eyes commenting, 'It's all right JP, it's harmless fun.'

Mike continued, queuing off Raj. 'So, JP, you were a fighter pilot yes?'

'Yes.'

'Were you a steely eyed fighter pilot?'

Slightly indignantly JP muttered, 'I did my part.'

Raj cut in again. 'Ah! So, were you so good that you could do your work without getting excited or scared?'

'Well, I don't know about that. I didn't take a dump inside the leg of my flight suit in combat, if that is what you are asking.'

Tom was watching with amusement letting the banter play out and Mike replied. 'I am sure your dry cleaner was glad to hear that. So here is the question. Would you like to participate in a little wager?'

JP completely out of his depth before now felt on more solid ground. 'Sure, what's the bet?'

Raj explained. 'Well, it just so happens that I can see we are all wearing Apple watches.'

Completely baffled again JP said quizzically, 'OK?'

Raj continued. 'Well, this is the bet. We keep our watches on for the whole project, aside from charging them. At the end of the project, we download our heart rates and compare them. The loser, is the person whose heart rate spiked the highest over the project length, starting from 07.00 tomorrow morning until 9 days' time when Max calls project complete.'

'Oh, I get it. So, whoever flaps the most, or panics the most, their heart rate will give them away. What's the bet?'

'That's easy, it's always the same. If we are successful, Max takes us all out to dinner at The Muthaiga Club. They have an extremely strict dress code. The loser has to go to the team dinner wearing the most goddamn awful bright yellow Hawaiian shirt.'

'I can't do that; I am a life member there! My family have been members there for years! You have to wear a jacket and tie, or they throw you out!'

Mike played up now and in his deepest voice said, 'Well if you're worried of losing then perhaps, we shouldn't play.' He left it hanging there until JP replied.

'No, no, I am in, and I won't lose.'

Mike grinned. 'Excellent. You looked like you were getting a little ruffled there. You know in 43 times of playing this game. I have never lost, have I Raj.'

Raj slapped him on the back. 'Do you know what Mike; you are so damn icy calm that I think Charly here could stand naked in front of you and your heart rate wouldn't flicker.'

Charly laughed as Mike looked extremely embarrassed. So, embarrassed in fact that Raj who knew him so well glanced at him oddly. Mike's discomfort was luckily hidden by Chris who had remained silent throughout, but who now piped up and said, 'Yep, that sounds fun. I'm in.'

Chapter 52.
November 14th, Mombasa, Kenya

At 05.55 in the morning the sun was rising in the East over the city of Mombasa. The dawn sunlight shone through the smoke and fumes of the city which was already well awake. It was impossible to sleep through the noise of the buses, the shouts of the fish markets and the howl of underpowered tractors pulling heavily laden 40-foot containers, hitching them up to the cabs that would pull them up the main road to Nairobi 500 kilometres away.

Chris had had a busy couple of days and had flown back down from Nairobi last night to sleep on the Sea Dragon. She was due to slip from the wharf in about half an hour or so, and Chris was standing on the bridge wing, water bottle in hand, settling his mind and enjoying the hubbub sounds of the port as it woke up. He had been there for about ten minutes when the door behind him opened and out stepped Miguel. Chris said a cheery 'Good morning,' and Miguel returned the greeting in his heavy Columbian accent.

Miguel and Chris hadn't worked together before. They had spent a couple of days together preparing the project stores earlier that week and had mutually agreed that they could respect each other, despite the fact that they came from completely different life pathways. As a young man, Miguel with his long black hair tied in a ponytail, and a deep scar on his left cheek, had worked for the Western Cartel in Columbia as an enforcer. Before the cartel had been closed down, he had been lucky to escape both its clutches and or arrest. He had moved to Kenya with a reputation, an unknown amount of cash and a newly acquired identity. Corruption at its best. Miguel had become one of the staples of Max's crews doing ad-hoc tasks whenever some of his rougher skills were required. He had built up trust with Max over a couple of years as an exceptional shooter. As far as Chris was concerned that was a skill that was perhaps needed on this job but, whilst he had to take Max's word on Miguel, he would keep a weather eye open.

They both stood there for a moment in companiable silence. Chris was back in his beige shorts, brown deck shoes and a beige short sleeved shirt. Miguel was wearing black three-quarter length cargo shorts with Caterpillar branded sandals and an old Columbian national football team shirt.

The Sea Dragon's engines started to warm up, demonstrated by an increase in the pitch of the background hum, a change in vibration through the hull and a massive smoker's cough like expulsion from the stacks above them. As Chris and Miguel stood and watched the ship come to life, there was some movement from the crew on the decks and by the shore party on the wharf. The gantry was stowed. Mooring ropes were loosed from rusty bollards, retrieved, and stowed. As the last one was let go the Sea Dragon gently pulled away from the wharf under the power of her own bow and stern thrusters. A further change in engine tone and the propeller spooled up providing forward momentum. The water was muddy under the hull and slowly a bow wave formed with a mixture of dirty water, scum, and grey foam.

The noise and change in vibration had woken Omondi and Bob and they joined Chris and Miguel on the bridge wing. Omondi appeared first, about 50 years old, Kenyan with short black curly hair. He was wearing blue jeans that were heavily faded, a grey T shirt, no socks and flip flops. To look at him, with his thin frame, yellowing teeth, and pockmarked face you would underestimate him. A sharp intelligence was behind those eyes that missed nothing. He had grown up as a sailor in the Kenyan Navy but had been seconded for most of his career to a number of international military training organisations. For the past five years he had specialised in capacity building for coastal navies and coastguards all around Africa. This trip would help him pay the bills at home before he could get back to his current contract role advising senior military officers in Puntland, on how to manage their coast guard assets.

Bob appeared shortly after. Another British ex Royal Marine senior non-commissioned officer. His last job before he left the Queens service had been running a successful search and seizure operation off a British frigate patrolling the Indian Ocean. Based on intelligence he had found 10 million dollars' worth of cleverly hidden narcotics in a sailing dhow headed to Mozambique. From there the drugs would have passed through South Africa and into mainland Europe. After that success he had been promoted and given a job training maritime search skills to new recruits. He had only left the Marines about a year ago but had already done a couple of tasks for Max. Bob was only about five foot six, but powerfully built in his chest and arms. He had short brown hair, grey eyes, and a slightly ginger goatee. If you told him that you thought it looked ginger though, then you had better be wearing your running shoes, if you didn't want a good 'kicking'!

The team stayed up on the bridge wing for about half an hour, whilst the Sea Dragon made her way out of the mouth of the natural harbour. The vessel started to roll a little more as she rounded the headland and took a course heading North East. On her port side was the coast of Kenya and on her starboard, about 1500 Kilometres away was Madagascar. After that, if you kept going you would hit the South Pole and there wasn't much else in between.

Chris broke the silence. 'I need another cup of coffee and some breakfast. Shall we go and grab a bite to eat before we have a chat about the project?'

With a verbal confirmation from all, the team went down the stairs to the main deck level and in through a hatch to find the galley, following their noses to the bacon.

Chapter 53.
November 14th, Hobyo, Somalia

'Abdi, how are the crew today?' John asked politely.

'They are all fine.' Abdi replied rather dismissively as with his tongue he probed a piece of breakfast that was still stuck in his teeth.

'OK, and how is Szymon specifically?'

'He is alright. The doctor saw him and gave him some drugs to manage the pain.' Abdi was covering. To be truthful he was a little bit worried. The doctor had told him that if they were near a hospital, they might have admitted Szymon and put him on an intravenous drip with a cocktail of antibiotics and perhaps even a steroid. The infection in his broken ribs seemed to be getting worse and there was perhaps the beginnings of a fever.

'Abdi, I need you to let me know if that changes ok?'

Still sounding non-committal, which worried John a little, Abdi replied with 'Sure. Now tell me where we are with getting me my money?'

'Well, everything is going smoothly. Remember I told you about the small ship that would come to escort the Hibernia, when it's released? That is on its way now as it takes three or four days to get to you.'

'Good.'

John continued. 'I need you to remember what we discussed Abdi. That ship and its crew are all part of the way for us to get the Hibernia III back. They are not to be attacked or obstructed. They won't come close to you, but you will see them approach after you have received your money. When you and all your men hand the Hibernia III back to Captain Oleksiy, then the smaller ship will come along side. But by that time, you will have departed, won't you?'

To be honest Zahi had tried to persuade Abdi to try to capture the rescue ship, but Abdi had ruled against it reminding Zahi that it was all part of the same business transaction and that they were trying to build trust for the longer term. 'Yes, we won't mess with your rescue ship, if your rescue ship doesn't mess with me and my ransom.'

'Good, glad to hear that. Now another reminder. We intend to deliver the ransom at about 09.00 your time on the morning of the 19th. I need you to let me know if you agree, as we are now entering the most important phase. This is all about getting you your money safely, and you releasing the ship, its cargo, and our crew unharmed. Do you agree to that?'

'Yes, the morning of the 19th is fine.'

'Excellent. Now, let's go through that morning's plan once more. It's important to make sure that we all understand what's going to happen.

Finally, Abdi had managed to worry loose the piece of food in his teeth, and he managed a slightly muffled 'OK.'

John and Abdi spent the next ten minutes going over the plan again, including the details of how the second and final proof of life check was going to be completed. At the end of the call when John had hung up, Abdi put down the phone receiver and reflected for a moment. Whilst constantly repeating what was going to happen was boring, to be honest he was getting quite excited now. He was looking forward to receiving the payment. They were getting so close.

Chapter 54.
November 14th, Athens, Greece

'How are you holding up?' Finlay asked John following the call to Abdi.

'Not too bad considering,' replied John. 'It's getting near the end game now, isn't it?'

'Yes, not quite so much for you to do from now on, but the nerves start to get to you at this stage. You can see the finish line, but there is still one more lap to go.'

'Yes, I certainly feel that. So, what happens next?' asked John.

'Well, I am now going to drop the delivery consultants a secure email and let them know that we have confirmed everything and that they should mobilise their air team. It gives them two days to do their final preparations and to fly to the bank here in Athens to collect the money.' Finlay was opening up his laptop as they were speaking, and John remained silent whilst Finlay typed.

After a moment Finlay had finished and he re-read his message out loud. Partly as a spelling check but also so that John would hear.

'Dear Max, Ref. Project Calico. Confirmation from our end that your air team should launch as per the agreed timeline. Delivery date as agreed is 09.00 on the 19th. Yours Aye. Finlay.'

He checked to confirm that he had Cc'd Chloe, had pressed the encrypt button on his email software and then he pressed send.

Finlay continued talking. 'Good, that's all done then. Nothing substantial for you to do now John for the next couple of days except to standby in the event that we get any calls from Abdi. We do still need to do the daily check in that we promised as well. To be honest I am a little worried about Szymon, but there is truly little we can do about that now. Your next major call is going to be on the morning of the 18th for another confirmation check and procedural run through with Abdi. He will also be feeling nervous, and we should take him through the plan one more time. Then, I would expect a very final call with him on the morning of the 19th just before delivery and fingers crossed, we should be all done.'

John spoke plainly. 'I am certainly looking forward to getting this finished.' He grimaced slightly to himself. 'And there was me thinking that my normal day job was stressful. I am now realising that it was a breeze compared to this.'

Chapter 55.
November 15th, Nairobi Kenya

The air team were back in the briefing room. Mike, Raj, Charly and JP the new co-pilot were all sitting in the front row of chairs. Tom was standing at the front behind the podium on the right and going through a stores list for what they needed to pack into the aircraft later that afternoon. The list was up on one of the big screens at the front of the room and the team were all providing their input while Tom typed. Much of the preparatory work had come from Mike who firstly had done a lot of the stores shopping when he had placed an order with the South African Agents a couple of weeks ago. Secondly, he was the guy who was going to put the loads together and so had put a lot more thought into it than the others. The team had finished covering the stores needed for the drops when the door opened, and Max walked in.

'Sorry to interrupt team. This will only take a moment,' Max said.

'That's ok,' said Tom, 'The floor's yours.'

Max didn't want to walk into the briefing room and cause a major disruption, so just stuck his head into the room and said 'Good morning all, I just wanted to let you know. We have an update from the negotiation team. Confirming that all is OK for a delivery on the 19th, so you are good to launch as planned tomorrow morning. If I don't see you before, good luck and I hope the trip goes well.'

The team members thanked Max as he ducked back out. A little frisson of excitement went through the room. They were definitely going now and that put a little more focus on to their current task.

Tom brought them back into the present. 'That's good news. Now, Raj, could you let us know how you got on with the cash transit cases?'

Raj said 'I managed to get hold of four large aluminium Samsonite suitcases on rollers. I collected them yesterday from the industrial area where I had them modified by welding aluminium loopholes on to each of the sides of the cases. We can use them to transport the money using the 'cash in transit' plasticuff seals that we will get from the bank in Athens. They are not going to stop a determined entry to the cases, but they will certainly be good enough to ensure that we don't have any tampering or illegal opening. You know, just in case anyone decides they want to steal the odd brick of cash.'

'Great, thank you. When we go to the bank in Athens, I will take one of those, Raj another, and Mike, you take two. So, finishing off now. Is there anything else on the project stores that we should make sure we take with us, anything for contingency planning?'

Raj again, 'Yes, I think we should take a quality digital camera with a good zoom as a contingency, just in case the onboard digital PTZ camera doesn't work for whatever reason. On the first fly past, you can use the onboard system and then I can use the manual. It might save us embarrassing ourselves.'

Mike agreed and so did Tom, who then said. 'Ok, anything else?' He paused a moment, allowing the team time to reflect, before continuing. 'Ok, Raj, Mike, Charly can you do your final checks and load up the aircraft this afternoon with everything we need?' They nodded. 'Let me know if there are any dramas. Otherwise as planned, Charly and JP will fly the Citation to Wilson airport tomorrow morning first thing. Mike, Raj and I will board there at 07.45 after we have cleared immigration and then we will be on our merry way to Athens.'

Chapter 56.
November 15th, Nairobi Kenya

The Citation was parked inside a hangar at Orly Airport with the hanger doors closed. By agreement with the owner, the vast and cavernous space was empty except for the single sleek white jet plane. There was no need for other casual airfield users to see what Raj and Mike were loading onto the aircraft. Charly had opened it up when they arrived and on ground power dropped the external drop hole door so that Raj and Mike could run their final checks. They had already checked everything once, and checked it again, but professional operators kept checking until all the contingencies had been thought through and tested. Charly had left them to it and gone off to do her final flight plan filing, leaving Mike and Raj with a trolley filled with kit and equipment.

The Citation model X, being a small corporate jet, was normally configured for 8 passengers. Charly had had the ground crew take out the rear four seats, to provide more working room in the rear of the aircraft. It would also provide a flat space for a couple of the team to be able to lie down and get some sleep if they wished. There were four executive seats left in the aircraft near the front, two on each side of the aisle and they faced each other. This was an executive jet, and the interior was cream leather and pale suede. The chairs were cream too and the rest of the internal trim was a luxurious rose wood panelling, similar to the type of trim in a top end automobile. The Citation X wasn't a large aircraft though and Mike certainly couldn't stand up to his full height in it. The aisle was fairly narrow too so as Raj and Mike were moving the stores down to the rear end, they had to shuffle awkwardly sideways. They felt a little odd lifting and partially rolling back the plush thick carpet in the rear to expose the fitted cargo D rings rivetted to the floor. They first laid out a cargo net on the deck, using the D rings and carabiners to secure one side of the net. Then they had brought in the four empty cash tubes for the drop and laid them on top of the cargo net: the intent, to close the net like an envelope around the tubes to secure them during the transit flights.

Raj had placed the four aluminium Samsonites that they would need to collect the money from the bank in the cargo hold as well as a couple of Pelicases with the jump stores and parachutes. None of that was needed on the outbound leg and they would bring it inside on the return leg once they had collected the quantum.

Mike had removed the internal floor panel above the drop hole again and he and Raj were just testing the drop procedure. Mike was on his knees facing the rear bulkhead behind which was the aircraft toilet. Between him and the wall the 24-inch-wide drop hole was just in front of his knees. Raj was sitting just behind Mike and they were talking through the best way for Raj to be able to pass Mike each load so that he could quickly drop them when needed. The faster they did this the closer the loads would be to each other as they fell into the water. At a hundred knots it was equivalent to 50 meters in transit per second, so a couple of seconds meant a hundred meters gap if they dropped two loads.

Mike was holding one of the three-foot-long tubes upright in front of him. The base was resting on the deck of the aircraft, just next to the drop hole and Mike was holding the upper part of the tube with his arms stretched out in front. Raj was next to him leaning forward and looking down the hole. Neither of them heard Charly enter the aircraft behind them near the cockpit.

From her perspective, it just looked phallic. 'Wow, Mike, I never knew that it was so big.'

Raj laughed and immediately grasped the type of view that Charly had. His laugh was slightly stifled though as his regular drinking wingman replied impressively. 'Well Charly, I give it a lot of exercise.' Mike was still holding the offending tube proudly out in front and had casually turned around to look Charly in the eye.

'Really, and is yours red and black striped like that one?' Charly had locked eyes with Mike and raised one eyebrow slightly coquettishly as she said it. Raj was beginning to feel like the aircraft cabin was just too small for the three of them. His jaw dropped open slightly as he waited for Mike's retort.

Mike calm and in full flirtatious mode replied with, 'Charly, mine is all prime black man, and do you know what they say?'

Raj groaned inwardly; he knew what was coming next as Charly asked the inevitable question. 'No, what do they say?'

'Well, once you have had black, there is no going back!'

Raj was cringing inside. He had heard Mike say that awful line on countless nights out. At best, the lady in question just walked away. Every now and then though he would get a slap for his efforts. Whilst seeing him get what he deserved was often a laugh, never in a million years had he thought Mike would make such a clumsy pass at Charly at work. Raj was wondering how had he missed all the signals?

Charly wasn't even remotely flustered by the exchange. Almost ignoring the fact that Raj was in the room, she turned back towards the cockpit saying clearly as she went, 'You know Mike I don't know much about what 'they' say, but one day I think I shall do my own research on that.'

There was silence for a few moments as both men digested the meaning of what she had said. Mike's dumb grin lost a little of its shine when Raj brought him back down to earth muttering. 'Dude? Seriously? Can we get on with our fucking jobs now?'

Chapter 57.
November 15th, The Indian Ocean

The Sea Dragon was well out into international waters heading North East. Yesterday and today had been spent supervising the crew doing some limited hardening of the vessel. Given the extremely low freeboard at the stern, which was only marginally above sea level, the team had agreed that efforts on hardening would be better spent on ensuring that the superstructure was a defendable fortress. Some of the stores that had been brought on board earlier in the week were now unpacked. Each of the team members had a set of Kevlar body armour, a Kevlar helmet, and a set of chest webbing with pouches for ammunition, water and some first aid trauma packs for gunshot wounds.

Ships stores that had now been installed included some coils of razor wire, to make any attempt to climb the external stairways and gain access to the bridge difficult. It would likely be impossible for a pirate to gain entrance to the crew quarters, or the Bridge given the exposure to the armed defenders who would be on the bridge wings firing down at them. Internally, it was agreed that any of the superstructure doors to the deck areas would all be welded shut except for one. That one had a clever secondary locking device to ensure that the door could not be opened from the outside but could be opened up from within to get access to the rear deck for work purposes.

On the bridge wings, ballistic blankets had been secured all the way around the rail and then held in place by thick gauge wire and well packed sandbags. In a small pouch on each bridge wing and to keep them safe from the elements, were a set of good quality mariner binoculars and a fairly primitive set of 1st generation night vision optics. Secured with rubber bungees and in separate, bright yellow, plastic storage jars, with bright red twist seal lids, there were 6 large maritime distress flares. These flares were multipurpose. Firstly, to provide enough light to engage targets at night and secondly, they could be used as a deterrent option if they needed to be fired in a direct fire role at any transgressors.

As of tomorrow, as the ship crossed into Somali waters, the team would work in two shifts of twelve hours. Two men on duty on each shift. Chris was teamed with Miguel and Omondi was with Bob. Captain Jammo had unpacked his weapons and they were now kept on a rack on the bridge, with the ammunition separated and stored in the Captain's safe. Chris had agreed with the Captain that there would always be a Captain's approval, as Master of the vessel, prior to the ammunition being handed out.

The duty security team would ensure that there was always one of them on the Bridge as an extra set of eyes. Ideally both would be on the Bridge at all times, but there was always a need to eat or take a piss and so there would be times when only one would be on lookout. This was supplementary to the vessel's regular Bridge team anyway and was sufficient for now. In the final 24 hours prior to the Hibernia III's release no one was going to get much sleep.

After the physical security measures had been put in place, Chris had gathered everyone together to discuss in detail the drills and operating procedures that they would follow in the event of a problem. Chris, Miguel, Bob and Omondi were all sitting on white plastic chairs out on the port bridge wing, enjoying the sun and calm wind.

Chris said 'I like how you have reinforced the bridge wings. That combination of steel plate, ballistic blankets and sandbags will certainly stop any 7.62, and we don't expect the pirates to have anything heavier than that. Certainly no 50 Cal or RPG's.'

Omondi in his languid, Swahili accent flavoured English agreed. 'Yes, anything with a higher calibre is most likely to be mounted on the top of a pickup truck or what's called a "technical" in Somalia. They could have RPG's I suppose but, in my experience, so few men have fired them that they are never going to hit a target unless they are right in close. In my opinion if they are that close, we will have engaged them long before then.'

Bob added with his southwest English accent, 'I would expect them to have to come in to within a hundred meters or so to have a chance of hitting the ship. They are in little speed boats that bob up and down like crazy in the swell. We are on a much more stable platform with rifles that can reach out and touch them accurately at 300 meters plus. They also won't have any armour to hide behind and will feel very exposed. If we haven't been able to persuade them to change course by the time that they get to within their effective RPG range, then we will really have screwed up. Critical for us is to keep our eyes open and be proactive.'

Chris agreed. 'Yes, that's a good point. The Sea Dragon has radar, but it's old. It might pick up skiffs on a flat calm day, but there is a risk that it might not, until they are close in. So, our constant vigilance is going to be important in order to make sure the ship is locked down and to ensure a reception party. That's going to be one of the key points I want to get across to the Sea Dragon's crew when we brief them later. Also, we need to make sure that they keep the discipline that we have discussed when they are working outside the superstructure. If we get attacked, and if everyone is inside, then we will be fine and can defend ourselves easily. If we are asleep and get boarded whilst one of our crew is out on deck and they are captured, then we will have some much harder decisions to make. I would much rather that we never had to go there.'

Chapter 58.
November 16th, Nairobi Kenya

Tom, Mike, and Raj were all sitting in a sweaty departure lounge in Wilson airport in Nairobi. Wilson had a reputation as having the highest number of daily movements of aircraft of any airport in Africa. Situated on the southern side of Nairobi, adjacent to the national park sat this disorganised but surprisingly well functioning airfield, where every day many hundreds of tourists would fly in and out. Fleets of Cessna Caravans took these tourists to the Masai Mara or elsewhere for the safari adventure of a lifetime, or the local equivalent of easyJet took business passengers to any one of a multitude of regional airports. Perhaps most oddly, the largest khat traders in Kenya had a huge warehouse in Wilson that every morning would send khat to Mogadishu and onwards into remote parts of Somalia. The team didn't know it, but a fraction of the khat that left Wilson every morning ended up being chewed and spat out on to the deck of the Hibernia III.

The team had already gone through passport control and were now sitting on sweaty plastic chairs, in a room that had no air conditioning. It was fine for now though; the heat of the day hadn't yet started reflecting off the black aircraft dispersal.

As they watched, JP wearing a pilot's uniform and a high vis vest entered the main hall through a glass door that went airside. He spoke to the security guard at the door and showed her the three tickets in his hand. JP waved the men over and they picked up their hand luggage. A brief show of their passports again and they walked out onto the tarmac following JP. There were probably 30 or so small aircraft parked outside being tended by a swarm of aircrew and ground crew getting ready for the morning runs to the Mara and beyond. The Citation, being larger than many of the other aircraft on the dispersal was parked about a hundred meters away. JP led them across the dispersal, following a yellow guideline marked on the concrete but ultimately having to thread their way through the last couple of parked Cessna Caravans, to get to their Citation. The men could see that its door, just behind the cockpit, was open. The stairs mechanism was hanging down, secured at the base, and then attached to the fuselage by two thick cords which also doubled as handrails.

As they approached, Tom, Mike and Raj waved to Charly whom they could see in her 'office' through the cockpit window. They climbed the aircraft steps ducking their heads as they entered.

'Make yourselves at home guys, I will see you in a mo. for a safety brief.' JP said as he left them to it and started to do a final external check. The men chose their seats, putting their hand luggage in the rear area, next to a couple of large blue and white cool boxes that had been loaded that morning.

Mike lifted the lid on them both and told the others what he saw. 'Awesome, we have one box full of cold drinks, sodas and water. The other is packed full of food. Sushi, sandwiches, coronation chicken and a number of salads by the look of it. We are not going to go hungry today!'

Tom looked over and grinned, 'Well you know, keep the troops happy by feeding them well!'

JP came back in at that point carrying a pair of bright red but well used tyre chocks which he stowed in a small locker just behind the cockpit. He turned around, raised the stairs, and closed the door. 'Right, safety brief. Usual drills, oxygen from here, seatbelts etc. There is only one exit from the aircraft and that is the door you just came in by. If you see me leaving, follow me as quickly as you can, trying not to let your apple watch get excited. The loo is at the back of the cabin there past all the drop stores. Does anyone get airsick at all? No? Ok then any questions?'

With a consensus of no, JP went forward to the cockpit and climbed into the front seat as Charly spoke on the radio getting permission to start.

Raj was already pulling his noise cancelling headphones out and his iPad. He intended to watch movies most of the way to Greece. Mike was an avid audio book listener and started listening to General Stanley McCrystal's latest audio book on organisational leadership. Tom's travel routine was work. He dug out his laptop and pulled out a table that was recessed into the wall. He also put some noise cancelling headphones on and caught up on paperwork. The bliss of these long trips was no Wi-Fi so no incoming emails could interrupt his flow. That said, he connected to blue tooth on his phone and made sure his inbox was up to date before they got out of 4G range. As the aircraft spooled up, the synchronisation completed, and he switched off his mobile device. He made sure his lap strap was done up, stretched out his arms and cracked his interlocked fingers. He took a deep breath and looked down at his screen. He was going to have a go at some of those longer documents that had been filling up his in-tray for a while. He barely noticed as the aircraft took off, banked left, and started climbing to the North.

Chapter 59.
November 16th, Overhead Khartoum, Sudan

JP was flying. Or perhaps the aircraft was flying itself on full autopilot and JP was the handling pilot. Charly had taken a short break for some lunch. She had joined the men and had sat down in the fourth seat which was available. The team were discussing the quantum and how on earth the insurers, who ultimately had to agree to pay-out, for any ransom, did the maths on what was a reasonable sum.

Tom who had dealt with a couple of ransom cases before, but not for shipping incidents, was hypothesising. 'Let's keep the numbers easy. Let's say the ship is worth 10 million dollars, and it is carrying five million dollars of cargo. The cost per day of running it is 10,000 dollars. The insurers need to work out a way to get to a reasonable settlement figure for them, whilst appeasing the owners, the families, and paying the kidnappers and whilst making sure that they don't cause inflation for future problems. If they try to settle too fast, the baddies will demand more, thinking that the insurer wants to pay to get it done promptly. If they settle too high, then next time the baddies again want more. But, if they offer too low a price, then the baddies won't accept, and the insurers lose another 10,000 dollars per day in running costs or lost revenue. They likely start to have to pay more in a final settlement to the owner for lost revenue and also in compensation for the crew if and when they eventually do get released. On top of that there are the reputation risks for the shipping company.'

Raj who was eating Sushi and easily keeping up with the conversation said. 'Yes, but now consider this. What if your cargo is oranges? '

Mike said 'What?'

'Oranges, what if your cargo is oranges? 4 million dollars' worth of oranges.'

Mike still wasn't there. 'No, you've lost me.'

Charly had got it though. 'Ahh yes. What if your cargo is going to rot?'

Raj added some pickled ginger and wasabi to his meal and continued, 'Exactly, your pressure to recover your oranges, within a couple of months, so that you can still sell them for a reasonable price, is going to force you to offer a higher price faster. If you don't get your oranges back, then you lose 5 million dollars on top of the lost running cost payments and crew compensation.'

Mike had it now. 'But it's a catch 22. You settle too high, and next time the baddies will want the same amount of money, even if this time its TV's or trainers.'

Tom took a drink of his Coke Zero and said 'Yes, and then you need to look at the value of the hostages. In some countries, like Nigeria, a person can be kidnapped and then a week later they are back at home with the family having put together a 3,000-dollar ransom.'

Charly piped up. 'That's not very much?'

Tom continued. 'In Nigeria for a local national that's a lot of money, it will hurt. For an expat, start adding a zero or three. But things go completely out of whack when families try to do it without any professional insurance company support. Sometimes governments can really screw it up. Take the French government. They regularly place massive public value on any French national who gets kidnapped. Multimillion-dollar ransoms get paid by the government, quickly because of media pressure and lobby groups, and then you see the president on the runway kissing them as they return!'

Raj wiped his mouth with a paper napkin. 'And that then screws up the market for the rest of the normal population, or the insurance company next time around. It also means kidnappers will target French nationals more often, knowing they will get huge payments. So, what is the value for the 24 hostages on board the Hibernia III?'

Tom replied. 'It's a good question, and a real moral problem. I think it's obscured by the massive value of the ship and its fuel cargo. I think in this case the value of each of the humans is relatively small. Certainly, the value of life in Somalia in terms of financial value is lower I suspect than it probably is in Europe.'

Mike spoke again. 'Well let's just hope that when we deliver this ransom the hostages are all still alive.'

Chapter 60.
November 16th, Athens Greece

The benefit of flying a private jet, however cramped it was inside, was that at a good international airport you could get the VIP treatment. A car had collected the team from the steps of the aircraft once it had arrived in Athens and taken them to the VIP terminal. Passport control had been ok, but the customs officer had looked at them strangely when they scanned 4 empty Samsonite suitcases on arrival. Raj had quipped that they were here for a bit of shopping and the customs officer, used to eccentric and wealthy foreigners, had waved them through.

The team were now at the Marriot hotel sitting in the bar having a stiff gin and tonic to help lift them from their post flight blues. Finlay and Chloe, dressed casually, walked in together and stood at the entrance scanning for the team. It wasn't hard to find them. Mike was the only huge well-muscled black guy in the bar, and Raj and Tom looked like security consultants wearing light cotton jackets and open necked shirts. They were all alert enough to nod to Finlay once it was obvious that that was who they were meeting.

'Hi, you must be Tom?' Finlay stuck out his hand and shook Tom warmly by his.

'Yes. Finlay, Chloe? Let me introduce you to Mike and Raj. Charly and JP aren't here yet though; they are taking some rest after that flight.

'Great to meet you.' said Chloe. 'I hope the flight was ok?'

Raj replied. 'Not too bad thanks. It is odd though, despite travelling on a multimillion-dollar jet, with as much leg room as we wanted, flying is still just tedious and tiring.'

Mike looked at Raj and said 'You are right there buddy; I was thinking that it might be better than normal but...' He tailed off as he saw Charly enter the bar. She looked gorgeous with her long blond hair clean, loose and blow dried. She was wearing a black pair of jeans tight around her petite figure and a blue and white checked top which was a cross between a bodice and waistcoat. It wasn't slutty, but it did show off a little of her well-toned stomach and long slender arms. Her green eyes lit up as she saw Mike and she grinned as she walked towards the group.

Raj, a little like a prep schoolboy spoke quietly out of the corner of his mouth at Mike. 'Dude you are drooling!'

Only Tom overheard him, and he looked quizzically for a moment at them both before rolling his eyes and stepping forward to introduce Charly to Finlay and Chloe.

Finlay, always a sucker for a beautiful woman was gushing. 'Charly, it's a pleasure to meet you. Chloe's vetting report says you are a world class stunt pilot!'

Caught a little off-guard Charly replied, 'Hi, um, yes, I used to fly for the Red-Bull team. What vetting report?'

'How exciting, oh but don't worry about that, perfectly normal don't you know. We made sure to do a little research on all of you. After all we aren't going to sign over a vast amount of cash to complete strangers, especially ones with such interesting pasts hey? Ha!' He tailed off with a slightly forced laugh to try to break the ice before continuing, 'Now, who wants what to drink?'

A vodka martini for Charly, she wasn't flying tomorrow, a white wine spritzer for Chloe and a beer for Finlay were promptly ordered. As they waited, the team went and sat down at a booth in the corner of the large, marbled bar area, there they could talk more freely.

Over the next hour or so, whilst they were all fresh, they confirmed the details for tomorrow's bank run. Then they relaxed a little and moved onto listening to Finlay telling his war stories about a number of different kidnap situations that he had had to mediate on. He was always discrete about who and when, but some of the more high-profile ones had made international news for weeks and so it was fairly easy to guess who the victims were. Tom thought Finlay was a little loud at times and hoped that he would be able to keep his mouth quiet for long enough during this project, so that operational security was maintained, and his team were not at risk. After all, north of six million dollars in cash was a tempting target.

Chapter 61.
November 17th, Athens, Greece

Epsilon Zeta Bank only dealt with high-net-worth individuals. It was situated between the Bank of Greece and the Hellenic parliament building in the centre of Athens though it was set back a little from the main road and pavement. The architect had obviously been allowed a large budget to ensure that the bank's headquarters building was opulent, and it tastefully alluded to the Greek culture of the Parthenon only 300 meters away. Its grand fluted columns, marble steps and colourful mosaics in the grand entrance hall were designed to impress even the wealthiest of clientele.

Tom, Mike, and Raj had arrived in a black chauffer driven Toyota Landcruiser that had collected them from the hotel. They had entered the bank through the large double doors towing their aluminium Samsonite cases behind them. Tom pulled one, Mike two and Raj the other one. As they entered, they were politely guided towards a luggage scanner and a uniformed guard helped them load them into the machine. He had lifted the first case expecting it to be full and was surprised when he almost lost his balance because it was empty.

After the scan they were guided to a soft seating area with a plush square of bright blue thick shag carpet. Tom sat on a cream chaise-long with golden threading. Mike looked at the other one and decided that a delicate Louis 14th antique didn't need his weight testing its age. He sat on a slightly more robust, French style armchair with gilded leaf patterns and tried not to break it. Raj took a seat on a pale cream and gold Ottoman. They sat there with their Samsonites standing next to them feeling not in the least bit at home amongst the marble splendour and brightly lit glass chandeliers. A smartly dressed bank assistant came over and offered them tea or coffee, which they ordered. As they waited Mike said. 'Hey Raj, you do know that you are sitting on a footstool?'

'What?'

'A footstool, or should I say, you are sitting on a poof!' Mike was enjoying himself now.

'Piss off!'

'Do you normally sit on poofs?'

Raj getting louder, 'I said, Fu…'

'Ah excellent, coffee!' Tom interjected in his clipped British accent as the assistant brought them their hot drinks. Tom was used to Mike and Raj being a little childish at times. They always cut it out when it was time to work though.

Five minutes later Chloe walked in accompanied by a man whom they hadn't met before. The man was obviously Greek and by his jowly face and expanded waist he looked like he enjoyed dining out. He was wearing golfing trousers, a sports jacket, an open necked pale pink shirt with a large medallion visible against his neckline. He beamed at them as he approached. Chloe introduced him as Mr Papadopoulos, the owner of the Hibernia III. The team had been expecting a signatory, perhaps a finance manager to accompany them today, and not the boss, but Tom recovered quickly by introducing the team to the shipping magnate. They made small talk standing in the foyer of the bank until 10.00 when a tall thin man in his late 50's and with obviously dyed dark hair but a greying moustache walked up to them. He was wearing a bespoke grey suit and spoke directly to Mr Papadopoulos as he arrived, shaking his hand. 'Mr Papadopoulos, good morning and welcome.' He wasn't obsequious or fawning, he treated him as an equal and Tom thought he must be the bank manager.

'Good morning Mr Nikolaou. You are well?' replied Mr Papadopoulos.

'Yes, thank you. I must say I was very intrigued to receive your request, but we have it all prepared in one of our side vaults. Shall we all go and discuss the matter downstairs?'

'Yes please.'

'And I assume that this is the team you told me about. Would you like them to come as well?'

'Yes, they will be assuming accountability for it once I have signed.'

'Very well, we had better take the stairs if that is alright, we won't all fit in the elevator. If you want to leave your cases there, someone will bring them down shortly.' With that Mr Nikolaou led them down a short corridor off the banking hall. He pushed a buzzer on the wall next to a reinforced door and looked up at the security camera. The door buzzed and he pulled it open holding it for all of his guests. 'Please continue down the stairs and wait at the bottom.' Everyone trooped down the stairway. Raj marvelled that this was also marble. It was pale grey with black flecks, and it complemented the old-fashioned bronze banister and rail. The stairs were purely functional though and after doubling back on themselves they arrived at the bottom. As Mr Nikolaou joined them, the door buzzed and Tom who happened to be in front did the honours this time holding the door for everyone to pass through. 'Turn left please,' instructed the bank manager. 'And now I must overtake you please.' He passed everyone and paused at a door on the right. He placed his palm on a pale green lit biometric sensor and the door opened automatically under pneumatic pressure. Whilst it had a wooden veneer on both sides, it was obvious that this door was strongly reinforced.

The windowless room had a large square table in the middle of it, and there were a number of chairs that had been pulled back and placed against the walls. On the table, 2 large cash counting machines were powered up. On a side table at the far end were two fine bone-china tea and coffee pots and a number of cups. As Mr Nikolaou walked to a phone mounted on the wall, he asked everyone to get comfortable and to help themselves to refreshments while they waited. Into the phone he said. 'We are ready in room 4.'

About 3 minutes later, whilst the team were still getting coffee, two banking staff entered the room bringing the 4 Samsonites with them. As those two staff left, another pair of banking staff wheeled in a large trolley. It looked a little like the type of sealed trolleys that go into airplanes. One of the staff handed a clipboard with paperwork to the bank manager. He looked at it, and then he examined the plastic numerical seals there were evident on the side of the trolley. He checked a serial number and then put the paper down on the table. He pulled a black and gold Montblanc fountain pen out of his breast pocket and signed one of the pieces of paper with a flourish. Mr Nikolaou nodded to the two staff members, saying 'You may proceed.'

A pair of what looked like nail scissors were produced by one of them and the plastic seal was cut. Through an ingenious process, the interlocking sides of the trolley were folded away leaving what now looked more similar to an open stainless-steel catering trolley. Sitting on the shelves, in cling film wrapped bundles was a huge amount of cash in newly printed one hundred-dollar bills. There were six individually wrapped packages of one million dollars, and a seventh package that was about half the size. The banking staff lifted the packages off the trolley and placed them on the table. The smell of newly printed money filled the air. The team, who all had a hot drink in their hand now, had naturally gravitated towards the action and were standing silently in a half circle watching the bank staff do their job.

Mr Nikolaou addressed Mr Papadopoulos in formal tones. 'Sir, as per your written request we have here the sum of 6,534,000 US dollars which you would like to withdraw from your account. I suggest that we now proceed to count the funds using the cash counters here. Is that OK with you?'

Mr Papadopoulos looked at the huge pile of cash and replied. 'I was wondering if instead you and I might discuss another matter, and I ask the team here to do the confirmatory check with your staff? I will ask Chloe here to verify for me.'

'Of course, no problem at all. Alexis, Georgy, please conduct a full count under the watchful eye of this young lady. Please bring the paperwork for our signatures when you are finished. Mr Papadopoulos, shall we retire to my office?' and with that they both left the room.

Chapter 62.
November 18th, Hobyo, Somalia

At the same time that Tom and team were in the bank, Abdi was onboard the Hibernia III having a different type of meeting. He had thought long and hard about this one and had consulted with Zahi about who should attend. In the end, Abdi had invited Yuusuf, the salty old man who was Zahi's helmsman and Tadalesh, the brave young man who had been with them when they captured the Hibernia III. The fifth person in attendance was Axmed, one of the original skiff Captains who whilst unsuccessful in the first trip out, had at least brought his skiff and his crew back alive. Axmed was thin, sinewy and with awful teeth, decaying and browned. He was quiet, but a deep thinker and as far as Abdi was concerned, totally trustworthy. That was important for what he was about to be asked to do.

The meeting was being held up at the bow of the Hibernia III, away from prying ears. So far Abdi had only told Zahi about the pending payment of a ransom. Whilst all the phones had now been taken from the rest of the pirates, there was still a nagging worry in Abdi's mind that somehow the secret might get out. The small group of men were all squatting under the shade of a vast anchor chain drum mechanism. Standing proud above them was a tall white thin tower which carried the forward navigation light. The hulking white superstructure of the accommodation was about 250 meters away at the stern of the ship.

After the culturally demanded greetings, Abdi opened the meeting by welcoming his trusted team. 'I know I have not told you the purpose of this meeting, and I appreciate that you are here and willing to listen. Before I tell you the purpose, I need you to trust me.'
Intrigued the men agreed and Abdi continued. 'I am going to ask you to stay on board tonight, and I am going to ask you to give me your mobile phones without question. Do you all agree?'

Yuusuf and Tadalesh had already surrendered theirs when Zahi had asked for it a couple of days ago, Zahi caught a little by surprise paused for a moment before saying, 'I have trusted you so far and look at the prize we are sitting on. I am happy to trust you until this is done.' He rummaged in his pocket for his phone and handed it to Abdi.

Axmed the only one with a phone left on the whole ship, other than Abdi asked, 'And when will I get it back?'

'If Allah is with us, then tomorrow afternoon.'

Intrigued, Axmed handed over his old Nokia whilst saying, 'I am in, what do you need of me?'

Abdi looked up to the clear blue sky briefly and shifted his feet slightly gathering his thoughts.

'Tomorrow my friends we get paid.'

Cries of delight, pats on the back, and big grins followed. Abdi let the men enjoy the moment before settling them down again. 'Believe it or not, tomorrow with Allah's blessing upon us, millions of dollars will fall from the sky.'

More whoops and cries followed and Tadalesh even jumped up and did a little dance.

Yuusuf, the old hand, not prone to such exuberance asked, 'And what do you need us for?'

'Come with me and I will show you.' Abdi stood up and went to the seaward side of the ship with the others following him. Standing there at the bow they had the expanse of the blue Indian ocean before them. The swell was low, and the sea sparkled. 'The four of you will captain four fishing boats that I have ordered to be here tomorrow morning with their helmsmen and you are going to be out there.' He pointed. 'Axmed and Tadalesh, your two boats will be up at this end, about five hundred meters apart, but in line with the bow. Yuusuf, you and Zahi in your own two boats will be at the stern, again 500 meters apart.'

Axmed asked, 'And then what?'

'Then, an airplane is going to come. It is going to fly over the top of the ship a couple of times, and then it is going to drop four separate loads by parachute. Each load will contain money. It will land in the water near the middle of the ship. It is the job of Zahi and Yuusuf to collect the first two loads. Tadalesh, you and Axmed will stay up here at the bow in case anything goes wrong and the airplane drops the loads too far ahead.'

Zahi said 'Wow, so we have to catch the parachutes?'

'No! And this is important. I am told that the packages will be well wrapped and must land in the sea, or they might sink a skiff. They are supposed to float. Once they have landed, you collect them. When you have all four you come back to the ship here and we will bring all the money to the Bridge. From there we will count it and distribute it.'

'Are we sure they will float?' asked Axmed, sucking at a bad tooth.

'Well, if they don't it will be an expensive mistake.' replied Abdi. 'Now, who has any questions?' There were lots.

Chapter 63.
November 17th, Athens, Greece

Back in the bank, Alexis, and Georgy, used the little nail scissor type devices to carefully cut the cling film from around the first million-dollar bundle of cash. As that skin came away, Chloe and the team could see that inside the bundle were ten separately wrapped 'bricks'. Each one contained one hundred thousand dollars. Each brick was further made up of 10 smaller bundles each marked with a value of ten thousand US dollars together with the bank's logo printed clearly. Alexis and Georgy started to work very efficiently as a team, with one stripping the bundles down and then loading a one hundred-thousand-dollar brick into a cash counter. The counter would then start whirring, splitting the brick into bundles of 10,000 dollars which either Alexis or Georgy would collect from the dispenser at the bottom before wrapping a new paper ribbon of paper around them.

They had only just started when Tom interrupted them. 'Alexis, Georgy, could you pause for a moment please?'

Alexis replied, 'Sure, how can we help?'

Tom said, 'Two things. One, I see that those machines are quite advanced. Are they able to record the serial numbers of the notes as they count them?'

'Yes, we do that as a process whenever we issue larger sums. We can email you an Excel file of the serial number of every single note if you wish?'

'Yes please, that would be great. Secondly, I don't think we should use your branded paper bands to seal the cash in its bundles. This money is going to be delivered to some people with whom you may not wish your bank brand to be associated. On top of that, we don't want them to look up your bank on the web and see that you look after extremely wealthy people, if you see what I mean?'

Alexis thought for a moment. 'How about we use rubber bands instead to keep the 10,000-dollar bundles separate, and then we wrap the 100K bricks in plain bankers' film again?'

Tom looked at Mike and Raj who both nodded at him. 'That would work for us. We can leave them in 100K bricks, no need to bundle them into the millions. Thank you for being flexible.'

Georgy stood up and said, 'No problem, I shall just go and get some packing materials and I will be straight back.'

Whilst he was away, Alexis went back to the very first bundle and started again after pressing a couple of buttons on the cash counter. He did a test run to make sure it was recording the serial numbers and then started to work his way through the mountain of cash on the table.

It took a while to process all that money. As the first bundles came through, they were placed on the far end of the table, where Raj who had opened up the first of the Samsonites started to stack them. The initial buzz that he felt as he picked up the first bundles, smelt the smell of newly printed bank notes, realising what it was worth, was intoxicating. However, after half an hour or so the job became surprisingly monotonous. It wasn't his and so it was just like monopoly money. Eventually they were down to the last half million. All four cases were now open on the table, three were already stacked with one point six million in each of them. The rest was all going into the last case.

The phone rang in the room and Alexis paused what he was doing to answer it. 'Yes?' he listened. 'Ok, please bring them in fifteen minutes.' He put the receiver down and spoke to the group. 'The cash in transit team are here. They will come in shortly, but we have plenty of time.'

The plan was that the cash in transit team would take the risk of transporting the money to the airport. They would secure it in their vault overnight and then arrive at the airport shortly before take-off. There was no point in the team driving around the city with a large amount of cash. Better to let someone else take that risk.

Eventually with the cash counted and stacked in the Samsonites, Alexis concurred with Chloe that the sum was correct. They walked down the corridor to the bank managers' office to get the final signatures completed leaving Georgy in the room with the team. It only took a moment, and then they were back. Charly now produced her own paperwork which she handed to Tom to sign. They had discussed it the previous night and it was a quite simple statement. It said that Tom had taken custody of the sum and that it was being transported by Tom to be used to pay a ransom for the release of hostages for humanitarian purposes. Tom took a cheap plastic pen out of his pocket and signed for the money. 'Wow, so there we go. I am now responsible for more money than I will ever earn in my lifetime.'

Shortly after, the 4-man team from the cash in transit company were shown in through the door. They also had their own serial numbered seals. After discussion with Raj, they closed the cases, and used their plastic seals to tie through the reinforced loopholes that Raj had added to the cases in Nairobi. For good measure, they then enveloped each of the suitcases in an additional extra-large sealable bank bag and used another of their seals to close those too. All the way through Mike and Raj monitored what they were doing. They tore parts of the tags off which had a duplicate of the individual seal number; these were handed to Tom. They recorded the numbers on the triplicate form that they presented to him to sign. Barely fifteen minutes after signing for responsibility for the money, he had handed it over to someone else, albeit temporarily. 'Well, easy come easy go!' Tom said as the guards started to cart the money away, leaving him with the top copy of the paper form. The cash in transit team left through an underground tunnel to a special part of the bank where cash in transit vehicles could park underground and do their business safely out of the public eye.

The whole process had taken all morning, and it was now pushing towards 14.00. After thanking the banking staff, they went out onto the street to find somewhere simple to have some lunch. As they stepped out, an icy gust of wind caught them. They looked up, and they were surprised to see ominous dark grey clouds. Tom called Charly. 'It's Tom, what's that weather looking like for departure tomorrow morning?'

'Well to be honest, this morning the forecast has deteriorated massively. I am at the airport now talking to the weather forecasting team. They tell me one of the largest November snowstorms in recent history is brewing and it's affecting much of our flight path. We should be okay, but it might be a little rough.'

Tom replied. 'Ok, I had better let Max and Finlay know.'

Chapter 64.

November 17th, Athens, Greece

It was early evening and Tom was back in his room at the Marriot hotel. He had a quick phone call to make before he could unwind for the night.

'Max, its Tom.'

'Hi Max, how did this morning go?'

'Well, we are all sorted on the quantum side. That all went smoothly. You should have seen that bank; the level of service was impeccable. We were waited on hand and foot! We had a bit of a win in that the banks cash counters could digitally read the serial numbers on the notes. The cashier is going to send us an Excel file with a complete list of all of them. It saves us doing a 10 percent record manually, so my team is happy with that.'

'Excellent.'

'Also, on the positive side, the quantum has been collected by the cash in transit company and Chloe took me through the paperwork for the EU cash export declarations this afternoon. I have signed that already and will carry a copy with me. She will get a copy notarised and submitted to the right authorities today.'

'Good.'

'On the bad news side, the weather has taken a turn for the worse. There is a hell of a snowstorm coming and it will be touch and go as to whether or not we can get away tomorrow.'

'Ah, that's not what we were expecting. What does Finlay say?'

'I am going to meet him for a drink this evening and we will discuss it, I will let you know how that goes.'

'Ok, just send me an email. I am getting onto the overnight flight tonight from Nairobi to Athens, so that I can be with the shipping team on the morning of the drop. Depending on what time you finish I may already be airborne.'

'No problem. If it's going to be tricky then I will work up a plan B. The fly in the ointment is that the cash in transit team don't work on weekends. If we can't get the cash out tomorrow, then we end up delaying the delivery by four days. Ultimately, if we can get out then we will, but if we can't, then Finlay will have to manage it with the opposition.'

'Ok, it's not ideal, but there isn't anything we can do about it now. Let me know what you decide.'

'Will do, safe flight.' And with that Tom hung up and went to take a hot bath to wind down and consider the options.

Chapter 65.
November 18th, Hobyo, Somalia

On the Hibernia III, Abdi had gathered all of the ship's crew together in the canteen. The TV had been turned off and the crew were all sitting on the comfy chairs, or on the floor in front of them, in a semi-circle. Abdi was standing in front of them. Zahi and a couple of his armed guards were standing alertly in one corner behind him.

The crew looked emaciated, exhausted, and demoralised. A poor diet of rice and beans had taken its toll over the past months. All the fresh food had been finished many weeks ago. The crew had spent truly little time outside and were pasty and gaunt. Their clothes were now dirty and grey, matching the bags under their eyes. A lack of sleep, tense days and the constant threat of abuse, meant that mentally they were as low as a human could be.

It was 08.00 local time when Abdi addressed them. As he studied his captives, he saw a range of expressions. At one end of the spectrum there were blank glassy eyed stares from those who had long since given up. At the other end, interest and keen attention from the Captain. Abdi addressing them was a novelty that hadn't happened since the ship had first been taken.

Abdi kept a laconic easy attitude as he spoke, trying to display indifference that was completely at odds to the excitement he felt inside. 'Your problems are nearly over,' he stated. Captain Oleksiy's eyes narrowed as he listened very carefully. 'I have agreed with the owner of this ship that I will release you if he pays me a ransom.' Everyone in the room perked up intently now. Neighbours turned to each other to check that they had understood correctly. Abdi gave them a moment and then continued. 'The owner has agreed and tomorrow the money will be delivered to me here.'

Captain Oleksiy spoke up over the increase in murmuring. 'Excuse me, did you say tomorrow?'

Abdi looked at him with eyes devoid of any emotion. 'Tomorrow. If I get paid what has been agreed, then I will let you go and you can take your ship with you.' As though refusing more questions he continued quickly, 'In a moment we are going to practice something that you will need to do tomorrow morning. The airplane that is delivering the money requires you all to be on deck when it flies past, so that it can prove that you are alive.'

Suspicious, Captain Oleksiy asked, 'And what is this thing you need us to do?'

Still very much in command here Abdi said quietly but dangerously, 'You will do whatever I tell you to do. However, in this case it is simple. You will all stand on deck, one meter apart in a long line facing out to sea. The airplane will fly low and take pictures of you all. When they are satisfied that you are all alive, they will drop me my money, and after I have counted it, you will be released.'

Captain Oleksiy, still the proud Captain inside said, 'Ok, we can do that, but Szymon hasn't been able to stand for a couple of days now. His chest is in such pain he finds it difficult to breath, let alone move.'

Pretending not to be worried, but actually being concerned in case this screwed up his payment, Abdi replied, 'I will deal with that. For now, he can stay here. The rest of you, behave. Don't do anything stupid over the next 24 hours and then you will be free. Captain, does your crew understand?'

The Captain looked at his team. 'Men, do you all understand what Mr Abdi has just said?' He paused before continuing. 'Good, don't do anything stupid. Let's go and practice this thing that we need to do tomorrow morning. Don't mess it up, don't give the pirates any reason to beat you. After it is done then we all come back in here. We need to talk about how we get the ship underway again if things go well tomorrow.'

Abdi looked at them all, judging that it was unlikely that anyone would screw around. 'Right, everyone out on deck just in front of the superstructure in a long line. Zahi, they are all yours.'

With that, Zahi took them down two flights of stairs to the deck level. They all trooped out of the door and into the heat and morning sunshine. For the first time in months there was a bit of cheer in the atmosphere from both the guards and the hostages alike.

Chapter 66.
November 18th, Athens, Greece

Ten o'clock in the morning and Tom, Mike, Raj and Chloe were standing just inside the entrance of the VIP departures building. They were there eight hours earlier than planned because there was a slight possibility that they might be able to fly out this morning. Tonight, was an absolute no with massive snow forecast to fall. Charly and JP had already gone through to the flight planning cell and brought forward their flight plan. If they could just get out of Athens then they could wait in Djibouti on the ground a little longer, still hitting the intended drop deadline. The pressure was on because the secure cash in transit service didn't operate on weekends. Either they got the cash today, or they had to wait until Monday and blow the delivery deadline out of the water.

Tom was looking up at the sky glumly. It was already snowing, and Charly had just called him and told him that the window of opportunity for mid-day was looking awful on the weather radar. The team had decided that it was better to accept the cash from the transporters and wait in the aircraft for the opportunity to leave. After all, airside in an international airport was fairly secure anyway.

Raj didn't like the cold. He had on every item of clothing that he possessed and still shivered every now and then. Mike laughed, used to Virginia Beach winter weather and regular snow from his training days. He couldn't resist the opportunity to wind Raj up. 'Raj, hey buddy, do you want to borrow my jacket?'

'No.'

'Seriously, it's OK. I have never seen a Sikh turn blue before.'

'I said no.'

Mike continued his goading, 'I think you should eat more fat. Protein is fine, but what insulation and fuel reserves have you got? Shall we see if we can order you a Big Mac and fries?'

'I would rather pollute my body by drinking engine oil.' Raj couldn't help but let a slight chatter escape through his teeth.

Mike laughed again but his retort was cut off by seeing the cash in transit van arrive. 'Look alive guys. Inbound.'

Lights on, windscreen wipers thrashing snowflakes clear of the armoured glass, the bulky grey and green cash in transit vehicle pulled up outside the entrance to the VIP terminal in a sloppy swoosh of slush.

Tom went out to speak to the leader and showed him his passport and the triplicate copy from the previous day. The cash in transit team followed their procedures and brought the four Samsonites into the departure hall. Everyone moved off to a corner of the hall where Mike and Raj assumed overwatch whilst Tom checked the seals on the bags. When they were ticked off against his form, he nodded to one of the guards to remove the outer bag cover. Then Tom checked the seals on the cases themselves. Again, all good. He signed the form and accepted responsibility for the cash again. The seals on the suitcases though he left intact for now. Giving thanks to the guards, the team lifted the Samsonites onto two trolleys. Tom texted JP and told him that they were ready to embark.

Only moments later JP arrived from a side door marked 'Crew only'. He had the tickets in his hands and started to escort the team to the uniformed single person behind a desk with a sign saying passport control. The men said goodbye to Chloe thanking her for her support. It had been agreed though, that she would wait there until the team had passed through customs just in case there were any issues. Passport control took a little while, mostly because of the different nationalities between the three men. That done, pushing their trolleys, they walked through to the customs desk a mere 20 meters further on.

By coincidence, the same customs officer who had been on duty when they had arrived was on duty again now. He recognised Raj, and the suitcases. 'Good morning gentlemen. Do you have anything to declare?' he said with a strong Greek accent. Tom stepped to the front pulling out reams of paper. 'Actually sir, we do.' He handed over the customs declaration form for the export of cash.

All credit to the customs officer, he hardly raised an eyebrow. He did however flick into consummate professional mode. 'One-minute sir.' He picked up a phone from his desk and called somebody. There was a short conversation in Greek, during which the customs officer referred to the forms a couple of times. At the end of the call, he hung up and addressed Tom. 'Sir, please wait a moment, I have asked my supervisor to come down and speak to you.'

A slightly nervous five minutes later, during which time Tom could see Chloe raise a questioning eyebrow through passport control, another customs officer appeared. This woman was in her mid-fifties, obviously senior and had a lot of gold braid on the epaulets of her black custom's uniform jumper. She spoke immaculate English. 'Sir, good morning. Can I have all of your passports please?' Tom, Mike, and Raj all took their passports out again and handed them over. 'And the cash declaration form please.' Tom handed that over as well. 'Please make yourselves comfortable, I will be back in a moment.' with that she left again.

There wasn't anywhere to make themselves comfortable. The men just stood there fuming next to two trollies with more than six million dollars and their hand luggage. It didn't matter how much legal advice you had, standing there waiting for a customs officer to do their job always made you feel like you were guilty. It was akin to standing outside the headmaster's office after some minor school rule infraction. You always thought that the headmaster knew about the bigger rule that you had broken the week before and this time you were for the high jump. The customs officer was away for about ten minutes and when she came back, she wasn't smiling. 'Sir, it says on the form that you are exporting this cash to pay a ransom?'

'The purpose of the cash is for the humanitarian release of hostages.' said Tom carefully.

'Which hostages?'

'Madam, I am not at liberty to say.'

'That is not a satisfactory answer.'

'Madam, I have taken legal advice and my lawyer is standing just over there. I am not a legal professional, but if you have any questions, we can ask her to assist?'

The customs agent hadn't expected that, and she knew that she had no powers to get more details as to the purpose. She did though have powers to hold the money pending further enquiry if she wished. She opted for the next best thing. 'I will go and speak to my superior' and again, she left.

This time they were left for nearly 45 minutes. During that period, a number of other VIP's were processed through passport control and customs. They looked suspiciously at the group of men with large aluminium cases with obvious cash in transit tags on them. By the time the woman came back, the two junior customs officers were almost looking apologetic.

As the senior officer approached, she said simply. 'This issue was elevated to the Minister of Interior. I have been instructed to tell you that you may proceed on this occasion, but...' She let that word hang for a moment. 'Greek banks will not become a routine stop for you. You will not risk our banks' reputations again. Is that clear?'

A bit irritated at being treated like a child, but keeping his external demeanour pleasant, Tom simply said, 'Thank you madam, have a lovely day.'

Mike and Raj started to lift their hand luggage first on to the luggage scanners. They passed through quickly and then came the cases with the money. Tom positioned himself on the other side of the scanner. He really wanted to take a photo of those bags being X-rayed but knew that it would be pushing his luck. The shell of the cases almost evaporated on the screen and instead he could see bricks and bricks of hundred-dollar bills, the metallic strips showing up as a defined black contrast to the transparent paper of the notes.

With the bags scanned, JP started to lead the team out of the door onto the dispersal where a minibus was waiting to drive them to the plane. The snow was falling heavily now, and the minibus was covered in it. As they left, the customs officer who had been on duty when they arrived spoke to Raj. 'Have a good flight sir, delighted to see that you managed to achieve all your shopping.'

Raj, recognising the sense of humour was able to retort with a wink. 'Thank you, a lovely experience. Sadly, we had to get a cash refund for a couple of items.'

Chapter 67.
November 18th, Athens, Greece

It was now early evening and it had done nothing but snow all day. The team had been onboard for all that time and the interior of the cabin smelt of consumed food and damp fug. A cool box lay open but most of the food had been eaten, and the bin was full of empty sandwich box carcases. The aircraft had been on ground power all day so that the lights and air conditioning systems worked as well as the particularly important de-icing systems. The window for departing had evaporated with the customs delay and Charly as the aircraft Captain needed to make a decision. The two pilots were sitting in the back of the aircraft with Tom, Mike, and Raj. Charly was speaking, 'Tom, the meteorological forecast is looking grim for the rest of the night. I think we need to abandon today's effort and plan again for tomorrow morning.'

'Thanks Charly, and how likely do you think it is that we will get out tomorrow?'

'Given the current weather picture we have perhaps a 30% chance weather wise. But I don't actually think it's the weather that will be the issue. Athens doesn't get much snow like this and whilst it has some de-icing and snow clearing equipment I just don't know if they have the capacity to clear the runways in the short period of time between the snow break and it starting up again.'

'That's very boring.' said Tom disappointedly.

'Add to that,' Charly continued, 'We are a simple private operator. If they do open up there will be a whole bunch of commercial jets that will get priority ahead of us.'

The team were all looking glum. They had spent the whole day waiting for an opportunity that just didn't present itself. On the other hand, there had been lots of opportunity to discuss standby plans.

Tom started to give instructions. 'Right team, there is nothing we can do about the situation so let's make the best of it. Raj, JP, and I will stay on board the aircraft. That keeps one of the aircrew air side and two of us can stay on as security officers to protect the cash which will stay with us. As discussed, I don't want to start hauling those bags between the airport and the hotel. I also don't want that customs lady to change her mind. She is less likely to do that if we don't keep carrying the cash back and forth over the border. Mike, Charly, you two are key for the flight and for the drop so I want you both rested. Head back to the hotel and get some sleep. What time do you want to be back on board tomorrow Charly in case we get a departure window?'

Charly looked at her notepad and did a quick mental calculation. 'If we are lucky then we might get a slot at about two in the afternoon. Mike and I will be back by mid-day, but I will check the weather at 06.00 tomorrow morning in case things have changed.'

'Fine, and what's the worst-case scenario? If we can't get out tomorrow?'

'This weather front will blow through by perhaps midnight tomorrow night. We could then fly and perhaps deliver on the 20th in the middle of the afternoon. Give or take an hour or so.'

'Ok, so let's organise more food, notify the airport that three of us will be staying on board and get transport for the two of you so you can get some good quality rest.'

General replies of yes, and no problem followed while Tom continued for the benefit of the team. 'In the meantime, I am going to give Max and Finlay a call and give them the bad news.'

Chapter 68.
November 18th, The Indian Ocean

That same evening, but 5000 kilometres away, the Sea Dragon, still far out at sea, had passed Mogadishu and was chugging her way North East towards the staging area. The time had just passed 21.00 and Omondi and Bob were on duty along with the vessel's night crew. Chris and Miguel were asleep down below and were due to stag on just before midnight.

The sea state was calm, with a slow, low, regular swell which didn't trouble the little vessel at all. There was a less than quarter moon that was still waning. A thin cloud layer obscured most of the stars and there was virtually no ambient light out there on the dark sea.

The helmsman was alert at the controls, but the radar operator was fidgeting a little in his seat. Omondi was out on the small bridge wing deck. He was wearing his body armour but not his helmet which was on a small table to his right. His binoculars were hanging by a strap from his neck, and he was holding the railing, looking out, enjoying the breeze and the empty blackness of the sea. Bob had just been to urinate in the heads, next to the bridge and as he came back in Daniel the radar operator called him over.

'Bob, come and have a look at this would you?'

Bob walked over to the ancient radar screen, a classic round circular glass with a sweeping white line pinned in the centre that rotated clockwise. The operator had turned the gain up to a high level, and as a result there was a lot of white clutter on the screen.

'What are we looking at mate?' said Bob in his Cornish burr.

The Kenyan radar operator replied, 'I wasn't sure, but I have been watching for about ten minutes. I think we have a small boat tracking towards us. I first saw it on the port side 10 miles out. Then as we maintained our course, I thought I saw it do a definite turn towards us. The problem is that whatever it is, it's low in the water, it's not a clear radar return.'

'Ok so where did you see it last?'

'There!' Daniel exclaimed as a clear white blip flared as the radar spun around somewhere above them.

'Yep, I saw that. Switch to five miles on the radar let's see if that gives us a clearer picture. Helm, can you call the Captain please. He should be up here for this.'

'Yes bwana,' replied the helm.

Daniel changed the radar range by turning a small knob. They both monitored the screen for a few minutes. With a boost in heart rate Bob saw the radar signature of something coming closer to them, but it wasn't enough to tell what it was. The object was now at about four and a half miles and definitely moving. The Captain arrived on the bridge opening the door just as Bob called. 'Helm, I recommend we switch off all external lights and when they are out, change course to 080.'

'Agreed!' called Captain Jammo walking over to the radar. 'Daniel what have you got?'

'Captain, something is following us, and closing rapidly!'

The external lights went out and the helm turned the wheel to get the Sea Dragon on a course that led directly away from the possible threat. The bridge was now bathed in a deep red night light. Bob headed outside and as he got there Omondi was the first to speak. He knew that killing the lights was one of the first responses to a suspicious approach. 'What have we got my friend?'

Bob replied, 'Something small, changed course and is actively pursuing us. Range about 4 miles out and direction almost immediately astern at about 190.'

Omondi picked up the night vision device, a simple monocle design, which relied a lot on ambient light. It wasn't being particularly useful at the moment, as there wasn't much of that. Still, he started to scan in the direction of the threat. 'Shall we wake the others?'

'Yes, better to be safe than sorry. Shout out if you see anything. We will put the others on the starboard bridge wing.' Bob went back inside. The tension on the Bridge seemed to have raised a notch or two. In his calmest voice possible Bob spoke to the helm again. 'Helm, please can you call Chris and Miguel to the bridge.'

'Sure bwana.'

Daniel and Captain Jammo were sweating over the radar. The blip was much clearer now, it pinged with every revolution, was 3 miles out and still on a course of 030. The Captain jabbed his finger at the screen. 'Look at that! Its fast, it's changing course, it's definitely coming towards us!'

Bob kept his voice calm. 'Captain, I suggest we get the additional ammunition out of the safe. We will use our normal rules of engagement and fire warning shots first if we need to.'

'Yes, yes! Get it, get it!' The Captain was getting a little overwhelmed. Chris entered the Bridge just as this last outburst happened immediately sensing the tension.

Bob was straight to action. 'Chris, small vessel, identified on radar only at this stage with likely hostile intent. No visual confirmation. Omondi is on the port side. Miguel, can you go on to the starboard bridge wing and monitor that side.

Miguel scooped down to pick up a set of body armour and to collect an L1A1, 7.62 self-loading rifle from the rack behind the Captain's chair. The other one was already out with Omondi.

Bob took Chris to the back of the room. 'Chris, I suggest that you stay in here mate and keep the Captain company, he is beginning to flap a bit. I will wedge open the bridge wing doors so that we can communicate across the Bridge.'

'Happy with that, well done.' If Bob had maintained an obvious level of calm, Chris exuded ice like control with his tone. 'Captain Jammo, if you are happy, I think we should maintain this course for now, the turn may have persuaded them to follow a false trail.'

'Ok Chris. Daniel, are they changing course or are they still following the same direction that they were before we turned?'

'Too early to tell Captain, another minute or two and we will know. They are only 2 miles out now.'

Bob departed to go and tell Omondi that news. 'Mate, only two miles out now, you should be able to see them.'

Omondis' voice was slightly muffled because his hands were holding the night vision device up to his eye. 'Nothing concrete yet. I thought I saw a bow wave a moment ago but, Yes! There! Directly astern! It's a small speed boat, and its turning... shit! It's turning towards us!'

Moments later Bob heard the Captain swear as well and in a higher pitched voice. 'Fuck! It's turning towards us, it's only about a mile now, can you see it Bob?'

Bob replied, but it was obvious who he was answering too. 'Chris, confirmed visual on a small white skiff. Low in the water coming at us quite quickly.'

Chris spoke to the helm directly 'Helm, with the Captain's permission, when I give the order, I want you to start weaving in the water, hard to port, hard to starboard. Don't set a rhythm, make the move jerky. Captain, I suggest you sound the alarm and get the crew locked down.'

'Yes, Helm, what he says, sound the alarm!'

With the alarm sounding throughout the ship. Chris was putting his body armour on, and his helmet. He and Bob both picked up an AK47 from the rack leaving it empty. Chris gave Bob a wink, 'It's quite exciting this isn't it?' They both giggled for a moment and then Chris went out to join Miguel and Bob joined Omondi.

Omondi had put down the night vision device and was now looking down his rifle sight. 'Got them visual, at about 800 meters.'

'Chris!' shouted Bob. 'I am going to send up a flare, suggest we give them a warning shot?'

'Send it!' called Chris through the open doors across the Bridge.

Bob quickly unscrewed the lid of the flare pot and pulled out a parachute flare. It was about 30 centimetres long, 5 in diameter, in a bright yellow tube and with a large red arrow pointing in the direction of travel of the flare. He twisted the bottom cover off to show the firing trigger, held the flare in front of him at arms length and depressed it.'

The swoosh of the flare was noisy, an almost obscene firework. It climbed to about 300 meters and with a slight pop, burst into an incandescent white light that began to float down on its small parachute. In a brightly lit cone below, the black water sparkled. Highlighted and exposed was a white skiff, twin engines roaring up foam behind. Three men on it, weapons clearly visible.

'Chris, you see that?' called Bob.

'Yep, we got it.' replied Chris. 'Captain!'

'Yes?'

'Positive confirmation of a skiff with three armed men. Intercept course for us. I am going to fire warning shots when they get to 300 meters.'

The Captain had stepped onto the bridge wing on the starboard side next to Chris. He paled at what he saw in the ghostly light of the flare. 'Ok!' he exclaimed and then promptly stepped back into the bridge.

'Miguel, Omondi, three warning shots each. If they get within a hundred meters, or if they fire at us, then you are weapons free. Bob, if they do fire, then you and I will go to auto on the AK's and get some weight of fire down!'

Bob called agreement whilst he unwrapped another flare and then launched it. The first one still had another 20 seconds or so of burn left, and for the period of the warning shots the light was doubled.

Omondi fired his three shots to the starboard side of the skiff. He aimed well to the right and didn't see the fall of shot in the water. He did see the reaction of the crew on the skiff though as they heard the bangs and the snaps of the shots as they passed. The pirates jumped out of their skins, probably not realising that this old bathtub had weapons on board. Miguel had paused for a moment, to see the reaction. It took only a moment. The man at the front of the skiff fired a full magazine in one burst towards the Sea Dragon. The muzzle flashes flared bright orange in the dark of the night. The team on board the Sea Dragon heard the firing, but no tell-tale pinging off the hull and no snap from any shots passing nearby. This pirate had watched too many movies.

Miguel took a breath and waited for the peak of the upswell, much like those who aimed cannons on the warships of old. As he hit equilibrium, he fired with the centre of mass of the skiff directly in his sight and at three hundred meters he wasn't going to miss. The pirate in the front fell backwards awkwardly crashed off the side of the skiff and into the water. Chris, Bob and Omondi started to fire as well. From this stable platform, at this rate of fire and at this close range they could see the fall of shot. It looked like mini fountains in the water in front and to the side of the skiff. Black holes appeared in the white hull of the boat itself, the two remaining men cowering low, cut the engine. It took but moments to persuade the pirates to call off their attack. The flare went out, and Bob popped another one up. They could just make out the skiff fading backwards into the night, settling lower and lower into the water. They didn't see any other movement after that.

Chapter 69.
November 18th, Athens Greece

Mike and Charly had elected not to drive all the way back into the city to the Marriott. Instead, they had taken a couple of rooms at the Sofitel at the airport. It was ten o'clock at night and they had just finished what had turned out to be a great meal. They had enjoyed the food and each other's company immensely. It was certainly a better option than the packaged sandwiches on the plane.

They were now sitting in the bar, which to be honest didn't have much of a soul. For a four-star hotel they had managed to decorate the bar a bit like a kitsch diner from the 70s, albeit with modern marble. There were lots of small square tables set too close together and each had four plasticky chairs over a chess board black and white floor. Charly and Mike were sitting in a small pink fury booth, one of a string that ran back-to-back down the centre of the room. From where they were sitting, they could look out of the large glass windows into the night and see the snow flurries falling. There was a general hubbub of noise, mostly business travellers, having late meetings. There were also quite a few single people, perhaps whose flights had been delayed, who were sitting at their tables with only an iPad or a laptop open for company.

Mike looked around and commented on what he saw, 'I am so glad that I don't have to travel the world selling stuff to people who don't want to buy it. I think living permanently in hotels would be so dull.'

Charly, who smelled amazing, or so thought Mike, said, 'But you do travel the world!'

'Yes, but usually with other people. Rarely on my own. And usually with a real meaningful purpose.'

'But surely these people feel they have a purpose?'

'I am sure they do.' Mike paused 'But look at that guy, nice suit, nice watch, watching some movie or other on his iPad. Where is his family? You could offer me a large amount of money and I still wouldn't accept that life.'

Charly looked at him, He looked so out of place in this room. Cargo trousers, tight black T-Shirt, big gold navy seal signet ring. And there he was sitting in a bright pink booth with her. She couldn't put a finger on exactly why, but she felt that of the 30 or so men in the room,

Mike was without doubt, 'the' man in the room, and that turned her on. She blushed thinking Mike could see right through her and changed the subject.

'So how are the guys in the plane getting on?'

'I spoke to Raj when we got to the hotel. They are all right. It's a bit cramped, but there is space at the back for two to sleep on the floor. I joked with him that when he wasn't on guard that he would have to decide to spoon JP facing out or facing in.'

'Ha-ha. You guys are funny. You are always winding each other up. Why is that?'

'Man stuff. We trust each other absolutely. We have done more tasks that I care to remember, and we just know how we both operate. We are never going to go soft on each other, so one of the best ways that we use to show we care is to take the piss. Does that sound odd?'

Charly had a flicker of surprise, not quite understanding and not knowing Mike well enough. She thought she might have made a huge mistake in her assumptions. 'Sorry, soft on each other?'

'Yes, you know. We aren't ever going to tell each other that we are best mates, even though we know that we are.'

Charly laughed and flicked her hair a little, 'Oh thank goodness for that.'

'What?' asked Mike?

'Well, being 'soft on each other' is a very English way of saying you fancy each other, you know, you are in love!'

Mike boomed out laughing and in his deep American voice said, 'Charly, I am not gay!'

Perhaps by sheer circumstance, as he said it, there was a lull in the noise in the room and his voice clearly cut through it. Most of the business travellers', men and women alike turned to stare at him. Charly blushed; Mike laughed louder. Charly started giggling too as the noise resumed and the travellers went back to their screens or their meetings.

Still giggling she said. 'You know there were a couple of disappointed faces out there amongst the guys, and some of those lonely ladies looked at you like cats that want the cream.'

Mike tried to recover his composure. 'Of course, it's OK to be gay, I just meant that I am not.'

'Thank god for that. For the record, I am not gay either.' She paused for a heartbeat and then said slowly. 'In fact, tonight, I think I would like to be that cat that gets the cream.'

Mike wasn't listening properly and had just raised his hand to call over the waiter that was passing to order another round of drinks. He paused, processed, and looked directly into Charly's open, smiling, but slightly nervous looking bright green eyes. He smiled strongly back at her, not saying a word, seeing a little trepidation there still.

The waiter came over and Mike said, 'Cheque please.'

Chapter 70.
November 19th, Athens, Greece

In the negotiation room at the Aphrodite Freight and Shipping Company offices, Finlay and John were getting ready to make a call that they would rather not. Finlay had been hoping to run through the final day script with John for onward discussion with Abdi, but the massive snow falls over the past 24 hours had put paid to that. The weather was so bad, it had been near impossible for John to get into the city from his home. Athens just wasn't set up as a municipality to deal with freak blizzards and snow. As a result, they had only had half an hour to practice the call and given the way it was likely to go John was feeling apprehensive.

The problem was that Abdi was expecting an airplane in about forty-five minutes and to get his cash. It was Johns' job now to break the bad news to him gently.

Finlay hit the record button as John picked up the telephone handset. He took a deep breath as the phone rang.

Abdi picked up sounding extremely happy. 'John good morning are you ready for our big day?'

'Good morning Abdi, how are things on board?' John replied.

'All is fine, we are all prepared. I am going to send the crew out on deck in about fifteen minutes. Is the airplane going to be on time?' Abdi asked buoyantly.

Fuck it, thought John, as he broke the bad news. 'Abdi, I have some bad news for you I am afraid.'

Suddenly serious, Abdi's tone changed completely. 'What do you mean bad news?'

'Abdi, I need to explain something to you. Something has happened which is completely outside my control. The weather in Europe has…'

Abdi interrupted him. 'Are you shitting me?'

Nervously John tried to continue. 'No Abdi, the weather, in Europe. There has been a massive snowstorm and the airports are all...'

Abdi was livid, pacing around the bridge, stretching the cable of the sat phone that was pressed up hard against his ear. He interrupted again. 'I don't give a camels turd about the weather! You promised me that my money would come today. We are all prepared. I was going to give you your ship back, and your precious crew! Where the god damned fuck is my money!'

Finlay winced, and pointed to the key word 'explain' on the white board.

John nodded and continued. 'Abdi, I would like to explain. We have your money. Its currently in an airplane, but the airplane is grounded in Athens because of the weather. It couldn't take off yesterday, it was outside our control.'

Incensed now, and not really listening Abdi blew a fuse. 'Control! Outside your control? I tell you what else is outside your control. Me! I am going to go and get me a hostage and execute him. In fact, I am going to execute one hostage per day until I get my money!'

Finlay rolled his eyes, completely calm he pointed to words 'death threat procedure' on the board behind him. John, surprised, mouthed 'really?' to which Finlay nodded.

John did the best he could to put authority into his voice though he kept it calm and not at all angry. 'Abdi listen to me. We have spoken about threats like that before. Do you remember what happened?' Silence at the other end as Abdi remembered it resulted in two weeks of no communication at all. John continued. 'I have told you that I will pay you a large sum of money, for the return of the ship, the cargo and all of the crew, alive. That deal still stands. It has been delayed by one, perhaps two days. If you don't want that to happen then I suggest we have a cooling off period and we speak again in two weeks' time.' John paused for a beat and then said. 'It's choice time Abdi. What's it going to be?'

Taken aback by the tone, that he hadn't heard at all from John throughout the last months, Abdi was stunned. Here he was, in charge of everything, but that man on the other end of the phone was telling him how it was. His first impression, as a hot-headed young Somali man was to tell John to go fuck himself. Strangely enough, it was the finance side of him that told him to think. His creditors were lining up, the family of the dead skiff crews wanted paying off. Six and a half million dollars was a lot of money. It was enough to persuade him to cool down a little. He asked in a petulant but calmer voice. 'So, when is the weather going to clear?'

'Thank you, Abdi.' John was immensely relieved, but he couldn't break off the call just yet. 'We may be able to get the plane out today, in which case we can deliver tomorrow morning. But if the snow doesn't clear, it will depart tomorrow, to be with you the day after. I promise you that I will call you tonight at 18.00 your time and give you an update. Does that work for you?'

'If it isn't out here in two days' time, then the deal is off. Does that work for you?' Abdi asked sarcastically before hanging up.

John put the receiver down and took a deep breath whilst Finlay pressed stop on the recording device. John looked at him shaking his head slightly and speaking quietly. 'Damn, that felt like a gamble. How did you know that he was going to agree?'

Finlay seemed quite cheerful when he replied. 'Well, you are never certain. It's all about character analysis, observations throughout the negotiation and all that. I think Abdi is under a lot of financial pressure. Simply put he needs the money. Now, that said, if we don't get that to him in the next few days, it might be enough to tip him over the edge and do something stupid. For now though, we have bought the team a couple more days, and we just have to see how the weather goes.'

John asked for probably the hundredth time 'I still don't know how the hell do you stay so calm!'

Finlay grinned. 'If you hadn't realised by now, my liver tells me I drink too much whisky and I smoke a lot of cigarettes. Shall we go and grab a coffee and then head outside?'

Chapter 71.
November 19th, Hobyo, Somalia

Abdi was sitting in the Captain's chair having just hung up the phone with John. He was on his own having told the duty guard to go and do something else as usual so that he couldn't be overheard. To put it mildly Abdi was extremely anxious. He just couldn't work out at what point he had lost control of the narrative. There he was, holding all the cards, or so he thought, and yet he wasn't able to do anything about the delay. He started to worry about whether or not John was telling the truth. Was there really money on the way? Or was this a scheme to get some kind of military intervention in place? He pulled out his phone and looked up the weather in Athens. The page loaded slowly on the 3G signal, but sure enough, the weather app showed heavy snowstorms and the news headlines showed the airport closed. The forecast did at least look like it might clear in the next 24 hours, but it was touch and go. Abdi was a little relieved to see that John might be telling the truth and he was mulling it all over when Zahi came onto the bridge.

Zahi was bright and cheerful, 'There are good conditions today on the sea. The guys are all ready and in their boats. Anything else before I go?'.

Abdi took a deep breath. 'It's not happening today.'

Zahi, his bubble burst, looked at him disbelievingly. 'Seriously? You are joking right?'

'No. There is a problem with weather. Apparently, our money is on an airplane that is grounded by snow.'

'That doesn't sound right. Are you sure it's not a trap? The plane is meant to be here in,' Zahi looked at his watch, 'about twenty minutes.'

'Zahi my suspicious friend, you read my mind. But, from what they just told me on the phone I think they are telling the truth.'

Zahi was obviously disappointed and a little incredulous. 'Shit!' he paused as a new idea hit him, 'Do you trust them?'

'Absolutely not. And this is what we are going to do about it. I want you to call Axmed, Yuusuf and Tadalesh back in. Then I want to you take three of the hostages and put them into one of the skiffs with Yuusuf and Tadalesh in it. They can then go and sit about 100 meters away in the water until we hear that the money is coming.'

Zahi nodded, 'I like that. It's an insurance policy. If the infidel think they can recapture this ship with the hostages, then they won't be able to take the ship and the skiff at the same time. How long do you think they will be out there for?'

'Perhaps one day, or two. We shall know more tonight. I am also more worried now about other 'interested parties' here in Somalia. It is possible that the news has leaked out. One of the neighbouring warlords or even the puppet government might try something stupid.'

Zahi considered that a moment before saying, 'Well let's have a double shift of guards. Lots of weapons visible on deck and up here on the bridge wings. That will dissuade any neighbourly visits and also be a visible deterrent to any hostile military that might be out there.'

Abdi was feeling disappointed. The adrenaline of anticipation that had kept him up through much of the night was now wearing off and he was fatigued. 'Zahi, you are doing well. Let's keep this going for just another couple of days. We are so close, and we will get there. For now though, I need to try and get hold of one of the skiffs that I still have out there trying to find us a new prize. I haven't heard from them for a day now, and they should have checked in.'

Zahi replied, 'I understand. Let me worry about this ship. I hope you are able to get in touch with the other team.'

'So, do I my friend, so do I.'

Chapter 72.
November 19th, Athens Greece

It was lunchtime. Tom, Raj and JP were all awake sitting in their first-class seats in the Citation. It had been a long and uncomfortable night with Tom and Raj taking it in turns to stay awake, whilst JP slept. As part of the aircrew, it was important that he got his rest, though that didn't stop Tom and Raj taking the piss out of the former Royal Airforce officer.

This morning JP had spoken to Charly who had a weather update which said that they were going nowhere quickly. It had been agreed that Charly and Mike should stay at the hotel for now until things improved. JP then spoke to the VIP flight ops and found out that they could provide a much better meal than packed sandwiches. That food had just arrived, literally delivered to the door of the aircraft by a catering service. The delivery man, dressed in a massive puffer jacket, gloves and woolly hat had banged in a muffled way on the aircraft door. With Tom and Raj on full alert taking up the positions that they had agreed beforehand, JP had opened the aircraft door. As he did so in came a blast of snow and wind, but also the welcome smell of a hot, king prawn curry with all the trimmings in separate aluminium foil takeaway cartons. The cool box with the soft drinks in was still pretty full and now the three of them were enjoying a good lunch.

They had been discussing how odd it was for them to sit there so calmly, with six and half million dollars in cash sitting in the Samsonites just a few paces away. JP swallowed a mouthful of the delicious curry, 'So have you ever been tempted to take the cash on any of your projects?'

Raj looked at him a little suspiciously, but Tom, knowing how wealthy JP was didn't blink. 'It's an interesting question. If you put the moral questions aside about the fate of the hostages, and the betrayal of your friends and employers; perhaps a better question is how much is enough?'

JP thought for a moment. 'Yes, I suppose it depends on what you are used to as a standard of living. I have never had to worry about money, so I don't know the answer. I suppose, already having enough as you put it takes the temptation away.'

Tom asked Raj. 'How much is "enough" do you think, for you?'

Raj swallowed some naan bread; he had succumbed to his no carbohydrate rule and was indulging. He licked some of the curry gravy off his fingers. 'Enough, if you have earned it legally, is the usual material things. A house, a well looked after family, good health etc. But, if you are talking about how much is enough if you are on the run, because you stole it, then 6 million is nowhere near the mark. Think about it. For years, your immediate family would be under surveillance in case you got in touch with them. Sure, you could get a fake ID, move to an island, or country where the rule of law is poor, drop off the face of the earth, something like that. But can you really spend what you got? Or are you making the choice to become a hermit, ignore your family for the rest of your life and just live off a private income whilst constantly watching over your shoulder?'

Tom smiled; 'But there is an error is your exceptional maths Raj. In this case, it wouldn't be six million. For us, if we left right now, it would be just over two million each.'

'Then it's definitely not enough!' he laughed.

Chapter 73.
November 19th, The Indian Ocean

It was just before midnight and Chris and Miguel were up on one of the bridge wings of the Sea Dragon conducting a shift handover with Bob and Omondi. Everyone was still buzzing after the failed attack the night before.

They were all standing out on the starboard side and they had closed the door to the Bridge so that they could speak freely. The vessel was barely making any headway and was almost idling. She had reached her staging area and was now just marking time, waiting for the main event. There was no point in burning extra fuel, and they might have to wait for a little while yet.

Bob, as the off-coming shift leader was leading the briefing and was just wrapping up. 'So, that just about sums it up. Nothing further seen of that skiff, and no other vessels seen for much of the day, certainly nothing closer than 10 miles. We did get a call on the sat phone from the Ops room in Nairobi. The aircraft still hasn't left Athens and the weather for today is looking like a whiteout. There might be a window tomorrow afternoon, and if that does open up, then we can look at a delivery date the morning after, so that makes it the 21st. Ops told me that Tom would give us a call directly once they are airborne and with a confirmation of that drop timing when he could.'

Chris who had been listening carefully nodded, 'Great, anyone got any questions about that before I move on to the contact yesterday?' There were shakes of the head from the other three team members. 'Alright, now comes the legal bit. We all took actions yesterday and all of us fired our weapons. It happened in international waters so it's outside any particular country's jurisdiction other than the flag state of the vessel. We need to be thorough though, and we need to write up our own individual statements of what happened. That includes the actions we took as individuals. Personally, I think it's cut and dried, but we don't have any video of the incident. From what I saw, I don't suspect that there is any evidence of the contact in terms survivors on that skiff but that's the only slightly dodgy bit. The Captain will have to write up his summary too, covering why we didn't check to see if there were any survivors or wounded. I am quite happy to answer that one in a court if it ever got to that point. Anyway, if you can all write up your statements, independently of each other, then I will send them off to Max's legal advisor. Once she has had a look then we can give them to the Captain. He is the one who needs to inform the authorities.'

Miguel asked in his thick Colombian accent. 'How is the Captain doing? He was really panicking yesterday.'

Chris replied, 'He will be alright, though, he is a bit shaken. He has been sailing up and down this coast for years and never had a problem. It was his first time in combat, so I think it's OK to give him a little bit of slack.'

Miguel asked what a couple of the others were thinking. 'Is he going to be cool when we need to cross deck to the Hibernia III?'

Chris smiled, 'Well as long as you don't need to shoot anyone again Miguel, we should be fine!'

Bob piped up. 'It was a bloody good shot that!'

Omondi nodded agreement and said 'Maximum range for the weapon, only lit by a flare, the target bobbing up and down whilst firing at us. That was ice cold.'

Miguel was quite happy to take the praise but was also modest dipping his head and shrugging his shoulders, 'We did well in the preparation. Secure, high position, fairly stable, plenty of time to prepare because we were alert to the risk. Not too much wind to worry about and no doubt in my mind that it was a clean shoot.'

There were nods of agreement from all on that one as the Sea Dragon continued to mark time under a waning pale moon.

Chapter 74.

November 20th, Athens, Greece

It was mid-morning and the snow had finally stopped falling onto the dispersal where the Citation was parked. It was still minus 5 out there, but the clouds were beginning to clear in the East and things were brightening up.

The whole team were awake, but it was Raj who was on watch when he saw a large black SUV with an orange flashing light on top, come towards the aircraft. The car was taking it very slowly, no snow chains and the driver not certain how effective much of the de-icing had been. 'Heads up Tom, looks like a vehicle coming our way.'

'Tom looked up from his laptop, folded it away and also watched as the driver uber-carefully stopped about 50 meters away from the multimillion-dollar aircraft. The back doors of the SUV opened, and Mike and Charly got out. Mike was carrying both of their overnight bags and Charly was carrying her flight planning bag. Mike was dressed in his standard cargo pants, a black t-shirt, and a very thin V-neck sweater. Charly was back in her Captains uniform of white short sleeved shirt and black trousers. It was Mike who looked coldest though. They walked purposefully but carefully towards the aircraft. Raj went to stand by the door, watching them through the small glass window.

Mike was first up to the aircraft and having not seen Raj, banged on the fuselage. Raj didn't move. Mike banged again and looked up. He could see Raj grinning down at him. 'Open the bloody door Raj!' he shouted.

Raj just continued to grin, cupping his hand over his ear, giving payback for Mike taking the piss out of him being cold a couple of days ago. He pretended not to hear whilst mouthing 'What?'

'Open the door, its bloody freezing out here!'

'What's the password?'

'What the fuck?'

'No that's not it. Look you might look like my best mate, but how do I know it's really you?'

'For god's sake. Open the door!'

'Yep, that's the one.' with a grin Raj relented, pulling the door lever, and letting it swing out. The stairs descended automatically and Mike, offered with a wave of his hand for Charly to go up first. She climbed the ladder as a blast of cold air entered the cabin, and a bubble of foetid warm air wafted out.

'Oh my god, it stinks of boys in here!' Charly exclaimed. 'What the hell have you lot been up to!'

'Morning Charly.' grinned Raj and bowing slightly 'Welcome to the palace of perfume! On special today, we have man-stink, two days with no shower, brewed nicely and bottled in a lovely little crystal bottle for that discerning lady!'

Charly smiled at him and walked past shaking her head and wrinkling her nose. As she passed, Raj stepped back across the entrance as Mike tried to climb the stairs. 'Boarding card please sir.' He asked politely holding out his hand.

'Listen you tube, it's really cold out here, let me in.' Mike said crossly.

'If your names not down, you are not coming in sunshine.' Raj continued the game, but Mike was done. He climbed the steps and threw the two overnight bags into Raj's midriff forcing him back with an 'Ooph!'

'Stow the bags you muppet.' Mike finally got access to the cabin and noticed the stink. 'Oh my god, don't tell me you ate a curry in here. It's going to honk all the way home!'

Raj, who was closing the door said, 'Well you are a bit grumpy today, I thought it was good news?'

Charly looking bright and chirpy cut in. 'Yes, it is good news. I have just had the meteorological briefing. The snow is definitely done. There will be a couple of hours whilst they de-ice and get the larger aircraft out, but by mid-afternoon today we should be on our way. We will need to go through a thorough de-icing protocol ourselves, but I reckon by 15.00 we should be airborne.'

'Excellent!' said Tom, 'I will let Max know.'

Charly asked JP to join her in the cockpit and they both went forward to conduct their planning and preparation. Mike went and sat down in one of the cabin chairs, he looked exhausted.

Raj went to speak to him whilst Tom got on the phone. 'Dude, you ok? You look exhausted. You've got great big bags under your eyes. Didn't you get any sleep?'

'Not much actually buddy, no.' Mike replied as he closed his eyes.

Chapter 75.

November 20th, Athens, Greece

'Abdi, its John, I have good news.' John blurted out excitedly almost as soon as he heard Abdi pick up the phone at the other end.

The positivity was immediately infectious, and Abdi replied, 'Hi John, are they going to be able to get out today?'

'It's better than that my friend. They took off about 15 minutes ago! We expect them to be with you at 09.00 tomorrow morning. Does that work for you?'

'Yes, Yes! We will have everything ready, that is good news!'

John was feeling really quite relieved. 'Great, I will call you at 08.00 your time tomorrow morning to do a final check, and after that all of your calls will be with the team on the plane. The person who will call you, will call himself Hermes OK?'

'Hermes?' replied Abdi?

'Yes, that's correct. Google is your best bet there Abdi.'

A little unsure, but still caught up in the excitement of tomorrow Abdi replied, 'I will look it up and we shall speak tomorrow, inshallah.'

John hung up the phone, he was grinning from ear to ear. However, he lost some of the gloss when he saw Finlay's face staring at him with a bit of a frown on. John asked him, 'What's wrong?'

Finlay mulled over his reply. 'It's OK. Well actually John, I might be being picky, the call was fine but there was one thing that grated on me.'

Throughout the entire long process of the negotiation John had never had a telling off by Finlay but he felt one coming now. 'What is it? What did I do?'

'Well John, you called that wanker on the other end of the phone 'your friend'. If there is one person in this world that isn't your friend, it's that dick head. Hostage takers are evil, manipulative little pricks that would cut your throat and rape your wife if there was no money to be had in keeping you alive. They can package it up and try to justify what they do as repayment for a grievance, a business transaction, or as part of a holy cause, but they destroy lives. Not only the hostages' lives, but all the family around them. Never call him your friend again.'

John looked devastated. 'Sorry Finlay. I got carried away. I guess I was happy that we could proceed. You're quite right; it won't happen again.' Upset that he had let his mentor down more than anything, John felt his emotional bubble had been truly pricked.

Finlay saw it happen and softened a little. He said brusquely 'It's alright mate. I am probably over-reacting. I have just seen too many of these go wrong near the end game. It gets to you sometimes. Let's give this one another 24 hours and then touch wood we can put it behind us.'

The snowy weather was long gone behind them and the Citation was cruising at just under 40,000 feet, above the Red Sea desert. The sky was clear blue above, but below them the yellow, fine dust particles blown up from the Sahara caused the landscape to be a muzzy brown smudge. On the port side, almost as though looking at a giant map from above, you could just make out the Red Sea: a long streak of dark blue in amongst the golden sand. The two 'rabbit ears' of the northern end with the spit of land, where Sharm el Sheikh sat, had passed by about twenty minutes ago. Outside, all was calm and serene as the aircraft cruised towards Djibouti for a rest and refuel. Inside the aircraft, it looked like an admin bomb had gone off. Forget about the smell of curry or body odour. The smells that hit the noses of the team now were of polystyrene, glue, silicone sealant, gaffer tape and that unmistakable smell of money.

Tom was sitting on one of the seats that he had rotated to face aft. His job was to monitor the packing from start to finish, and to be blunt, to make sure that one of those hundred-thousand-dollar bricks that he had signed for, didn't end up getting knocked accidentally into someone's bag.

Mike and Raj were sitting on the floor at the tail end with kit and equipment all around them. They had completed two of the loads already. Those two packed tubes and two empty Samsonites that had contained some of the cash in them had been pushed up the aircraft to sit just behind the pilots' deck to get them out of the way to create more space to work.

Packing materials were all around them. It looked a little bit like a massive craft and design project. Mike currently had one of the large nylon tubes between his legs. Before they had left Nairobi, at one end, the tubes had been sealed off with a base cap made of the same material and a strong epoxy resin. The base caps had had a couple of holes drilled through them and some D rings attached for the parachutes fastenings. Mike had placed the sealed end down on the floor, so the open end was facing up. 'Pass me that first polystyrene plug would you mate.' He indicated to Raj a 15-centimetre-thick disc of white polystyrene. Raj passed it, and Mike carefully placed it into the three-foot-long tube, pushing it all the way to the bottom.

Raj started packing money into bright yellow dry[...] was an open Samsonite on the floor to his right. Each d[...] take up to a million dollars but only if packed carefully[...] double bagged the bags, putting one inside the other to make as [...] as possible that there wouldn't be a leak. Next, he placed three bricks of money beside each other at the base of the bag, and then he used two more bricks which he placed at each end of the central block of three. It created a rough hexagon shape that was perfect for the cylindrical shape of the tube. As Mike and Tom counted, Raj added the second layer of cash, rotating it through 90 degrees to help even out the pressure on the bag. That done Raj folded over the seal of the inner bag and clipped it shut, then he sealed that clip with a plasticuff tag. He then did the same for the outer bag. Because of the meticulous planning, when Mike took that bag off him and lowered it into the nylon pipe, it fit snugly without too much movement. The next bag was going to take the rest of the contents of that Samsonite, another six hundred thousand dollars. Following the same process, but this time with five bricks on the base layer and one brick lying flat on top of them, they put another sealed set of bags on top of the first inside the tube.

Raj then passed Mike another of the thick polystyrene plugs to place into the tube, on top of the money bags. It would help with buoyancy, and it would stop them shifting about during descent. They glued that polystyrene plug in place. The final piece was one more plug, but this one had a nylon disc, perfectly cut to size already glued to it. Whilst Mike held the tube up, Raj got a sealant gun and put a liberal dose of silicon sealant, combined with an adhesive, and squirted it all around the inside of the tube where this last plug would fit. Trying not to get it all over his hands, or spilling it onto the awfully expensive carpet, Mike pushed the final disc into place and using a rubber hammer knocked it in gently. Sealant oozed out of the joins all the way around, but he wiped that off with a cloth. Now, the tube was sealed at both ends, solid, with no movement. All that showed on the outside were the two D-Rings sticking out of what was now the top of the tube. It looked like a good job.

Tomorrow morning all that was needed was to connect the parachutes, which had been packed prior to their departure from Nairobi, and things were good to go.

Mike cracked a big yawn and said, 'Let's get this last one done and then we can get some sleep.'

Raj looked at him suspiciously. 'Buddy, I would have thought it ould be Tom and I that would be yawning our heads off. You have just had two nights in a hotel. How come you didn't get any rest?'

Mike just shrugged his shoulders and gave a little grin.

Raj continued, 'Oh God, you pulled didn't you! Some poor businesswomen, or you pestered some poor local Greek lady! I bet you used that awful line of yours.' Raj did a reasonable impression of Mike's deep American accent. 'Once you've had black, there is no going back!'

Mike didn't say anything to that, he just shook his head slightly, picked up the last tube, and got to work.

Chapter 77.
November 20th, The Indian Ocean

It was ten o'clock at night and Chris was on the bridge wing of the Sea Dragon speaking to Tom on the satellite phone. With Chris a former Navy commander and Tom a former Royal Marine officer, there was always banter. 'Well Royal, good of you to eventually turn up. Only a couple of days late.'

Tom laughed, 'Well, you know us, we always enjoy a spot of snow sports, whenever the opportunity presents itself.'

'And there was me thinking you might have stopped off at a casino to let off a bit of steam and lighten the load a bit. Or did you decide to blow it all on dirty martinis and lap dancers?'

'Well, it has been an epic couple of nights, and needless to say we are all a bit tired.'

Chris leaned against the door jamb, so that Miguel who was on watch could hear the next part. 'And so? Are we all good to go for tomorrow morning?'

'Yes. 09.00 on the nail, but I will give you a call once we are airborne so that you can start your final approach to the vessel.'

'Excellent, well, try to get some sleep tonight and we shall speak tomorrow.'

As Chris hung up, he nodded to Miguel and then turned back in to speak to the Captain who was sitting at the chart table at the back of the Bridge. 'Captain, it looks like we are good for tomorrow morning.'

Captain Jammo who was still a little edgy, replied. 'Good, the sooner we get out of these waters the better.'

Chris asked patiently, 'How long do we need to transit to the Hibernia III tomorrow morning? Or rather, what time should we leave here in order to be there for 09.00?'

Captain Jammo looked at the chart in front of him and replied, 'About 4 hours, but there is a strong current so let's plan on 5.'

Chris seemingly absentmindedly walked over to the chart and had a quick look, but of course he was double checking. If the vessel made 8 knots, then 5 hours would be plenty. 'That's great Captain.' and then he added subtly, to make sure there was no doubt whatsoever. 'Are you happy that we start the approach at 04.00?' The Captain nodded and Chris continued cheerfully. 'Brilliant, I will make sure that all of my team are awake and fed before then. It's going to be a busy day tomorrow!'

Chapter 78.
November 21st, 15,000 feet over Somaliland

It was 07.30 on delivery day and the Citation had just taken off from Djibouti and was heading Southeast towards Somaliland. The team had had a restless night. Djibouti international airport was a dual-purpose facility. The Southern side of the runway was in fact one of the largest US military air bases in the world outside America. Home to some 4000 men and women it boasted cinemas, bowling alleys, its own Subway and even a Pizza Hut. The work side was constantly active. Fighter jets, Globemaster heavy lift aircraft and Predator drones operated constantly.

The northern side of the runway was commercial, but there were no more than a handful of flights per day to service the small civilian population.

Tom, Mike, and Raj had all taken it in turns to maintain a permanent watch system, splitting the ground time between them and getting a couple of hours sleep, in-between sitting in their executive seats. They were beginning to feel a lot less executive. JP and Charly had stretched out flat at the back of the aircraft and managed to get some sleep, though all were regularly wakened by the sound of F-16's spooling up for take-off.

The team had woken at 06.00 and then taken it in turns to use the tiny toilet cabin at the back of the aircraft. A quick wash of a face using the tiny hand sink, a brush of teeth using bottled water and a squirt of deodorant was about as much as was manageable.

The departure process was fairly painless, and as the aircraft was now in the climb and on the way to its delivery point Tom had some phone calls to make. The Sat-phone in the aircraft was plugged into an external antenna and so Tom could use it quite happily sitting at his seat. His first call was to Chris who picked up after only a couple of rings. 'Morning Chris, how are we doing this morning?'

'I was going to ask you the same thing mate. We are currently about ten miles from the Hibernia III making good headway. We will arrive in her vicinity as planned.'

'Good. As you can probably hear, we are airborne. Just departed and perfectly scheduled to reach the target area at 09.00.'

'Great, thanks for the heads up,' replied Chris. 'I will let the Captain know. I suppose we shall see you in about 90 minutes time then.

'Affirm. See you then and good luck.' Tom pressed the end call button on the Sat-phone and then pressed speed dial 1. As the phone rang, Tom felt the Citation do a slight course correction onto heading 130.

The phone at the other end was picked up by Max who said. 'Morning Tom. What's the update?'

'Hi Max. We are airborne and well into the climb. I have just completed a comms check with the Sea Dragon and they are heading into position now. We are on time to deliver as planned.'

'Excellent well done. I can see you on the satellite tracking system,'

'Good. I will check in with Abdi in about half an hour's time to make sure all is as planned and will then call you after we have confirmed proof of life.'

'Happy with that. Fly safe and talk to you soon.'

Max put the phone down on the board room table in front of him and addressed Mr Papadopoulos directly. The room had been silent whilst he took the call and there was an air of anticipation. 'Well, as you probably just heard, the team has taken off from Djibouti and all is well. No issues on the ground there at all.' Max leaned forward and pressed a button on his laptop. It was plugged in to the room's presentation system and the screen at the end of the room warmed up.

Max kept talking as it did so, looking at the faces sitting around him. Mr Papadopoulos was sitting at the head of the board room table with John sitting next to him. He had been invited in for the final show. Sitting either side of Max were Finlay and Chloe the lawyer. 'Tom tells me that the Maritime team are also in position, which is good, and both assets are now actively using their satellite trackers.' The screen had now warmed up to show the tracking software. Based on a standard Google map, which was zoomed out to show the Horn of Africa, there were three icons visible. The first was the Citation. Max hovered over the icon and a popup appeared showing its heading, height, and speed. The other two icons were quite close together, so Max zoomed in. There was a tag on the screen for the assumed location of the Hibernia III just offshore Hobyo and about ten miles to the west. Further out to sea was a small icon showing a ship. The tag said it was the Sea Dragon. Again, Max hovered on it and the popup showed her travelling at 8 knots towards the Hibernia III.

'We can keep this screen up and live on the board during the operation, but what I suggest now is that I give you a quick summary of what we expect to happen. From experience when things happen, they go quickly, so I might not have time to answer many questions. Is that ok with everyone?'

There were various nods and Max continued. 'We know that the assets are all in place now. John, how did the call go with Abdi this morning.'

John spoke clearly to the group. 'Abdi seemed OK. I ran him through the proof of life process again and he said that everything would be ready. I think we are good there.'

Mr Papadopoulos said, 'Good, well done.' And there were lots of nods around the table and further positive murmurs.

Max said, 'Great, the comms with Abdi will now be through Tom, until the end of the drop procedure. Let's go through that now and then we will have time for a coffee before the exciting bit.'

The Citation was in the cruise at 31,000 feet over Puntland and about 300 Kilometres Northwest of the Hibernia III. Charly had taken the aircraft on a slight dogleg to avoid entering Ethiopian airspace. The Ethiopians had much better radar systems than the Somali states and seeing as Charly had turned off her transponder when she left Djibouti airspace, she didn't want a couple of Ethiopian fighter jets waggling their wings at her. The Somali infrastructure was woeful and there was no way it would be able to pick them up if they stayed well clear of the single piece of 1960's radar hardware at Mogadishu international.

In the back of the aircraft, everything was ready. The carpet had been lifted up, but the floor seals were still in place in order to maintain the cabin pressure. The four black and orange delivery tubes had all been checked and checked again and placed carefully on the floor. Mike had rigged the four parachutes, by clipping them on to the D-rings at the end of the tubes. He had then used a fine parachute cord with a five-pound breaking strain to secure the parachutes to the top of the tubes. It was enough to hold them in place while manoeuvring them inside the cabin, but during the drop procedure, when the canopy deployed, they would snap and not impede the canopy release. The static lines had already been clipped to D-rings on the floor.

Tom had the satellite phone in his hand again. Speed dial 2 this time. It rang four times before it was picked up with a 'Hello?'

'Hello, is that Abdi?' asked Tom.

'Yes, who is this?'

'Abdi this is Hermes. I think you are expecting my call?'

'Yes good. Hello Hermes, what is your real name?'

Tom smoothed over what he thought was a bit of a stupid question. He heard an almost London accent speaking down the line, though it was definitely with a Somali guttural twang. 'Abdi, I think for this you should just call me Hermes, OK?'

'OK, whatever.'

'Abdi we are now one hour away from you, and I need to run you through a couple of things all right?'

'OK.'

Tom worked hard to keep the tone of his voice calm, and soothing. 'To be clear. I have the agreed sum, and it is ready. If all goes well over the next hour, then we will deliver that sum to you. In return, you are going to release all of the crew unharmed, the ship and its cargo.'

'Yes, yes, that is the agreement. I am a businessman. That is what I have said I will do.'

'Good. By 8.45, that's in 45 minutes, I need you to have all of the crew standing on the deck in front of the superstructure. They must not be wearing any hats and they must look clearly out to sea so that I can recognise their…'

Abdi interrupted him. 'Ok, its proof of life. I understand, I have gone through this many times with John.'

Hiding his irritation and still speaking calmly Tom said. 'Abdi. This is particularly important. If I am not able to confirm proof of life for all of the hostages, I may not be able to deliver the money. I am going to bring my plane down to sea level and pass down the seaward side of the ship to get a clear sight of all the hostages. That's why I need the crew spread out. Do you understand?'

Almost nonchalantly Abdi replied 'Yes, yes.'

'Abdi, I need you to give me re-assurance that when we are flying low beside the ship, that none of your men will fire their weapons at me. If that happens, we will fly away, and you will not get your money. Do you understand?'

Again, Abdi replied 'Yes.' Though in his mind he did fantasise for a moment about such a thing after the aircraft had dropped the money. He dismissed the idea promptly. After all, as he had just said, he was a businessman. He did make a mental note to make sure to remind the guards on the deck not to fire their weapons at the aircraft.

'Good. Do you have your skiffs in the water, on the seaward side? With one at the front and one at the back of the Hibernia III?'

'Yes. In fact I have two at each end.'

'Good, remember, they must not try to capture the loads as they fall. Someone could get hurt, or you could damage the tubes. They will quite happily sit in the water and then your people can pick them up after they have landed.'

'I understand.'

'OK, and the final one from me for now. You will see our resupply vessel approaching shortly. It has been told to stay within sight of you until you leave the Hibernia III. It will not interfere with the drop, and you are not to fire on it. Is that clear?'

'Yeah, I get it Hermes.'

'Right, please get your team prepared. I will call you on this number five minutes before we arrive. We will also have Channel 9 on VHF dialled up, but I suggest we only use it for emergencies. I assume you don't want other people to hear any of our conversations.'

'I agree. Speak to you in about 40 minutes.'

Chapter 81.
November 21st, Hobyo, Somalia

Abdi was standing on the bridge wing of the Hibernia III looking down in-front of the superstructure with the long hull stretched out away from him. Below him, under the watchful eye of eight of the Somali guards and managed by Hassan, 23 members of the ship's crew were all standing in a long straight line. The three who had been taken out to sit in a skiff the day before to make sure no funny business occurred, were looking very relieved. It was almost a party atmosphere down there for the crew and pirates alike. Other than the rehearsal, it was the first opportunity in a long time that the crew had been allowed on deck. Abdi had worried that some would be foolish and jump over the side, but he needn't have. They all knew that today a ransom would be paid, and so they would do their part.

There was one problem. Szymon the first officer was seriously unwell. Too unwell to go outside and stand under the morning sun. His ribs had a monstrous infection that the antibiotics that he had been given just were not touching. The doctor had been back to visit several times, especially when Szymon's breathing had become shallow, he didn't have the right drugs to touch this problem whatever it was. As a result, Szymon was up on the bridge, on a mattress on the floor. In order to make up the numbers on deck, Abdi was going to bluff. He had one of his guards' dress in the white shirt and black trousers uniform of the crew and he would stand out there on the deck, making the numbers correct at 24 for the fly by.

Abdi was feeling really nervous. Firstly, there was that infidel boat, standing off about three miles away. It was just sitting there ominously. The men and women on that boat had to have balls of steel to come and do what they were doing he thought. Abdi felt that it must be packed full of heavily armed and experienced fighters. He didn't know it, but he was wrong about that. He would have laughed though if he knew there were only 3 ex-military onboard, and one very mean Columbian. The thing that made him really nervous was that today was payday. Would he actually get the money? Would anyone try to interfere? Would someone try to double cross him? He just didn't know. The pressure was building, and it was making him sweat.

The phone on the Bridge rang. He walked back inside and picked it up.

'Abdi, its Hermes. Just to let you know, we are five minutes out. Are the crew all on deck and lined up clearly?'

'Yes, they are.'

'Good. Remind your men. We are going to come really close and low level. If they fire on us, we are gone.'

'I will tell them. See you in a minute. I have channel 9 on as well.' Abdi hung up the phone and then picked up the handset for the ship's intercom. He selected main deck on the switch board and blew into it. He heard a reassuring noise from the speaker just in front of the Bridge. Speaking in Somali he said 'Listen very carefully. The infidel airplane is coming now. It will come low, it will be near, it will be loud. You are not to fire on it. I tell you again. You are not to fire on it, or I will slit you bellies and throw you overboard to the sharks.' Switching to English he said. 'Captain Oleksiy. Tell your men to stand still as we discussed. The plane is coming. They need to count you now.' Abdi switched off the device and moved out to the bridge wing. He didn't know which way the plane was coming from, so he kept moving his head around. His eyes were searching in the clear blue sky whilst his mind was thinking about that rescue ship, that was obviously and malevolently watching him.

Chapter 82.
November 21st, The Sea Dragon, The Indian Ocean

Chris was standing on the Bridge of the Sea Dragon watching the Hibernia III through his high-powered maritime binoculars. With him were Bob, Miguel and Omondi. They were all in their full body armour and helmets and were carrying their weapons loosely slung over their shoulders. Captain Jammo was stressed, flitting between being outside and looking at the skiffs on the water, or stepping back on to the bridge and standing fussing over the radar operator. He wanted those skiffs to stay right where they were, and he was perspiring heavily.

The Sea Dragon was standing off only two miles away from the Hibernia III, a mere 5 minutes for one of those skiffs at top speed. Sea Dragon's engines were idling, just maintaining her position. Whilst Chris needed his binoculars to get a really clear picture, he could see much with his naked eye especially the 300-meter-long bulk of the super tanker. Slightly nearer in the water, Chris could see 4 stationary skiffs, pale grey rectangular shapes, low in the water, against a blue sea. There were two at the stern and two at the bow, just as they had been told to be.

Tom had checked in about ten minutes ago saying they were on the final run in, and Chris had briefed him to say he could see the hostages on the main deck of the Hibernia III. He had also told Tom that he could see a lot of armed pirates as well. The final bit of detail that Chris had discussed was the weather. It was a clear day, there was little swell, and the sky was an idyllic blue. The wind was negligible, and it was a perfect day for a drop.

Chapter 83.
November 21st, The Citation, Hobyo

The Citation had descended fairly rapidly from 33,000 feet down to 500 feet above the sea. The view out of the side windows was a little unnerving for Tom, who was convinced at one point that Charly wouldn't pull out of the dive fast enough. She had however bled the speed back well and was now flying at 120 knots, well above the 86-knot stall speed.

'You are having fun back there?' Charly called over the intercom.

'Are we having fun? Don't you mean are you having fun?' said Mike with a laugh. He wasn't even remotely phased by low level flight even with the gentle swell rushing past at about 140 miles per hour.

'Oh yes, I am definitely having fun. Look out at that lovely water!'. Charly waggled the wings, dipping them briefly so that the men could almost look directly down into the sea.

'Great!' said Raj deadpan as he recovered his balance. 'The accident investigators will get to this crash site and ask, 'Where the fuck did all this cash come from!''

Charly laughed and said, 'If you hadn't guessed we are now five minutes out. Time to earn your pay!'

Tom got onto the Sat-phone and dialled Abdi, who picked up after just the one ring. 'Abdi it's Hermes. We are five minutes out and are starting our run. We will pass down your port side at low level approaching from the stern. Can you confirm that all the crew are on deck and separated so we can count them?'

Abdi, lying because Szymon was lying down on the Bridge floor beside him said, 'Yes all the crew are on deck.'

Tom replied, 'Roger that. Make sure they are all facing the aircraft as we pass. Starting our run now.' He then called forward to Charly and said, 'Good to go!'

Charly acknowledged and then as the handling pilot gently lowered the aircraft to 150 feet above the sea. Glittering waves flashed past the cockpit windows so close that JP the co-pilot sitting next to her thought he could almost reach out and touch them. It had been a long time since he had flown a Tornado low level and feeling a touch nervous, he flexed his fingers and placed his hands on his knees near the controls.

Charly noticed and said, 'JP, do you want to fly this bit? You are going to be closest to the ship and its better for you to do the visual pass.'

Delighted, JP said, 'Yes. Sure. I will maintain the passing distance if you want to double check me on maintaining our height.' With that he placed his hands gently on the control column and his feet on the pedals and said, 'I have control.'

'You have control.' replied Charly as she took her hands and feet off the controls. Seeing the bulk of the Hibernia III now approaching on the starboard side she called back, 'One minute out! We are at 150 feet above the sea and will pass the ship about 300 feet away on our starboard side.'

In the back of the aircraft Tom was operating the high-definition external video camera using a screen that was resting on the table in front of him and a control box in his lap whilst sitting in his executive seat. He double checked to make sure it was recording. Raj was sitting by one of the rear windows, looking forward and in his hands was a high-quality digital camera. Mike was sitting opposite Tom holding a folder which had photos of all of the faces of the crew members so that they could confirm the proof of life.

Tom had slaved the digital video camera forward and had it locked onto the ship. He played briefly with the zoom so the system could auto focus, and he adjusted the panning mode so that he could move the camera as they approached. Everything was moving very quickly now.

'Coming abeam!' called Charly from the front as she looked past JP through the cockpit window on her right to the Hibernia III.

Raj could make out the stern of the ship now and he brought the backup camera to his eye. He let the autofocus adjust for the difficulty of shooting through the aircraft's round passenger window. There were still some traces of condensation from the rapid descent of a cold aircraft into the hot humid air, but it was clear enough for what he needed. He held his finger down on the button and started to take bursts of photos.

Tom had the best view. The digital video was simply impressive. Stabilised, crystal clear, he was nearly guilty of being zoomed in too far and had to adjust as he realised. Time slowed down a little as Tom watched intently. The white superstructure of the ship was filling the screen one moment and the next he was seeing a line of crew members all standing on the deck. He adjusted the camera and as JP kept the aircraft perfectly straight and level Tom could see the hopeful looking facial expressions of the crew flash past on his screen. Just seconds later they were past the ship and JP pulled the aircraft back up to 500 feet before starting a slow right-hand orbit.

Chapter 84.
November 21st, The Citation, Hobyo

'How did you do Raj?' asked Tom.

'I think I got some good shots. I basically held the shutter down for about five seconds. As long as the focus held, we should be good. What about you?'

'I think I got what we need but let's play it back now.' Tom turned the screen so that both Mike and Raj could see the replay. Tom froze the video as the first face came clear and he used the digital zoom control to adjust the image on the screen.

'That's the Captain.' said Mike pointing a finger to the photograph of Captain Oleksiy in the folder in front of him.

'Agreed and I would say that's 100%.' said Tom. 'Let's mark him as alive.'

Mike used a pencil and made a small tick mark next to the Captains photo and circled it as well to show that they were 100 percent certain. Meanwhile Tom played the next couple of frames until they came to the best focused shot of the next man in the line.

The team spent the next five minutes working efficiently ticking off the men that they could confirm as present and marking with a question mark if they were not 100% sure of the identity. Many had grown facial hair which made identification difficult. All the time that it took for them to work the Citation was in a gentle right-hand turn above the ship. They got about three quarters of the way through the video when the next face to be shown was obviously a Somali albeit wearing a ship uniform of white shirt and black trousers.

'Fuck. That's not a crew member.' said Raj.

'Agreed.' said Tom. 'Let's park that and come back to it after we have checked the rest of the crew.'

The remaining 4 crew members were quickly marked off and a final check of the uncertain ones showed that there was a sufficient match to say that 23 of the 24 crew members were on the deck and alive. The Somali being number 24 was a problem.

Tom took a moment to think and then spoke to Charly and JP. 'Guys, we have a problem with the POL. One person is missing. I am going to get on the phone to Abdi and ask him what the hell is going on. Can you keep the orbit?'

Charly came back to him. 'Sure, we can do a few more. Don't let them mess you around too much. We have a small fuel margin, but only about twenty minutes or so play time in total.'

'Roger that. How about you reposition downwind and prepare for another run. If this joker has killed a crew member, then the drop may be off anyway. If he has got him alive then we will need to get a photo and we will be in the right place.'

'Wilco.' said JP.

Tom picked up the Sat- phone and pressed speed dial 2. For some reason though the call didn't go through. He tried again. Still no joy and the phone screen now showed loss of acquisition of satellites. Cursing the comms, he put his headset on and asked Charly to patch him through to maritime channel 9.

'Abdi this is Hermes on Channel 9 over.' a hiss of static, a pause and then Tom repeated himself. 'Abdi this is Hermes on Channel 9 over.' A pause again with no reply until Chris who was also monitoring channel 9 came up.

'Hermes this is Sea Dragon. I hear you. Strength five. Out'

Tom internally thanked Chris for confirming that these comms were working. He just needed Abdi to reply now and he repeated. 'Abdi this is Hermes on Channel 9 over.'

'This is Abdi. What's the problem?'

Relieved about the comms but irritated about the situation Tom replied, 'The problem Abdi is that you didn't put all of the crew on the deck.'

'Yes, I did. You had all 24 of them.'

Keeping his temper Tom replied. 'Abdi time is short. I have a great picture of one of your Somali friends standing on the deck where I was expecting to see the ships First Officer. Tell me where he is, or I take this aircraft home and give the money back to the bank.'

There was a pause whilst internally Abdi swore to himself. How could the infidel know that he had done a switch? Was their technology that good? Abdi looked over at Szymon who was lying on the floor of the bridge and then shouted across to him. 'Szymon tell the man on the radio that you are OK!'

Szymon came out of his painful trance, took an agonizing deep breath, and then shouted whilst Abdi pressed the send button on the radio. 'This is Szymon. I am ok! I am hurt, but ok.'

Back on the aircraft Tom heard what had been said but wasn't having any of it despite the obvious Slavic accent. 'Not good enough

Abdi. I am going to do one more run. If I don't see the first officer and confirm that he's alive then we are leaving.'

There was a little panic in Abdi's voice now. 'OK! OK! Listen he is hurt, but he is alive. We didn't want to move him too much because he is not well!'

Tom, with complete authority in his voice said, 'Abdi. Get him onto the bridge wing on the ships port side and do it immediately. We will do another pass and I want to see his face clearly. Do you understand?'

'Alright! He will be there just now. I will support him!' Abdi went across to Szymon and manhandled him to a standing position prompting a cry of pain. Abdi was beyond caring though and dragged him out to the bridge wing propping him up against the rail at the far end near the hole in the floor that was the toilet.

On the aircraft JP had heard the radio conversation and called. 'Starting the next run, two minutes out!'

Raj picked up his camera and got ready for the next pass. Tom prepared the video recording kit again and in only moments they were back alongside the ship just over a hundred feet above the sea.

This pass was much easier. With only one face to capture, Tom slaved the camera forward and held it for the whole pass. Clear as daylight almost level with the aircraft was Szymon leaning up against the rail on the bridgewing. Pain obviously showing on his face as he was supported by a young Somali male.

Tom said over the maritime radio. 'OK that's good enough for me Abdi. Give me five minutes and then I will give you further instructions.'

As the aircraft pulled up, the team watching the screen saw the Somali head back into the bridge and then a few seconds later was the reply over the radio. 'OK, I understand.'

Tom removed his headset and spoke to Mike and Raj. 'Well, I would say that we have a 100% confirmation of proof of life. Do you both agree?'

Raj said 'Yes I agree. And I would add that we have 100% certainty of having a video recording of the head pirate too.'

Mike shook his head, half closing his eyes and said 'Yes. The muppet.'

Tom nodded. 'Do you know what? I think on one of the next runs we should take images of all of the pirates onboard that ship, as well as the ones in the skiffs if we can. You never know how useful that might be in the future.'

The men all grinned at each other as the Citation pulled gently back up to 500 hundred feet and turned downwind.

Chapter 85.
November 21st, Athens, Greece

Around the boardroom table of The Aphrodite Freight and Shipping Company sat Mr Papadopoulos, Max, Finlay, John, and Chloe.

There was now a buffet breakfast in warmed chafing dishes on a sideboard that had been left pretty much untouched. Nervous stomachs were not hungry, but coffee was being drunk by the litre.

The big screens still showed the locations of the assets though the refresh rate of the satellite-based system was only every five minutes. Max had added permanent tags to them as well now which showed their heading, speed, and height so they could see an almost jerky, slightly delayed picture of what was happening.

It was clear that the Citation had been over or near the same spot for the past fifteen minutes and as Max had briefed, they were expecting a call at any moment. The room was tense with waiting and there wasn't a lot happening. In the centre of the table was a VOIP spider phone. It had been still and silent for what seemed like an eternity. Max reflected that it didn't matter how many times he looked at it, it wasn't going to make it ring.

Five more minutes passed with staccato awkward chit chat before the spider phone shrilly broke into the room. Max leaned forward and pressed the speaker button.

In a clear voice, that belied the phenomenal distance between them, but spoke volumes of the power of digital satellite communications Tom spoke first. 'Boss, its Hermes.'

Max, understanding the need to not use names over clear comms said, 'Go ahead Hermes, you are on speaker to the main board room.'

'Understood. We have proof of life and I request permission to make the drop.'

Mr Papadopoulos answered in his thick Greek accent. 'Are you sure my crew are all ok?'

Tom replied, 'Well sir, I guarantee that as of five minutes ago the whole crew is alive. I do believe though that the first officer is very unwell. There was a bit of an issue during the proof of life run, but I won't go into that now as we are low on fuel. May I deliver the ransom?'

Mr Papadopoulos looked around the room, especially at Chloe, the insurers lawyer and Finlay the response consultant.

Chloe spoke first. 'As an authorised delegate of my company, I approve the delivery of ransom for the humanitarian release of hostages.'

Finlay was less formal and said, 'I agree.'

Max was there placid faced; this one wasn't his decision.

Mr Papadopoulos spoke loudly enough to make sure that Tom could hear, 'Go ahead, deliver the ransom and good luck. Please let us know as soon as it is done.'

'Will do, I will call you back within the next half hour. Hermes out.'

John, who hadn't said a word so far, grinned to himself. So far so good.

Chapter 86.
November 21st, The Citation, Hobyo

Tom hung up the phone and called out loudly enough so that the whole crew could hear. 'We have approval to drop! Let's set up on the approach run.'

'Roger that.' replied Charly as she did the spatial awareness calculations to work out how far out, she wanted to be to line up for the first drop run. JP had already started a gentle turn and had maintained a height of 500 feet. She approved of the line that he was taking.

Tom, broadcasting on the VHF radio on channel 9, knowing that Chris would hear the call as well called, 'Abdi, this is Hermes, over.'

He didn't have to call again before he heard Abdi calling back. 'Yes Hermes, this is Abdi.'

'Abdi, we are starting our approach to deliver the first 2 packages. I remind you that if any shots are fired, we will vacate the area. I also remind you that your skiffs should not try to catch the loads. Let them land in the water.'

Relief flooding his voice Abdi replied, 'Yes! Yes we understand. You may begin.'

'Ok, we are five minutes out.'

There was a double click of static which Tom took to mean that Chris was acknowledging discretely too by depressing his transmit button twice briefly.

In the back of the aircraft Mike was on his knees ready to unbolt the floor panel. 'Charly, can I remove the floor panel?' he cried.

Charly had a quick look to make sure that the cabin pressure was equalised with the external pressure and called 'Affirm.'

Mike using the electric screwdriver with an Allen key type fitting on the end promptly removed the four screws before storing them safely in a seat pocket behind him. He lifted the panel and now he could see the thin metal door on the exterior of the aircraft.

Raj came and joined him and between them they made sure that the tubes were lined up and ready to go. They double checked that the static lines were attached to the D-rings embedded in the floor and that the parachutes were still attached to the tubes. Double check, and double check again.

'Two minutes out, opening the rear door. Are you ready Mike?' called Charly.

'Two minutes out! Good to go!' he called. As he grinned at Raj the mechanical external door opened in a roar of air and revealing the glittering sea flashing by below.

Chapter 87.
November 21st, The Citation, Hobyo

From his seat on the starboard side, JP could see the approaching super tanker through his window. The Hibernia III was gentling in a calm sea of blue. Ahead, under the aircraft nose JP saw the first pair of skiffs, bobbing in the water, the people in them craning their necks up to see the aircraft pass overhead. He checked his instruments and called out '500 feet, 100 knots, ten seconds!'

Lots of things happened at once. Mike who was kneeling at the back with one knee either side of the hole in the floor called back 'Ten seconds!' He reached to his right and lifted up the first tube holding it between his knees above the drop hole.

Tom, who was in his seat with the external video camera recording the action, had been filming the vessel and trying to get images of the pirates. He only had a few seconds before he slaved the camera to the rear ready to record the release.

JP who was judging for the slight head wind waited until the aircraft was approximately halfway along the length of the Hibernia III before calling, 'Three, two, one. Drop! Drop! Drop!'

Mike called 'Dropping now!' as he eased the tube down into the hole and then he released it. It dropped rapidly as the wind caught it causing the static line to snap tight immediately and pull the canopy out of the rapidly falling package. The tube disappeared out of Mikes view behind the aircraft. He reached to his left, picked up another tube, with the assistance of Raj who was right beside him and then he lowered that through the hole as well. The process took less than three seconds. The only evidence was two static lines that were dangling out of the hole flapping in the slip stream. Mike quickly pulled on them to get the loose ends back inside the aircraft.

Tom called out. 'Canopy 1, good deployment!' then a slight pause, 'Canopy 2, good deployment!'

Mike and Raj turned around to look at the screen on the table behind them. Tom had a perfect image, two tubes dangling beneath their bright orange canopies gracefully gliding down to the water. Even as they watched, in the distance the rear most skiffs, blurry on the screen, gunned their engines to move up the length of the ship. JP started a gradual right-hand turn, ready to turn downwind for the final run.

Raj looked out of the starboard window and got a good view of the two loads as they floated down on orange canopies beside the super tanker. He called 'Five bucks says one of them cracks on impact! Any takers?'

Mike replied, 'I'll take that bet you bonehead.'

They both stared at the falling loads while Tom rolled his eyes but kept recording. As the first tube hit the water about 300 feet off the port bow of the Hibernia III it was more of a plop, than a splash. The tube entered the water cleanly, went under and then like an emerging black seal, bobbed back to the surface where it lay horizontal on the water. The first skiff was right there beside it as it did so and had nearly run over it in its eagerness to get there.

Tom zoomed in on the video camera and was watching a pirate in that skiff leaning over into the water. The pirate grabbed the lines of the canopy which were billowing in the water like some kind of giant orange jellyfish. The pirate pulled on the lines for what seemed to be an age before the tube itself responded to the effort. He needed help from his fellow crew member to pull the tube up out of the water and into the skiff. Tom called out, 'First tube captured and looks good!'

Tom panned the camera across to the other tube which was just being collected by the second skiff. With their loads secure the two skiffs revved their engines and started to head straight for the gantry ladder on the port side of the Hibernia III. Tom used the spare time to zoom right onto their faces getting perfect images. The aircraft was rapidly heading down wind by now and JP called again. 'Two minutes out!'

Mike who had seen where the two loads landed was pulled out of his observations. He jumped up to go to the drop hole again and replied, 'Two minutes out. Let's see if we can land them a hundred meters shorter this time. I don't think there was as much drift as we thought.'

JP replied, 'Roger that.' as he turned the aircraft around to line up for the next drop run.

Chapter 88.
November 21st, Hobyo, Somalia

Abdi's heart was racing as he was thinking that so many of his dreams were coming true today. Allah was throwing him blessings from the sky. He was standing looking up at the circling plane far away behind him as it turned to prepare for its next run. He looked down at the two skiffs that were pulling up at the gantry ladder, that had been lowered down to the water level. He cast a glance forward and saw that all the ship's crew, and most of his guards were leaning up against the side rail, watching the action unfold. He scowled deeply. He wasn't happy that Hassan had taken his eye off the ball and allowed the guards and crew to mingle so freely. 'Hassan!' he shouted. 'What are you doing? This isn't a fucking party! Get the hostages under control.'

Hassan looked up and then back at the confused mingle of bodies around him and he started barking orders. The crew were led back inside to the canteen area much to their disappointment, by very sheepish looking guards.

As Zahi approached in the lead skiff there was a large grin on his face. 'Abdi! What do you think?' he called whilst pointing at the tube with the parachute still attached. 'It's very heavy!'

'Well bring it up here Zahi, let's see if its full of concrete!' Abdi's scowl disappeared and was replaced by a smile.

Zahi stood at the front of the skiff and passed the parachute to two of the Somali guards who were standing at the foot of the gantry. When they had a firm grip, he passed the tube across and told them to carry it up to the Bridge. As the two young guards wetly struggled their way up the stairs carrying the heavy load, they paused a moment because the canopy got tangled in their legs. Zahi gathered the soaking wet bright orange parachute and followed them up the stairs like a bridesmaid following a garishly dressed bride. As the first skiff pulled away to stand off, the second arrived with Tadalesh. He too passed his tube across before following it up to the Bridge. Unseen and in the air above them, the process was captured by Tom on his camera, as the aircraft approached on its final run.

Abdi on the Bridge heard the radio squawk. 'Abdi, this is Hermes. We are starting our second run now.' He stepped inside and acknowledged the call before stepping back out to watch. As he stepped out, he just checked to make sure that there were no other skiffs in the area. The only ship in sight was the Sea Dragon, still stationary about two miles away. Abdi looked up and to his left astern as he heard the jet engines coming. He could see the sleek white shape of the aircraft only a couple of hundred feet above him. He felt he could almost reach out and touch the plane it was so close. As it passed almost directly overhead, he could see the dark hole at the back, almost like the anus of a giant seagull. As it continued, he saw the first package drop, and then moments later the second.

The first was fine, its canopy opening almost immediately, blooming like a flower, and drifting gracefully down. The second though was the one that caught his eye. It popped out of the aircraft, but the canopy didn't open well. There was some kind of twist or loop in one of the strings. Half of the canopy opened, and the other half twisted and fluttered. It didn't drop like a stone, but it fell much more rapidly than the first load and as it fell, it started to spin. It didn't fall for long and whilst it didn't freefall into the sea it smacked in at such a rate and with such a splash that Abdi winced.

The remaining two skiffs were already moving in to collect the loads. Again, the first was easy and was collected quickly. The second load was in a sorry state. It had landed only a hundred meters or so away from Abdi and he could see that it was damaged as Axmed, the skiff Captain dragged it carefully out of the water. The hard outer shell had obviously cracked but it hadn't fallen completely apart. Abdi could see some bright yellow material inside the device, but he wasn't sure what that meant. Knowing he was watching, Axmed looked up and shouted across the water. 'I think it's OK!' Abdi waved an arm in acknowledgement and turned to go back into the Bridge, just as the loads from the first drops were brought in with dripping wet canopies leaking onto the floor.

Chapter 89.
November 21st, The Citation, over the Indian Ocean

Mike was busy putting the floor plate back on above the drop hole. Charly had already closed the external door and with a final couple of twists of the electric screwdriver the plate was back in place. He and Raj then replaced the carpet over the top before sitting down next to Tom to watch the rest of the show on the monitor.

Tom was currently monitoring the last two loads as they were being transferred onto the gantry ladder and as the second load was moved across, he tried to zoom in as much as possible. 'It looks like the tube cracked, but that the bags kept their integrity. What do you think?'

Quick as a flash Raj piped up, 'I think Mike needs to go back to parachute packing school.'

'What the! That was just bad luck!' said Mike. 'Anyway, you helped me rig the parachute you dick.'

Delighted that he had got Mike to rise so easily Raj continued, laughing. 'Ah, but you owe me 5 bucks my friend.'

'What?'

'You took the bet.' Raj continued. 'If I remember correctly, I said, five bucks that one of them cracks on impact. You accepted the bet and called me a rude word.'

Mike scowled as Raj kept going. 'Then one of them cracked, nearly sending about one and a half million dollars to the bottom of the ocean. So, you owe me five bucks because you are a loser!'

Tom was laughing and then Charly called over the intercom. 'Tom have you got what you need? I think we need to head on home as we are getting close to minimum fuel.'

Tom looked at the screen and saw the final two loads being carried up onto the deck. He called back. 'Thanks Charly. We are good to go. We have proof that the money is onboard the Hibernia III.' He paused and then added for Mike's benefit, 'Just.'

Raj started laughing again.

Charly called back, 'OK, beginning the climb and heading home. It should take just over two hours.'

Tom putting the banter aside called Abdi on the sat phone. 'Abdi, its Hermes. That is the drops complete. I see you now have all four packages on the Hibernia III.'

'Yes Hermes, we do. I was a little worried about the last one?'

'So was I, but sometimes it can't be helped. We made sure that the internal packaging would have kept the money safe for exactly that kind of contingency. I am sure when you open it up all will be fine.'

'I hope so.' Said Abdi.

'To open them, your best method would be to use a hacksaw blade and cut through the tube about 5 centimetres away from either end. Do not cut into the middle of the tubes or you risk cutting the money.'

'OK.'

'We are leaving the area now. As per our agreement, you have 4 hours to confirm the amount of money and to leave the ship. My colleague in the Sea Dragon will now be monitoring Channel 9 and will move in at that time.' There was just enough of an edge to Tom's voice on the word 'will' to ensure that Abdi understood.

'I understand. I will speak to him on the radio when we disembark. Goodbye Hermes.'

Tom thought for a moment whether he should reply and decided against it. He hung up on Abdi without another word.

Mike and Raj were still bickering about the bet, but Tom zoned out and called Chris on the sat phone.

'Chris it's Tom.'

'Hey Tom, looks like that went as well as we could wish?'

'Yes, it was a little close on one of the loads. We nearly had an awfully expensive canopy failure, but I have proof of delivery, so I will hand over local command to you now. I have informed Abdi that he has 4 hours to vacate, and he agreed. If there are any issues, he will call you on Channel 9, but I was reasonably firm with him and I think he gets it.'

'Roger that. Safe trip back.'

'And to you. Good luck with the boarding. Stay safe.' Tom hung up.

Tom had one more call to make, and he was looking forward to this one. As he pressed the dial button, he could still hear Raj in the background.

'You know Mike, we should do this more often. More runs like that and I will be a rich man!'

Chapter 90.
November 21st, Athens, Greece

The situation around the table hadn't improved much over the past 30 minutes. No one had eaten anything, and nerves were frayed. The screens just showed the dots of the locations of the Citation and the Sea Dragon. It wasn't anything like the movies, or the military, with real time video footage. The leaders just had to let the operators get on with their jobs. Trust to their skill sets and their ability to use their initiative if anything went wrong.

John had drunk too much coffee and had been to the loo twice in half an hour. Chloe was fretting, with her reputation on the line with her employer for approving the use of a new method for delivery. Mr Papadopoulos wanted this all to be over and as soon as possible and for his staff to be safe. Finlay had been to the smoking room and chain smoked what must have been most of a packet of Camels in the space of fifteen minutes. Max, of all of them, was the most sanguine about the whole thing.

Finally, the spider phone rang, and Tom's voice came through. 'Boss it's me. Good news.'

'Great, well done. What can you tell us?' Max asked as smiles began to appear around the table.

'We have confirmation of all four loads on deck and can guarantee delivery of the quantum. I have confirmed with Abdi that he knows he has 4 hours to verify the count and vacate the Hibernia III and I have transferred local command to the Sea Dragon.'

Mr Papadopoulos spoke up. 'Excellent, I am pleased. Do you think they will leave the ship like they promised?'

Tom replied, 'The simple answer is that I don't know. It sounded like they intended to when I spoke to them. Whether they will do it in the agreed timeframe? Again, I don't know the answer.'

Max cut in addressing the Greek shipping magnate directly. 'We have agreed an escalation method using Sea Dragon if we have to. A little psychological pressure if needed, but that's a last resort.'

'OK, so now we have 4 hours, perhaps more, whilst we wait for them to count the money and leave the ship?'

'Yes, that's correct sir. Sea Dragon will keep you informed from now on as they have eyes on. We are now heading back to Nairobi.'

'Well in that case, thank you for your work. I know it wasn't easy and I appreciate what you have done.'

'Thank you, sir.' Tom paused. 'Boss, by the way. I have some good video footage of the whole delivery, which I will try to edit now and send you some of the highlights when we land.'

Max replied. 'Great, thank you. Let's chat later then.' He pressed the end call button on the spider phone and then spoke to the room at large.

'Well, that's the first phase complete. Let's give them some time and then we can see how it goes. Mr Papadopoulos, this next wait is also going to be stressful. I suggest we pause, have some breakfast and then we reconvene and go over the plans for the arrival of the ship in Mombasa, if all goes well.'

'That is a good idea.' said Mr Papadopoulos. 'All of a sudden the smell of that bacon is making me very hungry. I think I will hold off on any more coffee for now though.'

Chapter 91.
November 21st, Hobyo, Somalia

There was huge excitement on the bridge of the Hibernia III. Stacked on the floor, with soaking wet parachutes still attached, were four black tubes. A water stain was growing, as it seeped into the pale grey nylon carpet.

Zahi and Tadalesh were standing over the tubes and on the floor and beside them was a canvas tool bag, that they had pinched from the engine room. Yusuf had locked the bridge door to keep out any unwanted visitors and Abdi was giving direction. 'Let's start with the broken one.' he said.

Zahi and Tadalesh separated out the broken one from the stack and with a knife Zahi cut through parachute cords. He then dumped the canopy in a corner of the room, out of the way. The crack was extensive and a piece of what they could now see looked like a piece of extremely thick nylon pipe had sheared away leaving a yellow rubberised waterproof bag exposed.

Whilst Tadalesh held the tube steady on the floor, Zahi picked up a long hack saw blade and proceeded to cut through the tube as Abdi directed, about five centimetres down from the nose cap. After only a few minutes the nose cap fell away revealing one of the polystyrene plugs. Using a set of pliers and a screwdriver he levered out the plug to reveal the yellow bag within. With everyone crowding around, Zahi stuck in his arm and pulled out a yellow dry bag by the buckle that had been cable tied. It was heavy, but as he pulled it clear there were very obvious brick like shapes within.

He used the knife to cut the cable tie, undid the fastening and unrolled the bag. He opened it and peered in looking hopeful. With everyone watching him on tenterhooks he swore. 'Fuck!'

Worried and not being able to see Abdi asked, 'What? What is wrong?'

Without answering Zahi reached into the bag and with some effort pulled out another yellow dry bag, cable tied just like the first.

He repeated the process of unlocking it and this time after he peered in, he looked up at Abdi. With their eyes locked, Zahi tipped the bag upside down and out tumbled brick after brick of cash. They hit the floor with a thump, a hundred thousand dollars at a time, wrapped in cling film. The smell of money started to seep through the room as, to a man, they jumped for joy, shouted, exclaimed, and swore.

Whilst Tadalesh, and even the old and unexcitable Yuusuf were dancing around the room, Abdi bent down to pick one of the bricks up off the floor. 'Allah be praised!' As he unwrapped the film the ten bundles of ten thousand dollars each came loose. Even though he dropped one in his excitement he opened them up like a fan, showing his men what they had. 'Hundred-dollar bills!'

Abdi picked up the bundle that had fallen on the floor and walked over to the map table where he had set up three cash counting machines that morning. He had hired them from the local bank branch for an exorbitant sum, but they were all ready to go.

Abdi stacked the cash into a counter and ran it through the machine. He tried it a couple of times before he got it to work effectively and then finally got it to count to a thousand. 'Excellent! That bundle is 100,000 dollars! Let's open all the tubes and count everything first. Then, we shall use the machines to count the shares out for you and the guards.'

Zahi said, 'Let's put all the uncounted bundles on the left-hand side of the table, on the floor. All the counted money then goes onto the right-hand side. Tadalesh, stop your dancing and come here and help me!'

Tadalesh grinned and picked up the next tube from the pile, whilst Abdi started to unwrap the next bundle.

Chapter 92.
November 21st, Hobyo, Somalia

It had taken a couple of hours but Abdi, Tadalesh and Zahi had finished not only the count, but also the allocation of cash into lots, ready to pay the guards. The piles had been sorted and placed on the map table and the cash counters had been removed. All of the cash that wasn't being dished out now was packed into a couple of very large holdalls, back in its bundles of 100K. Abdi had hidden them for now behind the large pile of rubbish of dismantled tubes and damp parachutes.

On the left-hand side of the table was the largest bundle. One hundred and fifty thousand dollars. Some of the initial party atmosphere had faded, but it gave Abdi great pleasure to call his team up and reward them. 'Zahi, you are first!' Zahi stepped up to the table as Abdi continued. 'For being the first man up the ladder, for commanding your skiff so well, for organising and supporting me during this long and difficult project I give you this. You are now a rich man!'

Zahi held out his hands as Abdi put the brick and a half of money into them. 'Abdi, thank you for having the vision to make this happen. May Allah bless you and watch over you.' With watering eyes Zahi leant into Abdi and gave him a hug. Whilst it was made awkward by holding onto the bundle of cash that wedged between them, when they looked into each other's eyes, there was an understanding that they had achieved something great.

'Yuusuf, old man! You are next!' said Abdi quickly trying to hide the fact that his voice was cracking slightly. Yuusuf stepped up.

'Abdi, if you think I am going to go all mushy and squeeze you like a young woman then think again!' Yuusuf cackled showing his brown, rotting teeth.

'That's OK old man. Here you have earned this, and I hope you get to spend it all in your retirement.' Abdi handed over a hundred thousand dollars.

'Thank you, Abdi. All I have to worry about now is how much of this my family are going to demand from me!'

Half laughing, but also knowing that it was perfectly true, Abdi nodded. 'And finally, Tadalesh, this is for you.' Abdi handed over another hundred thousand.

Tadalesh looked a little stunned. To have such wealth in his hands in this life had never even crossed his mind. He stammered slightly as he said, 'Abdi thank you. I don't know what to say.'

'That's OK, you have earned it. You are one of the bravest men I know, but you must be careful with this money. Invest it, buy land, buy a pretty wife!'

Tadalesh was very embarrassed and not knowing what to do leaned in awkwardly giving Abdi a half embrace, before stepping away.

Abdi continued. 'Now my friends I will ask this of you. I would like you to make sure that your friends know that you have been well rewarded. But do not tell them how much this ransom was, nor exactly how much you have been given. Much of what you have seen me put in that bag,' Abdi pointed, 'is now going to be paid as blood money, to the families of those who lost men on my boats at sea. I have to pay the khat suppliers, the food vendors and a large sum must go to the man, who lent us the money to buy the original boats. Some of what is left will go to the elders of Hobyo to help develop the city, and yes, there will be some left for me.'

'Good, you have earned it.' said Zahi.

Abdi nodded and continued. 'This next bit is important. I intend now to buy more boats and send more crews out. I want to do this again, and again. My vision is to make Hobyo a place of wealth, a place where men want to come to work. I hope that you will want to continue your journey with me?'

Tadalesh was nodding furiously, but it was Yuusuf who spoke first.

'Abdi, you said it yourself. I am an old man. I am also your man. I don't want to go out to sea again, my bones hurt too much. I will happily help you in the future though, if you need help managing a ship when it is taken.'

'Thank you Yuusuf, I understand. I see you are saying yes Tadalesh. That is good news. I want you as a captain in the future. What about you Zahi? Do you remember what we discussed?'

'Yes Abdi, I will work for you. I will train your crews and manage your boats. I will help you make Hobyo prosperous and the place to be on the whole of the Somali coast, if Allah wills it.'

'Excellent! I am delighted to hear that. Now! Shall we pay the rest of the crew and hand this oversized bathtub back to the Captain!'

Over the next twenty minutes, man by man, the guards came up to the bridge. They were given 3000 dollars each, and there was an extra 3000 for Zahi's brother Hassan, who had worked as the guard commander. Except for a couple of men who kept the crew under guard, as each man was paid, they went down the gantry ladder to the awaiting skiffs, which then carried them back to the shore. Their voices were alive and excited by their new wealth as they sped away.

Chapter 93.
November 21st, The Sea Dragon, The Indian Ocean

The galley area below decks on the Sea Dragon was a simple affair. The tiny kitchen, always hot and stuffy and where the chef worked tirelessly was to one side. In a space not that much larger, there was a chipped white Formica table in the middle of a seating booth with worn and faded upholstery. There was a tall, battered, old, branded beer fridge in one corner filled with bottled water and soft drinks, and a standalone hot drinks machine in another. Finally, there was a single table onto which the chef laid his food when serving it. A snack of some kind was always available.

Chris was sitting in the booth having some lunch and a brew, when Miguel came in wearing his body armour and with his L1A1 on a sling over his shoulder. His long black hair was in a ponytail under his Kevlar helmet. As he spoke, he sauntered over to the fridge and grabbed a bottle of water. 'Chris, it looks like the first group of the pirates is leaving.'

Chris looked at his watch. 'Good, the four hours are nearly up. They were cutting it a bit close. Let me just wolf this down and I will come up on deck to take a look.'

Five minutes later Chris was on the Bridge, looking at the Hibernia III. Through his powerful binoculars he could see a small group of skiffs at the base of the gantry ladder. Even as he watched he saw one pull away with a number of guards sitting down holding small bundles of what looked like personal possessions wrapped up in cloth. It also looked like some of the guards were carrying other items pilfered from the ship, as they came down the steps.

Chris said, 'The thieving bastards look like they are looting the ship. Still, at least they are leaving.'

Miguel replied. 'Yes, I bet there isn't a TV left on there.'

Chris snorted his agreement as he picked up his sat phone and sent Max a text message. 'The opposition have just started to leave.'

A moment later he got the reply, 'Good, feel free to apply a little pressure if you wish.'

Chris thought for a moment before calling. 'Captain. If you would be so kind. In fifteen minutes, I would like you to take us closer in and then hold at 500 meters out.'

Captain Jammo, still rattled by the incident the other day said nervously. 'Mr Chris, really? Why don't we wait for them all to be well clear?'

'Captain, we don't want anyone to get any ideas. What happens if someone else decides to get on board, whilst we are sat out here bobbing around? We shall be quite safe. 500 meters is outside the effective range of the AK47's that they seem to have.'

'OK, OK. We can do this.' the Captain said, almost to himself.

'Indeed we can.' said Chris as he put the binoculars back up to his eyes. 'Miguel, would you go and make sure the others are fed, watered and alert. With any luck we will be boarding in an hour.'

Chapter 94.
November 21st, Hobyo, Somalia

Abdi had just dialled John on the Hibernia III's sat phone. Luckily, John had had the switchboard auto forward the negotiating room number to his mobile phone and he was still sitting in the boardroom when his mobile vibrated on the table. Abdi could hear the muffled tones of John as apologised to whoever was in the room with him.

'Hello, John, is that you? Its Abdi.'

Slightly unprepared and taken aback John replied. 'Um, hello Abdi. Is everything OK?'

'Yes, it's all good. I confirm that I have received the money. Everything that we agreed.'

'Ok, ah, great. How can I help?'

'You can't. I just wanted to say that I am leaving the ship now. We won't speak again.'

John sounding very relieved said, 'Right, well, I am pleased to hear that. I am pleased that you are doing what we agreed.'

'Fine, I just wanted to let you know. I am a businessman. I do what I say.'

Not really understanding the long-term implications of what Abdi was saying John said. 'OK, well goodbye Abdi.'

'Goodbye John.' Abdi hung up and then spoke to Zahi who was the only person left on the Bridge.

'Zahi, would you go and get the Captain for me please. Tell the guards downstairs that we will be leaving in about ten minutes and we will collect them on our way past the canteen.'

'Yeah, OK.' Zahi left the Bridge down the internal stairway.

Whilst Abdi waited, he looked around, staring down the vast distance of the super tanker in front of him for one last time. He reflected that he was leaving a ship with a hundred-million-dollar cargo, but he had come to terms, a while ago now, with the fact that he wouldn't be able to sell it anywhere and wasn't bitter. Perhaps next time we should target cargo containers he thought. Ones full of electrical goods. He pushed that thought from his mind for now, as the Captain came in.

'Captain. It is time.'

'So, you got everything you wanted?'

'Yes. We made an agreement, and your boss has paid us what we asked. I am going to leave the ship now, with my remaining guards.'

The Captain paused before saying 'So I am back in command?'

'When I leave yes. But here is the deal. You are to keep your crew contained in the canteen for one hour after I let you go now. We will get off the ship, and then you may continue. That ship over there,' Abdi pointed at the Sea Dragon, 'has people who will help you.'

The Captain looked at the ship that was holding position a mere five hundred meters away. 'Who are they?'

'Well, they have armed men on board and food and spare parts I believe. They have the ability to tow you if you can't move on your own. That ship was organised by your company.'

The Captain raised an eyebrow. 'Very well. I will give you one hour to leave my ship and then we will meet with those men.' The Captain looked around the bridge, with a critical eye and then it hit him. 'Where are my laptop computers?'

'We have taken them.' said Abdi.

'And where is my Captains Chair?'

'Well Captain. I have taken that too, as a little souvenir.'

The Captain looked at him and a slight look of disgust came across his face. 'I will leave you now. I do not want to meet again.' And with that he turned and went back down to the canteen.'

Abdi smiled, and then with Zahi, picked up the two guards from the canteen and made their way outside, down the gantry ladder. Both Abdi and Zahi were struggling a little carrying two heavy bags. I would be stupid now to drop this in the water Abdi thought as he descended. Having safely navigated his way down and into the last remaining skiff, he settled down onto his wet seat. On one side was Zahi and between them were the bags. Propped up in the bow was the Captain's chair, like some kind of odd figure head on ships of old, it led the way as the skiff pulled out and headed for shore.

Abdi didn't look back. That project was done, and he had won. It was time to look forward.

Chapter 95.
November 21st, The Sea Dragon, The Indian Ocean

From 500 meters away the maritime team watched as the last few pirates came down the gantry carrying a couple of heavy bags, got into a skiff, and powered away. The pirates didn't even look at the Sea Dragon as they headed towards the shore.

Captain Jammo had been having kittens since they had moved closer half an hour ago, pacing back and forth, fretting. At one point even Omondi had asked if he was feeling alright and had tried to help settle him down.

Chris looked at the Captain and said, 'Captain. I believe that is the last of the pirates. I would like us to go alongside if you please.'

Captain Jammo, took visible control of himself, nodded, and spoke to his helmsman. 'Take her in alongside the gantry ladder. Be careful not to damage it.' He then strode across to the tannoy that addressed the open crew area on the deck ahead.

'We are going alongside. The first boarding party will be Mr Chris and his team. Then I want to tie up alongside, just astern of the gantry ladder and use their gantry crane to cross deck the stores, once we have agreed with the Captain of the Hibernia III. I don't know yet if he wants us to pass him any fuel, but you should be ready to.' He looked down and saw a thumbs up from his deck master, who was busy checking the cargo nets on the deck, and the stores that were destined to be cross decked.

Chris turned to Omondi, ignoring the working processes of the ship and the chatter of the radio man trying to raise the Hibernia III, telling them that they were coming alongside.

'Omondi, this is where we leave you. Are you happy?'

Omondi, was very calm and self-assured, 'Sure Chris. All good my side. I will keep a weather eye out up here whilst you all cross deck.'

'Here is the Sat-phone. I will give you a call when we are established. Let's minimise Channel 9 now between you and me, especially now we know that local 'friends' might be listening.'

Leaving Omondi top side to watch the Hibernia III like a hawk, just in case there was some kind of trap or ruse, Chris, Miguel, and Bob went down to the main deck. Their bags were already packed and waiting amongst the loads that would follow them shortly. For now, they needed to get onboard as soon as possible and secure the crew and the ship.

The helmsman on the Sea Dragon brought her in alongside the gantry ladder. Chris looked up at the massive black hull towering above him. Her freeboard was taller than the Sea Dragon main stack and even Omondi two decks above him couldn't see over the rail. Omondi was fully alert, weapon up to his shoulder, prepared for a horde of unseen pirates to suddenly appear. He called down. 'Chris, no reply from the Hibernia III on the radio!'

'Roger that. We will need to do this the old-fashioned way. Miguel, you lead, I will follow. Bob, cover us from here until we reach the top of the ladder, then you come on up.'

Clambering across wasn't as easy as it could have been. Despite the relative shelter from the waves provided by the vast Hibernia III, the vessels were still free floating. The Sea Dragon was using its thrusters to avoid crashing into the gantry ladder, which meant that the helmsman was being a touch over cautious. Miguel couldn't just step over, especially given the differences in height between the deck and the base of the ladder. 'Omondi, we are too far away, I can't jump that!'

'One minute!' Omondi replied before he relayed it to the helm.

Ideally Miguel would just step across, but he could see that that wasn't going to happen. He gauged the movement of the waves, a slow shallow swell, but with a little roll it compounded the distance from the ladder. He had on his body armour, helmet and had his weapon and ammunition. If he missed his step badly, he was going into the water and would drop like a stone. If he cocked it up but managed to cling on, there was the danger of being crushed as the Sea Dragon rolled on the swell.

The Sea Dragon moved in closer. Miguel started to feel his way through the timing of the jump. He was standing in a small space cut out of the rail, one hand on it, one hand stretched out towards the Hibernia III. Salt and spray had made the deck slippery. He bent his knees anticipating the roll, gauging the distance to jump, spotting where his hands would grab when he landed. In towards the behemoth he rolled, then out again by a meter, then in. Next one he thought, and just at the trough of the roll, he leapt! He had milliseconds of wondering if he got it right and then with his hands making first contact about three steps up from the bottom, his feet landed on the grilled step he had been aiming for. A quick breath of relief and he adjusted his weapon, pointed it up the ladder and raced up.

Chris was next. His sea legs were a little better, but he had also seen some horrible accidents during his time, so had a better idea of what could go wrong. He took his decisions quickly. Priming for the jump for only a few moments before he leapt, landing relatively well but grazing the knuckles on one of his hands as he fumbled a grab for a slightly rusty handrail. He recovered and followed Miguel up.

Bob came next, and all went well with his jump until he landed. Having over egged the jump he almost went too far and crashed into the rail on the far side, closest to the hull. His weapon barrel caught on a step resulting in the butt going into his midriff and winding him. Aside from the swear words, he managed to call out that he was OK and would be up in a moment.

As previously planned, the team made their way straight up to the Bridge racing up the internal stairs. To their surprise, the ship was empty. It was an eerie feeling, that they didn't see a soul on their way up to the Bridge. A deep sense of foreboding hit Chris, but he couldn't work it out. They had seen the crew on board during the proof of life and they had seen the pirates depart. Where the hell was everyone?

Standing now on the Bridge, Chris gave some quick orders, 'Let's start with the superstructure. We move together, clearing each floor. Make sure there are no pirates left and see if we can find the crew. Bob, if you are alright, it's your turn to go first especially as you have an AK and its better suited indoors than Miguel's long.'

'Yep, I am good.'

'It doesn't need to be said but be cautious. Don't fire unless you are certain it's a threat. There are meant to be 24 crew members around here somewhere. Perhaps the pirates tied them up.'

Over the next fifteen minutes the team worked their way down the floors, entering each room before moving on. During that clearance they saw things that disgusted them. Rooms ransacked. Personal possessions tipped out of draws and thrown on the floor. In the Captain's room, which was just below the Bridge, some of the pirates had obviously taken a shit in his living space and then using his clothes smeared it across the floor and walls. The stink was bad, the moulds and fungi growing in the humid, fetid air hinted at lethal airborne diseases. They moved on quickly.

Shortly they came to the canteen and on entering found the crew. Eyes wide with fear turned quickly to relief as Bob who was at the front lifted his barrel and grinned at the crew.

'Afternoon Men! Consider yourselves rescued!'

There was no mass hysteria from the crew as their freedom finally came. They were exhausted, fatigued, and stressed to hell. Good friends hugged each other, shook hands, or patted each other on the back.

Leaving Miguel to guard the corridor, Chris stepped in and having identified Captain Oleksiy walked over to him and offered his hand.

'Good afternoon Captain Oleksiy, I am Chris.'

'Hello Chris, thank God you are here, we are so glad to see you. Thank you for what you have done today.'

'Not at all. Firstly, is everyone all right? What about your injured man?'

'My first officer is very unwell. We need to get him some medical help as soon as possible'

'We can help with that. We have a doctor standing by on the phone and we have a comprehensive trauma and drugs pack with us.'

Oleksiy interrupted and called to Szymon. 'Szymon, do you hear that? These men have drugs and a doctor lined up.'

Szymon lying on one of the couches gave a feeble smile as Chris continued. 'We have a number of stores with us that we would like to get across to you and then it would be good to get underway. I think we have some grace time with the pirates, but there is no point in hanging around, if you get my meaning?'

The Captain turned to his crew and gave a short speech which ultimately expressed relief to them about the release, but also said that they must save the celebration until they were underway. He allocated a number of tasks. The engineering team needed to start an emergency check of critical systems and report back, on how long before they could be underway. The deck crew needed to get the stores over from the Sea Dragon. The bridge crew needed to check if they needed any fuel, what systems they had and navigate a course to safety; he paused there and consulted with Chris, who confirmed the destination was Mombasa.

Chris asked if one man could be spared to take Bob around all of the rest of the ship spaces, so they could conduct a rudimentary clearance. Having got his crew to work, Chris then asked the Captain to accompany him to the Bridge.

For the next twenty minutes whilst the crew started to shake themselves out and get back to work, Chris briefed Captain Oleksiy on how his team would support the crew as it made for Mombasa. As intended, Chris made sure the Captain knew he was back in charge of his own ship, but even as he was talking to him, he was gauging if he was capable in his mental state to command several hundred thousand tons of shipping, into one of the busiest ports in the Indian Ocean. Satisfied that he was thinking clearly, Chris suggested that they should call the Shipping company and give them an update.

Miguel was already on the Bridge wing facing shore side, where he maintained an overwatch of the small flotilla of pirate skiffs moored up along the beach in Hobyo. They were less than two kilometres away and he could see them clearly with his naked eye. At one point he heard the distinct sound of celebratory automatic gunfire.

Chapter 96.
November 21st, Athens, Greece

It had been a long day in the boardroom in Athens. Mr Papadopoulos had been in and out all the afternoon. After all he had a huge empire to run and whilst this was particularly important to him personally, he needed to keep the wheels of his empire rolling.

The time had been spent confirming the plans for the vessel on its arrival. They had an approximate schedule now and the most important thing was to get the crew medically checked out and reunited with their families. The crew would be getting a lot of time off, but the ship was an expensive asset and needed to undergo maintenance, so it could get back out on the ocean waves and earn its keep. A different crew was being lined up to take it out for its next charter; after all, every day lost was costing the Company $100,000. The relief crew would be flown out to Mombasa in time to meet the ship when it arrived.

Max was still in the room with John, Finlay and Chloe and it was sheer coincidence that Mr Papadopoulos's secretary popped her head in as the spider phone rang on the table. When she heard Captain Oleksiy's voice, she rushed to get her boss.

John led the call as the Operations Manager, and after greetings, well wishes and an update on the state of the crew, the boss walked in. Naturally, the Captain repeated the key messages for him.

'I am delighted that you are OK Oleksiy.' said Mr Papadopoulos. 'You must pass my absolute best regards on to the crew and tell them that we will help them with medicals, counselling, whatever is needed. Perhaps most importantly though tell them that I am flying their families out to Mombasa, so they will all be there to meet you when you arrive in a few days' time.'

After Captain Oleksiy had expressed his gratitude and before the call was ended John spoke. 'Oleksiy, I am sure you have much to do. Once you are underway, and have had a chance to assess, can you send us a list of breakages, missing items, things that need maintenance?'

'I will do John. I can tell you the top of the list will be new toilet pumps. They haven't been working for months now, but I won't get into that here!'

All sorts of thoughts were going through the minds of those in Athens as the call was ended, but fortunately that was cut short as Mr Papadopoulos nodded to someone standing outside the door. In came a waiter carrying a silver tray with glasses, an ice bucket, and a bottle of vintage Bollinger champagne. As the waiter prepared the drinks Mr Papadopoulos gave a heartfelt thank you, that ended nicely with the pop of a champagne cork.

Chapter 97.
November 21st, The Hibernia III, The Indian Ocean

Captain Oleksiy was getting to grips with being in command again and his crew were spooling critical systems up so that they could get underway. Chris and Bob on the other hand were in the canteen dealing with an extremely sick First Officer Szymon.

Using an iPad that was connected to the ships satellite based WIFI, they were using a direct video link to a doctor in Harley Street in London. Bob was a trained combat medic, and whilst his bedside manner was more suited to stabbing adrenaline into a patient's chest and thumping a seal over a sucking chest wound, he was highly knowledgeable, albeit little practised. Luckily, in this case though the doctor was in charge. Under his direction Bob had taken blood pressure, which wasn't good, put a glucose and saline drip in, because Szymon was dehydrated, undernourished and weak. Now Bob was rummaging through his bag for the specific antibiotics that the doctor said were needed immediately. At least these ones were the right type and were authentic, unlike the counterfeit crap that the Somali doctor had probably unknowingly given Szymon. The final thing administered was a massive dose of ibuprofen, its combined pain killer and anti-inflammatory were essential for dealing with the swelling and pain of broken and infected ribs. Bob was kind enough to let them take effect, before asking Szymon to sit up so he could strap up his chest with a series of tight bandages.

Despite the massive amount of pain, it was clear that Szymon was in much better spirits mentally now, knowing that someone was caring for him properly and that within a few days they would be in Mombasa, on the way to an international hospital somewhere. It wasn't long before he was in an exhausted but drug induced sleep.

'Have you seen the state of some parts of this ship?' said Chris as Bob packed away the trauma kit.

'Some of it. I saw that place outside on the deck which was covered in spit. Fucking disgusting if you ask me. All of that black phlegm that's dried in the sun. It will just breed disease. And they all just continued to sit in the middle of it chatting and khatting. No wonder they only have a life expectancy of 56.'

'Yes, and they were spitting inside in the corridors and cabins too. Disgusting! The Captain's cabin was particularly special. Quite literally shit everywhere. I swear somehow someone managed to wipe their arse on the curtains.'

'Grim!'

'The other thing that pisses me off is that they just left rubbish everywhere. Mouldy food just trodden into the carpets, wrappers everywhere. I think the galley needs to be disinfected with a flamethrower.'

'I am amazed that we don't have more cases of crew malnutrition. Scurvy even!'

'Yes, thank god we brought enough multi-vitamins. Whoever in ops thought of that one deserves a medal.' said Chris.

'You wonder what would have happened to the crew if this had gone on for much longer. Aside from the physical side, I bet this lot will keep the company shrink employed for years to come.'

And that was probably the greatest tragedy of all thought Chris as he made his way up, to make sure that Miguel could get a break.

Chapter 98.
November 21st, The Hibernia III, The Indian Ocean

It was late into the evening now and Chris and Captain Oleksiy were sitting in the canteen having a cup of coffee. The room had been scrubbed to within an inch of its life by the galley crew and several of the additional hands. Caustic soda, bleach, whatever was needed, the porthole windows were wide open, but the air in room had a chemical tang, which was welcome after the stink. At least one room was liveable in now.

The engineering team was busy at work, priming here, checking there, and had promised that the screws would be turning anytime now. The crew not involved in engineering, or in cleaning the galley, had spent the early evening cross-decking the supplies from the Sea Dragon. Four great cargo nets had been hoisted up including fresh food, soft drinks, contingency spare parts, bottled water and even ten cases of beer and half a dozen cases of vodka. The vodka was a local brand from Kenya and not a Ukrainian brand, but it had probably generated the biggest cheer, when it was seen landed on the deck.

Professional to the last, the crew had agreed to hold off until the critical work was done, but with the chef in the kitchen preparing a king's feast, a bottle or two would get cracked open that night. With the cross loading of stores complete, the Sea Dragon had taken up station just behind the Hibernia III, offset by about three hundred meters.

'How are you feeling Captain?' asked Chris.

'I am very tired. I want to eat and go to bed, but I need to make sure my men are ok first.'

Chris nodded but repeated, 'I understand, but how are you feeling? The last few months must have been difficult for everyone but especially you?'

'They have. I believe I have seen the absolute best and the very worst of human nature in the past few months. I don't know if I will ever understand how one human can treat another so badly. To them we were just a commodity, no more valuable than a thing, a possession they could trade. They would think nothing of pointing a weapon at us, kick us on the ground when we were not threat. I am certain that if the ransom had not been paid, or was not enough, they would have executed some of us.'

Chris nodded, being an active listener, whilst Oleksiy continued. 'But then on the other side I have seen some members of my crew show sides to them that I would never have believed. Take our steward as an example. He is from the Philippines, small in stature, always serving with a smile on his face. Not, you would think, a courageous man. But I saw him be, not by standing up to those criminals, but by continuing with his job. Keeping a brave face, cooking, cleaning whatever was allowed by the pirates to keep this room clean and the crew fed. On the other side, I saw some of my supposedly strong Ukrainian colleagues fold under the pressure of continuous pirate threats. Their stress, anxiety, a feeling of helplessness, a loss of power, and just being numbed to the core overcame them. I fear that it has done irreparable damage to them. Some who thought they were so strong, were broken in their minds. Not of course their fault, who knew how we would react personally under such pressures. For me? I am glad that this has ended, I don't know for how much longer I would have managed. For a time, I was just so angry! Frustrated that I had allowed it to happen. It took me some time to realise that there was nothing I could have done to prevent it, that I too was helpless.'

Chris agreed, knowing how difficult it must be culturally for the Captain to talk this way. 'I hear you. I think everything you have said there is very normal, there is nothing to be ashamed of either for you, or for any of your crew members. I also think that trying to get the crew back to a sense of normality, as you are already, is the best thing for now. When we arrive in Mombasa, I know there will be counsellors ready to help.'

Oleksiy continued, as though he hadn't heard, with more determination coming into his voice as he spoke, 'What I do know now though, is that I am going to do something about this criminal group. If no one does anything to stop them, then they will do this again and other crews will suffer in the same way. I don't know how yet, but I want to do my best to keep other crews safe. To prevent this from ever happening, again!'

In the quiet calm after that statement a vibration change occurred in the hull of the ship. The Captain sensed it immediately and stood up. 'Good. The screws are turning. We must be ready to depart.'

Chapter 99.
November 22nd, Hobyo, Somalia

After the highs of yesterday, today had been a tough day for Abdi. He had taken a room in his father's house and had paid for extra militia men to guard it overnight and to provide a visible deterrent by day. There had never been so much money in Hobyo before, let alone in one house and news would spread quickly on the bush telegraph.

Yesterday he had sent messengers to all of the main suppliers that they should present themselves today with their bills for payment. There had been a small queue since morning prayers. Khat traders came first in order of rank or trade value. Abdi was staggered to learn the final amount that was due. Nearly 25,000 dollars went to them. Next the food vendors took nearly 10,000 dollars. He had about the same again in total bills from other service providers. The welders who had made the ladders, the trader that provided the fuel for the skiffs, various miscellany and the list seemed endless and expensive.

Next up were the families of those pirates who hadn't returned and who were now assumed dead. The cultural law was clear. Blood money was due for each death and Abdi was liable. He had asked his father to meet with the families during the last week to negotiate. Abdi thought his father should at least earn some of his 'tax' and his father had agreed to negotiate. In line with tradition, the blood money of one hundred camels was to be paid to the family for each man lost. Abdi had winced at that, but had eventually agreed. He had insisted though that he would pay the cash price equivalent, rather than scrabbling around the traders to buy hundreds of the animals.

Dalmar had died on Zahi's skiff, and two complete crews had gone missing, now presumed dead on other skiffs. At the market rate of 600 dollars per camel that put Abdi at just under half a million dollars out of pocket for blood money for the seven lost men. Of course, he couldn't disrespect the families either, as they came in to collect their dues and so his whole morning had passed in offering his condolences and finally sealing the bargains.

After a light midday meal with his family, where Abdi had given his mother and sister 5000 dollars each for their cooking in support of the pirates onboard, his father raised the subject of his 'tax'. Having seen the size of the bags and the money flowing out of Abdi's possession he got greedy. 'Abdi, I think the town of Hobyo deserves a larger piece of the earnings from your little project.'

Abdi nearly choked. 'What? For what purpose? I am already paying a huge sum to you for city improvements.' They both knew that that was a euphemism. Sure, some of the money would go on community projects, but large amounts would stick to the leader's fingers as they were implemented.

'It's not enough. How much did you receive from the plane in total?'

Abdi was determined not to share the final figure. 'That's for me and The Associate to know only. Nobody else does so why should I tell you?'

Despite the name dropping his father wasn't deterred. 'Because I am your father, I am your clan chief!'

Abdi was still petulant, 'But why should I pay you more than you agreed with me before this all started? We had a bargain!'

'I have changed my mind. You will tell me. How much did you get paid?'

Abdi took a risk. He did some quick maths in his head. 'Five and half million dollars.'

Abdi's fathers' eyes widened, and he took a deep intake of breath. 'Allah be merciful. You got that much?'

'Yes. My idea worked well father.'

'It certainly did. Now listen to me, my son. You will not tell that to anyone else. You will give me half a million for the elders and I to distribute as the city tax, and you will give me another hundred and fifty thousand, to repay me for your London education. I think that is fair.'

Trying hard to contain his glee, Abdi realised that his father was demanding almost exactly the sum that Abdi was already going to give him anyway under the old agreement. 'Very well father. I will do that, but next time if we have an agreement, we will put it in writing.'

As they continued to eat, they both knew that writing it down would be worthless. Both felt they had outsmarted the other and won a small victory.

Chapter 100.
November 22nd, Hobyo, Somalia

That same evening in Hobyo was a celebration. Preparations, organised by Zahi, had been going on all day and a fire was now burning brightly on the beach down near the shoreline. Traders had heard about the cash windfalls and had set up stalls selling everything from trinkets to electronics. They couldn't quite work out though, why there was no demand from the pirates, for brand new televisions.

Several goats had been slaughtered and were being cooked on smaller fires to the side. The whole town appeared to have turned out and there was a party atmosphere. Zahi was the centre of the party, and along with Tadalesh would tell anyone who listened for the thousandth time of their exploits at sea. They frequently interrupted each other embellishing details. The fathers of eligible daughters were sitting with them, assessing the most successful men, and trying to vie for attention or favour.

Later into the evening, with bellies full, Zahi was sitting on the sand with his younger brother Hassan. Hassan had put his crutches to one side and taken off his locally made leg. He had been wearing it a lot on board over the past couple of months and he was chaffed and sore.

'Hassan, what are you going to do with your money?' Zahi asked.

'Well, I thought I might buy myself my own boat. Then I would pay someone to go and fish it for me.'

'It's a good idea. A steady income with luck. You know, if we are fortunate and catch another ship, I am sure that I could ask Abdi to let you guard it again?'

'The money is good, and it is much less risky than what you did. I don't expect I could climb a ladder to capture my own ship, so I will never be as successful as you brother.'

'I don't intend to do that again. Abdi has offered me a job training the new teams that will go out, and I have accepted.'

'Good, that means you will be able to be here and help look after father. Of course, you might also find yourself a wife too!'

'Ha! I wanted to talk to you about that.'

Hassan stared at him and then Zahi realised why and continued quickly. 'No! not about a wife! I meant about father. Now that we have some money, I think we should get him to a good doctor. See if he needs surgery. Certainly, get him the drugs he needs. I think we should also prepare a dowry for our sister so that she can marry.'

'That would be good, brother. Generous of you.'

'And for you. I would like you to go to someone who makes good prosthetic legs. Get a good one made that fits you well, is comfortable.'

Hassan looked at his brother, immense gratitude showing in his eyes. Neither of them trusting their voices just stared into the dying embers of the fire, content for their family's new future.

Far, far, above them, noiseless and persistent was a drone. It circled constantly and used a range of sensors on board. The first, a day night camera with a zoom so powerful it could read the time on your watch. The second, a thermal camera, though it was less useful tonight with the heat of the fires. Then, a clever piece of electronics that could spoof cell phones, collect their cell and IMEI numbers storing them for the future in one of a million databases. Using triangulation from its wide orbit, the system could estimate with reasonable accuracy which phone belonged to which of the faces it was photographing below.

In Djibouti, the drone operator sitting at her terminal pressed a button on her comms console to speak to the duty intelligence officer. 'Lieutenant, its Sargent Graves. Reference Task TS58GU. Task is complete and I am bringing the platform home. We have our data and it's uploaded ready for your team's analysis.'

Chapter 101.
November 25th, The Hibernia III, The Indian Ocean

The Hibernia III had been underway for just over 96 hours and was crossing the maritime boundary into Kenyan waters. All the way down the Somali coast, the Sea Dragon had trailed her with both vessels providing each other some mutual protection. The 12 knots they had cruised at was easily within the capability of the Hibernia III, but the Sea Dragon had been working hard to maintain position.

They had taken a relatively straight line and had tracked about twenty miles off and parallel to the Somali coastline. That was enough to stay well clear of most of the local fishing boats that were out at night, fishing with simple kerosene lanterns as their only markers.

The crew of the Hibernia III had been hard at work. Both inside and out they had spent much of their time cleaning. It was a cathartic process, washing away the filth of the past using high pressure hoses, chemicals and scrubbing brushes. Whilst they could remove the smells, stains, and traumas from the physical environment, for many of the crew they were just as deeply etched in their memories. No amount of chlorine-based bleach was going to help there.

When they weren't cleaning, they were assessing the damage. What goods had been stolen and what work needed to be done by better equipped servicing teams in Mombasa? The list was long, but top of it for the Captain was the potential need for the ship's hull to be cleaned. Month's stationary in a warm tropical sea wasn't the best thing for his ship despite modern anti-fouling paints.

The good news was that in a couple of days they would reach Mombasa and the announcement that they would be seeing their families there had improved moral considerably. With the stores delivered by the Sea Dragon, the team had eaten well for the past couple of days. Fresh vegetables and fruit, red meat, beer, and vodka had all gone down well. Best of all though, Szymon appeared to be responding well to the antibiotics and was sitting up of his own accord.

With the primary escort and protection task done, it was time for Chris, Bob, and Miguel to leave the ship and cross deck back onto the Sea Dragon taking the weapons with them. The weapons were registered to Captain Jammo and it just wouldn't do for them to enter Kenyan waters on another vessel, too much paperwork and bother irrespective of the need or circumstances.

At five that evening as agreed, the Hibernia III slowed down to the minimum to keep underway and the Sea Dragon pulled up alongside. With the crew managing the gantry ladder properly it had been lowered to the right height, to enable the team to disembark a little more safely this time. Standing at the top of the ladder with their bags having already been lowered on a rope, the team said goodbye to the crew. Everyone, except the duty bridge team and a couple of the engineers had come to say goodbye.

Captain Oleksiy said what much of the crew felt. 'Chris, Bob, Miguel. We are deeply grateful to you and your team for all that you have done for us. You stood up to the face of evil, and you took risks that many men would cower away from. Importantly, and a testament to your courage, you did it for other human beings whom you had never met before that day, when you walked into our canteen armed to the teeth. The skill with which your air team delivered the ransom, the detailed planning from your operations team to get everything in the right place at the right time was incredible. To you Bob, for saving Szymon's life with your medical treatments, Miguel your professionalism on the Bridge on guard protecting us all and to you Chris for your leadership and care for me and my crew. We would like to thank you for everything that you have done. Sadly, as would be traditional, I have no gift to give you now. I promise though that I will send your team a small memento, when I eventually get back to the office. It will never repay what you have done for us, but perhaps it will be a positive reminder of how grateful we are, as a crew.'

Chris replied on behalf of the team in a voice learnt at sea and loud enough to carry to the assembled crew. 'Captain Oleksiy and the crew of the Hibernia III. Thank you for your kind words and thoughts. It has been an honour for us to be able to help you out of this dark moment, and one that I am sure is one of the worst experiences you will ever have. Over the past couple of days, I have had the opportunity to speak to many of you and I would just leave you with this thought. The pirates that call themselves men, and who preyed on you and who made victims of all of you, have not changed fundamentally who you are as human beings. Being a victim does not make you weak, being a victim here is not your fault. You are still the same person that you were three months ago before the attack. You are decent human beings, providing in many cases for your families. Do not let what happened to you here at the hands of criminals, overrule who you are inside, break your confidence, drag you down. In short do not let them win! You are safe now, safe to get on with your lives. I can't recommend enough using the counselling services that are going to be available to you in Mombasa and beyond. For all of us men, it's difficult to ask for help, sometimes even culturally unacceptable. I would urge you to overcome that though if you can. I promise you that it will help you in the longer term.' Chris paused to let that sink in, before continuing: 'We are now entering Kenyan waters, and you are safe. We wish you all the best for the future and whilst now we will leave you, we won't go far, we will escort you all the way to Mombasa.'

There followed a round of thankyous, handshakes, and embraces and then the team went down the gantry ladder stepping lightly across to the Sea Dragon. As they looked up one last time, they could see Captain Oleksiy at the top. He gave the team a final nod, and then turned away heading back to the Bridge.

As the Sea Dragon pulled away to resume her position astern Omondi leant across the rail from two decks up. 'Lovely speech that Chris. Right from the heart mate.'

Chapter 102.
November 26th, Hobyo, Somalia

Over the past couple of days, Abdi had become a little nervous. He had received a call from the Associate who seemed remarkably well informed. The message didn't come through his father, who had originally introduced them, the Associate had called him directly on his cell phone. Apparently, this morning he was flying in for an update and there was 'much to discuss'. This time Abdi's father was not invited.

Abdi was sitting in the back of his families battered old white land cruiser again. On the seat beside him were two large canvas bags of money. He wasn't driving this time. He had someone else to do that for him now. He also had two escort pickup trucks, one at the front and one at the back. Partly it signified Abdi's new status, and partly he wanted the 4 men with the guns in each one to guard him and the money until he could hand the bulk of it over.

He had a sense of déjà vu as he drove down the long track to the airport just North of Hobyo. Once more he found himself waiting until, in a cloud of dust, the expensive looking white private jet with the red sash ribbon paintwork pulled up on the dispersal. The door opened outwards with a soft hiss and there was the same pretty oriental flight attendant to welcome him in. Before he had even set foot in the aircraft though the attendant had asked him if he was carrying a mobile phone or any other electronic devices? If so, then please could he leave them in the car.

Abdi did so and then he hauled the heavy bags up the steps one by one. The stewardess insisted on glancing inside each of the bags. As he entered the cool body of aircraft trying not to damage it with his heavy bags, he was surprised by The Associate appearing at his elbow. This time he was smiling. 'Welcome Abdi, I see you have had a busy time of things over the past few months.'

Caught off balance by the welcome, but also seeing The Associate standing up, he was astounded at how short he was. Abdi remembered him as bald-headed and thin but hadn't remembered him being perhaps a nudge under five feet tall. It seemed so out of place for a man of such audacious power. Abdi placed the bags on a couple of the executive seats and then held out his hand in the western way, but The Associate just looked at it, leaving it grasping the air and moved on. 'Come and sit Abdi. I would like you to tell me your story. Mind you, I only have half an hour before I need to go to West Africa so just give me the broad overview.'

'Yes, um I am sorry, but I don't know your name.'

The Associate had turned to go back down the aircraft and to sit at his desk at the rear and as he went, he said, 'That is quite alright by me Abdi. Now, continue.'

Over the next twenty minutes standing uncomfortably like a schoolboy in front of the headmaster Abdi told him everything that he could. Plenty of astute questions were asked and answered but when he started talking numbers and financials The Associate waved his hand. 'Have you put a ledger in the bags?'

'Yes, and I brought all the money, including what we agreed was my share. I wanted to check with you that the agreement was still in place for future projects?'

'Yes indeed. The terms are fine. This time from the proceeds you are to take half a million dollars as my stake for the seed capital for your next enterprises. How much is your 25 percent of the net profits worth before that deduction?'

'Its 1.2 million dollars.'

'Good! You are now a rich man. Congratulations!' The Associate grinned.

Abdi couldn't work out the catch yet, so was still cautious. 'So... to be clear. You want me to continue the project? You want me to take half a million from your share, to buy more boats, train more men and capture more ships?'

'Yes.'

'And then I take my money, and I do with that what I wish?'

'Yes Abdi, that part is now your money. I reward people who are successful and who are loyal to me. And you are both aren't you?' There was a cold look in his eye and a sharp tone to his voice with the last sentence.

'Definitely... Sir.'

Switching back to a more genial tone The Associate said, 'Good, well it's time for me to go. You should use one of your bags to take your share and then get on with your business. I will call you again when I need you.' The Associate looked down at his desk at a newspaper he had there, having dismissed Abdi already.

Abdi turned a little awkwardly and went to the bags. He had to tip the contents of one out onto the floor and he counted seventeen bricks carefully putting them back into the bag. He left the remainder lying in an obscene untidy pile on the pale leather executive seat. 'Goodbye Sir.' he said and feeling quite unsettled he went out the door with his bag, into the heat of the day.

Chapter 103.
November 26th, The Hibernia III, Mombasa

The Hibernia III had arrived in Mombasa just after dawn. She had picked up a port pilot and then made her way up the main deep river channel that for hundreds of years had sheltered shipping and made Mombasa the successful port that it was. She passed the old town part of the city on her starboard side, just as rush hour was getting underway and the dense brown fug of fumes combined with the blaring of horns, to make a noisy assault on the senses.

Up in the sky above them a helicopter was circling, a stabilised camera on a pod hung just below its port side skid and it was relaying the images of her arrival to television networks around the world. The news of the Hibernia III's capture had been a small sensation. Her release a few days ago was a good news story, to be shared as widely as possible.

She passed the Kilindini port on her right, where numerous cargo ships were alongside unloading containers, using the massive cargo cranes that towered proud on the jetty. As the channel opened out inland, she nudged on through to the Kipevu oil terminal, where she had been scheduled all those months ago to deliver her original cargo. The unloading terminal was free, and she pulled alongside where a well-practiced team collected her mooring ropes and tied her off. Almost with a sigh of relief she settled there at the end of her delivery run at last.

The oncoming Aphrodite Freight and Shipping Company crew were already standing there on the jetty ready to embark and assume their duties. There was also another team, which included Mr Papadopoulos himself, some of the company management, a medical team and also a sprinkling of diplomats and intelligence service officials. The suits were realising their mistake in the heat and humidity. Mr Papadopoulos confirmed that the families, which had been flown out, were all in the Tamarind Hotel in the Old Town, where they would meet their loved ones later that afternoon.

Captain Oleksiy had received a communication from the Ops team on how today would go and he had briefed his crew. There would be an address by Mr Papadopoulos first thing, followed by the Ukrainian Ambassador. Then they would all get a quick medical check. After that, in a process that was guaranteed to last less than an hour, the crew would receive a short debrief from the Ukrainian intelligence team, a brief from the company HR manager and also a brief on dealing with the media.

Szymon was first and he was taken promptly by ambulance to get medical attention.

For the rest, it was a long but understandable process, and as the day wore on Captain Oleksiy had to maintain his professionalism. For now, what the crew really wanted, was to get off the ship get to the hotel and see their families. He had to remember his vow to help future crews to avoid suffering the same fate again. Eventually the hot debriefs ended, though with some clear requirements that the medical support, especially for mental health, would continue tomorrow at the hotel, as would the intelligence debrief for some of the senior crew.

Having finished the handover and with all the crew ready, they descended the gantry steps to the jetty, where a couple of minibuses were idling. As the Captain's feet touched the ground, for the first time in months, he looked back up at his ship. 'See you soon,' he thought.

As they left the port the voices of the crew rose in excitement, happy and looking forward to meeting up with their loved ones. They barely noticed, as they exited the gate to the port, that they drove past about 20 reporters and film crews whose cameras were beaming more images around the world.

They didn't know it, but the journalists missed a scoop. At a little jetty further inland, an odd-looking foreign crew disembarked from a small work horse vessel called the Sea Dragon. It had arrived a couple of hours after the Hibernia III had entered the channel.

The Sea Dragon had settled quietly up against her jetty and a team of mostly white faces had disembarked and gone to the immigration office to register their arrival. A black Mitsubishi Pajero had picked them up and whisked them off to the Mombasa international airport, where they caught a late afternoon flight up to Nairobi.

Chapter 104.
November 26th, Hobyo, Somalia

Zahi had had a couple of days off. Once he had gotten over his irritation that the fathers of eligible daughters kept trying to corner him each time he went out into the town, he realised that he quite liked his newfound infamy.

Shopkeepers paid him respect when he went to their stores, though he hadn't been splashing his cash around. He had only bought himself a new t-shirt and a good pair of sandals. Fishermen crowded around him down at the beach basking in the glow of his success. Of course, the fishing captains had another purpose too. Abdi had selected fifteen of them, the strongest and the bravest and he had created a cadre of trainees to become future skiff captains. Those who had been unsuccessful in being selected were naturally disappointed. It was some consolation for them though that with nearly a quarter of the eligible fishing crews now being used for purposes other than fishing, the value of their catches should increase in the local markets. They were contented to make a little more at the end of each month, local economics at work.

Zahi's other problem was recruiting the warrior for each crew. He hadn't yet really put his mind to it, but he needed to work out how he was going to select the new 'Dalmar's'. There were plenty of young men who could talk it up and who carried a gun, but how many of them really had courage? How many of them had actually been in a firefight? How many of them could go to sea without constantly throwing up like Dalmar had, to the point of almost being ineffective? How many of them could be trusted? How many could he take from land, and not leave Hobyo unprotected? He resolved to chat to Abdi about that the next time he saw him. If Zahi was infamous, then Abdi was a rock star now and he could solve that one.

There were other logistical problems too, that had to be considered. Abdi wanted to send ten more skiffs to sea next month and had already placed the orders with the same company in Dubai. His volume purchase had come with discounts that the finance and bartering side of him had enjoyed. With the skiff that had survived the last season, that would increase the odds of capturing some good prizes. It was out already with Axmed and his own crew. They were 'fishing' again.

Zahi was sitting, near the end of his lesson with his 15 new recruits under the shade of a flame tree, on the edge of the town overlooking the sea. Its bright green leaves and its' burst of bright red flowers a clash of colour, compared to the pale desert sands.

'Tell me, what qualities must a good skiff captain have?'

There were lots of answers called back at him.

'Bravery!'

'Knowledge!'

'To listen to his crew and not boss them about!'

'Good navigation skills so you can find your way home!' there were titters of laughter.

Zahi let them continue and then said, 'Yes many of those are good. How about loyalty?' there were nods from his students and so he continued. 'Have you ever had millions of dollars in your hands? How about 200 million dollars' worth of ship and cargo? What do you think it was that meant that I brought my ship back here once I had captured it? I could have taken it myself!'

'Because you didn't want Abdi to hunt you down and kill you?'

Zahi nodded, 'Perhaps, but perhaps I needed the support of the clan? I couldn't guard the ship, negotiate the ransom, and collect it all on my own, could I? The clan is everything. We succeed together as a family, not by stabbing anyone in the back. Now I want you to think about that and tomorrow we will move on to tactics and how to take a vessel quickly and effectively.'

The class dispersed and went back to their day jobs chatting amicably, leaving Zahi under the tree, mulling things over. He had had plenty of time to think about how to take ships in a better, lower risk way. There were not too many answers. He had already ordered new climbing ladders from the blacksmith. Lighter, longer and with more effective curved hooks on the end to help them stick to the rail when pushed up. Then he had changed the design of the grappling hooks remembering how hard they had been to throw. Much lighter, less metal, thinner but stronger knotted ropes attached to them. He made a mental note to get them sooner rather than later, so that the new crews could start practising with them. His biggest concern was buying weapons. He had a man coming tomorrow, who dealt with such things. Abdi had warned Zahi not to buy all from the same man. If their clan suddenly bought 40 new AK47's and a lot of ammunition, then that would raise eyebrows with their neighbouring clans and conflict could start. Much better to do it subtly, from different merchants. All arms dealers were sharks though and Zahi didn't like dealing with them. That said, one had offered a couple of RPGs for sale, and they were reasonably priced. Perhaps a couple of them would be a good idea? They scared the shit out of Zahi, so they were bound to have the same effect on those shipping crews. Zahi smiled to himself at the thought.

Chapter 105.
November 27th, Nairobi, Kenya

It was early evening in the leafy green suburb of Muthaiga on the Northern edge of Nairobi. Some of the colonial gloss had worn off in the past twenty years, as many of the large ten-acre plots had slowly but surely been subdivided and turned into luxury housing for the rapidly growing Kenyan elite class and the diplomats. One place that had changed extraordinarily little during that period was the most private members' club in the country. The Muthaiga Club had kept its charm throughout, superb staff and excellent food meant it was exactly the right place for the team to gather and to have their celebratory post mission supper. Tom had booked the regular table in the corner of the dining area, out on the patio. The Club required jacket and tie for the men and skirts for the women to eat there. It was old fashioned, but that was its charm. Due to the cooler evening, there were a number of charcoal braziers lit. They added to both the warmth of the air and the glow of the ambiance. All in, around the table, there were the five members of the air team, the four maritime team members and Max.

The post project debriefs, held in the briefing room at Orly Airport earlier that afternoon had run through everything task related from start to finish. What worked, what didn't, what could be improved and what needed to be dropped entirely.

One of Tom's operations staff had had an opportunity to take the video footage from the drop and had cut it into a pretty slick marketing piece with some rousing music. Tom had shown it at the start of the debrief. It was a great sales tool for any future customers, to prove that the organisation could help resolve novel problems. It didn't show the tangled canopy, but that didn't stop Raj taking the piss out of Mike.

The feedback from the Aphrodite Freight and Shipping Company had been really positive. Max had met Mr Papadopoulos before he flew down to Mombasa and been congratulated on a project well done. Apparently, Max would be sent a 1/100th scale replica of the Hibernia III as a mark of appreciation 'to be put somewhere on display'. Max didn't quite know what he would do with a three-meter-long model, but was sure the team would enjoy a fun permanent reminder of Project Calico. More to the point, Max had persuaded the shipping magnate to provide him with an anonymised Reference, for potential future clients.

Now around the dinner table they were reflecting on how much fun it had been. Well, perhaps not the couple of days spent waiting in the snow, but certainly the planning, testing and delivery phases had been good fun for the air team. Chris and the maritime boys reflected that the vessel collection had been harrowing at times, but also immensely rewarding to see a successful conclusion.

As was tradition, Raj pulled out the results of the team's heart monitor competition. He had downloaded the history from every one's smart watch and laid them out on a time graph. It was always fun to go back over events and a couple of them stood out. With grand ceremony Raj had organised a tray of Jägermeister shots as fines and one of the waiters had just placed it down on the table. Beside the shots he placed an awful, garish yellow Hawaiian shirt. The penalty for the loser to wear for the rest of the night.

It was always done in a good-natured way, and it was a good way to decompress. Raj usually managed to get everyone to take a drinking fine for something. The ransom drop itself naturally had an elevation in nearly everyone's heart rates. JP had the piss taken for his heart rate spike being the highest during the drop and there was lots of banter that he was meant to be a steely eyed aviator. The first shot glass was placed in front of him.

Next up, Chris was nominated for a definite increase during the firefight with the pirates. His comment of 'Come on chaps, I have never fired a rifle in anger before!' didn't save him.

Miguel got a special mention for his ridiculously calm heart rate during his shoot, so much so that everyone jokingly accused him of having taken it off during combat. He got given a shot of Jägermeister for blatantly cheating, which he took good naturedly.

Tom got fined for what was worked out to be high stress during the customs clearance when leaving Athens. Max had asked him 'What was he afraid of? Going to jail for ten years for money laundering?'

Bob, tried to accuse Raj of not being fined, and so Raj fined him for being gobby to the fines master.

After the easy ones had gone, it got more interesting and Raj couldn't work it out. 'Mike. What did happen on the night that we were all snowed in, in Europe?'

'Why?' Mike replied.

'Well mate, your heart rate ramped up massively. You were as cool as a cucumber throughout the whole drop, but something happened when you were in the hotel that first night?'

Mike went a little quiet and Raj continued thinking, perhaps he had blundered.

'Sorry mate, are you having flashbacks again?'

The rest of the table lost a little of the sparkle and the team all looked at Mike with the care and compassion that all good soldiers and ex-combatants had learned was needed at times.

'Umm no mate, I haven't had those for a couple of months now. The counselling really is working.'

Slightly relieved Raj continued. 'Good to hear that buddy. So, what was it, did you go to the gym that night or something, overdo it?'

'Something like that.' Mike replied, cagey still.

Raj though was beginning to become a little suspicious at his best friend and then it dawned on him. 'Oh, for fucks sake! You pulled didn't you!'

Mike rolled his eyes but didn't deny it and Raj continued. 'There we were freezing our nuts off in the aircraft and you were getting your nuts off in the hotel! Charly, why didn't you make sure he went to bed early!'

Grins were beginning to appear around the table as Raj went further, 'Which local tramp did you find, and how the hell did you do it?'

'Raj, let's leave it buddy, go on just give me the fine.'

'No way. Look at this, everyone else kept their rates below 130 for the whole trip, and you peak in the middle of the night when nothing else was going on. I mean look at this,' he held up the chart on his phone, 'Everyone else was tucked up fast asleep… Hang on…' he paused, 'Charly? You went to 120 at about the same time…' Raj stopped talking. He looked at Mike, then he looked at Charly. His jaw dropped and then he said, 'No way!'

Charly who hadn't spoken a word until now took a sip of her drink, looked at Raj demurely and with a raise of her eyebrow she said, 'Well you know what they say Raj. Once you've had black there is no going back.'

The whole table erupted in laughter so loud and so infectious that much other conversation in the restaurant paused, heads turned, and waiters smiled. After a moment, the pleasurable babble of voices resumed and continued late into the evening.

Chapter 106.
December 14th, London, United Kingdom

'It's all a bit spy novel this isn't it?' Max asked the casually but warmly dressed middle aged woman, as he sat next to her on a cold wooden bench in Hyde Park in London.

'Is it? I am just out having my lunch break Max. Oh look! By good fortune I have bumped into my old friend from Dubai.' The intelligence officer took a bite of her cheese and pickle sandwich. 'It's lovely to see you again Max.'

'And you.'

'I hear you are doing well for yourself. Resolving lots of thorny issues for governments and commercial clients alike?'

'It's extremely rewarding for us.'

'Look, Max, I will be blunt. Whilst we do appreciate your efforts, the powers that be don't want that particular trick of yours with maritime piracy to become a regular habit. There are concerns that flooding that part of the world with such large sums of money might destabilise her Majesty's agenda in the Horn of Africa.'

'Well thanks for the heads up.' said Max. 'However, if the need is there, then I will help resolve the problems. Perhaps her Majesty's staff should look at solutions to the more deep-seated issues in the Region?'

'Max, that's not the answer I expected.'

'Well, if we don't do it, then someone else will.' Max continued, 'Whilst we are at it, I will let you know that we are currently working on a project to release some of the UK foreign aid workers that have been held onshore in Somalia.'

'Max that is most disappointing.'

'Well, again. I am aware of HMG's position on not making substantive concessions to hostage takers, but the French government paid to get their people out last month, and why should British nationals die, because someone in Whitehall turns their nose up at getting them released?'

'Our consular services are working that problem Max.'

'No, they are not. My network says that the Embassy in Nairobi has done bugger all for the past month on this. The families have asked us to help them, and we will do so. Now do you want the intelligence from this last project of mine or not?'

Realising she wasn't going to win this one, she said 'Yes, we would please. What did you get?'

'On this drive are a complete list of the serial numbers of each hundred-dollar bill. That should help your financial division and the Treasury trace the flows. Next up, there is a file in there with good images of each of the pirates that we could photograph, including a collection, on whom we believe to be the lead pirate, who negotiated with us, called Abdi. There are about 30 photos of other pirates too, but they are nameless. As a bonus, there is also a recording of the Abdi's voice, taken during the negotiation phase. There are notes from the crew debriefs, talking about some of the other names, characters, backgrounds etc. Much was collected by the Captain of the vessel during his ordeal. He said he was willing to view the photos and put names to some of them if you want to go down that line. However, that's not my business.'

She took a sip of her coffee. 'That's a lot of good raw data.'

'Yes. The serial numbers alone should be useful.'

'Max, on behalf of HMG, thank you for this information. Also, on behalf of HMG I can advise that there is a new group of fundamentalists that are coming to prominence in Somalia, called Al Shabab, a spin-off from Al Qaeda. It would be catastrophic if they were to receive funding on this scale. Are we clear? We want you to be careful?'

Max stood up, adjusted his trousers, and looked down at his old friend. 'We always are. I think we know a little bit about that group already, so do let me know if you would like me to fill you in? By the way, lovely to see you. Next time let's at least make it dinner, shall we?'

As Max walked off into the park his mobile rang.

'Max it's Finlay.'

'Hello Finlay, is everything ok?'

'Well, it's a spot of bother actually. Are you able to come to London in the next couple of days?'

'By sheer coincidence I am here already.'

'Really? That's bloody marvellous!'

'What's the problem?'

'It's those bastards in Hobyo. They have captured another one. Long and the short of it is - this one is full of frozen meat. Five million dollars' worth. Chloe is having kittens.' Can you come into the financial district tomorrow to meet the owner?'

'I would love to. Send me the address by email, would you?'

'Thanks Max, you are a life saver.' Finlay hung up.

Do you know what? I really think I might be, thought Max, as he strolled off through the park in the brisk cold winter air.

Chapter 107.
January 5th, Hobyo, Somalia

Abdi was standing on the beach talking to Zahi. The sun was brightening in the morning sky and the fishermen who had been out overnight were putting their boats away for the day. The boat boys were doing the hard work of resetting nets, tidying things away and washing down any fish scales from the hulls. The boat captains were carrying their produce up the beach in battered old cool boxes ready to go to market.

In the bay, anchored up, was the captured cargo vessel, a large white refrigerated ship with a green hull below the water line. Axmed had come good and was now managing the vessel with Hassan. Abdi had been in negotiation with the shipping company for a couple of weeks now, but they were playing a difficult game again. He had taken some time out today, to come and inspect the new equipment that had just arrived, giving himself a mental boost.

Ten new skiffs were lined up on the beach. Even as they watched, the selected crews were busy, taking wrappings off engines, mounting them over the sterns, checking fuel lines, allocating the stores such as fuel cans, and safety equipment.

'What do you think Zahi?' asked Abdi.

'I think the crews are nearly ready. I think they are hungry to succeed and having a monument to success like that in front of them is a good motivator.'

'Good. The weather forecast is reasonable for the next two weeks. I think we should send them out.'

'I would like two more days with them if that's OK? The fighters have only just arrived, and I want them to connect with the skiff crews. They also need to practice boarding and using the grappling hooks. Otherwise, we have all we need. The weapons, the fuel, the sat-phones, the ladders. Everything is in place.'

'Ok, two days then, perhaps they can use that ship, to practise their boarding drills?'

Zahi looked at Abdi respectfully, 'I hadn't thought of that. It's a really good idea. Better than trying to snag a tree branch on land.'

As Abdi and Zahi started to move amongst the new equipment, talking to the new Captains, checking they were prepared, above them a drone circled way up out of sight.

Sargent Graves, sitting at her console in Djibouti, was watching the live feed of its cameras, whilst she set the autopilot of the machine to a standard orbit.

'Lieutenant, it's Sargent Graves. We have a development on Task TS58GX. Sharing the feed to main screen now.'

In front of her and in front of five other operator desks in the room, the main screen lit up. The Lieutenant, sitting at a desk at the rear of the room acknowledged and looked at the main screen.

'Roger that, have we ID'd those two men?'

'Yes Lieutenant. The one on the left is called Abdi, he is the pirate Negotiator and the one on the right is Zahi, suspected to have been the primary pirate on the Hibernia III attack.'

'Thanks. That looks interesting. That's ten new skiffs and crews. It looks like that is a considerable escalation of capability. Write it up Sargent Graves. Good work.'

'Will do sir, I suspect we are going to be pretty busy over the next couple of months on this.'

'You said it Sergeant.'

Acknowledgements

As a first-time fictional author, learning the ins and outs of writing and self-publishing was a fascinating journey to undertake during The Pandemic. For me what started out as a journey to stop looking at so much social media, or even playing computer games, became a cathartic process that I thoroughly enjoyed, and I know it has helped put some old daemons to rest.

I loved learning something new and I loved the creativity of writing. So much so in fact that there will be more on the way from me as in the near future. (Sorry!)

For this book, I want to thank my family, for allowing me to slink off to my study, long after my normal working day had finished and do my 'hour a night' which frequently became a couple...

I also want to thank both Terry and Siri, my parents, for the comprehensive editing that they did for me when they had so much else on their plates.

Finally, to those courageous people, often taken for granted, who risk their all to bring others to safety; thankyou for all that you do, every day.

About the Author

Rob Phayre has spent nearly 20 years living in Africa, thriving on the multitude of cultures and seeing first-hand the beauty of the African natural world. He has worked as a security and crisis leader for a number of organisations and companies and had the privilege of running a couple of them. Prior to moving to Africa, Rob was a British military pilot and served in most of the usual places.

To find out more and see Robs other book releases visit www.robphayre.com

To leave feedback or ask questions about this title visit Robs author page on Goodreads.com

Printed in Poland
by Amazon Fulfillment
Poland Sp. z o.o., Wrocław